BEARER
OF THE CHOSEN SEED

BEARER
OF THE CHOSEN SEED

BY CAMERON ROYCE JESS

Illustrations by
Caitilin W. Pelletier

INSCAPE PUBLICATIONS
PORT WILLIAMS, NOVA SCOTIA
2003

Printed and bound in Canada by AGMV Marquis.
Cover design and typesetting by Olivier Lasser.

National Library of Canada Cataloguing in Publication.

Jess, Cameron Royce, 1943 –
Bearer of the chosen seed / Cameron Royce Jess

ISBN 0-9732414-0-3

I. Title

PS8569.E74B43 2003   C813'.6   C2003-902863-1
PR9199.4.J48B43 2003

Inscape Publications
P.O. Box 401
Port Williams, Nova Scotia
B0P 1T0
www.inscapepublications.com

Publisher: Chris Alders
Shipper-Receiver: David Beach
Distribution: Derrick Boone
Communications: Paul Fitzgerald
Webmaster: Kathy Leighton
Editor: Larry Powell

ACKNOWLEDGEMENTS

This is a testament to people in my life who have demonstrated long-suffering patience, faith and caring:

My "old literature prof", Jack Sheriff, who taught me so much and who never let me give up

My agent, Chris Alders, who never gave up working to make this book happen

My editor, Lawrence Powell, for seeing the forest despite all the trees

My friends who forgave me for turning my back on the "real" world in order to write

Malcolm and Sally for meeting a brother's needs

Holden and Gaea, for never begrudging the sacrifices that a writer's children are called upon to make

My soul-mate, Linda, for everything

From things that have happened and from
things as they exist and from all things that
you know and all those you cannot know, you
make something through your invention that
is not a representation but a whole new thing
truer than anything true and alive, and you
make it alive, and if you make it well enough,
you give it immortality. That is why you write
and for no other reason that you know of.

Ernest Hemingway (1899–1961)

Chapter I

DESCENT

Sanctuary Island, June 2001

'La voilà!' Leo leans back on his elbows against the low-slung boom, everything about him jibing at me. 'Mon Dieu, it looks like La Sorcière's coming out for a sail after all! She's running a half hour late, but that was to be expected!'

He's perfectly right, of course. Nothing has changed between us, not even the bad in-joke of calling me names in our ancestral French. The shock of unruly hair has turned white as snow, but under the weathered skin the muscles still ripple smoothly as hand over fist he unfurls the genoa. 'So, ma petite sorcière, welcome aboard! Or are you going to plant yourself there on the dock? You do look paler about the gills than I remember you.'

So intense the rush of déjà vu that I fondly picture turning on my heel and letting him sail down the Bay all by his lonesome. Except that I'm seven years older now. It belongs to another life, that last occasion the two of us went sailing together.

That was the time I executed a perfect swan dive over *Lizette*'s splintered taffrail. Cut the water clean as a knife and swam all the way back to this same ramshackle dock. Can't even remember now what made

1

me do it, but I'll never forget shivering streams of water against that gull-plastered post over there. This old bastard never did come back for me; he just kept on sailing away from what little was left of our life as a family.

Not that I've ever let Leo get me down — beyond the shedding of a few therapeutic tears, that is. I haven't knocked around the world for nothing the way he has. Along with the degrees and diplomas, I've accumulated a lot of experience dealing with dinosaurs like him. Unlike him, I insist on getting something out of whatever I put my mind to. Not that the method in my madness is all that obvious this morning. I mean, how does one rationalize subjecting oneself to yet another spiritual flogging by this impossible man? 'Step lively now, ma petite sorcière! Time to shove off!'

Just like always, I feel him taking control of everything around me. As if summoned, the freshening wind catches hold of the flapping jib and flings it billowing. Frantically, I slip the aft mooring line free of its bollard and leap aboard. I trip over a sheet-block and lurch drunkenly into the cockpit. Just barely, he catches my forearm in the steel grip I remember so well. He looks at me like I should feel grateful he just saved me a trip to the orthodontist. 'Let go of me, Leo! What the hell's wrong with you anyway, casting off like that?'

'Hell, you're bleeding all over my deck, and we're not even out of the harbor yet!' He draws a first-aid kit from under a cockpit seat and tosses it at me. 'So much for Philippe's tales about how you've gotten to be quite a sailor down under! It's high time you got yourself back on your sea-legs, ma sorcière.'

'Leo, you know I've never liked you calling me that. So why do you do it?'

'You might just as well ask me why I breathe.' He turns away dismissively and starts unlimbering the mainsail.

Somehow I go on being calmly rational with him. I keep telling myself it's a lot like dealing with a child. 'Leo, I've come down here to be with you this morning against my better judgment. The least you can do is afford me the courtesy of an answer. What is it about you that makes you delight in provoking me?'

'Try thinking of me as the personification of the primeval male urge to animate the essentially female cosmos. 'Tis our sole reason for being, you might say, our duty as men to quicken that which is feminine and inert.'

'Oh shit on your cosmic duty!'

'Yup, just like old times, all right — you resort to scatological vulgarity the moment I do my best to answer the questions you pose me. I blame Philippe for daring to hope that things had changed. He led me to believe that you had matured enough to handle a pet name or two.'

'First of all, Philippe doesn't know squat about me. We haven't seen each other a dozen times since you deserted. Secondly, Leo, I'm not your pet. I never was. Thirdly, I'm not a witch. Fourthly, I come bundled with a perfectly good proper name. It's Marie, in case you've forgotten it.'

'For Chrissakes, who do you think it was gave you that name anyway?'

I'm not about to let a bit of obscure historical trivia distract me. 'All the more reason you should use it, Leo!'

'Ah, but you forget what an utterly spontaneous person I am! The name "Marie" is never what comes to mind when I set eyes on you. The moment your mother plunked you squalling in my arms, the phrase that sprang unbidden to my lips was "La sorcière de la mer"… my little witch of the sea.'

'Leo, I've heard you tell that story so many times! Fact is, you didn't have the balls to write "Sorcière" on the birth certificate, so let it be.'

He serves up a forlorn smile at this. 'What's a mere male to do when a female of the species exercises her maternal veto?'

'You could have talked Mom round if you had really wanted to. As I remember, you could talk her into just about anything.'

'Not into something like that, I couldn't. I remember it well how she bared her fangs and went for my jugular. Positively ferocious she was as only a female defending her young can be. Kept harping about the name given a daughter being so much more important than that given a son. "The only real name she'll ever have in this world, Leo" were her exact words, as I recall. Which didn't keep her from insisting I do the honors. So you can imagine how she jumped for joy when I suggested naming you after my most distinguished ancestress.'

'I don't get it. Why should *your* ancestry mean anything to her?'

'Well, your mother believed in genealogical continuity. It was an article of faith with her that each of us is the receptacle of all those who have gone before.'

'Like each of us is a kind of burial urn, you mean?' I know it's bitchy of me, but I simply can't resist saying such things when people give me such perfect openings. The mother I knew and loved was way too down-to-earth for all this sentimental claptrap!

He pretends he didn't hear me. 'Deep down, your mother was a bit of a witch herself, you know. I think she knew we were dubbing a future doctor of philosophy.'

'Too bad she couldn't be here to see her vision brought to pass, isn't it?' Too late I bite my tongue. My God, I sound as corny as he does! So much for keeping my guard up!

'Dr. Campagna, there's pride enough swelling in my bosom for both your mother and me!' He spoils the effect of it all with a mock salute, but even so it's plain to see I've got him squarely where I don't want him. God damn it, his eyes are starting to shine! Perhaps some small part of him really does mean it. But I've been taken in too many times to let him do it to me again.

'You didn't show up for the convocation, Leo, so piss on your pride!' The last thing I care to share with this long lost man is the nostalgia wafting up around us with the morning mist off the Bay. 'Where did you dredge up this sad excuse for a sailboat anyway? I keep getting this crazy mental picture of you scraping it off a coral reef somewhere. Let me guess, you salvaged it off that island at the bottom of the Red Sea.'

'See what I mean? There's no earthly way you could have known that! I haven't been in touch with anyone back here for years!' The amazed blue eyes blink free of tears. 'But then, you were always talking to voices in your head, ma petite sorcière. Your mother and I — we used to regale each other with stories of how psychic you are.'

'So sorry to dash your fond illusions, Leo, but my good guess — assuming you're not pulling my leg — was supposed to be funny. It has nothing whatsoever to do with being psychic.'

'But you weren't guessing, ma sorcière. You spoke of what I did out there with all the assurance of some-one who was there to see it done.'

'Leo, please don't try to snow me! It was you who insisted that I be trained to think logically, remember? Short-circuiting my irrational feminine predispositions, I believe is what you called it. So how about practicing what you preach for a change? Short of theft, how else could an old vagabond like you have come into posses-sion of a twelve-meter aluminum yacht?'

'That hardly explains the Socotra reference.'

'What Socotra reference? I couldn't even retrieve the name of the island, for God's sake — only an image of it sitting like a stopper at the bunghole of a sink. Think, Leo: this boat looks like it's come through a shooting war. What more likely place for a shoot-up these days than the Red Sea? Credit me with some deductive capabilities, even if I am only a woman.'

Running a hand along the battered cockpit coaming, he turns on me that wistfully disarming smile that I had hoped never to see again. 'She's still beautiful in spite of all she's been through, isn't she? Just like your mother stayed beautiful till the very end despite everything.'

Now he's really getting under my skin! 'You have the gall to compare this empty beer can with Mom? All those dents along the bow section look like plugged bullet-holes to me. And not a lick of paint anywhere except for my name slapped like a skin-flick marquee across the transom. I'm not flattered, Leo.'

'You flatter yourself, ma sorcière. This boat was named for dear old Marie, the same as you were.'

'That piece of news is supposed to make me feel better? My God, Leo, what a floating wreck this is! You've really outdone yourself this time. How did you ever sail it half way around the world?'

'So she's somewhat the worse for wear!' A plaintive note creeps into his voice. His tragic flaw is a boundless and utterly uncritical love for sailboats. If only he could have loved the people in his life the same way! I can't count on one hand the times he loaded the family down with floating albatrosses like this one. 'These are the marks of living life to the full, ma petite sorcière; these scars are what give *Marie* her distinctive character.'

'The character of a bag lady, you mean! Why don't you paint her up like one of your whores and tattoo *La Sorcière de la Mer* across *her* stern!'

'Actually, I did think of doing that, but then it struck me that formality is as important in the naming of one's sailboats as in the naming of one's women. Besides, there's only one Sorcière de la Mer.' And saying so, he winches in the genoa sheet. *Marie* takes off down the Back Harbor stretch like a two-year-old mare fresh out of the barn in the spring.

Strange how equine analogies spring to mind whenever I'm around sailboats. I like to think it's because deep down I'm a very terrestrial creature in spite of having grown up on the sea. Knowing myself secretly guilty of such heinous familial heresy kept me from freaking out whenever well-meaning friends and relatives tried to tell me I take after this unbridled man. Not that I need such puerile defenses to ward him off any more. He's been gone way too long for that.

He doesn't offer to apply the band-aids. Not that I'm about to let him touch me anyway. What he calls "female complaints" always did roll off his back like water off a duck's. How sad that Mom would shrug me off whenever I tried to sympathize with her lot. Oddly memorable phrases like "my man's no woman's fool" would come tripping off her tongue. On one occasion, she even told me that Leo was "the challenge that makes my life worth living." Whatever that's supposed to mean.

I curl up as best I can in the uncushioned cockpit the better to think about her and the cross he made her carry. Maybe all she was trying to tell me was the painfully obvious: that Leo was just plain challenged and needed her to look after him. God knows he's sure gone to hell in a basket since she died!

'Hey, Sorcière, that's the North Atlantic out there, you know, not the South Pacific. The Zen of sailing these waters doesn't come from lying around tanning your curvaceous hide. Here, put this on.' I heave myself up on my elbows, and he snaps the bundled lifejacket at me like a football. Poof! It strikes exactly where he means it to strike. Then he flashes me his patented evil grin and goes back to hoisting the mainsail.

All the while he holds the tiller clamped between his bony thighs. Too late I catch myself wishing its extension would rear up and thump him where it supposedly does a man the most good. Sure enough, the rudder hangs up hard. Thump! It's all I can do to keep from giggling like a giddy schoolgirl.

Yet he doesn't even so much as flicker an eyelash as the sailboat bumps over the snag. So much for it being so painful. He just looks at me and grins. 'I see you've taken to wearing dear Marie's old ring. You didn't use to wear it.'

'It was too big. I had to have it resized. It's still really too clunky for a woman to wear, but I like it.' I start putting on the familiar faded-yellow lifejacket that Leo custom-designed to fit Mom. All its adjusting straps have been seized, but I'm damned if I'll give him the satisfaction of complaining about too tight a fit. I wouldn't put it past him to deliberately rig it this way for my benefit. Back in the old days, he couldn't get enough of twitting me about how much larger in the bust I got to be than Mom. No end of ingenious suggestions and innuendoes! Oh this man could come up with a thousand ways to provoke you without even trying!

I get myself all snugly buckled up before it dawns on me that something rather significant is missing from our little equation. 'That birthday gift I gave you the year before Mom died – where is it, Leo?'

'What birthday gift?'

'The life-vest – the one with the built-in auto-inflation device. It cost me a small fortune, you know.'

'Oh that. Sorry, I lost it overboard a while back.' Now Leo knows that I know he's way too seasoned a sailor to ever just lose anything overboard. He takes his time cleating off the main halyard before checking to see whether his lie will wash. 'Why do you look at me that way, ma petite sorcière? You think I bother wearing a life jacket now that your mother is gone?'

I've never had it in me to humor that dark underlying streak in him. No more can I bring myself to offer up the obligatory cliché about how he still has Philippe and me to live for. Truth is, we've never been close to him, my brother and I — not since when he used to carry us about the deck on his shoulders and feed us his to-die-for fish chowder after we came in from sailing. But those are not memories I care to dwell upon. God knows he's made it clear enough over the years that he doesn't have much use for them either. So the best I can do is gesture bravely at the sea and sky around us. 'Oh do stop feeling sorry for yourself, Leo! You're still free to sail all this. That's more than most people can say.'

Just in time, I restrain myself from slipping "at your age" into that pathetic little speech of mine, but his mind's too perverse to have missed the inference. From the corner of my eye, I follow the lingering way his glance trails from me to the hard-drawing sails and the cold-green island-speckled waters of the Bay. It's as if he wants to drink it all in one more time. 'I know what you're thinking, Sorcière, but don't go getting your hopes up just yet.'

'Talk about flattering oneself, Leo! Do be a good boy and go put your life jacket on! If you fall overboard, somehow I just don't see myself soloing this empty beer can of yours back to port. You should have let me teach you how to swim while you had the chance.'

'Real sailors never learn to swim, Sorcière — you know that.'

It always amazes me how he can state the most preposterous things and still keep a straight face! 'I've heard you say that often enough, but I've never understood why.'

'It's analogous to the notion of a captain going down with his ship. A true sailor who needs to swim has already lost all he has to lose. So, ma petite sorcière, if I

do go overboard, just keep on sailing and don't look
back. There's no call to look at me cross-eyed like that!
What better way for an old sea-dog to go?'

'Jesus Christ, Leo, pray spare me the theatrics! Go
put your lifejacket on, okay?' I move from the cockpit
to escape the oppressive aura of him. I grip the stain-
less steel port shrouds with both hands. 'I know you
think me a coldhearted bitch, but do you really think I
could do such a thing?'

'I think of you as a witch, not a bitch, remember?
Think about it, Sorcière. I'm no longer part of this
world. Haven't been since your mother died. So I'm
more than ready to leave it. I only came home to see
you and Philippe one last time.'

I close my eyes to squeeze back the tears. 'Oh, that's
so damned thoughtful of you, Leo! It really is!'

'You don't believe me, do you?'

'Hey, Leo, it's me, the real flesh-and-blood Marie!
I'm the one who knows you from way back!' He looks
me straight in the eyes as though he can't quite believe
his ears. Then for the first time, I savor the sweet sensation of not being the one who has to turn away.

He stands up, shaking his head and rubbing his
grizzled jaw with the back of his hand the way a
punchy boxer might. How come I didn't notice the cane
he keeps tube-mounted inside the companionway till
he draws it forth? 'Here, take the tiller, will you? Keep
her headed south by southeast while I hoist the stays'l.'

Marie needs more sail like we need more holes in
the head. I'd say she's already surfing well past her
rated hull speed. She may look broken down, but she
dashes like a thoroughbred through the swells sweeping the open Bay. Close-hauled like this, all that
damned staysail does is make her heel a lot more than
she needs to. The cold choppy waves slop over her
gunwales and douse me with a fine spray. I lick salt
from my lips. It tastes a lot like blood. Why do I bother

feeling angry as I watch Leo drag one stiff leg forward? The whole point of this man ever doing anything is the overdoing of it. He has sailed his whole life through on the verge of knockdown. I shout at him over the sail-twisted wind. 'You haven't changed the least little bit, have you?'

'I sincerely hope not, ma petite sorcière.' He pulls his navy blue tuque down over his ears. Mom knitted that ratty old thing for him years before I was born. I watch the spray bead like so many pearls in his bushy gray beard and eyebrows. It's as if I'm sharing *Marie's* cockpit with one of our seafaring ancestors. Nothing ever really changes in the Campagna family. There's something timeless about the way he licks his sun-chapped lips as he works the winch and talks to the sail. 'Just knowing that life's slings and arrows haven't shot me down like most people shoot themselves down before they reach the end — that's my one consolation for having lived.'

I'm one of those Shakespearean spear-chuckers he's alluding to in his cryptic fashion, of course. Okay, I admit it: there was a time just after Mom died when I did my best to do what she couldn't. She and Philippe always accepted that changing him just couldn't be done, but I never did, until he finally just sailed away. Not that I harbor any regrets over his going, mind you. Living my own life to the full has taught me to be thankful for small mercies. There's no way I could ever have become what I am if he had remained part of me. He's like a vestigial organ that one must cut off to survive.

No, there's definitely no point in trying to change him this late in the picture. With Mom gone, he has no one left to hurt but himself anyway.

In token of truce, I pull his grandfather's brass spy-glass out of its kapok case. I put it to my eye and try to imagine myself a pirate of yore on the lookout for prey, the way Philippe used to do as a boy while I looked down my sisterly nose at him. A few white sails ghost across the entrance to the Bay. Out beyond the barrier islands looms the gray North Atlantic, a vast malevolence blocking out the sunrise and threatening to pirate all my dreams. 'Fess up, Leo. You're taking me somewhere, aren't you?'

'Hey, you're not psychic, remember?'

'If I were really psychic, I wouldn't have to ask where we're going, now would I?' And suddenly I don't have to ask. I remember all too well why I jumped overboard that last time we went sailing. 'Leo, don't go getting morbid on me again, okay?'

I hate that unrelenting smile of his. 'You've never yet made it out there, have you, ma petite sorcière?'

'For the perfectly good reason that I never-ever wanted to make it out there.' I succeed with some difficulty in modulating the rising pitch of my voice. Pent up anger shudders through my inner core, but I refuse to let it get the better of me. 'Leo, it's just conceivable that we could make it through this day together and go our separate ways with pleasant memories of one another. Let's just day-sail around the Bay the way we planned to do, okay?'

'The way you and Philippe planned it, you mean? He chose not to come along, you notice, but there's no easy way out for people like you and me, Sorcière. This time we're making it all the way back to where our story begins. You're going to have your nose rubbed in what's waiting for us out there — unless of course you take it into your head to go swimming again.'

Which is definitely not a valid option this far out from shore; the water's too cold this early in June for even an expert swimmer like me to chance it. So to keep from feeling shanghaied and maintain some semblance of control, I set myself to stay at the helm all that long sail down the Bay. He knows me well enough to know he'd have to force me to give over, and I know him well enough to know he'll let me steer so long as I stay on the course he sets. Not that I have any illusions what would happen if I make a break for it. Hell hath no fury like this man when he's really crossed. And all the while, he just stands there as cool as you please on the foredeck, looking straight ahead. One hand bracing his blackthorn cane, the other light on the forestay as though he fancies himself *Marie*'s carved figurehead.

Under his feet, she plunges onward like a champion headed for the finish line. Even I can't help admiring the way she takes everything in her stride in spite of all the slings and arrows she's had to endure along the way. Who was it put those bullet holes in her bows, I wonder?

Hey, how come it never struck me before how many damned islands are out here in this Bay? They all look pretty much the same from a distance. Yet it seems like I've always known without knowing that Sanctuary isn't like any of these other islands. We Campagnas made it different spilling our blood there more than two centuries ago. Good God, it feels like I've got a carrier pigeon's brain or a GPS implanted inside my skull!

So I don't need Leo or the chart to know which island to head for. When it finally opens up from the pack, I recognize it immediately from the shiver that runs up and down my spine. It's like I hear a voice calling me across the water from this postage stamp of an island. Really, it's nothing more than two heavily wooded hummocks joined by a strip of beach and a tidal marsh.

I point *Marie* up into the wind as Leo clumps his way back to the cockpit. 'Not yet, ma petite sorcière. I'll have you sail her right into that little pocket-cove, if you please — over there on the sandy beach side of the *barrachois*.'

He has to be pulling my leg. 'Shit on that, Leo! That cove's got to be too shallow for a boat this size. *Marie* will never make it in there!'

13

'She has done it once already! With her centerboard up, this boat'll navigate in a heavy dew.'

'Centerboard?' What the hell's wrong with me, anyway? How could I possibly have steered this boat all morning long without noticing she's a lift-keel? Has Leo really put me off my stride that much?

I let *Marie* have her head. Slowly she heels over as Leo winches the heavily ballasted wedge of aluminum up into her belly. 'La voila! Time to jibe, ma petite sorcière.'

Talk about me being a witch! It still amazes me after all these years how Leo works the sails like a bloody warlock! The main boom hardly jibes at all despite the stiff breeze shoving us along. And then as if he's charmed it somehow, the wind just goes away. Wing on wing, *Marie* glides into the little cove like the old gray mare coming back to her stall. It's quiet in here with these heavily wooded ridges enveloping us. Still as a millpond and so clear you can see all the way to the bottom. Nothing down there but the odd bottle and beverage can. Somehow the Twenty-First Century hasn't quite overwhelmed this island yet.

I help Leo set the plow anchor and stow the sails. Then I kick off my boat-shoes and execute one of my patented swan dives over *Marie's* stainless-steel pushpit.

Turns out, there's not quite enough water for the graceful exit I was hoping to make. I have to fend off the rocks with my bandaged forearms. The water is even colder than it looks, but I stay submerged till the shock of it drives me surging to the surface for a warm breath of air. I could probably wade ashore from here, but I swim faster than I sprint. So I start crawling for the sandy ribbon of beach. There's a dull splash behind me. That will be Leo launching the dinghy. I morph into a barracuda and go streaking through the water.

Shivering cold in dripping wet jeans and T-shirt: how's that for a fitting way to climb ashore on Sanc-

tuary Island for the first time? For right here is where
my refugee ancestors staked their first claim on this
New World of ours. Fleeing religious persecution, we
Campagnas came to this island hoping to make a fresh
start. Well, we didn't exactly get off to one, did we?
Downright amazing we're still alive and kicking two
and a half centuries later.

It's even more beautiful than I expected it to be, this
island of ours. So why even as a child did I fear to come
here? Somewhy I've always had this stupid idea that
something or somebody awful is waiting here for me.
Somebody who might tell me horrible secrets about
who or what I really am. Things I still don't want to
know. But hey, I'm a big girl now. Whatever comes, I
can take it or leave it.

Ah, feel that dark warm sand squishing up between
my toes! A good enough beach here for a quick-dry in
the sun, but no time for that, what with Leo close on
my heels. Besides, I didn't think to bring a bikini. Hell,
back in the land of Oz, we never bothered with any
bikinis. So why should I bother here?

I tug off the wet clothes, undergarments and all,
and leave them piled like a cairn on the beach. Just the
sight of them should be enough to keep Leo at bay for a
while. And now there's nothing left to keep me from
pretending I am the original Marie — or the original
Eve, for that matter. Let's see, where would you tell
your husband to situate your new home? Ah, but I don't
have to pretend anymore, do I? I am Marie's namesake,
ergo I am her living repository, as Mom would have it.
Build it up there on that high knoll, Luigi.

Who the hell ever said that? It's for sure the original
Marie wouldn't have talked like that. Her English probably wasn't much better than my French. Anyway, what
difference does it make what language she spoke? Just
use the universal translator straight out of Star Trek
and have done with it. *Build the house high up there on*

that knoll facing the entrance to the Bay, Luigi. Build it as high up there as you can build it. From way up there, we can see coming a long way off whatever they send after us.

They? Oh yes indeed, it came as no real surprise. We were expecting somebody nasty, Luigi and I. But even from up there the view wasn't good enough to save us. Fact is, looking out to sea was the wrong direction for what was coming after us! So much darkness and pain might have been avoided if I hadn't left it to others to watch Luigi's back. But it ill behooves those who come after us to think they could have done any better. They're the offspring of our darkness and pain. If we hadn't made our mistakes, they wouldn't be alive to make theirs, would they?

Hmmm, this water tastes a bit brackish. I remember now: Luigi told me to spit it out when we took our first walk down here. We still have to drink that awful ship's water, but he's promised me a well. Men are so dilatory when it comes to getting really important things done. And where's the path he had the Lüneburgers blaze for us along the edge of this pond? Gone now. Nothing here but us brambles, rocks and brush. It's as if Luigi and I never lived here at all. As if Nicole and the children hadn't roamed all over this island day after day. Damn good thing I don't need help to get where I am going. Not much farther to go — ouch! That hurts! I goofed big time not bringing my boat shoes along. At least there's no fear of getting lost so long as I keep heading for that knoll up there.

'Marie! Where are you!'

Meanwhile back at the beach! Just when I'm really getting into the spirit of this place, the dinghy bumps ashore and shatters the illusion. From the plaintive note Leo's sounding, I'd say he has found my clothes. He really wants me to answer him this time. No more of that "ma petite sorcière" shit. Ah, but it's too late to do your act of contrition, ole boy. Pray consider your cosmic role successfully performed in having dragged me this far. Whatever it is that made you bring me here, I mean to beard it in its den alone — not with you dragging your game leg along behind me.

Good God, my shattered virginity for a machete to cut through all this brush! What's this off to the right? A veritable palace in the midst of the jungle, no less! Covered in vines and thorns like Sleeping Beauty's Castle. Except this one's been built of factory-cut logs. Must have been quite a splendid summer retreat once upon a time, but look at it now! Rotting and tumble-down. Definitely not the ancient humble abode I'm looking for. But it does mean that someone else was living here not so long ago. Someone else failed to make a go of it here. Must be a curse on this island.

No curse, Madame. I don't much care for strangers, that's all.

'Marie! Where are you!'

Keep going. Mustn't look back now or I'll crystallize into a pillar of salt or something. Nothing here but these sharp rocks and brambles to hurt us anymore. Oops! Damn near lost a nipple on that one. There really is a point to wearing clothes, Virginia. Thank God it isn't much further to my lookout point. But which way through this jungle? Don't struggle. Just let that slight breeze at your stern push you along like a sailboat.

I'm waiting for you up here, Madame Campagna.

Who are you? Your voice sounds vaguely familiar, but I can hardly make it out. Whisper louder, please. God, what an imagination those two bundled into you, *Sorcière de la mer*!

Finally, light ahead at the end of the jungle! Like suddenly it's all opening up into a sort of waist-high meadow of tickly things. Ah yes, I remember well these lovely thistle blooms and brown-eyed susans. And there's the patch of juniper and milkweed. My knoll's straight ahead. A beautiful place for our house, if I don't say so myself. Even Luigi says he likes it up here, despite having to have everything packed all the way up from the cobblestone beach. He's building it for me in the shade of this magnificent ash. Hey, wait a minute! That can't be! This tree wasn't here before. The Luneburgers clear-cut all the trees up here that one time we went over to their village for the day.

Don't you remember, Madame? You planted this ash here and that staghorn sumac over there the day after you came back. I remember how angry you were.'

You say I planted these two trees? You must be mistaken; that yonder tree's too large for a sumac. I thought sumac never get to be much more than glorified shrubs. And what bright red leaves this one has! Why, it isn't even summer yet.

What do you expect, Madame? I watered it with my own blood.

You did? Just who the hell are you, anyway?

Don't you remember me, Madame? But no wonder, you left me here such a long time ago.

Are you accusing me of abandoning you?

No matter. I forgive you.

Yes, I've been gone a long time, haven't I? That's why everything seems wrong, including you. You're Nicole, aren't you?

So you do remember me?

Oh I remember you, Nicole, but you're coming on a bit too strong for my liking. Get behind me, O figment of my imagination! Hey, what's this? A ruined basement by the look of it. All that's left of my new house — the one the Luneburgers were building when they came for us. All that's left of our stay on this island. We lacked the mortar to hold these Cyclopean rocks together, but here they still stand, perched one on top of the other after all these years. And look, more foundation stones laid down there near the water as if someone had been building barns or something. No, I remember now. This is all that's left of Louis' beloved trading post ... and the storehouse. That's where it all came to an end ... almost.

'Marie! Where are you?'

Leo again, intruding upon my *recherché du temps perdu,* but thank God he's holding back, afraid to go beyond the cairn and stumble upon a naked woman in the altogether. Not just any naked woman. What was it he once called me — a frustrated Electra, wasn't it? God, how men do delude themselves with all their theories about what makes women tick!

Wait now! Here's something strange — these weathered sticks crisscrossed at my feet? They're covering up something. It's a pit, a trap for catching animals! No, silly goose, this is Luigi's well! The one you nagged him to build. It must have been a surprise for me. See how he had his workers line it with rock? Poor man, he never got around to building a proper well house. My God, I could have fallen in so easily — one more step! And no way out; it looks deep and the dark water is a long way down. Waiting here like a trap for someone to step on this leaf litter and go crashing through. 'Tis a wonder no one's ever been drowned in this.

No one's ever been drowned in my well, Madame. I myself was no longer alive when they threw what was left of me down here.

Then you were with me when they came?

Mais oui, Madame, I was here with you till the very end.

Till the very end, you say? Yes, oh yes, for you it was indeed the very end. Certainly what happened here put an end to all we were hoping for, didn't it? But everything for me is still a blur of shadows, Nicole. Help me to see things just as clearly as you did once before. For that is why Leo brought me back here, isn't it? He knows who I am! He brought me back here to remember things as they were.

How else can the lost promise be kept if the Chosen Seed does not remember? I am a well of memories, Madame. To relive them, all you need do is come down into me.

But you are so very deep, Nicole. So very deep and dark. The last of the Dread Maidens. I was always afraid of you, just as I am afraid of you now. Seems like you were always forcing me to learn that which I would rather not learn. I'm not being fair to you, am I?

Fair enough, Madame. Fair enough. Why else do you think I am still waiting here but to set things right between us?

But I am afraid, Nicole, so very afraid of you. How will I ever be able to free myself from you if I do as you say?

That is as may be, Madame. This time around, learning what you need to learn from me must be your free choice. You have come a long way and are past forcing, even by a Dread Maiden. You alone must decide whether the risk be worth it — the unfolding of this dream for which we have both waited so long. Only know this — we shall both be free of one another from this moment onward, whatever you decide to do this day. If you go from me now, I shall not be here waiting for you, should you ever come this way again.

Seems like you are giving me no more choice than you gave me last time. You always make me feel like I'm jumping off a cliff into the darkness! Do you think I am such a fool as to let you do this to me again?

Come back, Madame! You must come back!

Get back to the beach and put your clothes back on before you do something stupid, Girl. Don't look down. Just keep walking away from this haunted place. That reflection off the water is blinding me. Wait, there's the cliffs. I'm walking in the wrong direction. Feel dizzy like I'm going to faint.

'Marie! Where are you?'

That's Leo calling me! Go back the way you came before it's too late! Try not to run! 'Leo, I'm coming! Wait up!'

Try not to trip over these sticks! Omigod, I'm falling!

So nice of you to join me, Madame. I thought you would never come, but better late than never!

Chapter II

REFUGEE

Isle of Jersey, December 1755

As before, morning light awakened her to fearful wonder at her strange surroundings. How came she here to musty tapestries and long corbelled windows? She was safe now, her husband assured her. Yet when awakened from nightmares, she did not feel safe.

She slid from under the embroidered lilies of the heavy counterpane and lowered her bare feet to the oak floor. It felt warm after the stone flagging of the seminary, and the dark walnut paneling of the walls enclosed and protected her from the cold. *Yet wood can burn: I do not want to be trapped and burned!*

The long flannel nightgown tripped her as she dragged her lame foot into the sunlight. What did they call this cold blue sea? Ah yes, Baie de St. Aubin. This whitewashed town that gave her refuge was called St. Helier. And looming just barely visible in the distance, that gray ominous coastline was her beloved France.

That she was Marie Campagna, the wife of a merchant of considerable means, was the hardest of all to comprehend. There, just down the street, was the barnlike Huguenot church where she had wedded Luigi Campagna just three months ago. This was his fine house she dwelt in. Two of those ships anchored off the tidal flats belonged to him.

The square tower of the Catholic parish church still dominated this 'English town'. How powerfully it pulled at her in spite of everything. Madame Campagna hugged her arms about her and looked to the great turreted fortress standing guard across the harbor. Elizabeth Castle, they called it, after the English Queen who had built it to safeguard the island from the 'papists'. The stout stone ramparts and cannon comforted her, but she still felt the old danger lurking outside, waiting to get in.

Her eyes turned to the English man-of-war lying at anchor before the Castle. Her husband had explained that such formidable fighting ships were the real defense of the island, that no French army could cross the tidal races so long as the British Navy guarded La Passage de la Deroute. Yet she longed to be gone from here. The danger was much too close. Perhaps, if they traveled far enough, she would be safe and could allow herself to remember....

Madame Campagna listened warily to the industrious sounds emanating from her antechamber. Her ear cocked to the wall and holding her breath, she could even overhear the dovelike whimpers of Nicole's two-year-old son and the chiding maternal responses. At first the presence of Guillaume had seemed to irritate her husband. Yet slowly he had come to share her joy at the way the servant-child filled the great empty house.

Luigi Campagna's own three children were much older and far away in England with their great-uncle. The thought of her three stepsons passed like a shadow over Marie's mind. She thought of the first Madame Campagna, Eloise Le Masson, and devoutly wished her alive again. That way, she would be spared the burden of another woman's cross.

Surely Luigi Campagna deserves better of me than such thoughts. God knows he asks for very little. The black-habited nuns prepared me to expect much worse from my future husband. Of course, secluded nuns know nothing of austere Huguenots, whose needs are clearly different from those of worldly Catholics.

Indeed, Marie knew very little about her Calvinist husband. At least not the things women generally think it important to know about men. It was all very well to own ships and a house, but how came a Huguenot by an Italian name? *And who were his parents, his brothers and his sisters? And why is he so determined to take his sons and me to the New World? He says we will be safe there, that our enemies will never find us there.*

Her husband had been reluctant to answer her questions. All she had managed to learn was that Luigi Campagna was born a Genoese but had lost his family during a bloody revolt on the island of Corsica. A family of Huguenot merchants from Marseilles had sheltered the orphan and eventually helped him recover much of the Campagna property. The Christian charity of the Le Masson family had manifestly impressed the young man. He had converted to the persecuted religion and married the daughter of the family.

Marie heard his rich baritone invade the antechamber. *He is not a young man anymore. The wrinkles are deeply etched around his blue eyes, and those unfashionable gray whiskers have overgrown his face. Shall I never persuade him to trim that rat's nest? I know! I shall give him that ivory-handled shaving-kit as a birthday gift, the one Nicole showed me at Antoine's. Hah, something has excited him!*

His brisk rapping irritated her. She turned back to the morning sunshine and her spectacular view of St. Helier. She thought it wrong for a woman's husband to knock upon her chamber door, but surely it was up to him to set things right between them. 'Entre, Monsieur, s'il tu plait.'

'Madame, c'est ici!' French was pouring from his lips as he burst through the door, but Luigi Campagna bethought himself and paused to form his racing thoughts into halting English. One must adapt if one is to survive, he was fond of saying, and he wanted them both to be fluent in English before embarking upon their great adventure. 'I have here a letter from my late wife's uncle, the one with a position in the British Foreign Office.'

'Sir Yves Le Masson?'

'Yes, him.' He stumbled on, advancing uncertainly into the room. 'He writes to inform us that His Majesty, King George II, has finally granted us the charter to set up a trading post on an island in Nova Scotia!'

'And this savage island of yours — does it have a name, Monsieur?' Marie tripped over the awkward words. She disliked the harsh foreign tongue almost as heartily as she loved her lilting native French, but there were so few ways she could think to please her husband. She caught hold of the parchments he kept waving at her the better to partake of his enthusiasm.

'No, Madame, not yet! As I promised you, it belongs to my lovely young bride to name the island.'

'It must be given an English name, of course?'

'Yes, of course! We dare not offend the English by giving a French name to a place so recently conquered from our former countrymen.'

'So we can expect to find conquered Frenchmen there, Monsieur?'

'Yes, Madame, but rather a strange lot of Frenchmen, according to Uncle Yves. Even the French are inclined to disown them, and he's warned me to have nothing to do with them. They're devout Catholics, you understand. They consider us Huguenots the spawn of Satan.'

'It sounds just like here.' Marie gestured at the distant coastline.

'It will be different there, Madame, I promise you,' He seized both her hands with a passion so Italian that it both shocked and pleased her. In such moments she wanted to trace his face with her fingertips to discover whatever made it so alive. It had to do with the eyebrows, she decided. Like festoons of exotic fungi, the great coarse white hairs bristled forth from their tamer dark cousins to obscure the darting sea-blue eyes. She had been revolted by such profusion at first, but one could follow the course of each hair as though it lived a life of its own.

'Bien, Monsieur. Let us call our new island home Ile de la Sanctuaire.'

'Sanctuary Island.' He mused, cocking one eye shrewdly. 'Yes, it does sound much better in French, but still, the translation should offend no one.'

Guillaume raced into the room with Nicole in hot pursuit. Luigi Campagna snatched up the squealing child and swung him high to the ceiling. For a moment their pooled laughter filled the chamber, but again Campagna bethought himself, extending the squirming Guillaume to his mother and looked askance at his wife. 'My apologies, Madame. I abuse the privacy of your boudoir. Pray excuse me, for there's a great deal to do.'

'There's no harm done, Monsieur.' Marie searched vainly for English words to reassure him, but her husband bowed and was gone.

'I'm sorry, Madame.' Nicole clutched Guillaume to her breast to prevent his pursuit of their master. 'This child of mine will be the death of me, I'm sure.'

'It's all right, Nicole — we mustn't let little things upset us. The Master is right: a great deal lies in store for us in the days ahead. We must prepare ourselves accordingly.'

'This voyage the Master is planning in such a great hurry, Madame. Does it not frighten you that we must cross a great ocean in winter?'

'Such things are inevitable, Nicole.' Marie wondered if she were being tested, for it was not like her maid to express such doubts. 'The plans of men always frighten women, but in the end one has to go along with them, is it not so? However, the Master and I will understand if you decide not to go with us.'

'Mais non, Madame! Haven't I followed you across all of France? Would I desert you now?'

'Bien, but you have Guillaume to think of, Nicole. Perhaps you do not wish to take him to some heathen place far across the sea. Have you even so much as heard of this Nova Scotia before? Certainly, it is unlikely that we shall ever see this Isle of Jersey again.'

'Excuse me, Madame!' Nicole drew herself up as only she could. 'What call have I given you to talk to me like this? Why, begging your pardon, Madame, but Guillaume thinks as much of the Master as though he were his own father. I'm not about to take him away from the only family he's ever likely to have!'

'Ah, Nicole, what a caution you are!' Marie filched a handkerchief from her sleeve to dab at her eyes. 'But what would I do without you?'

'Ah, Madame, that is a question I often ask myself! You live so much in dreams that a feathered Indian might sneak up and cut off your lovely black tresses — and you none the wiser! I have to go along to help the Master protect you. The Lord knows he'll have his hands full with that awful crew of pirates he's signed on.'

'Nicole, you must stay away from those sailors. Just look what happened last time!'

'Ah Madame!' Nicole smiled and continued stroking her son. 'It's amazing what fine things come from such scalawags, is it not? And besides, how else am I to learn to speak that awful tongue of theirs? Which reminds me, a strange sailor in the market gave me a letter for you.'

'A letter? For me?'

'Pour Madame Campagne, he said. I weren't too sure at first because he spoke with a Brittany accent. He had the nicest brown eyes, though, and a lovely way about him for a common sailor.'

'Well, where is it? — this letter you say you have for me.'

Nicole retrieved a sealed envelope from the folds of her apron. 'It looks important, does it not?'

Lacking an apron, Marie placed the letter on her night table. 'Thank you, Nicole. I'll read it later.'

The disappointment writ large on the maid's Gallic features left no doubt that she had expected to be her mistress's confidante in the matter of the letter. Not for the first time, it crossed Marie's mind that she had made a mistake in permitting a virtual friendship to develop between them. They had been through so much together. She would still be a prisoner back in France if not for the courage and fidelity of this young serving-woman. 'We have much to do, you and I. We are two women about to cross an ocean alone, except of course for a score or so of men. That means we shall spend the rest of our lives regretting all the things we leave behind.'

'The Lord made men to think only of their brandy and guns.' Nicole sniffed, seemingly mollified to conspire with her mistress on a womanly level. 'Even the Master asked the other day why you needed to take along so many needles and spools of thread. I had to bite my tongue, I did.'

'Now that we are sure we are going, we must work harder still, you and I.' The young mistress had to work hard at playing the role fate had so mysteriously assigned her. In suppressing the delight she took in her maid, it never occurred to the Huguenot merchant's wife that she possessed the soul of a sculptor. She often caught herself studying the planes and angles of Nicole's face. Its distinctive beauty had already been somewhat marred by hard experience. *Yet it is precisely the lines and that odd scar that define and ennoble her.*

Yes, ennoble is not too strong a word! Where else could such a wondrous visage be shaped but in the France I am leaving behind forever?

'The Lord knows there are worse things to be doing than spending the master's money.' Nicole produced her penned list, oblivious of her mistress's thoughts but warmed by her presence. 'We'll be needin' a lot more flannel, I think, and more bolts of good Irish linen wouldn't go amiss either. This Nova Scotia is a cold and savage place, by all accounts.'

'Bien, Nicole.'

'And you must buy those wonderful Swedish razors for the Master. If his beard makes it unscathed to Nova Scotia, there'll be no shaving him for sure.'

After Nicole and Guillaume had sailed off to discharge a hundred and one critical errands, Madame Campagna considered her mysterious letter. The thick vellum envelope lay on her morning table, exuding disturbing emanations. She could think of no one likely to communicate with her in such a manner. Her past had been utterly erased, had it not? Clearly the right thing to do was to place the sealed letter in the hands of her husband and attend upon his judgment. Yet she had known Luigi Campagna for only a short time, and it rankled innate feminine sensibilities to wholly absolve herself of responsibility for her own actions. Besides, her curiosity was overpowering.

The unfamiliar wax seal, bearing the impress of a rampant lion, yielded reluctantly to the letter-knife. The faintest odor of an exotic aromatic reached her nostrils as she unfolded the parchment. The script was written in a bold hand remarkable for the grace of its unadorned Roman characters. Madame Campagna sensed a masculine presence even before she began to read the elegant French:

Madame,

We are not acquainted. Indeed, wiser heads have determined that we continue strangers to one another. Yet it is of crucial importance that our paths cross on a single occasion. I wish I could explain further, but the danger for us both is too great to pen such confidences.

Accordingly, I ask your indulgence in meeting with me, alone, under cover of tomorrow's night at the Hermitage of Saint Helier. Trusting in our common destiny,

I remain,

Chevalier Guy de Bouillion, Keeper of the Faith

Madame Campagna's slender hand trembled as she replaced the folded letter on her morning stand.

Chapter III

EXCURSION

Saint Helier, December 1755

The ultimate disciples of discipline had taught Marie to honor and obey. Utterly bereft of any sense of personal volition, she read her mysterious letter to her myopic husband during their candlelit meal that same evening. 'May I leave it to you to keep this appointment with a stranger, Monsieur?'

'Mais non, Madame, you yourself must be the one to keep it.' With masculine aplomb, the Huguenot sampled vintage Bordeaux from the cask delivered that morning from his brig, *Felicité*. 'Far from his being a stranger, I take this Guy de Bouillion to be the one we've been waiting for so long.'

Luigi Campagna's outward composure failed to relieve Marie of her misgivings. Indeed, the slight tremor afflicting her husband's wine goblet convinced her that he must have anticipated events, even if he had not actually authored them. Clearly, the letter had not arrived by sheer coincidence on the same day as notice of the land grant from the English King. She could not keep her rising anger from manifesting in her voice. 'So then, Monsieur, you know this gentleman who signs himself "Keeper of the Faith"?'

'Au contraire, Madame, I've not even so much as heard of him before.' Luigi Campagna performed the awkward language shift with a flurry of his thick peasant-like fingers. 'But you need not look so perplexed. Over the years, the Societé's minions have become much too adept at compromising even the most faithful of our brethren. We have learned the hard way that the left hand must never know what the right hand is doing.'

'Yet you seem quite certain of his identity.' Marie set aside her glass. She relished the full-bodied wine, but a few sips were always enough to cloud her mind. 'How can you be so sure this letter is not meant to deceive us?'

Luigi Campagna shifted in his high-backed chair and coughed discreetly into his napkin. 'There is a sign concealed within the text, Madame.'

'A sign to which you are privy, Monsieur? Ah, so I was supposed to show you the letter.' Marie pressed her own lace napkin to her cheek. 'What if I had not?'

'It would indicate lack of prudence on your part.' The wine gleamed darkly on Luigi Campagna's lips, a droplet forming in the inner beard wreathing the cleft of his chin.

'So, indeed! Along with everything else, I am being tested.' Marie did not try to keep her voice from shrilling this time. 'And you expect me to accept all this on faith, Monsieur?'

'What better grounds for acceptance is there, Madame?' Campagna's face remained a smooth mask, but his neck flushed darkly. 'What else is there for us in this world but faith?'

Not for the first time, Marie dared to wonder whether all men were given over to religious fanaticism. Certainly the ones she had known so far in life gave every sign of possessing that trait in common. *Yet have a care with your casting of stones, Madame Campagna. For better or for worse, your life is entrusted*

34

to this man. To date he has borne that trust rather well, has he not? Yes, but more like a father than a husband. He has risked his life to save you from the others, has he not? Yes, but more for the sake of his brethren than the sake of his wife. 'Bien, Monsieur. I shall do as you instruct me. What other choice is there for such as me?'

'By God's grace, even the most humble of his creatures is given choice.' Luigi Campagna held his glass up to the candle the better to appreciate the Bordeaux's fine play of color. 'But only He knows from the beginning of Time which choices we will make.'

His words dragged Marie down the sinkhole of memory. A child, she did penance on her knees in the wintry courtyard of the priory — that same priory where all her memories began. Gray-spotted, the figure of Father Jerome danced above the thin snow, his cowled head blotting out the weak sunlight. *For the sake of your soul, Holy Church has redeemed you from eternal perdition, Marie. Never forget that your parents died unrepentant heretics. Your request to know more of them is a sign that the Evil One still has power over you. Pray for God's Grace, my child.*

In numb horror, Marie watched the image of her confessor resolve into that of her husband. 'It is no part of mine to make this choice for you, Madame — neither this one nor the choices that must surely follow. You alone must choose which way you are to go.'

'Then I shall pray that your guidance sets me on the right path, Monsieur.'

'Every care has been taken to make it so, Madame, I assure you.' Luigi Campagna let his fingers brush hers for the briefest moment. 'Do not fear. Each approach to the Rock of the Hermitage shall be guarded. You will be safer whilst there than you are here in this room with me.'

'It is not my safety I fear for, Monsieur.' Marie struggled to keep her voice even, though she had long despaired of ever seeming more than a flighty girl to her husband. 'It is rather a question of fearing to go on dwelling in this dark cave. Is your conscience clear that you have told me everything?'

'You know everything I know, Madame, other than certain details that would endanger the lives of other people.'

'Such as who these brethren of yours really are?'

The Huguenot sighed like an expiring saint and glanced about the shadow-streaked walls. 'I shall repeat my general instructions once again if you wish it of me.'

'That would be good of you, Monsieur. Pray pardon a poor woman's inability to grasp such things.'

'Very well.' Luigi Campagna drank deeply of his goblet as though it were the well of memory itself. 'My brethren contacted me in the usual manner to offer me a commission. It was made plain to me that I must prepare myself to travel to the ends of the world in the fulfillment of it.'

'To the ends of the world?' Marie leaned forward till the candle illuminated her widow's peak. 'That is a long way. You must have considered such instructions highly extraordinary, Monsieur.'

'Madame, it was merely a matter of freeing a young woman of our faith from the papists. Such things I have done before at the bidding of my brethren.'

'Did your first wife require such a service?' Suddenly Marie felt herself hot on the scent for some clue to the mystery of it all.

'Eloise? Mais non! We knew each other as children in Marseilles, long before this latest time of troubles.' Campagna threw up his hands in protest. 'Do you think I make a profession of marrying fair ladies in distress?'

'You married me, Monsieur.' Marie's breath fluttered the candle. 'Did your brethren order you to do that?'

Campagna managed a Gallic shrug. 'I was advised that taking you to wife would greatly assist matters. It is not that unusual a procedure. This way little trace is left for the Societé to follow.'

'What else did they order you to do?'

Campagna shrugged eloquently. 'They instructed me to discreetly sell or else abandon my property in France. I was further instructed to fetch my sons home from the papist schools they are forced to attend. I have smuggled them abroad, as you already know. Finally, I was myself commanded to flee the kingdom once you were safely delivered into my hands.'

'Your brethren ask a great deal of you, Monsieur.'

'You must understand, Madame: I have wanted to leave France ever since Eloise died.'

'To go to this frozen wasteland of yours?'

'Only since coming to this Isle of Jersey was I told Nova Scotia would be our destination. It is not so bad a place by all accounts, Madame. We should be quite safe there.'

'You forget there's a royal bounty on your head, my husband. Your three ships and this fine house are not all that invisible on this little island.'

'I admit I was somewhat clumsy in extricating myself.' Again Luigi Campagna sighed deeply. 'Yet let us thank God for small mercies, Madame. I am quite lost in the crowd of the many heretics the Societé hunts all over Europe. As for yourself, there's no reason to believe they have yet discovered your true identity.'

'And pray, what identity is that, Monsieur?' Marie rose off her chair. 'All I know is that I am Marie Campagna, and Marie Campagna is nothing more than the wife of a Huguenot outlaw with a price on his head, is she not?'

'I am sorry, Madame.' Luigi Campagna was nothing if not patient with her. 'I know even less of your past than you remember.'

'The brethren told you nothing of me, Monsieur, do you swear it?'

'I swear it, Madame: I do not ask unnecessary questions, for it is better for such as me not to know such things lest I betray them. I only know your deliverance must be of great importance to the unfolding of God's will.'

'This Guy de Bouillion must share your opinion.' Marie handed her husband the letter. 'Perhaps he knows who I am.'

'That is one of the reasons you must go to him.' Her husband presented the stiff parchment-like paper to the flame. 'Guy de Bouillion undoubtedly holds the key to your whole affair, Madame.'

'My whole affair? You speak as though you were not truly part of all this, Luigi Campagna. What of us? Are we not truly man and wife?'

'Our marriage is legal under English law, Madame, I assure you. We are not living in sin.'

Silence enfolded the Campagnas as the parchment burned between them. Marie watched the Huguenot's stubby fingers deftly manipulate the flames without getting burned. *Indeed, your husband has done this many times before. He is an agent of the brethren, whoever they are. You are simply another mission and your state of matrimony only a ruse. You must never forget that, Marie Campagna. You must never delude yourself that you truly belong to this man. Yet you must learn to pretend so, if you are to survive.*

Marie repressed the hysteria welling in her throat as she waited for permission to withdraw. Yet still her husband's gaze remained fixed upon the guttering flames and ashes of the letter. Grown weary of staring past him, she crossed to the double window that looked out upon the roadstead of Saint Helier. There mounted on a pedestal stood a great brass telescope. Though not the kind of man to fix his eyes on distant stars, Luigi

38

Campagna was an accomplished celestial navigator. He had seemed to take delight in discovering the planets to his young bride.

Adjusting the eyepiece as he had taught her, Marie swiveled the telescope to the horizon and swept the harbor. The brief December twilight was failing; the shadows of Elizabeth's Castle were rapidly lengthening. Yet the Rock of the Hermitage was still clearly silhouetted in the waning light. She could just make out the solitary hermit's cell carved into the living stone near its tall summit. It struck her as a most incongruous place for a married woman to meet a total stranger.

What manner of man is this Guy de Bouillion? What do these so-called brethren want of you?

Nicole entered the dining room to light more candles and to pour tiny cups of coffee. Since becoming a wife, Marie had acquired a taste for the bitter beverage, just as her husband had assured her she would. How the nuns would chastise her for such indulgence, and Father Jerome condemn her for it to a thousand prayers in the snow. Yet she had known a kind of security in that cloistered place. Would her life ever know as much certitude again?

Marie waited till the maid had left the room. 'Bien, Monsieur, I shall obey you in all things, of course. Who knows? It may be that your reclusive friend is the hermit of the place.'

'That is extremely doubtful, Madame.' The Huguenot permitted himself a rare smile. 'The hermitage has been desolate for years.'

'Am I to assume that Nicole knows as little about this matter as you do?'

'I do not take your meaning, Madame.' Campagna hunched his shoulders again in the time-honored manner of a husband under fire.

'You are truly her master, are you not? It was no accident she found and guided me to Saint Malo after your false Franciscan was killed. You placed her in that inn to cover such an eventuality, didn't you, Monsieur?'

'Really, Madame, your suspicions will be our undoing!' Campagna cast about him with furtive eyes. 'Of one thing you may be certain: your maid Nicole is absolutely to be trusted.'

'You made such a display of hiring her for my sake.' Marie sat down and began sipping her coffee. 'What a simpleton you take me for!'

'I need Christ's atonement for many sins, Madame.' The Huguenot's voice turned hoarse with emotion. 'Disservice to you or contempt for your person is not numbered among them!'

'That much you have given me no reason to doubt, Monsieur.' Marie chose to grace her husband with a smile. 'Was there ever such a man and wife as we are?'

'Si, Madame.' Campagna labored visibly to calm himself after the storm. 'We are not the first to endure such times as these.'

Nor will we be the last. So long as this world persists, there shall always be those who suffer and die for what they truly believe. Yet you are not such a one, Marie Campagna, for you are sure of nothing. Only for the sake of your dead parents do you endure this madness. Who were they to have been so drawn into this nightmare? 'I could wish your wife were a braver woman, Monsieur. It is sad to be so afraid to live, is it not?'

'Believe me, Madame — there are much worse things to face in life than what we face.' Luigi Campagna reached out but could not quite bring himself to touch her. 'Have faith in God!'

That night Marie slept fitfully, dimly aware of her maid and husband hovering watchfully on the edge of her dreams. They tried but could not hold her back from sinking into the dark liquid terror on which she drifted. A young handsome man, a prince judging from the manner of his dress, came riding out of the high northern mountains into sun-drenched plains. She knew — though she knew not how — that some terrible fate awaited him there.

Once more, the morning sunlight brought a measure of relief from her nightmares. She rose with anticipation, somehow sure that she was drawing measurably closer to ending the doubt and fear she had always known.

The walnut case set out on the morning stand reawakened her slumbering fears. A brace of 'lady's companion pistols' nestled inside. Their fanciful Milanese workmanship could not disguise their deadly purpose: one shaped in the form of a pitcher-pouring nymph; the other a crouching, howling satyr. They were gifts from her Huguenot husband. 'With these miniatures at hand, you needn't feel helpless, Madame. They look too small to harm anyone, but they're quite lethal for all that.'

The last thing Marie required was such an assurance. It had been all she could manage just to indulge Campagna's desire to teach her to load and shoot the pistols. He had declared his wife a promising markswoman, but inwardly she knew herself quite incapable of firing the weapons in anger or even self-defense. Certainly she had no intention of bearing arms to the Rock of the Hermitage. Hadn't her husband given assurance she would be perfectly safe there? She closed the lid and slid the ornate case within the bottom drawer of her chamber commode.

Nicole had a steamy bath waiting for Marie. A chill passed over her before slipping into the warm water. She contrived to avoid the full-length mirror, knowing her body only too well. She was much too thin to be beautiful, and there was also the matter of her stiffened, deformed foot. No wonder Luigi Campagna had not consummated their marriage!

Madame Campagna remembered sadly a portfolio of Flemish lithographs hidden in the study of Father

Jerome. The young girl had discovered therein several nude women of truly wondrous proportions. Fortunately for her, the priest had never caught her spying among his treasures. What foolish compulsion had often driven her past fear to invade the priest's study? What had she been searching for in those marvelous but forbidden books? Ah yes, Father Jerome had been right to warn her against the incorrigible carnal nature of womankind.

Marie remained in her nightgown past noon. Nicole had difficulty persuading her mistress to lunch on poached quail eggs served upon a lightly toasted baguette fresh from the bakery of Saint Helier. Guillaume's merry antics and the promised reward of a coffee induced the young woman to consume half of her small portion.

Once or twice, Marie's mind wandered to Luigi Campagna. Was the Huguenot merchant down at the harbor readying his brigantine *L'Espérance* for their Atlantic crossing? More likely still, he was arranging for the coming rendezvous with Guy de Bouillion. It somewhat comforted the young matron to feel her husband at work insuring her safety.

Marie dressed carefully in a gabardine skirt and cloak that had once belonged to Eloise. The garments were slightly too big for her. A pair of the dead woman's soft kid boots and a fur-trimmed bonnet completed her accoutrement. The mirror image bemused both the young woman and her maid.

'Ah Madame, you're much too beautiful to be the wife of a merchant!'

'Don't be silly, Nicole. Look how thin and ugly I am!'

'Actually, you're the spitting image of the Marquise de Montcalm-Gozon. I saw her once at her husband's chateau at Saint Veran.'

'Whatever were you doing at the chateau of a marquis?' Marie still did not know quite what to make of Nicole.

'The general, that's her fine husband, hired me to teach the children English.' Nicole did not even so much as bat an eye while telling her wild tales. 'I was fixed to become governess, so I was, but her ladyship got an earful of my Langue d'oc accent and sent me packing.'

'That's terrible, Nicole! I'm so sorry for you!'

'Oh I didn't much mind, for I found those butlers and footmen an impudent lot. Not a true man among them, Madame, so help me God. Give me one of the Master's sailors any day.'

'Nicole!'

'Madame, it be God's truth! Serving marquises and such is no fit work for a proper man. It drains the spunk out of them, it does.'

'Really, Nicole, I've heard enough!'

'Yes, Madame, but if you pardon my saying so, there's a lot you would do well to learn about men.'

Or about women, for that matter. Other than you, Nicole, I've known only sworn virgins. Hardly women at all, those black-habited creatures from another world. Father Jerome once called them angels. Whatever they are, I shall never be free of them.

'Ah, if only men could all stay like this one.' Marie dandled Guillaume on her knee.

'And so they do, Madame, in a manner of speaking.' Marie marveled at how Nicole's vision of the world contrasted her own. How strange that she and Nicole had never discussed the letter, even while it was driving them both down a common path as if there were no turning back, no other choices for either of them.

As though reading her thoughts, the maid turned suddenly upon her, a roguish look in her eyes. 'You will be taking your pistols with you, of course, Madame.'

'No, Nicole, you know how I hate them!' Marie drew herself up as resolutely as she could manage.

'But the Master gave them to you! Faith, Madame, the loving work that's gone into them! They've got those new-fangled rifled barrels and everything.'

'I gladly give them to you. Don't argue with your mistress, Nicole. They're mine to give, aren't they? Who deserves them more than she who saved me from worse than death?'

'Madame, I just happened to be on hand when needed.' Indeed, the maid had never fully explained how a Huguenot serving-wench at a small inn near Toulouse "just happened" to prevent a young fugitive from being captured by her pursuers after her guide was murdered.

'Oh Nicole, I keep having awful dreams about how those evil men killed Brother Abélard!'

'He was only a paid agent posing as a Franciscan, Madame!'

'Yes, but he was the first man I've ever liked. I'd be back in the nunnery if it weren't for you and him.'

'But you act so sad, Madame! Sometimes you make me think you'd really rather be back in the nunnery.'

'I still suffer these terrible dreams, Nicole. It's because of the dreams I knew I was a prisoner in that priory. I often dreamt that I would escape someday and go find my parents.'

'This meeting today — I hope it will turn out to be something better than dreams.'

'I hope so, too, Nicole. As for these pistols, they've given me an idea! They're very valuable, aren't they? Perhaps we can sell them and provide you with a fine dowry.'

'I am sworn never to wed, Madame.' Nicole spoke with such a matter-of-fact air that her mistress simply couldn't credit the assertion.

'Of course you will wed! Why, a comely young woman like you! You said yourself Guillaume needs a father. And judging by what I see, you certainly need a husband! When we get to Nova Scotia, I shall put my mind to it. I'm sure even there we shall find many fine Christians in need of a good wife. Don't argue, Nicole.

You're to leave off those awful sailors and be bedded with a proper husband. That's final!'

The maid only smiled and went to fetch her mistress's cloak.

A fine carriage and four waited in front of the house. The breath of the dappled grays steamed the frosty air. Cutlasses dangling from their waist, a pair of sailors standing in as footmen clung precariously to the boot of the vehicle. Looking extremely disgruntled at finding himself a coachman, Jacques Sabot, sailing master of the *L'Espérance*, clambered down from the driver's seat. He knuckled his forehead and assisted the two women to mount. A huge pistol butt poked out from his makeshift livery as he did so. Only when all was set to go did he venture to speak. 'The master said to make it look like a Sunday outing, milady — so Sunday outing it is.'

An hour was spent making a circuit of the island. Peasants bowed and scraped at what no doubt seemed to them a splendid equipage of touring gentry. Marie thought their splendid blond cattle looked rather less impressed.

The pale sun was already low in the west when the coach approached a tiny cove situated just beyond the roadstead of Saint Helier. Sabot halted the horses and escorted his passengers down a steep set of steps to a makeshift fishers' dock.

Yet another of Luigi Campagna's seamen grinned up at the two women from a fishing dory. Nicole had seen fit to prepare Marie for the sight of Hugo Forth. A lurid scar from chin to ear gave a malicious cast to the coxswain's bluff English features. Marie saw him wink at Nicole over her own shoulder while steadying their entry into the boat. 'Just make yourself comfortable, ma'am. There's a spell of hard rowin' in store fer us.'

Marie sat herself in the bow of the dory to avoid eye contact with the disfigured sailor. Positioned to better advantage in the stern, her maid subjected the hapless

Hugo to a barrage of teasing banter and alluring glances. Mercifully, her antics did much to distract her mistress from the disquiet seething in the pit of her stomach.

Too soon, the Rock of the Hermitage rose up from the gathering mist and shadows. The coxswain expertly slid the dory into place alongside a stone jetty. Quickly he leapt out and secured the painter to a rusty spike, extending his arm to Marie. 'The gentleman's already arrived, ma'am.'

'He's already here? Where's his boat?'

'We seen him trekkin' across from Ole Bess's Castle at low tide. Dropped off there by a tender from Captain Vigot's old brig, 'e was. Not to worry, ma'am. 'E's a proper French toff by the cut of his jib.'

The coxswain's remarks reminded Marie that the Channel tides would soon ebb, that by morning the island would become a peninsula extending out from the Isle of Jersey. Reluctantly she placed one foot on the slippery rock of the jetty.

'I think I'd best come with you, Madame!' Nicole seized the rusty spike, holding the dory steady against the fractured rock. 'Now that it's come to it, I don't fancy leaving you here all by yourself.'

'The Master says I'm to go alone.' Marie drew her warm habit more closely around her. 'Don't worry, Nicole. I'll be safe enough, if I don't get lost.'

'The Rock ain't big enough fer to get lost, ma'am.' Hugo leapt into the dory and thrust it off with an oar as if fearing where the women's conversation might lead. 'Just go up the path till ye come to the hermit's cell. Now mind where you step — there be bluffs up there where a body could drop straight down into the sea.'

Biting her lip, Marie turned and began climbing the rock steps. When she looked back, the fog had already swallowed the fishing dory. The young wife of Luigi Campagna hiked up her skirts and hurried onward, conscious of her lameness as never before.

Chapter IV

COMMUNION

Rock of the Hermitage, December 1755

Climbing the Rock was for Marie very much like playing a part in the morality plays the black nuns had staged at the priory. Once or twice an ill wind shoved her off the giant steps cut into the black putrid stone. Malicious sprites rose up from the shadows and snatched at her stiffened foot, trying to trip her into the gnashing jaws of the rocks below. Yet always, a providential glow lit her starless way up the steep twisting path. Cold pure sea-breath filled her lungs with the courage to press on. She brushed past clawing brambles, whose dark shadows fled before her. Rallying the last of her strength, she reached the windswept summit.

Something intense and powerful waited in that lonesome place. Gasping for air, Marie felt its breath stir the hairs at the nape of her neck. She felt no malice in that touch; only a profound sadness, as though the presence despaired of reaching out to her. With a whip-like twist of her body, she let go her fancy and turned her face to the Hermitage.

The hermit's cell had been carved from the Rock's utmost pinnacle. A slatted wooden shutter and door were its only signs of ever serving as human abode. Glimpsing a flicker of light within, Marie breathed deeply and knocked. She had not yet exhaled when the door jarred open. 'Qui passe?'

Marie's heart filled with misgiving. The tender whisper and the slender silhouette that partially revealed itself in the doorway could well have been that of a woman. 'Je suis Marie Campagna. Et vous, Monsieur? Vous êtes le Chevalier Guy de Bouillion?'

'À votre service, Madame!' Marie drew another much-needed breath as the young man clicked his heels together and bowed. She was speaking to a young man who spoke excellent Parisian French. One gloved hand drew her into the light of the candle within. The other reached up and deftly tipped the riding bonnet from her hair. 'Yes, the perfect likeness of your mother!'

The stranger heightened Marie's confusion by doffing his wide-brimmed hat and bowing deeply from the waist. Adjusting to the candlelight, her eyes beheld a tall stripling of a man, whom she judged to be several years younger than herself. He was clean-shaven and wore his reddish-gold hair unfashionably long and flowing about his shoulders. A court sword hung from the broad silver belt that cinched his narrow waist. 'You knew my mother, Monsieur?'

The young man smiled sadly and shook his head. 'Only from her portrait, Madame.'

'I don't remember my mother at all.' Marie turned away from the stranger's too intense stare. 'Sometimes I think I see her in my dreams, but I can never be sure it is her.'

'You have only to look in a mirror, Madame.' The stranger fumbled in the fob of his waistcoat.

'I don't even know her name, Monsieur.' Marie choked on a torrent of shame and infinite regret.

'Lizé, her name was Lizé.' The young man placed a heavy object in her palm. 'Lizé de Noguet.'

'Lizé!' Marie echoed the name wonderingly, gazing at the lion rampant seal glowing red in the candlelight. 'It's a good Christian name, is it not? And what pray is this, Chevalier?'

'Tis a gift she gave to your father before you were born.' The signet ring hinged open at the youth's subtle touch. 'She would have been about your age when she sat for this portrait.'

Looking at the monochrome cameo inside was exactly like looking into a mirror. Hair so jet black it seemed tinged with blue, and skin so alabaster white it hurt Marie to gaze upon it. She snapped the lid shut. 'She is not at all as I imagined her to be!'

'Well, you are exactly as I imagined you to be! Pardon me, Madame: one small doubt still lingers.' The young man knelt down. Marie suspected him of performing a chivalrous act till he took hold of the boot that encased her right foot. He straightened in satisfaction at her lame recoil. 'Yes, all is as it should be! Now I am perfectly satisfied you are the one I seek.'

She was not about to forgive him for taking such liberties with her person. 'I cannot say confidence is mutual, Chevalier. I really have no idea who or what you are!'

Again the youth clicked his heels together. 'You and I are cousins, Madame.'

The casually spoken words staggered Marie. 'We are cousins?'

'Distant cousins, as reckoned by those whose business it is to keep track of our parallel lineages.' De Bouillion stepped backward appraisingly. 'But in some ways we are closer to one another than any cousins who ever lived.'

Marie exerted all her senses in trying to peer beyond the casual aristocratic arrogance, but the young man remained a blank page to her, little more than a semblance of what she had expected a kinsman to be. She hastened to remind herself that she had not come to this place with the least idea what to expect. 'I can see that you have not lived as I have lived, Chevalier.'

'Yes, I'm sorry I have been so much more fortunate than you, my dear cousin.' De Bouillion seemed to take Marie's comment for a reproach. 'You must try to understand: I've been surrounded always by the Templars — all of them wonderful knights, really. They indulged my every whim while teaching me whatever I needed to learn.'

'And I have lived always in a dark prison!' Marie made no attempt to keep the bitterness from edging her voice. 'Tell me this, Chevalier: how is it a stranger was sent to teach me my mother's name?'

'The game we have played so long was almost lost at the time you were born, dear Cousin.' De Bouillion's voice wavered and broke as though he were at a loss where to begin. 'Not even after the murder of the Emperor were we taken so unawares and brought so low. Both our lineages were almost extinguished.'

'After the murder of the Emperor? Both our lineages? What are you talking about?' Marie took a step forward, but the young man amazed her by shrinking back from her grip on his lapels till he was leaning against the stone wall of the cell. 'I beg your pardon, Chevalier, but I have waited so long! You must tell me who I really am!'

'Alas, dear Cousin, you were a dove helpless in the talons of a bird of prey.' De Bouillion rattled on as though entranced. 'Only your utter innocence kept you from being torn apart.'

'You speak in riddles, Chevalier.' Marie half-turned as though to go. 'Answer me fair or I shall leave this place. Is your band of wondrous knights and my husband's brethren one and the same?'

'Shh-h! First, I must make sure you weren't followed here.' The young man put an eye to a crack in the shutter. Watching him in the flickering candlelight, Marie decided his profile was extremely fair. 'We must be careful, Madame: even now the cause we stand for hangs by a single thread.'

'I know not what cause we stand for, Chevalier, but my husband takes every precaution for our safety, I assure you.'

'Ha! Luigi Campagna is one of our most trusted agents, but he is not a Knight Templar.' De Bouillion made a dismissive gesture with his gloved hand. 'If it comes to that, he could not even save himself. The foe of the Chosen Seed is beyond his comprehension.'

'You forget, Chevalier, it was my husband who rescued me from those you fear so much.' Marie decided a matter so touching her husband's honor was worthy of even more emphasis. 'He watches over us as we speak. You may rest assured we are safe here in his hands.'

'Madame, Luigi Campagna has been kept ignorant of your true identity.' De Bouillion sighed wearily as though Marie's naïveté taxed him greatly, but he did not leave off surveying the darkness outside the Hermitage. Taken in profile, she could see he was indeed little more than a youth. She would have to make allowances for him. 'Your husband is highly esteemed by us, but you must never forget he is no Knight Templar.'

'I know nothing of Templars.' Marie was suddenly all indignation. 'Luigi Campagna is the noblest, kindest and the wisest man I have ever known, and you, Guy de Bouillion, are nothing more than an arrogant boy!'

'Cousin, your experience of men is necessarily somewhat limited.' De Bouillion left off his vigil to face her. 'Do not be fooled by his seeming to be kind and gentle. Luigi Campagna kills for us when occasion warrants.'

'Be that as it may, Chevalier, I think you would greatly profit by making the acquaintance of such a man!'

De Bouillion seemed not to catch her meaning. 'That must never be allowed to happen, Madame! Our instructions, both his and mine, strictly forbid us ever to come into the presence of one another. Never forget, Marie de Noguet, he is your husband only in name.'

Something left unsaid by the young man robbed Marie of speech for a moment. She felt the ground giving way beneath her feet, even though she had long suspected her marriage of being no more than a sham. Yet she picked herself up and hastened onward through waves of pain. 'You called me Marie de Noguet, Chevalier. Was that my father's name?'

'No, Madame, but it is one of your many rightful names.' De Bouillion smiled in the posing of his odd riddle. 'As is customary among us for reasons of security, your mother never took the name of your father. You must always keep your name secret, even from your husband. You must continue to be known as Marie Campagna till we come for you again.'

Marie refused to be drawn off the scent. 'Chevalier, what more can you tell me of my father?'

'Very little, dear Cousin! I'm afraid I am not even permitted to tell you his name. The trace of him vanished from Templar records soon after his last meeting with your mother.'

'Last meeting?' Marie had not come so far to be brushed off so easily. 'You speak of them as though they were never man and wife.'

'They were not strangers to one another, Madame. According to our records, your father and your mother were brought together not less than three times.'

'Whatever do you mean, Chevalier?'

De Bouillion's voice took on a tone of awkward empathy. 'Apparently your mother had difficulty conceiving you, Madame. Unfortunately, their final meeting aroused the Societé's suspicions.'

'My head is spinning!' Again Marie turned her back on the young man. 'Chevalier, are you telling me that my parents never married?'

'Not one another — no, certainly not!' Guy de Bouillion made it sound as though Marie had suggested something indecent. 'Lizé de Noguet was later given a husband to protect her during the raising of her child.'

'That would make him my stepfather, would it not? What was his name, Chevalier?'

'I forget it, assuming I ever knew it. In any case, his part in the scheme of things is not important — just another of the many who have sacrificed themselves over the centuries to keep the line of the Chosen Seed intact. He disappeared long ago into the dungeons of the Societé. Have no fear, Madame: we can be sure his marriage to your mother was never consummated.'

'But why not?' Marie felt like throttling the young man for the casual way in which he stated the most outlandish things. Beyond that, she had caught her first inkling of the reason for their meeting. 'What kind of people would consent to live such a travesty?'

'Your father was a Knight Templar, just as I am.' Guy de Bouillion drew himself up proudly. 'All of us are sworn to keep the Faith until the appointed time. Just as your mother was a Bearer of the Chosen Seed, Marie de Noguet, so you must be.'

'But what if I choose not to be, Chevalier?' Defiantly, Marie drew herself up to match him. 'I am sworn to nothing. I have not been trained from infancy, as you obviously have been, to bear my part in these clandestine affairs of your brethren. Do not forget that I was shaped and taught by black nuns and a Jesuit priest. Countless "Hail Marys" and morning communion were my daily fare.'

'God's will be done! As you say, Madame, the choice is yours to make.'

'Answer my question, Chevalier.' Once again Marie took the liberty of seizing his cape. It came away in her hands. 'I am sworn to nothing. What if I refuse to become one of you?'

'How can I truthfully answer such a question, Madame?' The self-declared Templar looked suddenly at a loss how to proceed. 'Surely the answer lies between you and God. However, certain considerations do spring to mind, if you would care to hear them.'

'I am listening, Chevalier. Anything is better than this pit of darkness I have been cast into!'

'Dear Cousin, your escape from the priory has fueled the Societé's suspicions as to who you truly are. Left to your own devices, you couldn't hope to avoid being hunted down by them.'

'That much I've already gathered, Chevalier. Tell me something I do not already know!'

'Cousin, you are the only surviving female of your line just as I am the only surviving male of mine. The Knights keep a register of all who have kept faith throughout the centuries. One of my first tasks as a young student was to learn that register of all our fore-bears by heart.'

'What do you mean to suggest, Chevalier?'

'Without you, our sacred mission is ended. Would you condemn all those who kept faith over the centuries to have done so in vain! Your parents' names are both inscribed on that role of honor.'

'You are unfair, Chevalier! You mean to leave me no choice, invoking the memory of parents I have never seen!'

'Ah, Cousin, there is always choice.' The youth spoke as if reciting his catechism. 'Alas, there is only one right choice for such as you and me. Do you think your poor parents found it otherwise? Do you think that I myself might not wish to live as do other men?'

Bitterness edged the callow voice as De Bouillion gave a nod at the door. 'Even now they hunt me out there. Sooner or later they must catch me whether I succeed with my mission or not. Think you I would not prefer to bear my noble heritage proudly rather than go skulking through the night till caught and killed like a thief? Cousin, our ancestors were royalty!'

She glanced down at the fingers clasping hers. 'My mother and father were of royal blood?'

De Bouillion tightened his grip. 'Yes, I can see it in your eyes, dear cousin! You do understand the choice of blood that must be made! You see it in me as clearly as did your mother see it in your father!'

'Do not overreach yourself, Chevalier! All I see right now in this poor light is that you are left-handed. A rather sinister trait for one who thinks so highly of himself, is it not?'

He did not seem at all baffled by her play on words. 'All the Chosen males of my line are left-handed, Madame. It is written in our motto, *"by our left hands thou shalt know us"*. What the world sees as a mark of the Devil, we know to be a true sign from God.'

'So you would have me believe that you come here as my father came to my mother.' She broke off haltingly at the sheer unthinkableness of it all.

'Indeed, and let us hope there is no need to place you at risk again.' The young man began unbuttoning his waistcoat with his right hand. 'As Bearer of the Chosen Seed, you shall go with your steward of a husband to a much safer New World.'

'And bear your seed there, Chevalier?' Marie turned incredulous in a flicker of the candle. 'What should ever become of such a child?'

'Whatever comes, the child must not bear my name lest she not live to become a Bearer of the Chosen Seed like her mother before her.'

'What, Chevalier? You are certain even of the sex of the child!' Marie rolled her eyes at the young man in wonderment.

'It is a future Bearer that is needed, Madame. You are the last fertile female of the Chosen left alive.'

'Do tell! And just how much longer must we, mother and daughter, keep on bearing our burden, Chevalier?'

'Till the World calls out for the Chosen One at the Time of the End.' De Bouillion spoke as though he were giving her street directions. 'Fear not, dear Cousin! Have faith that at the appointed hour your role as a Bearer of the Chosen Seed shall be fulfilled.'

Marie no longer doubted whether all men were fanatical. She pulled her hand free from the youth's grasp. 'You spout utter madness, Chevalier! I cannot wonder that the Societé seeks to rid the world of you!'

'On the contrary, it is this world that is mad.' De Bouillion inscribed a circle before her eyes. 'Look out there and know I speak the truth. Keeping the Faith gives meaning to our lives. We of the Chosen Seed are blessed with meaning in a meaningless world!'

'Father Jerome taught me that men like you are Satan incarnate!' Marie drew back from the young man. 'He warned us that daughters of Eve often receive visitations from such as you, that you seek not just to violate our bodies but also our souls, that surrendering to such evil is to merit eternal damnation!'

'So, dear Cousin, it would seem that the time has come for you to judge between the Jesuit and the Templar!'

'It is not for me to judge such things, Chevalier de Bouillion. Father Jerome would say your left-handedness is itself the very mark of the Devil upon you!' It was Marie's turn to step backward till she was pressing against the stone wall. 'If he were here, I do believe the good Jesuit would burn you to ashes with a sign of the Holy Cross.'

'Fair enough!' The youth crossed his arms and bathed Marie in a baleful smile. 'Try dispatching me back to Hell and see if it works.'

Hesitant at first but then with conviction, Marie inscribed a cross in the space between them, but the young man's slender body did not waver before the sign. 'You tempt me to a sin of pride, Chevalier! I am not holy enough! A priest is needed to perform such works!'

'Dear Cousin, you are a pure virgin, are you not? Who better than a virgin to invoke God in defense of her virtue?'

Again and again Marie signed the cross, her determination mounting with each stroke till the youth spread his arms wide to her. 'Alas, dear Cousin, were you the Bishop of Rome himself, I would still endure.'

The reference to the pope drove her to her knees. She had presumed to destroy him with papist evil, had she not? Father Jerome would indeed be proud of her. She felt herself utterly confounded. 'Forgive me for what I tried to do to you, Chevalier! So be it, then! I am only a weak woman! Take what you want of me and go!'

'You mistake me, dear Cousin.' De Bouillion took up his cape from where she had tossed it on the floor and crossed to the door. 'I want nothing from you at all. I came that we might together fulfill our destiny — nothing more than that. The burden lies heavy upon us both, but I would not have you fear me. Our Faith cannot be kept by doing evil to one another. Adieu, Madame.'

'Where are you going, Chevalier?' Marie's eyes blazed at him in astonished anger. 'Will you abandon me in this desolate place after bidding me come here?'

'Pardon me, dear Cousin, I forget myself.' A trace of self-mockery illumined De Bouillion's features as he gallantly extended his right arm to her. He seemed to be withering into an old man before her eyes. 'Come, Madame Campagna, the least a failed Keeper of the Faith can do is escort you safely back to your husband.'

She would not meet him halfway. 'Your reason for coming here does not convince me of what I must do, Chevalier: you have not told me all you came to tell.'

'That is because I find you are neither ready to believe nor to conceive.' Right hand upon the latch, the youth bid her follow him with a flicking of his fingers. 'Perhaps our Dread Maiden failed this time to see into the heart and body of her charge. But more likely I am the one who has failed his test of faith. Come, Madame, this cell is too cold and the danger too great for us to stand here prattling like children.'

'You have not yet told me who I am!' Marie sank to her knees upon the stone floor. 'How can you expect more from one so kept in the dark, Chevalier?'

'I take your point, but you must also take mine. I dare not place you in a position to betray us if you choose the dark path.' De Bouillion came to her and made to lift her up. 'Clearly, dear Cousin, you need more time to escape the black nuns. God willing, I shall still be alive when you are free of them.'

She came to him then, her desperation mounting. Gently but firmly, she tried to take the cape from his shoulders. 'Soon an ocean shall divide us, Chevalier. I could wish it otherwise, but something tells me there shall not be another time for you and I.'

'Some things divide more deeply than any ocean, Madame.' Again he drew back from her, but she would not let him go.

'Pray pardon me, Chevalier.' She whispered the words in his ear. 'I am confused and frightened, but one thing above all is clear to me: I cannot let my mother and father die in vain.'

'An insufficient reason for what we must do, Madame.' The youth remained immovable as stone despite her hands upon him. 'Have you no faith?'

'Ask that question of Father Jerome.' Marie laughed bitterly. 'I know nothing of such matters as you men love to dwell upon. I only know I would rather mate with you and then cross an ocean with Luigi Campagna than remain behind with those who murdered my parents.

You expect a great deal from me on faith, Chevalier. May I not expect something on faith from you?'

He took a long moment to ponder her words. 'You are right, dear Cousin. We are given no choice but to trust one another and do the best we can.'

Yet still his immobility persisted as though he waited for some sign. She closed the door and placed her hand on his left arm. 'You must help me do this, Chevalier. You were right when you said I have no experience of men.'

'And I no experience of women, if the truth be told.' A comely blush overtook him at having to confess so much. 'We are both virgins, you and I.'

Marie felt the tension ease from her limbs. She would have laughed aloud if not for fear of offending the young man. Quite plainly, he was going to need all the help he could get. She spread his cape and her own cloak upon the stones. 'Chevalier, I have heard it whispered behind the backs of nuns that God wills this work be pleasant.'

'Indeed, dear Cousin.' He graced her with a nervous smile. 'And I have heard it said that a woman is more likely to conceive if the deed be done with joy.'

'Then our duty is clear, Chevalier!' She drew him down to her with what she hoped would pass for a smile.

Lurching over her, he bumped her nose with his mouth. 'With your permission, dear Cousin.'

Their lips brushed as lightly as the wings of butterflies, but Marie felt a faint tingle in her frigid toes. She returned his kiss, inhaling the clean youth of him, and his arms tightened like steel bands around her. Instinctively, she drew him quickly beyond all control. His hands came groping for her, but her heavy clothing was a restraining web.

Clumsily, she stripped away his waistcoat, dimly aware that her riding outfit suffered a similar fate at his hands. The laces of his shirt stretched open, and warm male odor swamped her like a tidal wave. For one nauseous moment she tottered on the brink of panic before drowning in the rankness of him.

She had never touched maleness before. His spider-thin body was a wonder to her: long strings of muscle and bone beneath a veneer of pale skin. What now seemed her opulent flesh she pressed against his trembling limbs.

The overwrought youth was so lost in discovery of her that she knew instinctively she must guide him or lose him forever. She was ready for him now, but his unnatural hardness appalled her. Near the end she froze at the impossibility of it all until he lunged bull-minded at the obstacle. There was searing white-hot agony in the quick of her being, but she knew the battle won and arched to meet him. Filled with wild pain, she begrudged nothing.

His ascent lasted mere seconds, barely long enough for her grinding pain to ease; yet she shared his conquest of the peak in absolute determination that their fleeting moment not be lived in vain. It seemed a lifetime that she held him skin to skin, giving warmth, easing his precipitous descent from the summit.

'Dear Cousin!' He eased back, courteously aware of their respective positions. 'How goes it with you down there?'

'It goes, Chevalier, it goes, except that you press me to death against these stones!'

He kissed her throat tenderly and rose quickly from her. She felt grateful for the guttering candle as she wiped blood from her body. They dressed one another in silence like two truant children. He dutifully embraced her, and she warmly returned his kiss. A vision of her husband guiltily seized her mind, but she hardened her will and dashed the image to pieces.

'We must go now, Madame.' Already De Bouillion was busy peering through the shutters, re-engaging his ancient enemy.

Marie fleetingly wondered at his unease, for she herself had no time just then for misgivings. The young man had become the sun around which she revolved, and for a brief moment she had known herself his sole world, but now she felt herself in danger of being quite forgotten by him. 'Not yet, Chevalier! You still have not told me who we are.'

'First I must hear you swear the Keeper's Oath. For that we shall need witnesses.' De Bouillion pulled her to him and kissed her lips. 'Come, Marie de Noquet, my good Capitaine Vigot will be waiting for us at the far end of the island.'

The sky had cleared and a thin crescent moon sailed through wispy clouds across the eastern sky. A few bright stars lit the way as they slipped furtively from the Hermitage and scurried down the path. The wind had vanished and the sea had declared a truce upon the Rock. Square-rigged masts ghosted quietly in the anchorage. De Bouillion squeezed her hand and pointed at the ship's boat waiting far below. 'It seems God is with us. I must learn not to give so much cre-dence to my forebodings.'

Marie was still attending the softness of her lover's whisper when two of the shadows solidified upon the path in front of them. His sudden hard grip upon her arm told her who they were and what they were there for. She whirled about and shrieked in terror at a third shadow overtaking them. Steel scraped chillingly as de Bouillion pulled his sword free and placed his back to the rock.

'Have no fear, messiers! This boy is no true Templar.' It was the deepest male voice and the most guttural French accent Marie had ever heard. 'He's one of their drones who's sworn not to kill.'

'Capitaine Vigot, is that you?' De Bouillion lowered his sword point to his feet as if in token of surrender.

'The same, Chevalier.' The owner of the deep voice lit a torch and stepped forth out of the shadows. 'See how awkwardly he holds his little dress sword in his left hand? It's double pay for us all if both be taken alive.'

'I-I trusted you like a father!' De Bouillion seemed to choke on his words as he slowly reared his sword and assumed the *en garde* position. 'May you burn in hell, Vigot — you are a traitor!'

'It's true the Templars paid me well enough to deserve your trust, Chevalier de Bouillion, but no sane man refuses the Societé when it comes making offers. Is that not the truth, Mendez?'

The shadow blocking retreat chuckled and slid closer. 'The Jesuits are famous for their miserliness, Señor Capitaine, but God help those who haggle with them! Don't tell me this is the strumpet they seek?'

'Show respect, Spaniard!' Vigot spat profusely and ground the tobacco-stained spittle into the pathway with his heel. 'Think you the Templars would waste the boy's sacred seed on a street trollop?'

'Her lungs are good enough, Señor Capitaine — I am still *hors de combat* from hearing her scream, but there's a spavin in the filly's left leg!' Mendez used his cutlass as a pointer. 'Even heretics ought to take better care of their brood mares.'

'Watch your tongue in the presence of a lady, Spaniard!' Vigot stroked his dark beard thoughtfully. 'Didn't the priest mention something about her escaping from a convent near Toulouse?'

'Christ's blood!' Mendez's sour visage broke into a grin. 'Compadres, this may be an untried baggage we have on our hands!'

'A virgin heretic, perchance.' The third man smacked his lips. 'Surely those celibate priests will not begrudge us a small bonus.'

'You may be sure she is no longer a virgin, messiers.' Vigot waved his cutlass ominously. 'The boy's man enough for that much, at least. Never trifle with a Jesuit's meat, Minot. If you care to live long enough to cut another purse, I'd advise you to keep your hooks off the wench.'

'Are we going to stand here bickering the rest of the night?' Mendez unlimbered his cutlass arm with a practiced flourish. 'There must be a dozen armed picket boats floating around this island. We must get away from here before dawn breaks if we've a mind to get away at all.'

'Good point, Mendez.' Vigot drew his cutlass from its sash as though he meant to lead by example. 'Relieve the boy of his sword, Minot. He's harmless enough.'

'I bid you perform that service yourself, M. le Capitaine.' The footpad fervently made the sign of a cross. 'I take no man's word when it comes to crossing blades of cold steel.'

'Oh, very well, if I must!' The sea captain waded in, waving the torch and feinting with his cutlass. Marie caught her breath as the youth spun awkwardly to one side. Seemingly almost by accident, De Bouillion's court sword steadied at the last moment and passed through the flesh of his opponent's thigh. 'By the moldy hymen of the Virgin!' Vigot's face shone pale in the moonlight. 'I believe you are forsworn, Chevalier!'

'Nay, captain.' De Bouillion flicked his sword rather more fluently in twisting away from Vigot's riposte. 'My oath permits me to defend this lady. Too bad it was not your bowels I pricked just now!'

'Enough talk of double pay, Señor Capitaine!' At sight of blood, an evil cast had settled upon Mendez's glinting eyes. 'Let us make short work of this young buffoon and get out of here.'

Minot nodded and spat his pigtail on the rock. Marie sensed that this was the most dangerous of the trio. The little man bore a long wicked poniard in his right hand and a heavy cape wrapped around his left forearm with a dagger held in down-stroke position. He shifted sideways, attempting to cut Marie off from her protector. De Bouillion clumsily whirled into his path, shielding Marie, an unprepossessing thrust of his sword forcing the cutpurse back onto the defensive.

'Look out, Cousin!' The youth pirouetted like a dancer to parry Mendez's lethal swing. Another thrust and parry spun the Spaniard's cutlass over the cliff to the rocks and sea below.

'Matre di Dios! You deceived us, Señor Capitaine!' Mendez lightly caught the toss of Vigot's weapon. 'Someone has trained this young cur to fence!'

'It is I who have a right to be angry, Spaniard!' Seated comfortably above the fray on a rock step, Vigot cast about till he found a fissure in which to set the torch. 'Ah, such a pity! It's a sad pass this world's coming to when one of the Templar Chosen will shed blood.'

Mendez leaned on his cutlass and watched his leader work at binding his broad leather belt around his wounded thigh. 'Jesu Christi, Señor Capitaine! There you sit on your fat arse like the Grand Turk himself and expect us to do your work for you.'

'I'm hors de combat, messieurs!' Vigot held up a hand covered in blood. 'I'll stand you a bumper and drink to your health when this deed is done.'

'By our Savior on the cross, someone's going to drink more than my health for this night's work!' Minot edged along the rock face, questing for an opening. 'Mendez, you poxed Spanish bastard — one chance is all I need.'

'Bueno, you Parisian gutter rat! Let me see if I can oblige you.' Mendez swung the cutlass in a wide covering arc, moving in cautiously with exaggerated feinting moves.

De Bouillion easily parried Mendez's slashing attack and riposted. Blood streaked across the Spaniard's cheek as Minot, the street-rat, seized his chance and moved inside. As the deadly poniard struck home, the youth caught him on the point of his sword and ran him through. For what seemed to Marie an eternity, the two men stood holding each other, weapons buried in each other's vitals. Cowering against the rock, she would have sworn they exchanged smiles before they crumpled at her feet.

'A good fight, Spaniard, was it not?' Vigot's question was punctuated by the piercing scream.

'A clumsy way to make a living, Señor Capitaine.' Mendez stared in amazement at his own blood dripping through his fingers. 'At least there's no need now to share with Minot.'

'Give the cut-purse his due. He died well enough.' Vigot raised an eyebrow as Marie threw herself upon de Bouillion. 'Now, my friend, mercifully finish the deed while she wails for her lover.'

'Why not take her alive as you planned, Señor Capitaine? We can't drag both bodies down to the boat in our condition.'

'Too late for that. We need take just enough to prove the job's done.' Vigot used his teeth to finish cinching himself up. 'Hurry, Spaniard, that last scream will be heard all the way to Paris.'

'Tis such a pity to have to do this! You're a pretty little strumpet, game leg and all.' Her throat numb, Marie looked up to see the assassin standing over her. It needed gritting her teeth to keep from fending off the coming stroke with her forearm. Mendez winked at her as he swung.

Out of the darkness a cloaked projectile knocked the blade aside. Mendez was still crossing himself when his startled face exploded. Something heavy dropped on the smooth rock next to de Bouillion's outstretched hand.

Marie's smoking satyr pistol grinned up at her luridly in the torchlight.

'For the love of Jesus, Nicole, did you need to make such a mess?' Vigot shakily rose to his feet as the maid approached him. 'You blew poor Mendez's head off!'

'Double-charged with grise-shot, the better that no one identify him.' Nicole leveled the bronze nymph. 'Look at him well, Captain Vigot. For you'll soon be his twin in hell!'

'Old friend, you were always one to think of everything!' Vigot coolly ignored the cocked pistol held to his bearded cheek. 'You were always the best. I showed you some good times in my bed, no?'

'You couldn't service the bunghole of an empty wine-cask, Captain.' Nicole pulled the trigger.

Sobbing, Marie found herself tugging at de Bouillion's inert form. The maid came and stood over her with the torch in her hand. 'I knew it weren't right to leave you here alone, Madame.'

'Nicole, I think they killed him!'

Together they rolled the young Knight Templar onto his back. His waistcoat was soaked with blood, but his eyes blinked opened and focused. His left hand reached up and left a crimson trace across Marie's face. 'Now I would hear you swear to keep faith, O Bearer of the Chosen Seed.'

Guy de Bouillon awaits at the Rock of the Hermitage

Chapter V

MARIE'S DREAM

Far below in the slanting sunlight of the Grand Piazza, long-shadowed Neapolitans stroll the *passeggiata*. Up and down, up and down they parade slow and easy. Often they pause to gently greet each other.

So they have done for a thousand years. So they will do a thousand years from now. Not even the cutting off of Barbarossa's last scion disturbs the timeless rhythm of this people. What folly to think they would welcome me as their king!

And yet they welcomed my father's father. Did he look the part when still a boy they raised him to their shoulders and proclaimed him their king and emperor? They stood foursquare with him in the face of scheming popes and traitor priests and foreign armies. They followed him to the marches of Germany and the deserts of the Holy Land. They did not forsake him, for he was their Stupor Mundi. As for me, I am only the German boy-prince.

From deep inside the thick stone walls, the red-haired prisoner hears the rumble of a portcullis opening. He closes his eyes and tries to think only of his family's glorious deeds while the chains rattle and the rusty hinges squeak and turn. Tooth-pocked lips trembling with cold anger, he spares no glance when his

69

gaoler bursts into his cell. 'Young Prince Conradin, I bring a priest of God to confess your sins.'

'Am I not betrayed enough by them already?' The youth flings himself upon his stone cot. 'Have done, Angevin, for I have done with priests.'

'By all the saints, call me no Angevin!' The gaoler spits his disdain.

The young Hohenstaufen waves his left hand dismissively. 'If not an Angevin dog, then I mark you doubly a traitor.'

'I am no traitor, Sire, but just an old man who does what he must to keep a crust of bread in his wife's mouth. Why, as a lad, I served with your grandfather at Cremona. Now there was a prince of princes, our Frederick. Now that you are lost to us, I fear the world shall never see his like again. I see you are somewhat shaped in his mould, young Conradin. Alas for what might have been!'

'Would that I had never been born to shame his memory!'

'Would indeed that you had not, young prince!' Gaolers are not in the habit of arguing with Hohenstaufen princes. 'I pray you, Your Highness, receive the good father confessor lest you die unshriven and go straight to Hell.'

'Get thee hence, fellow, and take this priest of Satan with you. My stomach is weak this evening.'

'Alas, spurning the church was always the Hohehstaufen downfall.' The warder sadly shakes his head. 'The cardinal has ordered your grandfather taken down, horse and all, from the Grand Piazza. It is whispered they will use him to cast bells for the Cathedral.'

'Let the Curia destroy every likeness of him; it will avail them nothing in the end. If only my own stamp were set upon this world as indelibly as his!' The young prince hides his face against the stone lest the gaoler see him shed a tear. 'By the Immaculate Virgin, I curse you, warder. May the French usurper, Charles of Anjou, hang you high from his gibbet till crows pick your bones clean.'

The gaoler yelps like a stricken dog and beats a hasty retreat. The curses of a Hohenstaufen are not to be taken lightly. Yet he halts at the door and lets the priest slip past him into the cell. For what seems a long time the cowled figure stands silently gazing at the prone figure of the prince. 'Pray hear me out, Your Highness, if you value the name of Hohenstaufen.'

The cleric's voice reverberates from the blank stone walls as though a tocsin were striking, but the young prince will not so much as turn his auburn head. 'We Hohenstaufen understand that nothing but lies and perfidy comes from black robes. They tell me my grandfather used to say that the only good priest was a dead one.'

'Yet your grandfather also used to say that nothing is ever as it seems.'

Slowly the prince sits up and stares back at the robed shadow in the dim light of the single candle guttering high upon the wall. 'You yourself seem of somewhat better quality than the others sent to plague me. Tell me your name, priest.'

'I would not deceive you, Your Highness, unless you force me to it.' The cleric draws back the black hood. 'Names of such as me are not so important that I should risk the telling of it.'

'By the holy wounds of Christ!' The Prince makes the sign of the cross fervently as his grandfather would never have done. 'Whatever your name, I can see you are no Angevin.'

'Nor am I a priest, Sire, if the truth be told.'

'Nor even a man for that matter!' Again the Hohenstaufen crosses himself. 'You are one of my grandmother's Dread Maidens!'

'That cognizance will serve, your Highness.' The visitor ventures a rueful smile that matches rather well the silver streaking her jet-black hair. 'Who else could have made it inside these Jaws of Hell but such a one?'

A light begins to shine in the face and eyes of the young prince. 'Send this dog away, Dread Maiden, for I would speak with you alone.'

'Your Highness, this man deserves better of his rightful King and Emperor than to be called a dog.' Even while admonishing the prince, the black-garbed woman sinks to her knees and pays him homage. 'He has risked his all to bring me to you this evening.'

'So I would ask his pardon if only he were of gentle blood.' The young Hohenstaufen deigns to offer the gaoler a curt nod. 'Fellow, I give you leave to go about your rounds while we speak.'

The gaoler bows and hurries out, right glad to be excused from such high and dangerous proceedings. 'Dread Maiden, is it possible that you are come here to save me from the scaffold?'

Sadly the woman of the rueful countenance shakes her head. 'Sire, the Pope and Charles d'Anjou have drawn the noose tight round your royal neck. Not even their master in Hell could work it loose. In the morning, Sire, you will surely be done to death in the piazza below this window.'

'I knew in my heart that all was lost, but a condemned man never ceases to hope.' The youth sinks again to his hard bed. 'So tell me, Dread Maiden, why risk you your life to see me?'

'Yolande would have wanted it so.' On her knees the visitor shuffles closer to the cot as though some power is reaching out from within her to enfold and protect the disconsolate boy.

'Yolande? Twas for my grandmother's sake the Hohenstaufen were brought down to this!' The prince beats his arms about him to keep off the cold dampness of his cell. 'Perchance we would still be Roman Emperors and Kings of Sicily if she had not lured us to think that God had chosen us to save the world.'

'In her right you are King of Jerusalem as Frederick was crowned before you.' The Dread Maiden places her two hands upon his knees. 'I am come here because your grandmother would not want you to die thinking you are the last Hohenstaufen.'

'How can that be?' The prince throws back his head and utters a hollow laugh. 'The Pope has proclaimed us a den of vipers. Has he not betrayed this city and all of Sicily to the French? Even Germany we have lost to the Guelfs. Have not all the others of Frederick's seed been hunted down and killed? Even my father's bastards were not spared.'

'Highness, you forget the young damsel whom you have made heavy with child.'

'Do you speak of Mathilde de Noguet, Dread Maiden? That was but a moment's dalliance. God is my witness I never intended to wed her. She gave up her virginity without a whimper. She is no fitting vessel for Yolande's Chosen Seed.'

'Your Highness, those who had you in charge thought otherwise.' Not for a moment will the Dread Maiden let go of him despite the youthful bitterness he keeps spilling over her. 'They prepared against this evil day by placing her near you.'

'Dread Maiden, you know such a lowborn child cannot be recognized! Mathilde's lineage is not worthy to bear our seed.'

'Nay, your Highness, in her veins secretly flows blood nobler than your own. Those who know better than you chose Mathilde as a fitting vessel to bear the seed of the Hohenstaufen.'

'Be that as it may, the child is still a bastard for all that.' For the first time in a long time, a Hohenstaufen smile lights the prince's wan features.

'And that, your Highness, is the real reason I have come to you.' The Dreadmaiden draws a sheepskin parchment from her habit. 'This document requires both your signature and your seal. It provides for your proxy marriage to the Lady Mathilde. Thus the Chosen Seed she carries will be recognized by you and made holy before all the world.'

'I have no signet-ring.' The prince holds up the cauterized stub of a forefinger. 'Mine was cut off me at Tagliacozzo.'

'I have brought you the signet-ring of your grandfather, Frederick II Hohenstaufen. Several good men and a sister of mine have died to keep it safe. Highness, is this ring of his not yours by right?'

'It is.' The prince draws himself up and slips the heavy gold ring upon his middle finger. 'Dread Maiden, if I do as you ask, tell me to what fate I condemn this lady and the unborn child?'

'You should have asked that question of her before you blessed her with your seed.' The woman takes a short quill and a vial of ink from a pouch at her belt.

'You answer me, Dread Maiden!'

'Very well. By signing this, you condemn them to be fugitives all their lives. You condemn all those who come after you to hide like thieves in the night till it be time for the Chosen One to arise.'

'Ah yes, the fabled Chosen One that the troubadours love to sing about! And will this blessed event come soon enough to avail any of us now living?' The prince's voice fills with youthful derision.

'Nay, Highness. First, many centuries must pass.' Clearly, the Dread Maiden does not shrink from the prospect. 'Many generations of the Chosen Seed must arise before the time of the Beginning.'

'Ah, then it is but a small thing you ask of me!' The prince signs his name with a regal flourish. 'I pray you tell me this: does the Lady Mathilde freely consent to bear such a thankless burden?'

'The lady consented when she gave herself to you.' The Dreadmaiden reaches out and collects the hot wax dripping down the wall on her sleeve. 'And so in time will your child consent. Those sworn to keep faith with the Hohenstaufen stand ready. As your grandfather commanded, the Templars have searched out and prepared a Sanctuary in a hidden land for the Hohenstaufen's most sacred treasures.'

'The Templars? Those devilish monks of war were always the Hohenstaufen's worst enemies!'

'Highness, as your grandsire would say, nothing is ever as it seems. In sending me to you, the Grand Master expressed the hope that these tidings will lighten your final hours. Your lady and seed will be well cared for by the Brethren.'

'I tell you this, Dread Maiden, I prefer my fate to theirs.' The prince sets his grandfather's seal in the wax from her sleeve.

Somewhere outside the tower a bell begins tolling the hour. The nameless woman rises from her knees. 'The watch changes. I must be gone from here else all is forfeit.'

'May God go with you, Dread Maiden!' The prince holds out his ring to be kissed like the true Hohenstaufen he is. His serving woman looks weary, but she presses her crescent mouth against the rampant lion. Then she slips the loose ring from the extended finger and disappears down the passageway.

Dirty and forlorn, the boy-king turns and looks out his darkening window. A few last rays of sunlight strike the gilded cupola high above and reflect into the shadowed cell. It seems to Conradin there stands beside him a glorious form, its golden raiment and diadem gleaming. An approving smile lights its lined visage.

Shivering, the boy drops to one knee and speaks to it. *Ah, Your Majesty! Promise me your Chosen Seed never to abandon.*

Never, son of my son. We shall wander with them for as long as they must wander. Your Mathilde shall not have conceived in vain, we promise you.

Then I am at peace. And the boy-prince lowers his coppery hair to receive the royal blessing.

Chapter VI

L'ESPÉRANCE

La Manche, December 1755

A rolling sea heaved Marie awake to find her cheeks and pillow wet with tears. And still the spectre of a boy-prince languishing in a prison cell lingered before her eyes. The succession of vivid images culminated in the stark spectacle of a headless and bleeding trunk kneeling on a scaffold, the headsman holding high his red-haired trophy.

She turned on her side at hearing a strange noise: Guillaume humming and rocking to and fro against his pale sleeping mother in the adjoining berth. Responding to a smile, the child clambered across to her and immediately began to tug at the gold signet-ring hanging from a matching chain around her neck. His clever little fingers soon sprang the hidden lever, revealing the cameo portrait of Lizé de Noguet. Sight of her mother brought the memory of Guy de Bouillion back in a rush, his face indistinguishable from that of the decapitated prince. Hugging the sleepy child to her breast, she began once more to silently weep.

Why do you weep, flesh of my flesh? All is well.

Marie felt strangely certain of having encountered that same powerful presence before. *Who are you to address me in so familiar a fashion, Monsieur?*

A true friend who has long watched over you, Marie of Hohenstaufen.

What true friend would call me by a false name, Monsieur? More like, you are an evil one sent by the Devil himself to take advantage of an innocent young maiden!

Have you forgotten what has happened to you, Marie Campagna? You are no longer a maiden and not nearly so innocent as you once were.

What an insolent swine you are to say such a thing! You must be one of those beastly Templars who sent that miserable boy to plague me!

Miserable boy to plague you? Is that the best you can say for one who died in your service? We should have thought you would consider Guy de Bouillion to have acquitted himself rather well.

Guy de Bouillion was brave enough, I admit. With a jolt of pain Marie relived how he had fought to the death for her.

A worthy successor to his Hohenstaufen forebears. A pity though that he could not have lived longer and gained more experience of life … and of women. I take it you did not find him sufficiently ardent, Princess Mine.

I will not speak lightly of the dead to a stranger! Feeling naked, Marie pulled the bedcovers up around her neck. *And by what right do you call me familiar names? You trouble me, Monsieur!*

Please forgive us, dear child. No one ever accused us yet of harboring a subtle wit. Nor should we have come to you so soon. You are still in a state of shock. We will come visit you again when you have fully recovered yourself. Adieu, Princess Mine!

The voice faded out of her dream.

Nicole was bending over Marie when she reawakened. She glimpsed the maid's careworn face an instant before it broke into a smile. 'Let us sing Hosannahs, Madame! You've finally decided to wake up! I was beginning to wonder how a body could sleep so long as you!'

'I — I've been dreaming the most terrible dreams!' Marie bolted upright and banged her skull on a deck-beam. The sharp blow brought tears to her eyes, but with them came a perverse sense of relief. She would have preferred coffee to the pewter mug of hot steaming tea her maid proffered her. 'Thank you, Nicole. How long have we been at sea?'

'For a day and night, Madame, though it seems more like a year to me.' Marie scanned the maid in vain for some indication of the ordeal they had just come through together. 'The Master says we'll reach Plymouth before noon. I trust we'll both feel much better when we get our feet back on dry land, Madame.'

Marie was not interested in casting her thoughts forward. 'Nicole, I remember there being a young man on the Rock. Or was he just an awful dream?'

'But no, Madame, you were not dreaming! A young man died in your arms, as real as I am standing here.'

'Oh Nicole, my poor head's gone all foggy! I think perhaps I'm running a fever!'

'Well, I stand witness you have every excuse for that.' The maid put a comforting arm around Marie.

'Nicole, you were there with me at the awful end. The young man made me swear something when he was dying, didn't he?'

'Yes, Madame, you did swear a terrible oath! It made the hair stand up on the back of my neck, it did.'

'A terrible oath to do what?'

'To bear your heavy burden no matter what happens till the Keepers come again and demand that burden of you.'

Involuntarily, both Marie's hands sprang to her nether regions. 'Oh Nicole, how could you just stand there and let me swear such a thing?'

'Madame, what's a poor maid to do? I thought you were going to die on me as well as the young chevalier.

There was his blood all over you. Ah, such a likely lad he was, too!'

'Nicole! Don't start!'

'Sorry, Madame, I'm after forgetting what the Master said.'

Marie hated this sense of being constantly managed by those around her.'And just what did the Master say?'

'Not to be talking to you about the Knight Templar.'

'Did he now? I expect you know all about Templars, don't you, Nicole?'

'Not much to know, Madame.' Nicole sniffed indignantly. 'It's said they go to sit at Christ's right hand for keeping the faith. If that be so, your young man's in good company right about now!'

'I sincerely hope so!' It comforted Marie to reflect that Nicole was probably right, but then she took alarm. 'My young man, you called him! Oh Nicole, you must help me remember what happened out there on the Rock!'

'Not much more to tell, is there? After you swore the oath, the lad asked us both to pray for him, and then he passed over.' Nicole spoke matter-of-factly as though describing a walk in the country. 'He was glad enough to go, Madame. He was suffering so much pain and spitting up blood. Pierced through the lungs he was, but you weren't about to let him go off that easily. Oh no, how you clung to him! I think you'd have passed over with him, if I had let you. From then till now, you've been out of your head most of the time.'

'Nicole, we didn't just leave him there on the Rock, did we?'

'The Master buried him behind the church where you and he were wed. He won't be bothered with this evil old world anymore, Madame. As for them that murdered him, we just rolled their carcasses into the sea.'

'Nicole, it's coming back to me now! You shot those men dead with my very own pistols!'

'Just the traitor and the spy.' Nicole assumed an air of maidenish modesty. 'You gave the pistols to me for my dowry, remember?'

'But I didn't expect you to slay men with them, Nicole!'

'I did no great mischief, Madame. If there is any justice in this world, those two villains are sizzling in hell. They'll be turning nicely on a spit alongside that cutthroat the young Chevalier spitted before he died.'

'It's not our place to judge the dead, Nicole!' Marie felt called upon to strike a moral tone; her maid's Christian principles clearly needed a lot of shoring up. 'We should leave that to God in heaven who has preserved us. As my good husband says, we must trust in Him, wherever we are.'

'Amen to that, but we daren't tarry in Saint Helier, whether God be with us or no.' Nicole had never been one to suffer preachers gladly. 'The Master weighed anchor on the next tide, never mind that his women-folk were not near to being ready.'

'Where are we bound for, Nicole?'

'For Plymouth to finish victualing before crossing the great ocean, God help us!'

'What, do you mean to say we're already on our way to Nova Scotia?'

'That's right, Madame. After Plymouth, we don't set foot on land till we reach the other side, God willing. The Master says the Societé won't stand a beggar's chance in a whorehouse of ever finding us again.'

'Nicole! I'm sure my husband never spoke in such a rude way!'

'Begging your pardon, Madame, but all this water makes me loose in my speech. God's truth, I'd rather be back on the Rock with those cutthroats than bobbing around out here!' The maid suddenly turned prim and proper. 'We'd have been given fins and tails if the Lord wanted us to go to sea.'

'Ah, but think about it, Nicole: without ships, there'd be no sailors!'

'God preserve us from harm, that's true!' The maid feigned alarm at the thought of a sailorless world. 'But I still say, as sure as God made men to please us, a ship's no fit place for a woman. We should wait on dry land for the poor pent-up creatures to come sniffing after us.'

'Nicole, you are hopeless!' Despite her best resolve, Marie couldn't help giggling.

'Ah Madame, it's good to hear you laugh again!'

'God wills that life go on, Nicole.' Despite the platitude, Marie stifled her mirth. Her mind turned to Guy de Bouillion and the oath she had sworn. 'Now you must help me get dressed; I'm still feeling a bit poorish.'

'Ah Madame, you do well to rest while you can. You'll be needing your strength to mind those stepsons of yours.' Nicole herself seemed actually to relish the prospect she had called to mind. 'We're to collect all three of them from their great uncle at Plymouth. Oh, Madame, what a handful they're going to be! They'll turn this ship upside down if we let them.'

'They dislike me so, Nicole!' Marie felt she had enough to worry about without having to deal with stepchildren. 'I'm the reason the master sent them away to live with their uncle.'

'Madame, you weren't yet yourself when we fetched you to Saint Helier.' The maid began sponging Marie's face with cold water. 'We can't be blaming boys for missing their natural mother.'

'The truth is, Nicole, that I've no wish to be their stepmother!' Marie worked at unsnarling her long dark hair. 'Stepmother — just the sound of it makes me cringe! What a thankless task to ask of any woman!'

'Well, Madame, it's not like you've got any choice, is it?' Nicole snatched the brush away and began applying vigorous strokes to her mistress's hair. 'Heaven knows it could be a lot worse. You could be still stuck away in that dark nunnery. You were well on your way to becoming an old maid! Sir Yves Le Masson is a wonderful old man to be sure, but those boys need a mother. You'll find it'll go a lot better with them this time; they'll be older and you're a lot closer to being a full bloomin' woman yourself! You just wait and see.'

Marie bit her lip and hurried on to her next worry. 'The master, Nicole, what of him?'

'Your husband's worrying himself sick over you, Madame, if that's what you mean.' Nicole swung the brush as though it were a cleaving weapon. 'He blames himself for you almost getting killed. And so he should, if you ask me.'

'No, Nicole, it was Captain Vigot who betrayed the young Chevalier.' Marie blushed furiously, unable to suppress the associated memory. 'Those assassins followed him to the Rock, not me!'

'Well, Madame, I do keep telling the master there's not much sense him worrying about spilt milk.' Nicole stepped back to survey her handiwork. 'But he won't listen to me. He's in an awful funk for a God-fearing man, he is. It needs his wife to talk to him.'

'Yes, I suppose I must.' It was not a prospect Marie at all relished. She suspected there was a great deal more to her husband's poor state of mind than the matter of her close brush with death. 'We can't have him getting sick on us, can we?'

'Not if we want to reach Nova Scotia with body and soul still holding together, Madame.' Nicole raised a knowing eyebrow. 'I wouldn't trust that Jacques Sabot to navigate his way out of a tavern!'

'And who are you to say such things — a Lord of the Admiralty?' Marie considered it her duty to work at keeping her maid in her proper place, albeit she suspected her efforts were doomed to failure.

'Sailors say the sea is a woman, Madame. If that be so, I don't trust Jacques Sabot to sail us across an ocean.' Nicole bit her lip and refused to say another word on the matter of the sailing master.

It took Marie some time to accept that she was embarked upon a voyage of no return to the edge of the known world. Her only previous experience of the sea had been a short run at night aboard a fishing smack crossing from Saint Malo to the Isle of Jersey. On that occasion Luigi Campagna had stowed both her and Nicole in a stinking fish locker. Both had been terribly seasick. Both had emerged from the ordeal with a visceral dread of ships and the sea.

Marie was unable to walk the first few steps without her maid's assistance. Yet her queasiness vanished miraculously with her first breath of fresh salt air and sight of the weak December sun.

They found Luigi Campagna pacing his quarterdeck. At sight of the Huguenot, Marie suffered a paroxym of guilt. She could dimly imagine what fearful penance Father Jerome would have laid upon her for the sins committed upon the Rock of the Hermitage. But the doom a rock-ribbed Calvinist would prescribe for her was quite beyond the young woman's reckoning.

'There's the Eddystone lighthouse, Madame.' Her husband pointed his telescope at a grey speck in the distance. 'Just a few hours more and we'll be safe to Plymouth!'

Marie looked round at the wonder of it all. A bone in her teeth, *L'Espérance* was dashing through the green white-capped waves. Men born to the sea were racing up and down the ratlines, hauling on halyards and shouting to one another. 'Luigi Campagna, I've never seen anything so wonderful as this before! How beautiful your ship is!'

'She's only a little brigantine to be sure.' Her husband's steaming breath had coated his beard with frost.

'Like most of her kind, she's built lean and mean to serve as a privateer. Her hold's too small to serve for a regular merchantman, but I traded a full brig for her because she sails so well.'

'She's utterly the most beautiful thing I've ever seen!' Marie looked up and spied the scarfaced coxswain perched on lookout duty high in the rigging. He sent her a wave and a knowing wink.

Luigi Campagna seemed to grudgingly approve her genuine enthusiasm. 'A trim sailing vessel is the most beautiful thing ever fashioned by the hand of man, Madame. Mind you, not every woman thinks so.'

Marie thought of the Huguenot's first wife, Eloise. She exchanged a meaningful glance with Nicole, who promptly dropped a curtsy and withdrew. Since her husband still would not look at her, she addressed herself to the white billowing sails. 'I promise to love this sea of yours, Monsieur.'

'It's hardly mine, Madame!' Her husband graced her with a knowing mariner's smile. 'Wait till we're caught in the teeth of a full gale. Then we'll see how much you love it!'

His manner was much more distant than it had ever been, but Marie was determined to win his forgiveness for the terrible wrong she had done him. 'Thank you, Luigi Campagna, for saving me once again.'

'You'd do better to thank Nicole.' Campagna raised his eyeglass to his eye. 'If she hadn't disobeyed me, you would be lost to us, that's for dead certain.'

'But she killed two men, Monsieur!' Marie uttered the accusation as a harsh whisper. 'Women are made to give life — not take it.'

'Nicole was the instrument of God's will.' The Huguenot looked askance at Marie from under his frosty brows. 'Leave it to Him to judge and forgive her, Madame.'

'If that is so, Luigi Campagna, let me ask you this: can you find it in your heart to forgive me for what I have done?'

'Madame, it is I myself who needs to ask your forgiveness. I nearly let you be killed!'

'You are not responsible for Vigot's treachery.' Marie lightly brushed his shoulder.

'I should have left nothing to chance.' Her husband flinched away from her touch. 'De Bouillion was only a boy. Who should know better than myself how far the Societé's hand reaches?'

'But that is not what troubles us most, Monsieur.' Marie could not bring herself to look at him in saying so much.

Nor would her husband look at her. 'And what might you be saying to me, Madame?'

'That what troubles us most is that which should lie privy between a husband and a wife.'

The ensuing silence endured a very long time for Marie. It was only her steady eye upon him that finally compelled Luigi Campagna to speak. 'Madame, what kind of hypocrite would I be to judge you for doing what you had to do?'

'That may all be true, Monsieur, but you are my flesh and blood husband for all that!'

'Ah yes, your husband!' There was gall and wormwood in the way he spoke the words. 'I would rather you did not remind me of that just now.'

'Perhaps the Templars ask too much!' Having come so far, Marie would not let go of him, even though she felt desperately afraid to be probing so deeply in the dark gulf dividing them. 'Perhaps there's a limit to what even they should expect of ordinary men and women.'

'Madame, do you remember Abraham and Isaac?' Luigi Campagna took on a patriarchal air in turning back to Marie. 'God commanded the old man to kill his only son. He expects no less faith from you and me.'

Marie could not rest content with parables. 'Tell me, Luigi Campagna, what will it mean to you if I do bear the young Templar's child?'

'Madame, I pray each night it will be so.' Luigi Campagna turned once again to the sea. 'You may be sure I shall raise him up as if he were mine own son.'

'The Keeper told me the child would be a girl, Monsieur.' In saying so, Marie felt she was taxing her husband's faith almost as severely as God taxed Abraham's.

'Boy or girl, it makes no difference, Madame.' The Huguenot took on an aspect of the utmost conviction. 'All that matters is for the child to grow up and serve the Lord.'

'But what if after all this I am not pregnant, Luigi Campagna? Can you and I go on from there as man and wife?'

'Do not trouble your head about that, Madame.' The Huguenot's rueful smile reminded Marie of how Guy de Bouillion had once smiled at her. 'I have it on good authority that you are indeed with child.'

'Nicole told you that? How is it humanly possible to know such a thing so quickly?'

'Madame, I leave all such mysteries to womankind. However, it should comfort you to know that your serving maid is expertly trained in these matters.'

'It comforts me not at all!' In an effortless flash of feminine spirit, Marie traveled from a mood of penitence to one of anger. 'You hide too much from me, my husband!'

'Give thanks for divine mercy in protecting you so long from the awful truth, Madame.' Luigi Campagna set his shoulders as if to weather a blow. 'The events of the last few days will have taught you that much knowledge brings much pain — sometimes too much pain to be endured.'

'There can be no greater pain than the emptiness I feel, Monsieur!'

'Your sense of emptiness is about to end, Madame.' Marie sought in vain for a hint of irony in the Huguenot as he cast about for a misplaced chart. 'My sons join us tonight, God willing. It is my fondest hope that you will become a mother to them.'

'I greatly fear I shall not be capable of mothering them as you might wish, my husband.' This time it was Marie who needed to stare at the distant headlands. 'Grateful as I am to you for all you've done for me, I could wish your children a better guardian angel than I am likely to prove.'

'Let us leave this matter in God's hands, Madame.' Luigi Campagna came behind her and placed his great hands on both her shoulders. 'I know that the black nuns held you in their clutches o'erlong.'

'Do not blame the nuns, Monsieur.' Marie cast up her eyes despairingly at the grey light of dawn. 'I have no calling to be a mother, I fear!'

'I remember what it is like to be young.' The Huguenot softly chafed the flesh of her arms. 'You are a woman, Madame. Loving children will come to you, whether you will it or no.'

'Monsieur, did you not know that the Jesuits school-ed me to Acquinas and Aristotle?' Once more Marie felt driven to anger as she turned on her husband. 'I may be a woman, Luigi Campagna, but never doubt I am capable of thinking for myself!'

'It never occurred to me to think otherwise.' The husbandly protest was uttered in vain.

'Which makes the indignity you heap upon me so much the greater, Monsieur: you take my lack of choice for granted because I am only a woman!'

'Madame, it is God who disposes which roles we are given to play.' The Huguenot took his hands away as if suspecting his touch of incurring his wife's anger. 'Your destiny as a mother is firmly set in His celestial scheme of things, just as it is mine to play Joseph to your Mary.'

The Huguenot only succeeded in angering his wife further. 'Take notice, Luigi Campagna: I intend to make up for lost time and live my life to the full in this New

World we go to. I give you fair warning that I shall not be content with a Joseph for a husband!'

Luigi Campagna studied his wife earnestly before speaking. 'I truly share your hope for the future, Madame. Yet for all that, I am already a father many times over and know whereof I speak. You will soon be a mother, God willing. The child that is coming will be a very special child indeed. It cannot help but curtail its mother's freedom.'

'On the contrary, I declare that my freedom shall be its birthright!' Marie's eyes turned wild with some strange power welling up within her.

'May God grant it, Madame.' Luigi Campagna folded his telescope with a heavy sigh. 'And may God preserve us both from presumption and pride.'

Marie spent the afternoon basking in pale sunlight and the balmy air flowing into the Channel from the Southwest. Hugo the coxswain brought her a folding deckchair, but she preferred to exercise her lame foot with many turns about the quarterdeck. More than anything, she enjoyed watching the crew work the brigantine's hermaphrodite rig. Minute by minute, amid the smells of hemp and tar, she felt her strength and sense of well-being returning.

Ever so cautiously, as though the mere thought of it might drag her soul down to perdition, Marie let her mind return to her sinful intimacy with Guy de Bouillion. Much to her surprise, she could discover little trace of guilt within herself. Her lover was dead and buried, but she remained alive upon the deck of a spirited brigantine crossing La Manche to England. Her only regret was that she was leaving France behind forever.

Dear God, what is happening to me? Is this what it means to be transfigured? Is this how Nicole knows I am pregnant? Wherefrom comes this sense of power? I feel as though my lover did in truth commit his spirit to me, as though I bear a legacy bequeathed down to me through centuries. I am become Life itself, shaper of a world to come!

Chapter VII

EXODUS

Plymouth, December 1755

Adverse winds delayed *L'Espérance* from reaching port till mid-afternoon. Sails luffing, the brigantine faced into the wind and picked up her mooring like a graceful damsel entering a tavern full of jostling cutthroats and pirates. Dozens of rough and ready naval and merchant ships bellied up to the Hoe of Plymouth or swung from their anchors in the harbor. Swarming over them all like body lice were hundreds of sailors, red coated marines, stevedores and roustabouts. Marie had never seen anything like it before.

Her husband quickly briefed her after returning from conducting business ashore. 'The English are spoiling for a great war, Madame. Already the Four Horsemen of the Apocalypse ride through the streets of this town.'

'A great war?' Constrained to stay aboard ship by her protective husband, Marie had spent the entire morning spying out the harbor with his telescope. 'Luigi Campagna, who will fight this war?'

'Just about every prince in Europe and even some beyond.' The Huguenot rolled his eyes in dismay at the magnitude of it all. 'Of one thing you may be certain,

Madame: these English will join whichever side opposes the French. Already the two fight each other in the Indies and America.'

'America, you say?' Marie hastily rummaged through her vague smattering of geography. 'Luigi Campagna, this Nova Scotia of yours is in America, is it not?'

'Madame, it's only one small and remote corner of a continent much bigger than all of Europe.' Her husband touched her shoulder soothingly as one might touch a child. 'The English seem already to have matters well in hand there. I have just heard that the Acadians have all been expelled, every last man, woman and child of them.'

'The Acadians?'

'L'Acadie is the French name for Nova Scotia.' Luigi Campagna enjoyed teaching his young wife things which could safely be explained. 'Don't you remember? We spoke of the French peasants who were settled there last century.'

'Ah yes, I remember now: you told me these *Acadiens* were all Catholics.'

'The French government refuses to let Protestants immigrate to its colonies!' Luigi Campagna could not conceal his bitterness at the forces that had driven him from his native land and declared him an outlaw. 'The Jesuits contrived to make it so, even though it was good Huguenot merchants who first claimed L'Acadie for France way back in the time of King Henry! But the wheel of God has a way of turning. France has lost L'Acadie precisely because they would not let Huguenot merchants and artisans settle there and make it strong! Now the Acadians are driven from their adopted land just as we were driven from our native France.'

'And we dare go there to take their place? I pity them, Monsieur! At least you left France of your own choice.'

'We Huguenots fled rather than give up our religion. What choice is that?'

Marie had learned not to argue with her husband when he became so heated as this. 'Luigi Campagna, what will happen to these Acadians?'

'I am told the British unceremoniously loaded every last one of them on ships. They are now scattering the whole lot far and wide throughout their other dominions.'

'But Luigi Campagna, I know from the priory that peasant folk live rooted to their land! It is a part of them. They cannot take leave of their homes so easily as you or I!' Marie took up the spyglass once more and trained it on a T-shaped structure dominating the skyline from high atop the Hoe itself.

Her husband was more troubled than he cared to admit. Huguenot or not, he had not been born a Frenchman for nothing. 'These Acadians were taken unawares in their papist churches, I am told, but a few die-hards have escaped the British noose and have chosen to make a fight of it. It will go that much harder for them and their families, I fear.'

'May God in heaven take pity on us all!' A presentiment of evil seized Marie as she stared through the telescope. 'Dear husband, I fear we go to a land already drenched with innocent blood.'

'Yet it makes no difference where we go, Madame.' For once, Luigi Campagna did not bother to dismiss his wife's forebodings. 'This war will spread to the four corners of the civilized world, I fear.'

Marie shuddered as she stared at the human bodies hanging in chains from a gibbet. Ravens and crows perched upon the cross-bars. She lowered the telescope and returned her husband's brooding gaze. 'Then why do we bother crossing an ocean at all, Luigi Campagna? Short of death, escape from this grim vile world of ours is an illusion!'

The Huguenot gazed at his wife in mild consternation at the disturbance he had wrought. 'Madame, it is God-fearing Christians like us who make the difference in this world.' He took the telescope from her hands as if she had seen too much. 'This desolated land of the Acadians needs us. It will become less grim and vile by virtue of our presence there.'

Her husband's words rang hollow in Marie's ears. As if sensing her mood, Campagna went off about his business just as Nicole came on deck with coffee. Seeing her thus, Marie found it impossible to reconcile the meek serving woman with the avenging fury who had rescued her from assassins on the Rock of the Hermitage. The maid's winsome manner and forthright gaze seemed more brazen than deadly.

'Madame, had you any idea so many sailors were to be found in one place! Look, Madame, see that one there on the dock with the red sash and the gold ear-ring flashing? Does he not make you wish you were a maiden again?'

'Nicole! You are simply incorrigible!' Which indeed she was by any standard Marie knew how to apply. Although attached to the Huguenot cause, Nicole clearly considered herself exempt from the strict moral laws binding other Calvinist women. The mistress simply did not know what to make of her extraordinary maid.

It was nearly noon when the Campagna children arrived with their great-uncle aboard a lighter loaded to the gunnels with trade goods. Sir Yves Le Masson clambered onto the quarterdeck with the aid of an ivory cane. Marie remembered Luigi Campagna's story of how the baronet, as a young Huguenot refugee, had served before the mast on a British vessel trading to the Orient. He had come back to pursue his fortune ashore in London, and somehow he had found his way into His Britannic Majesty's Service.

'My dear Madame Campagna, how lovely you are!' The old man kissed her hand with all the gallantry of a French cavalier. 'What a lucky young devil is this kinsman of mine!'

Sir Yves Le Masson was ninety-one years old, but a profound and lively intelligence still lurked behind his genial blue eyes. He made a point of formally introducing his charges to Marie as though it were their first meeting. 'Madame, I present your husband's eldest son, Philippe.'

The twelve-year-old bowed stiffly. Jean and Louis were introduced in turn. Their stepmother, not that long removed from the convent, could easily imagine the thoughts of the three young boys as their stern father admonished them. 'As you know, my dear sons, I have wed this gracious lady since you were last with me. I expect you all to treat her with the same respect and devotion you accorded your cherished mother.'

Philippe visibly winced at his father's injunction. The two younger boys simply nodded obediently. Despite having been taught it was something a woman should never do, Marie felt obliged to make a little speech. 'My dear step-sons, we four are all bound together now by the affection we hold in common for your father. We must learn to love one another as we do him.'

The tousle-headed Louis, whose difficult birth had occasioned his mother's death, was the first to respond. 'Madame, we three sons of Luigi Campagna welcome you onto his ship. We are glad to have a mother again!'

'We shall try to be worthy sons to you, Madame.' Jean stepped forward with an air of scholarly dignity and knelt to kiss Marie's outstretched hand. Clearly relieved to have done so well, he could not resist admonishing his younger brother. *'L'Espérance* is not a full ship, Louis. She's only a brigantine.'

As for the eldest son, he simply smiled and bowed again.

'Philippe, can you say nothing to welcome your new mother?' Luigi Campagna's paternal philosophy did not allow of much latitude in the deportment of his sons.

'Welcome, Mother.'

'Thank you, Philippe: you cannot imagine how happy I am to be here with you and your father.'

'Very well, my sons. You may go see what God has provided for our voyage to the New World. Mind what the crew tell you and see that you don't fall overboard. The sailors tell me the harbor's full of great hungry sharks.'

Sir Yves accompanied the three children forward, and soon all four were busy renewing acquaintance with Jacques Sabot and other members of the crew. Luigi Campagna glanced at his wife's troubled frown and took her hand in his. 'It's going to take some time, Madame.'

'I feel we are cheating them, Monsieur.'

'Cheating them? How so?'

'By demanding that your sons accept me as I am. Children are not so easily deceived, you know.'

'Madame, all they need accept is that you are my true wife.'

'My true husband!' Marie indulged her flair for the dramatic. 'Listen, can you not hear how false ring my words? As for you, Monsieur, you still address me as "Madame"!'

'And so I called their mother to her dying day!' The Huguenot evinced a trace of frustrated impatience. 'Eloise was too fine a lady for a vulgar man like me to address her otherwise — and what was true of her is even more true of you, Madame.'

'What? Eloise bore you three sons — and you still called her "Madame"?' Marie could not restrain herself from rushing in where another wife would have feared to tread. 'She must have loved you with all her heart, Monsieur.'

'She never once told me so.' The Huguenot cast about him as if he wished to find a reason for absenting himself from so troubling a conversation.

'You Huguenots are hard men to tell such things, Monsieur. Did you ever once speak of love to her like a proper Frenchman should?'

'I'm not a foppish courtier to be writing sonnets and love songs!' Luigi Campagna looked quite beside himself at what her question implied. 'I'm a plain-speaking merchant who follows the teachings of Jesus Christ and Jean Calvin!'

'Yet you must have loved her, Monsieur. How could it be otherwise for a young husband with a young bride from Provence?'

'I was born in Genoa, Madame!'

'Italian blood is reputed to be the hottest of all, Monsieur.' It salved Marie's own sense of frustration to thus torture her husband.

'I neglected to have her portrait painted.' Luigi Campagna's eyes moistened at making the admission. 'Her face blurs in my memory, but at times I smell the maquis in her hair as we sailed along in her father's barque.'

'Aha, I was right, Monsieur! You did love her!'

'That cruise we took off the coast of Corsica was our wedding trip, you understand. I didn't have time to spend on such things in those days, but her father insisted on it in the marriage contract, hard-nosed sea-trader that he was. Please understand, Madame, it was for the father's sake that I married the daughter, for I owed him everything.'

'Still, Luigi Campagna, I can tell that you loved his daughter for her own sake.'

'It may be as you say, Madame.' The merchant turned away, for there were tears running down his cheeks.

The old baronet returned to them with a lively gleam in his eye. Marie managed a curtsey this time despite her lame foot. 'Sir Yves, your nephew-in-law has rescued me from a fate worse than death. I would like you to know how eternally grateful I am to him.'

'That is as it should be, my dear, for he was himself rescued from a similar situation by my dear departed brother.' Obviously quite taken with Marie, the old man spared an amiable glance for the younger Huguenot. 'Luigi Campagna, in saving such a lady from the papists and taking her to wife, you may consider your moral debt to my brother paid in full.'

'Uncle, my debt to your family is beyond repayment.' The merchant essayed a formal bow, a social grace he normally eschewed as belonging to a nobler class of men. 'Wedding this lady is far more reward than I deserve for the little I have done.'

'My nephew is a good and virtuous man, Madame Campagna, but he was not always so gallant.' His eye atwinkle, the old gentleman affected an aside to Marie. 'Do not let him neglect you as he neglected my niece. Often the young devil has gone off for months at a time to far off lands.'

Marie's husband rose quickly to the bait. 'Sir Yves, I swear to you I need no reminder of such things. If she were still alive, I would do my best to set matters right between us!'

'Luigi Campagna, you are not a youth anymore.' The baronet drew a deep breath and proceeded to take full magisterial flight. 'You will understand me when I tell you that a long life like mine is full of such regrets as yours. And if you be at all like me, most of your regrets will have to do with failing in your service to the women in your life. Yet I believe my dear niece in heaven asks nothing more of you than to take better care of this second gift from God than you did the first.'

Marie was quite taken with the old baronet. 'Sir Yves, I see that I shall need you to come with us to Nova Scotia! That way I can be sure of him doing as you have bid him!'

'Alas, Marie, I do not expect to see Yuletide roll round again. As much as I yearn to go on one last sea voyage, I know all too well this little sojourn aboard your lovely brigantine must suffice me. You see, I promised my own late wife to take my final rest beside her at Saint Martins-in-the-Field.'

'Then, kind sir, what can we do to make your stay with us comfortable and happy?'

'Let your fine young maid show me to my cabin, my dear, for I grow weary. As I remember, she has a way with an old man's feet that would soften the horny hooves of the Devil.'

Luigi Campagna struggled daily to provision *L'Espérance* for her Atlantic crossing. A widening range of ships' staples and other trade items were in short supply due to enforced requisitioning by the Royal Navy. Repeatedly, the rising tide of war obliged the methodical Huguenot to reshape his plans.

One night, Luigi Campagna fumed aloud in the brigantine's great cabin. 'This is the third major war the English have fought with the French this century! How many times must these two old enemies come to blows before it ends?'

'My dear nephew, our two nations stand for opposing ideas as to how our world is to unfold.' Sir Yves Le Masson spoke with the conviction of a man who has reached a state of inner clarity. 'It is only in the natural order of things that they go on warring till those ideas are resolved into an ongoing unity.'

'Till France is no longer Catholic, you mean, or, God forbid, the Protestant cause has been destroyed by its papist enemies.' Marie felt a pang of disappointment at realizing her husband was not capable of dialoging with Sir Yves on so exalted a philosophical level.

'Till such differences no longer matter is what I mean to say.' Sir Yves looked straight at Marie as if expecting her to go where her husband could not follow. 'Till then, my children, we Templars must keep faith with those who have gone before us.'

The baronet's pointed words made Marie glance up from her petit point and meet the old man's eyes. *Why didn't I realize the obvious before? The reason of his visit here is not a matter of familial connection at all.*

'Yes, Marie, now you know.' The old baronet had waited till Luigi Campagna had gone on deck to finish speaking to her. 'Not for nothing have I spent my lifetime as a "translator" in the service of a foreign country.'

'I begin to see!' Yet Marie was far from sure she approved of what she saw. 'Posing as a simple Huguenot, you use your position with the British government to advance the interests of the Templars.'

'That's true, but there is full reciprocity, my dear. Both the British Government and the Huguenots benefit from my work. The diaspora of French Protestants throughout Europe has provided a ready-made intelligence network for my Anglo-Saxon employers. The information I bring them is vital to the very survival of the British Empire, as it shall soon come to be known if our Mr. William Pitt has anything to say about it! It is only fair that in turn we Huguenots should be assisted to find our way in the strange cold world the French King has cast us into.'

'But I very much doubt that either the British or the Huguenots suspect a third partner at play in this deceptive game of yours.' Marie cast her disapproval straight in the old man's teeth. 'Do they have the slightest inkling that the information their spy master provides is couched to abet Templar designs?'

'I am impressed, my dear!' Sir Yves' blue eyes were the only element still alive in his wizened mask of a face. 'These are very astute observations for a young woman who grew up in a cloister to make!'

'Do you forget, Sir, who it was that taught me to think!'

'Ah yes, I did forget the Jesuits for a moment! The things we speak of are rather like mother's milk to such a one as you, aren't they?'

'I know manipulation and deception when I see it, Monsieur.'

'My dear, do not imagine neither my British employers nor my Huguenot agents to be suckling babes in the wood. Both learned long ago to judge information and friendship by its source.'

'What I don't understand is the reason behind all this intrigue, Sir Yves — unless it be done for its own sake. Even less do I understand my own part in it all.'

'I do wish I were at liberty to explain it all to you, my dear.' The old Huguenot heaved a heavy sigh worthy of his adoptive nephew. 'Alas, all I am authorized to tell you is what you will need to know in the coming months.'

'Authorized by whom? The Grand Master and Council of the Knights Templar? I was taught that your brethren were destroyed long ago for dabbling in witchcraft and worse!'

'My dear, our order was originally formed with the blessing of the Pope at the time of the early Crusades.' Rather absentmindedly, the baronet began unscrewing the handle of his cane. 'Our original mission was to protect pilgrims traveling to the Holy Land; inevitably, we became a great deal more than that.'

'Yes, seekers after filthy lucre and delvers into black magic if I remember my history lessons.' Marie kept after the old man in the hope he would reveal something more of what the Templars had in store for her.

'As our English hosts would say, my dear, the Papist Church has given us rather a bad press.' Sir Yves seemed to lose track of his own thoughts as he literally pulled his cane apart. 'Certainly this much is true: we Templars became immensely wealthy — and not just with filthy lucre. As you suggest, we learned many things along the way that good Catholics are not supposed to learn.'

'So much so that you incurred the envy and enmity of all the Kings of Christendom.'

'Your statement is true as far as it goes, but there was a much more important reason to wipe us off the face of the Earth. That is what the French King set out to do in Anno Domini Thirteen Hundred and Eight.'

'Because it was discovered that the Templars were secretly harboring something extremely precious and dangerous! That's the real reason, Sir Yves, isn't it?'

The old baronet chuckled and drew a long cylindrical object from within his cane. 'Indeed, Marie, you weren't brought up by Jesuits for nothing.'

'Sir Yves, Guy de Bouillion told me very little of all this; only that he and I are part of something called the Chosen Seed, parallel and interchanging bloodlines descending through many centuries.'

'You and he represent more than just bloodlines, Marie. Here, take this with you to the New World.' The old man spoke with fierce sadness, as if in rendering up the object in his hand he was rendering up the inner core of his being. 'Guard this well but do not open it yet.'

Marie stared at the cylinder with great liquid eyes and drew back from it. 'But what is it, Sir Yves?'

'It is documentary proof that the Chosen Seed is still alive and well, that the battle against the forces of darkness can still be won!'

'The forces of darkness!' Marie took the wax-coated scroll in both hands. 'If so, why must we ourselves hide in the dark?'

'Because our time is not yet come, my dear! Our enemies hunt us to the death to keep such a time from ever beginning. More than once, they have almost succeeded in hunting us down.'

'Sir Yves, can that be why I suffer from awful dreams?'

'Indeed, such dreams are part of your burden, Marie de Noguet. Those who came before you have often reported such visitations. One cannot live amid such great contending forces without being touched to the quick by them. Can you tell me of what happens in your dreams?'

'Terrible things, but I also hear the voice of a man, and such a man he is, Sir Yves! He dares speak to me as though we were on familiar terms, as though perhaps I were his daughter! When I accused him of being the Devil, he only laughed at me.'

'So you converse with this man in your dream?'

'He's not a mere man, Sir Yves, but at least a king, I think. We spoke only briefly, but he promised to return soon. I fear to sleep lest the promise be kept.'

'Marie, you may sleep in peace. I swear to you that this new friend of yours is not Beelzebub come to steal your soul.'

'New Friend? Sir Yves, do you suggest that this man in my dream is something more than a figment of my mind?'

'Yes and no, Marie. Suffice it to say that those who are gone beyond this world watch over you. Indeed, the hope of us all, past and present, goes with you to your sanctuary in the New World.'

'Sanctuary?' It struck Marie that this was the name she herself had given in a moment of pure fancy to their new home in Nova Scotia. She also remembered that this same mysterious uncle had somehow obtained the royal charter to the island for them. 'Monsieur, what can you tell me about this Nova Scotia across the sea to which we go?'

'Only that long centuries ago we prepared there a refuge against need for the Chosen Seed. The great Templar treasure was hidden there for safekeeping till the Chosen One opens it at the time of the Beginning.'

'That hardly explains why you are sending me alone to bear a child in such a place!'

'You are hardly alone, my dear.' The old man waved his cane at her as though bestowing a blessing. 'In rescuing you, your husband has won the right to become a Templar and protect you for the rest of his natural life. I shall invest him tonight with a similar oath to the one you have sworn. Last but not least, never forget you have been given Nicole to keep you safe.'

'Nicole? Sir Yves, Nicole is only a maid servant!'

'Would you try to deceive an old man, Marie? I know you suspect the lass of being much more than that.'

'Very well, Sir Yves, I know she's no ordinary serving-wench! At first I even thought she was my friend.' Marie tried to repress the painful anger welling in her throat. 'What exactly is she?'

'Nicole is the last of her kind, my dear. Let's just say we don't make them like her anymore. She can never be your friend, but you will find her extremely good company for all that.'

'Good company? She is a trained manslayer, Monsieur, is she not?'

'At a pinch, but she has many other accomplishments, I can tell you!' Sir Yves expressed himself fervently as if knowing whereof he spoke.

Marie thought she might as well laugh as cry. 'Sir Yves, does she really massage feet?'

'Ah yes! Like an angel, my dear!'

'Perhaps then you are right, Sir Yves. Perhaps I am not traveling in such bad company after all.'

Just as Marie began looking forward to life in the New World, it suddenly became doubtful that *L'Espérance* would ever depart Plymouth. Rumors were rife that the British had begun issuing letters of marque to privateers and were about to seize every available vessel for the war effort. The situation grew so critical that Luigi Campagna felt obliged to keep his crew confined below decks lest they be pressed into naval service.

His final decision was not long in coming. 'Ready or not, we must make a run for it. Each passing day increases the danger of this vessel and crew being com-

mandeered by the British; each delay increases the like-
lihood of encountering French pirates on the high seas.'

'There is also the little matter of an ocean crossing
to consider.' Sir Yves spoke from his many years of seafaring experience. 'Soon the great icebergs will drift
south. Nephew, either you must leave Plymouth immediately or else you must wait for spring.'

Luigi Campagna shook his head. 'I agree, but the
English will never give us permission to leave port.
Their shore batteries can cripple us at will if we should
try to flee the harbor. They are just biding their time
before snatching us up!'

'How fortunate that I decided to see you off!' Sir Yves
toyed with his empty cane. 'I know the port captain
quite well, Nephew. Fortunately for us, he is a scoundrel
and a taker of bribes.'

The two men exchanged knowing Huguenot smiles.
'May I count on you to see to the matter, Sir Yves?'

'Consider it done, my nephew.' The baronet clinked
the gold guineas in his heavy purse.

Sir Yves proved as good as his word. A naval pinnace flying the Union Jack escorted *L'Espérance* past
Plymouth's batteries that same evening. Headsails set,
the brigantine surged out into the white-capped Channel
as though anxious to cross an ocean.

Sir Yves stood alone on the barren headland near
the guardian lighthouse and waved his ivory cane in
farewell. Marie waved her shawl and shed a tear for
the kindly old man, remembering their last words to
one another. 'I fear I shall never see you again, Sir
Yves!'

'In that case, be assured I also shall come visit you
in a dream.' Marie thought he kissed her cheek rather
too fervently for an old man. 'Never forget, my dear,
that we are all depending on you. You are the Bearer of
the Chosen Seed.'

Chapter VIII

FREEFALL

La Manche, December 1755

Dawn found *L'Espérance* beating past the Lizard. Strong warm sou'westerlies forced the brigantine onto a pounding series of long tacks as her captain attempted to weather Cornwall and slip into the open waters of the North Atlantic. Luigi Campagna glanced dutifully at the skies above. 'Give thanks to the Lord, Madame, that this brigantine sails like one of His angels to windward! I intend to hug this Cornish coastline and so give Brittany a wide berth. Once we make it past the Isles of Scilly, we can show our heels to our pursuers.'

Garbed from head to toe in heavy oilskins, Campagna's three sons thought it great sport to huddle in the lee of the foremast and yell at the top of their lungs into the blinding spray. Marie voiced maternal alarm, but their father simply lashed them to the mast with makeshift sea-harness. Much to her surprise, the boys proved immune to the dreadful seasickness that claimed Guillaume and his mother. Several of the crew were also laid low, much to the disgust of Jacques Sabot. 'What kind of sailors be these we've shipped aboard, M. le Capitaine? Why, even your good lady has a stronger belly than these Jonahs of ours!'

Only sheer determination to turn the tables on her prostrated maid prevented Marie from becoming acutely seasick. Her stomach heaved amid the sound and smell of vomiting in the claustrophobic quarters of a pitching sailing vessel. Poor little Guillaume finally cried himself asleep in her arms.

Though green of countenance, Luigi Campagna never left his station near the helm. His wife pleaded with him in vain to take some rest. 'I'm always weak-bellied when first to sea, Madame. It lifts after a spell. I'll be fine once I see *L'Espérance* safe through these narrow waters.'

Once past the Lizard's treacherous reefs, the lithe brigantine began close reaching in a nor' westerly direction. It was soon necessary to strip bare the square-rigged foremast and beat to windward under the reduced power of the great gaff-rigged mainsail. Clawing her way across the concave coast of Cornwall, *L'Espérance* was overtaken by night still far from Land's End and the open Atlantic beyond.

Marie collected her stepsons and took them below for a hot meal. The cook sang rollicking sea-chanties as he ladled *pot au feu* into the wooden bowls of the young wind-burned seafarers. A Huguenot refugee from La Rochelle, Pierre Lazar's colorful repertoire was the perfect end to the perfect day for the three young Campagnas. Exhausted and happily oblivious of their stepmother, the boys went off early to their fishnet hammocks.

Marie stayed close by Nicole and her child. Their misery stretched endlessly through the long howling night as *L'Espérance* fought her way against wind and current. Between bouts of nursing, Marie tried to sleep, but her quicksilver mind kept returning to her husband standing watch overhead.

What manner of man braves war and pirates and sea to carry a friendless woman across an ocean? Why would someone his age, whose life consists of bills of lading and account ledgers, risk everything for some strange cause? I don't even think he truly knows what it's all about. As he says, we have only faith to live by. Indeed, what else but faith could inspire such devotion in a man?

Oh come now, Your Highness, your husband is by no means that exceptional.

What do you mean, Monsieur? The voice thrust her on the defensive despite her firm resolve to ignore it.

So many like him have slipped through my fingers over the centuries. The unseen presence expressed itself with an air of fatigue. *This Huguenot's own ancestors were Ghibelline partisans of mine in Genoa. Some of them suffered their eyes to be extracted and their bodies roasted on spits rather than betray the House of Hohenstaufen to the Church. Think you your Luigi Campagna could withstand such a test?*

I won't listen to you, Monsieur! Marie covered her ears with her pillow. *I know you're just a dream.'*

That's true, Your Highness. The voice sighed inside her head. *How pleasant to be more substantial, but you're not yet ready for that. When we get to this Godforsaken New Scotland, I warrant you'll be glad enough of civilized company.*

You've been there, Monsieur? Marie was curious in spite of herself.

Never yet, Princess Mine, but I've read many reports over the centuries! We go to a tiresome land, I fear. No plots or murder or treachery to speak of. How could one ever feel at home in such a tedious place? I can't imagine what my Templars were thinking of in condemning you to exile there.

If you don't like it, Monsieur, you should stay in Europe!

Alas, Europe has gone to rack and ruin as well. Our beloved Sicily is reduced to a heap of ashes. Frankly,

Your Highness, we sometimes wonder why we linger at all in this world. I swear, if we had it to do again, we'd be sorely tempted to go down on our knees to His Holiness and trot blithely off to oblivion.

Monsieur, your hindsight is pointless! Innocents like my cousin and my mother lie dead because of you!

Hindsight is always pointless, Your Highness. As for innocence, it is an overrated commodity, much like virginity. It has forever been true that the sins of the parents are visited on their children, as mine are upon you.

Be gone, Satan! Marie screamed it at the top of her lungs and once more banged her head. *Father Jerome taught me that you would quote scripture to me! Get thee out of my head!*

Pale and wan, Nicole was shaking her. 'Madame, wake up! You've been dreaming again.'

The second dawn out from Plymouth brought first sighting of Land's End by Hugo. The scar-faced sailor seemed to live high in the rigging. Not even Jacques Sabot possessed the intestinal fortitude to long endure such tossing about. Far below, the sons of Luigi Campagna rode the waves after eating a hearty breakfast. Pierre Lazar had liberally seasoned the fresh mutton chops and onions with tales of his voyage as a cabin boy all the way to Pondichéry in an East Indiaman. He had laughed at Marie's maternal concern for her three stepsons. 'Do not worry so about them, Madame. Their father was not born a Genoese for nothing.'

Under a blue sky and a rising sun it seemed to Marie that the seas subsided somewhat, but the sou'westerly gusted as strongly as ever. *L'Espérance* was forced onto a long southeasterly tack past the deadly reefs radiating out from Wolf Rock. Great spumes of spray breaking over the sea-crags signaled danger.

'I'd like to dash through yonder reefs and run for it!' Though clearly uneasy, Luigi Campagna no longer showed the least sign of seasickness. 'But it's far too risky. We have to make it past the Isles of Scilly. I feel like a netted fish out here.'

His worst fears were realized an hour later as they completed their southerly tack and prepared to come about. 'Mahon!'

'Mahon?' Jacques Sabot echoed Hugo's cry of alarm from the helm. 'Surely the papists wouldn't dare — not here under the very noses of the English.'

'War may have already been declared, Monsieur Sabot.' Luigi Campagna glanced at Marie. 'Or perhaps we are simply too great a prize to resist.'

One arm looped around the mainmast's port shrouds, Luigi Campagna extended his brass telescope and began patiently to study the approaching craft. The heaving deck made it difficult to train the telescope on the tiny speck stuck on the horizon. 'What is it?' Marie could stand the suspense no longer. 'Luigi Campagna, what is a mahon?'

'This one's actually a big lugger by the look of her.' Her husband was nothing if not composed in the face of her womanly scrutiny. 'She's hull down on an intercepting course, I should say.'

'From the cut of her jib I'd say she's out of Brest, M. le Capitaine. And you may be sure she's chock full to the gunwales with corsairs.'

'No doubt, Monsieur Sabot.' Marie felt a subtle chill radiate outward from her husband. 'The only trick these wolves know is to lunge from their den, snatch up their victim and scuttle back to safety before more powerful beasts of prey can interfere.'

The sailing master took a determined grip on the brigantine's wheel. 'With a fair wind, M. le Capitaine, *L'Espérance* can outrun any lugger ever built.'

'Unfortunately, we stand off a lee shore, Monsieur Sabot. This string of reefs and islands is a pirate's weir. They've got the weather of us, no matter which way we turn.'

'Then, M. le Capitaine, let us stand and fight. With five guns to our broadside, we outgun them.'

'Mere six-pounders, Monsieur Sabot. Yon pirate has twenty-pounders mounted in the bow, each capable of crippling us with one good hit. She'll come straight in and board us, and God help our crew if we've drawn blood.'

'God help us anyway, M. le Capitaine. Better a quick death than spending a long war in the French galleys!'

'I doubt that's an option for the likes of us.' The Huguenot tightened his lips in what passed for a smile. 'If war has not yet been declared, they'll not wish to leave any trace of their piracy. Monsieur Sabot, I'd be obliged if you'd crack on every yard of sail she'll carry.'

'Our square sails won't draw on our next tack, M. le Capitaine.'

'Then hold your course to the last possible moment.' Cold and stern, nothing about Luigi Campagna bespoke his Latin blood. 'We're going to need every inch of sea-room we can make for ourselves.'

In moments, the foremast's ratlines were crowded with sailors. Great white expanses of sail billowed above the brigantine's decks. Hugo even set topgallants high above the great fore-and-aft-rigged mainsail. *L'Espérance* picked up her skirts and closed the gap between the two vessels till Hugo made out the *fleur de lis* flying from the lugger's masthead.

'M. le Capitaine, I believe we're coming in range of his guns.' The sailing master's bravado had utterly deserted him.

'Very likely, Monsieur Sabot. Can we make way with our square sails on the next tack yet?'

'Maybe, M. le Capitaine, but the slightest shift of wind will drop us dead in the water.'

'Then steady as she goes, Monsieur Sabot. This pirate would be a fool to waste powder in these seas.'

A white puff of smoke from the bow of the French privateer punctuated his words. Marie and the children

marked the fall of the shot not far ahead of the brigantine's tossing bows. The muffled roar of the gun came
faintly to their ears. 'May all their saints roast in hell!'
Only Marie's presence kept the sailing master from giving full vent to his feelings. 'That's at least a thirty-
pounder they fired at us, M. le Capitaine, or I'm spawn
to Satan!'

'Once again, you've correctly sized up the situation,
Monsieur Sabot. I didn't know they made culverins that
big and long. It would seem there's more to yon privateer than meets the eye.' Luigi Campagna lowered his
spyglass and sent Marie a warning glance. She quickly
made her way forward and collected the excited boys.
Philippe vehemently resisted her efforts to herd them
through the aft companionway.

'I pray you, Madame, let them stay on the quarterdeck for now if that is their wish.' Luigi Campagna gathered his three sons to him. 'If worse comes to worse, I'd
rather my sons not drown like rats.'

The wife of Luigi Campagna was still busy settling
the children when Nicole and Guillaume, both deathly
pale, joined them on the quarterdeck. Seeing the satyr
and nymph tucked into the maid's sash made Marie
recall what Sir Yves Le Masson had said of her. *This
maid of mine will fight to the death rather than surrender. God help some poor pirate this day.*

The French lugger's second shot kicked up sea
spume a cable length off the port beam. Luigi
Campagna watched the great ball of iron skip across
the waves. 'Monsieur Sabot, can you bring her about
now without losing way?'

'M. le Capitaine, I'll huff her to Nova Scotia myself if
I have to.'

'Hard huffing that would be, Monsieur Sabot. Just
bring her about, but take care you don't send her into
irons.' Again, sailors raced up the ratlines. Wind
snatched curse words from their mouths. Marie could

only marvel at the consummate teamwork of it all. *L'Espérance* came about splendidly on her new tack and went tearing back toward the rugged cliffs of Scilly.

'Very good, Monsieur Sabot. We'll make a sailing master of you yet. Hold her steady as she goes.'

'We can hold this course till hell freezes over, M. le Capitaine ,but ....'

'But what, Monsieur Sabot?'

'M. le Capitaine, I know these waters like the back of my hand. What with current and leeway, we'll never beat our way clear of the outer reefs.'

'In any case they still have the weather of us, and with that big fore-and-aft rig, they'll breast the Isles long before we do.' Luigi Campagna paced up and down. 'Let us pray the winds shift, Monsieur Sabot.'

'Aye aye, M. le Capitaine.' But the sailing master did not seem too happy to leave the matter in the hands of God.

'Monsieur Sabot, have the men unlimber our stern chasers. They're mere toys, but it can't hurt to teach the Societé a little respect.'

'Aye aye, M. le Capitaine.' Sabot seemed vastly relieved that Luigi Campagna was not yet reduced to praying.

The next shot passed harmlessly astern. The French gunners had been thrown off-target by the change of tack. Mutual congratulations were still in progress when the bow-chaser's twin drenched the deck with spray. Marie saw the great thirty-pound ball open a trough through the waves and couldn't help imagining its effect on the thin shell of the graceful brigantine.

The crew cheered when the first stern chaser barked out a Parthian challenge, but not even Hugo marked the fall of the shot. Its twin sent its six-pound ball skipping beneath the bow of their pursuer. Luigi Campagna nodded encouragingly at his wife and sons. 'Our stern's a much better gun platform than their bow.'

The third round from the brigantine's port stern chaser drew first blood. Hugo reported flying splinters of wood and smoke rising from the bow of the pirate ship. Yet the ragged cheer sounded hollow to Marie's ears. Everyone aboard the brigantine could not help being keenly aware that the pattern of cannon-shot was tightening as the space between the two racing ships slowly closed.

'The Lord is with us!' Luigi Campagna handed off his telescope to Sabot with an air of triumph. 'That last shot knocked their starboard bow chaser off its stanchions!'

Marie could not shake her sense of inhabiting a dream. *So our chance of being splintered into kindling is halved, thanks be to God. But we have certainly maimed and mutilated men on that French ship. Are their lives so unpleasant that men will risk such fates in order to kill others? Look at them: our crew relishes their fear. Even my husband, this man of God, comes fully alive only now as he stares death in the face. Is this need to experience death why we must hang men from gibbets and burn women at the stake?*

Marie looked round and found that the closest of the Scilly Isles had crept up on them. Waves were breaking against the weathered cliffs. On the heights, she made out a stone cottage and white dots sprinkled upon the emerald green of an island meadow. How incongruous this pastoral backdrop to the grim drama playing out on the waters below. A gaping hulk and a tilted spar still hung upon the reef lurking out from the cliffs.

Turning round, Marie saw that the gaff-rigged lugger had drawn closer, its great trapezoids of rust-brown sails filling the sky. She could make out the cutlass-waving corsairs swarming on the crowded decks. She even heard their chorused cheer as another huge cannonball churned up the waves beyond the fleeing brigantine. She mumbled a simple prayer of thanksgiving. If not for the heavy seas, she felt sure the mahon would have already scored a crippling hit upon them. 'Luigi Campagna, has this vessel been sent after us by the Societé?'

'Unless I mistake the feel of her, Madame.'

'Your Father Jerome is there on the quarterdeck.' Nicole leaned out past the railing and pointed. 'Look, Madame, see his mantle flapping in the breeze.'

Marie strained her eyes trying in vain to distinguish any of the forms clustered near the helm of the pursuing ship. *What incredible vision this woman possesses. Has she been somehow trained to see what others cannot see?*

'You are right, Nicole, and Gérard himself is with him!' Luigi Campagna hunched forward, straining down the barrel of his spyglass.

Marie experienced an acute sinking sensation. Huguenots only spoke of Father Gérard with fear and trembling. Gaspard Gérard, he who never gave up the chase of heretics till his quarry was rotting in an unsanctified grave or sweating in the galleys. Gaspard Gérard, hunter extraordinaire for the glory of Church and God.

A fresh cloud of smoke billowed from the bow of the privateer. Marie heard a whooshing sound overhead and a hole gaped magically in the great square foresail.

'M. le Capitaine, I believe the frogs have their starboard bow chaser back in service.' Sabot seemed to take a morbid delight in stating the obvious.

Luigi Campagna raised a massive eyebrow. 'Need I remind you, Monsieur Sabot, that you and I are frogs?'

'M. le Capitaine, it's a hard thing to keep in mind when the bastards be trying to sink you!'

'They are trying to dismast us, Monsieur Sabot.' Luigi Campagna spared a glance for Marie. 'Think you we'd still be afloat if they were not determined to board us?'

Yes, I am the reason for this. The lives of all these men are forfeit for my sake. These four children will perish or worse. And one thing is certain, Nicole will not let herself or me be taken alive.

Twice in rapid succession the stern chasers scored hits, but no more cheers resounded from the brigantine's crew. The lugger's chain-mailed bow brushed off the six-pounders like so many mosquitoes. Small puffs of smoke billowed along the deck as the massed corsairs began discharging firearms. Marie watched Hugo load with grapeshot the four unemployed guns of their starboard broadside. *Thank God, it will soon be over. What is the point of it all?*

Luigi Campagna gritted his jagged teeth and stared up at the sails. 'Prepare to jibe, Monsieur Sabot. We are going to run before the wind.'

The sailing master stared from his captain to the reefs guarding the channel between the isles and back again. 'Run before the wind, M. le Capitaine? There be nowhere to run unless we fly!'

'You prefer to stay here, Monsieur Sabot, and entertain these frogs? If we pass betwixt the islands, we'll come safe in the Road under the guns of the English battery.'

'Aye, M. le Capitaine, but we'll scuttle her on a reef for sure!' Albeit reluctant, the sailing master turned and barked at his seamen.

Luigi Campagna seized the wheel from the helmsman and ordered Hugo and his men to run out the starboard six-pounders. *L'Espérance* pivoted and headed straight for the reefs guarding the channel. Seconds later, a cannon ball crashed into the waves on their port beam.

Again smoke mushroomed from the bow of the lugger. The crash of shivering timber resounded overhead, and the mainmast's uppermost cross-yard came crashing to the deck. Great splinters of wood flew across the deck like javelins, and a young Basque sailor dropped to his knees, holding both hands to his midriff.

Marie, pressing the faces of her stepchildren to her bosom, saw pink and yellow intestines unfold like strings of sausage. All she could hear were the youth's high-pitched screams, her mind frozen as stiff as her limbs.

Now the distance between the two vessels closed rapidly as the surging lugger overshot the jibing brigantine. Plumes of smoke danced raggedly along the waist of the pirate vessel as the crew of *L'Espérance* exposed themselves in trying to clear the wrecked rigging. Marie flattened the children to the deck. She looked anxiously to her husband for some assurance that hope remained, but the Huguenot's beetle-brows never wavered from the opening channel. When she looked up, Nicole was standing over her, extending her squalling child to her with both arms. 'Please take the child, Madame. I've work to do.'

Guillaume stopped crying instantly in Marie's arms. He seemed to take more comfort from her than he did from his mother. She clutched him tight to her breast, only her eyes following Nicole as she knelt amid the wreckage and cradled the head and shoulders of the disemboweled sailor in her arms. She spoke softly, and the white trembling lips of the stricken boy parted in a smile. Then her slender arms wrenched viciously. There was too much noise for Marie to hear the sailor's neck snap, but she felt it. Gently, the maid lowered the limp body into its pooling blood.

Drawing herself erect, Nicole walked forward to the bowsprit, looking neither right nor left. Contemptuous of her cumbersome gown, she climbed outward through the rigging of the Huguenot vessel till she stood in place of the absent figurehead. She seemed to Marie an austere, windblown counterpart of the pagan goddess flaunting her bare breasts from the bow of the onrushing lugger. Fierce marveling corsairs saluted her with their cutlasses and grappling hooks as she turned and pointed her left hand at them. The gesture seemed to cut a swathe through that teeming deck of men.

So close did the vessels pass one another on their differing tacks that two black robed men now stood plainly visible on either flank of the gaudily dressed helmsman. The taller one stood immobile, arms folded above the fray, but the other made the sign of the cross and extended his rosary as if to ward off Nicole. Except that the cross did not point at the maid.

Marie met Father Jerome's grey eyes and read the promise of retribution there. The remaining strength drained from her limbs. She felt herself being drawn by the priest across the water. A penitential prayer slipped from her numb lips.

Praying, she witnessed Nicole whip the long-barreled pistol from her sash. Fire and smoke belched from the nymph's pitcher. The helmsman collapsed between the two priests as the brigantine's broadside came to bear. Marie closed her eyes and listened to the screams as grapeshot raked through the ranks of the corsairs.

Next moment the pirate ship had passed from view. Marie gazed at the two men standing before her as though they were creatures from another world. Holding the bottom end of the sailing chart unscrolled, Jacques Sabot pointed with a thick forefinger at the circled notation. 'According to the chart, M. le Capitaine, a fishing dory would be like to scrape bottom passing though this bloody channel!'

'No need to blaspheme, Monsieur Sabot.' Luigi Campagna seemed genuinely annoyed by his sailing master's profanity. 'Just give me every stitch of sail she'll still carry. Make her heel and God willing we shall make it through the Channel into The Road.'

'M. le Capitaine, this vessel draws close to ten feet! This chart shows less than a fathom of water up ahead!'

'Monsieur Sabot, you know as well as I do that these Admiralty charts are marked for low tide. Look around you and forget the chart. The tide is just beginning to ebb and the moon is full. We'll make it through unless you snag us on a hidden reef. I think you'd better get yourself forward and pilot us through.'

Marie turned round to find the privateer dead in the water. The great rusty sails were luffing in the wind. The slain helmsman's successor had attempted to match the brigantine's maneuver and thereby bring the lugger's guns to bear once more. Instead, the great mainsail had jibed, snapping spars and parting stays. Painfully, the lugger began to make way again under a jury-rigged sail. Luigi Campagna's dark eyes shone like sparks whirling up from a bonfire. 'This frog thinks to corner me in the channel entrance!'

L'Espérance was rushing through the water under full sail with the prevailing half-gale behind her. Jagged rocks gnashed up at them like ravenous sharks on either beam. So threatening was this danger that the straddling fall of two more cannon-shot passed almost unnoticed. The sailing master turned and frantically cupped his hands to his mouth. 'Hard a-lee!'

Luigi Campagna spun the wheel hard.

Seawater roiled across the deck. Marie clung to the children and waited for the terrible crash that never came. *L'Espérance,* wind gone from her sails, floated on a placid pond amid the Isles of Scilly. 'We're in the Road, mon capitaine!' Jacques Sabot shouted it from the bow as though he were announcing the Second Coming. 'Christ's blood, we're safe in the Road!'

'I bid you calm yourself, Monsieur Sabot.' Luigi Campagna watched as the first gun of the little English battery billowed smoke from the cliff. He put the spy-glass to his eye and watched the lugger come about and begin to limp away from danger. 'We mustn't tempt the Lord our God with a thousand leagues still to go!'

Chapter IX

LANDFALL

Atlantic Ocean, Mid-winter, 1756

L'Espérance left the Old World far behind in the following week of storms, but Marie could not so easily shake off her reoccurring dream. Night after night, a freshly severed head lay in her lap. Gouts of blood still oozed from its nose and mouth. On each occasion, the same familiar presence lay heavy upon her. Finally the head spoke to her. *Observe the hawk-nose and the cleft chin, Your Highness! Even after so many generations, the family likeness is still quite strong in me. Did you not find me a handsome lover?*

Monsieur, I know you are not Guy de Bouillion! Sir Yves Le Masson warned me that you are merely some long dead king sent to haunt me!

We are not just any long dead king, Princess Mine! In addition to successively gaining the crowns of Sicily, Germany and Jerusalem, we tricked that wiliest of popes, Innocent III himself, into crowning us Holy Roman Emperor. The least you can do is show respect for so illustrious an ancestor.

Bien, Monsieur, I will call you anything you like! Only make this awful head go away!

We think the least you should do is call us "Sire." Don't you?

Bien, Sire, now make the head go away!

Marie drew a deep breath at suddenly finding her lap empty. *There now, what do you say, Princess Mine?*

You mock me, Sire!

Mock you? How else should one address a princess of the Hohenstaufen blood royal?

I am nothing of the kind! And you, Sire, are nothing more than a figment of my dreams!

Why are all the women in our family so stubborn? Just once, we should like to come upon an exception that proves the rule! Not to complain, Princess, for we find you a breath of fresh air after all those tiresome ladies-in-waiting that plagued our court! You remind us of our saucy Saracen lovelies. Life would have been quite unbearable without them.

Saracen lovelies? You admit to the keeping of infidel mistresses, Sire?

Actually, we kept a regular harem, eunuchs and all. A veritable battalion of dusky houris worthy to staff Mahomet's Paradise. Ah, Princess, there's one we remember with particular fondness: she was as exquisite a jewel as the pearls that came with her. A matched set gifted us by our old friend, al-Kamil — he was the sultan of Egypt in our time.

Your poor wife!

What has the Empress Yolande to do with our harem, pray tell?

You just admitted you were unfaithful to her, Sire!

Actually, your ancestress quite approved of our respective living arrangements. That way she didn't have to countenance some little slut flouncing around the palace.

Enough, Sire, get you behind me! And do not trouble yourself coming here again!

Au revoir, Princess Mine!

Fifteen days sail past the Scilly Isles, sickness overtook the wife of Luigi Campagna. Nicole had no trouble diagnosing Marie's condition, much to her chagrin. 'I don't feel the least bit pregnant!'

'Then why did you puke all over this silk camisole the Master gave you?' The maid held up the soiled garment for her mistress to see before stuffing it in the canvas bag of dirty wash.

'I'm seasick!' Marie began to weep profusely. 'I suffer disturbing dreams, Nicole.'

'Seasick, my left buttock!' The maid crossed her formidable arms and sniffed. 'I'm the one who gets seasick, remember? As for your dreams, Madame, they but confirm you are with child.'

'It's quite impossible, Nicole!' Marie felt so sorry for herself that she began whimpering. 'I couldn't possibly have gotten pregnant. The chevalier and I spent so little time together.'

'Time enough! A woman is ready to conceive when she is ready. You were in season that night on the Rock, Madame.'

'How dare you say such a thing to me! Wild horses couldn't have dragged me out there if I'd the slightest inkling what you terrible people had in mind! I'm not pregnant, Nicole!'

'Madame, we left nothing to chance.' Nicole took up the clean bundle of washing and began folding it into piles upon Marie's berth. 'The timing of your meeting with the young Templar was carefully conjoined with your body rhythms to insure the outcome.'

'So that's why you're so certain I'm pregnant!' Marie fairly hissed out the words.

'It's my duty to make sure of all things.' Nicole seemed not at all perturbed by Marie's histrionics. 'What's done is done. What would Sir Yves and the Master say if we took you all the way to Nova Scotia only to find you are not with child?'

'Nicole, I shall never forgive you for this!'

'Would you prefer to endure all this for nothing, Madame? That would indeed be something to blame me for!'

'I am not a brood mare!' Marie blushed at recalling how the assassins had spoken of her. 'How dare you and Luigi Campagna treat me so?'

'Because it is our duty to do so, Madame.' Just for a fleeting moment Marie thought she glimpsed the hint of a crack in the maid's impregnable defenses. 'Your husband and I are sworn to serve the Chosen Seed.'

'If that is so, why did you and Luigi Campagna let Guy de Bouillion die on the Rock?'

'His identity had been betrayed, Madame.' The maid turned haggard before her mistress's eyes as though looking into a void. 'He himself knew it was only a matter of time before the Societé caught up with him. His appointed task was fulfilled. For him to go on living would have endangered the Chosen Seed.'

'So I guessed right: you stood by and let him die!' Marie shook her head sadly. 'How heartless you are! Is that what it is to be a Templar?'

'I am no Templar, Madame.' A tremor ran through Nicole as she recited her litany. 'I am the last Dread Maiden of God. I have but to hear His command and I obey.'

'He told you to slay the young pirate and spare those blackened Jesuits?'

'Madame, it is true that Monseigneur Gérard deserved slaying most of all, but the Master needed help to effect our escape from the pirate ship. So God guided my hand to strike down the helmsman.'

'Yours is a very practical God, Nicole. Did he also tell you to put that young sailor out of his misery?'

'A voice did come to me, Madame, but it was that of Normand Bedard himself. He deserved that much grace from the woman who once shared his bed.'

'Is nothing ever as it seems?' Marie's hands flew to her temples. 'Tell me, is Guillaume truly your son?'

'He is my natural son, Madame.' The maid turned to go as if suddenly aware too much had been said.

'Certainly he's no son of young Bedard. You're much too purposeful a woman for that, Nicole — if indeed you are a woman at all.'

'Woman enough that sometimes I act without purpose, Madame.' The maid smiled mysteriously before mounting the companionway.

Marie spent most mornings schooling her stepsons. After these fatiguing ordeals, she sometimes refreshed herself by promenading in the brisk noon air. Whatever the weather, she was sure to find Luigi Campagna on deck shooting sun-sights. Her husband's bearded face bespoke serenity while thus navigating them across an ocean. How his wife envied him those intimations he seemed to receive of some divine purpose unfolding around them!

'An amazing new invention, Madame!' He held out his gleaming brass quadrant to her. 'After millennia of dangerous guesswork, a navigator can now determine exact longitude.'

He explained how the instrument worked, but quickly lost Marie in the theory of it all. 'What a brilliant mind it would take to conceive such a device, Monsieur!'

'And great craftsmanship to fashion it!' Her husband's thoughts came down to Earth with a jolt. 'This English invention was made possible by French savants and artisans forced to flee their country. One more sad legacy of France's intolerance of its Huguenots.'

Each day, Luigi Campagna dutifully logged his navigational observations on the great chart of the Atlantic Ocean he kept pinned to the table in the Master Cabin. Scores of ornate arrows were carefully inscribed upon the chart in red and blue ink. These markings compared his dead reckoning calculations with the results of his celestial observations. What all his arrows had in common was the targeting of the oddly shaped landform guarding the northern coast of the American continent. Across that expanse of land and sea the name "L'Acadie" had been stricken out and "Nova Scotia" lettered in.

Driven by a fierce winter gale, *L'Espérance* raced towards a land of boundless forests roamed by noble savages hunting strange beasts beyond counting. Or so Marie imagined it would be. *One could easily become lost in such a vastness. One could disappear, never to reappear. To what strange tails do the mouths of all these great rivers lead? What do all these mythical symbols signify?*

It finally struck Marie that Nova Scotia was not just another of Luigi Campagna's navigational doodlings. The peninsula, along with its large islands and vast continental reaches, had magnitude and extension comparable to England or even France. The deeply indented coastline gave promise of Greek-like diversity despite an almost complete dearth of place names.

'Luigi Campagna, just where in Nova Scotia are we going?' The Huguenot indicated a large inlet which bore lettering in his own precise hand. 'Baie des Mahonnes.' Marie sounded out the French words carefully. 'Mahonne, that is what you called the pirate craft that chased us, is it not?'

'Upon the Middle Sea, all pirate craft are called mahon, Madame.' As always, her husband delighted to explain such things to her. 'Perhaps the Acadians named this bay for some strange ship that sought refuge there in the remote past. I much doubt pirates still frequent such a place; the English navy is too close at hand.'

He pointed at another deep inlet across which was printed the name, "Halifax." Yet Marie still suspected the Huguenot of leaving much unsaid. She remembered Sir Yves' reference to the Templar treasure. 'Why do we go here, Monsieur? Why did you pick this place to set up a trading post?'

In answer, Luigi Campagna unscrolled a smaller chart. 'See? Close by our island is a settlement founded recently by His Britannic Majesty, German George. The Indians and the Acadians call the place Merliquesche, but the German and Swiss settlers recently marooned there have renamed it Luneburg. Poor devils!'

'Marooned there? Are these colonists transported convicts, Monsieur?'

'They might as well be, Madame. I am told this land they were dumped upon will grow little or nothing. Being simple peasants, they are liable to starve.'

'Is that why you've brought so much flour and salt pork along, so that we may share it with these poor people?'

'We also carry beads, axe-heads and pots.' Luigi Campagna's expression reflected a typical merchant's aversion to being thought an altruist, especially by his wife. 'Look, Madame, see how these rivers and lakes converge on the Bay? For centuries the Indians have come here in canoes to barter and trade with the Acadians.'

'But the Acadians are gone, Monsieur!' For once Marie had no difficulty projecting her husband's line of thought.

'Exactly so, Madame. There is a place already carved out and waiting for us in this new land. By the way, I am told the Indians love to haggle in French.'

'Bien, Monsieur! Perhaps I may render you good service once we get there, for I also love to haggle.'

'I should never have guessed it, Madame!'

Stung by the ironic tone of her husband's response, Marie determined to give as good as she got. Father Jerome's tales of Jesuit missions to the New World came to mind. 'But we will need priests to hear the savages' confessions, will we not?'

'There will be neither priests nor confessions at my trading post, Madame!' The Huguenot refused to crack a smile. 'There'll be no need for the Indians to barter their souls when they trade with us.'

Marie resolved herself instantly into a model of wifely sobriety. 'Just what do they trade, Monsieur?'

'Furs of wild animals, of course, but also they bring their handicrafts — wonderful baskets, I'm told, and a few semiprecious stones carved into amulets. There's a good market for such curios back in England and the Low Countries.'

Marie surveyed the small chart afresh. 'Luigi Campagna, look at all the islands! Which one is our Sanctuary?'

The Huguenot indicated a wasp-waisted crescent shape with his forefinger. 'This one here, Madame. Unlike most of the adjacent islands, it's blessed with fertile soil. We shall plant staple food crops and trade them with the Germans and Indians. Just here is a landlocked anchorage. It's somewhat shallow but it should be adequate to harbor this brigantine.'

'Luigi Campagna, how did you come by all this knowledge? Have you been across this ocean before?'

'Nicole can best answer your questions, Madame.' Luigi Campagna knit up his eyebrows as if his wife had once again trespassed upon forbidden territory.

Marie stamped her lame foot. 'Why must you always leave me to the tender mercies of a serving-maid, Monsieur?'

'Madame, you know very well that Nicole is no ordinary maid.' The Huguenot began scrolling up the chart. 'You would do well to heed her, just as Sir Yves bid you do.'

The notion that the baronet had reported their private conversation to her husband completed Marie's mood of chagrin. 'Why do you always hide from me when I try to talk with you?'

'It's not an easy thing to be the husband of such a strong-willed woman as you, Madame.' Luigi Campagna permitted himself the faintest of smiles as though her evident fury delighted him. That made her even angrier.

'No doubt, Monsieur, you found it far easier to husband Eloise!'

'What would you have me say, Madame? You know very well that I hold you a treasure beyond price.'

'A treasure beyond price? What does that profit either of us, Luigi Campagna?' Marie moved to squarely confront her husband.

'As you can see by looking, Madame, I am almost done with worldly treasure.' The Huguenot ran his fingers through his long beard. 'An old and graceless man dare not hope for the honor you have done me by becoming my wife. You may rest assured I will faithfully serve the Bearer of the Chosen Seed till my last breath is taken.'

Marie was suddenly all concern. 'Luigi Campagna, what talk is this of dying?'

'All worldly things come to an end.' The Huguenot elevated his quadrant. 'I am old enough to be your father. At some point, Madame, you know well as I that our crossed paths must part.'

'Luigi Campagna, forgive me all my selfish ingratitude, I pray you!' Marie seized him by both arms, genuinely dismayed at the thought of losing her husband. 'I would not know how to get along in this world without you!'

'Madame, it heartens me to see you grow stronger each day,' The Huguenot gently but firmly tugged himself free from her embrace and preceded her up the companionway. 'See those clouds? There's a devil of a storm brewing off the Carolinas.'

Watching Luigi Campagna make his way forward, Marie counted her blessings. *How skillfully my husband navigates across this winter sea. What tribulation could ever exceed his strength? He even forgives the weakness of his foolish wife.*

That surge of remorse carried Marie back to the Rock of the Hermitage. *Guy de Bouillion spoke of a lineage descending through many generations, preserving a template of something precious. My mother and father are part of that pattern. They all died believing Chosen blood flows in our veins, that our unborn child is the Seed of a prophesied leader who will one day save the world. Dear God, to even think such a thing possible must surely be the ultimate blasphemy!*

Full realization of who she was came to Marie in a wave of shock and horror. *This unborn child is the result of a colossal fraud sustained across centuries to clothe a myth in flesh and blood. My child's fate will be determined accordingly. No wonder the Societé hounded my father and mother to their deaths. Holy Mother Church has no choice but to pursue us both till the line is extinguished. How Father Jerome must regret showing me so much mercy! I should have stayed cloistered! Yet what choice now remains to me but to stay in the keeping of my husband? And he is himself a pawn of the Templars? What will Nicole do if she suspects my lack of faith? Would she even care so long as I continue to serve as the bearer of this Accursed Seed?*

The wife of Luigi Campagna no longer felt affinity for her handmaid. Having witnessed for a second time the ease with which the woman killed others, Marie lived in constant dread of the moment when the deadly Dread Maiden would strike again. Yet she felt her husband had left her no choice but to turn once again to Nicole for enlightenment.

She chose to broach such matters while being assisted with the many bows and laces that made up a lady's proper dress — not an easy task in a tiny ship's cabin tossing on the high seas. 'This Mahonne Bay to which we go, Nicole. What can you tell me of it?'

The maid looked at her askance. 'Do you think, Madame, even your husband could have persuaded me to cross this God-forsaken ocean if I had done it twice already?'

'Be that as it may, Nicole, I'm sure the Templars briefed you well on this pirate lair we go to.'

'Pirate lair, Madame? It was not pirates who first frequented this Mahonne Bay.'

'No? Then why was it named for pirate ships from the Middle Sea?'

'Ships often came there from the Middle Sea, but they were not pirate ships, Madame. Those who came gave it that name to make others steer clear.'

'Then what ships were those that first came?'

'Why, Templar ships of course, Madame. Didn't Sir Yves tell you?'

'Why would Templar ships want to come here, Nicole?' The maid stuck a pair of straight pins in the corner of her mouth and went on tying bows. 'The Master said you would be willing to answer my questions, Nicole.'

'Did he now? That was very good of the Master.'

'Nicole, don't you think I have a right to know these things?'

'Madame, I can only tell you what I am sure Sir Yves Le Masson has already told you. Long ago, a secret refuge was prepared for the Chosen Seed.'

'To serve what end?

'Why, to safeguard the greatest treasure in the whole world, Madame: the Templars' treasure.'

'How long ago did they find this island, Nicole?'

'Why, Madame, as I understand it, Templar ships found their way to this America two centuries before the Basques and Portuguese and us French came to fish these waters.'

'The Templars, they kept their discovery secret?'

'For as long as they could, Madame, but such secrets cannot be kept secret forever.'

'So why do we go there now?'

'Why, to take up our place of refuge, Madame. Of course, it will not be the same sort of refuge that the Templars of long ago planned it to be.'

'Always you speak in riddles, Nicole!'

'Do not worry about it, Madame. Things will turn out less strange than they presently seem.'

'I wonder!'

Nicole gave herself over to domestic matters as though genuinely trying to re-establish rapport with her mistress. Yet their talk of bed linens and children's clothing, once so full of feminine vitality, grew stilted and forced. Marie sensed the chasm between them yawning ever wider. She could not forget that this only friend she had ever known had blood on her hands; no amount of washing clothes would remove such a stain.

So Marie went seeking answers from the crew. Pierre Lazar was the only one of the lot who had previously ventured beyond Europe's coastal waters. He sang songs of shipwrecked sailors roasted alive, of sea captains rescued by Indian princesses. Hugo called their destination the land of 'Ultima Thule', where snow never ceased to fall, where great glaciers choked the treeless coasts and monstrous leviathans engulfed full-rigged ships. All that Jacques Sabot could tell her were tales of pirates robbing honest merchantmen for no better purpose than hiding their fabulous treasures in the ground.

Savage winter gales and high waves never ceased to oppose *L'Espérance's* ocean passage. Guided by Luigi Campagna's masterful hands, the intrepid brigantine took it all in her footless stride till came the morning when she emerged from a bank of fog to find herself surrounded by pack-ice. 'I've headed us further south than usual, but it is tempting God to cross His ocean in the middle o winter.' The Huguenot grimly surveyed an iceberg so huge and high that it seemed some new continent to Marie. 'We must pray that he will forgive us and let us pass safely on his service.'

In the shadow of the deadly ice pinnacles, even the irreverent Jacques Sabot knelt to pray, his frostbitten fingers pointing to heaven.

Luigi Campagna's sons came closest to satisfying Marie's need to learn. Inspired by the tales of the crew, Louis sketched droll monsters that helped exorcise his step-mother's fantastical fears. Sir Yves had given Jean an old leather-bound volume entitled *Description geographique et historique des costes de l'Amerique septentrionale*, a most colorful account of early life in Acadia. Reading the book aloud, the foursome conceived an image of a land no less strange than the stuff of the sailors' yarns.

Philippe sketched a composite of Nova Scotia from various map fragments belonging to his father. He and his brothers spent many mornings poring over the makeshift chart. Even Marie, who had always depended on men for geographic orientation, worked hard to acquire her own sense of place.

Thirty-one days out from Plymouth, Luigi Campagna was still sketching arrows across the Atlantic. Already the brigantine had sailed safely beyond treacherous Sable Island where pounded countless wrecks and the bones of those who had failed to cross the great ocean. The lookout sighted gulls and other seabirds. Excitement grew palpable among the crew. Philippe assumed an authoritative air as he surveyed his father's chart. 'As I make it, we will sight land tomorrow.'

His father raised a bristling eyebrow at his son. 'God willing, that is!'

Marie waited till they were alone to question her stepson further. 'Philippe, what do you look to find in our new home?'

The boy spoke up promptly as if he had already given much thought to the question. 'A place to become a man, Madame. '

'And what will you do when you're a man?'

'I shall run away to sea, with or without my father's permission. I shall become the master of a full-rigged ship much grander than this brigantine, perhaps even a fleet of such ships.'

'And will you someday return to us?'

The young Campagna shook his head. 'I shall write my father once a year as long as we both shall live.'

That response was altogether too much for Marie. 'And your brothers, won't you miss them?'

Philippe considered the matter at length before replying. 'I wish them well with whatever way they choose to go, but their way will not be my way.'

'Does nothing bind you to your brothers at all, Philippe?'

Again the boy shook his head. 'God willed that we be born of the same father and mother. Yet in our hearts, we are no more than strangers thrown together.'

'But what of your mother?' Marie bit her lip before proceeding. 'Will you not hold your brothers dear for love of her?'

'Our mother is dead, Madame. She abandoned us.'

Philippe's words left his young stepmother speechless. She yearned to enfold the boy in her arms. The impulse set her limbs atremble and only made him withdraw further from her. 'May God take pity on your soul, poor dear Philippe!'

'And may God punish your wickedness, Madame.'

'My wickedness, Philippe?'

'For marrying a man old enough to be your father. I can see you do not love him the way our mother loved him, Madame.'

That night, *L'Espérance* was tossed and lashed by monstrous seas and winds. Marie did not even bother to undress. She simply threw herself full-length inside her lee-boarded berth and slept till the wind subsided.

Thick mists still shrouded the dawn when the wife of Luigi Campagna stumbled onto the ice-clad quarter-deck. Heavy skirts and the dull ache that never left her right foot made her progress forward to the bow painfully slow. A castle of ice, *L'Espérance* drifted wakeless above the grey water. Marie clasped tightly the signet-ring that hung cold between her breasts.

From its perch in the rigging, a bedraggled cormorant cocked its head and stared down at her. *Are you a harbinger of land ahead? O merciful God, let us prevail here and not be lost. Let us count for something in your scheme of things!*

The prayer still trembled upon her numb lips when the bank of fog parted before her eyes. The hueless dawn unveiled rocky cliffs, imperturbable and serene despite colossal waves breaking upon them. 'Helmsman!' Her words were snatched away by a sudden gust of wind. 'Helmsman, strike the bell! I see Nova Scotia straight ahead!'

Marie & Nicole and Guillaume

L'ESPERANCE

Crossing the Ocean

Chapter X

WILDERNESS

Luneburg, March 1756

A lover of snug anchorages, Luigi Campagna knelt down among the passengers and crew thronging his small quarterdeck. To an oft-repeated refrain of "amen", he offered up praise to God for bringing his vessel safe through Atlantic ice and storms.

Looking little the worse for wear, *L'Espérance* tugged at her anchor like a graceful gray swan. So deep and narrow lay the little harbor between its surrounding hills that her jaunty stern sometimes swung near the rocky shore. So near indeed were they to land that little Louis beseeched his father to run out the gangplank so that he and his brothers might go play in the snow.

They had dropped anchor soon after darkness had fallen the night before. Only a few flickering lights and coals glowing on exposed hearths had guided them to harbor. Nor had their hail roused any welcome on shore.

In the early light of morning, the settlement of Lüneburg stood clearly revealed on the knoll rising up steeply from the water's edge. It was already more than an hour past sunrise, but those on shore had yet to give the slightest sign of noticing a tall brigantine at anchor in the harbor below them. Amid a growing atmosphere of not knowing what to expect, Luigi Campagna decided to row himself ashore in his small captain's gig.

He looked every inch the prosperous merchant as he set off in his long sealskin cloak and the plumed hat that his womenfolk made him wear. Marie watched him splash his way over the gunwales and onto the cobble beach. He thus became the first of *L'Espérance*'s company to set foot on this New World.

Through the telescope, it looked as though the Huguenot were instantly mobbed by figures springing up at him out of nowhere. The ragged Lüneburgers drifted round him like a pack of ghouls. Marie feared for her husband's safety till a file of redcoats quickmarched through the dirty snow to salute him. They formed up around the Huguenot and escorted him toward the tattered Union Jack fluttering above a bivouac of army tents and whittled stumps.

Back on *L'Espérance*, Jacques Sabot kept up a lively commentary on matters ashore. He loudly pronounced unseaworthy every last one of the boats and coracles drawn up along Lüneburg's waterfront. The sailing master had even worse to say about the dozens of log lean-tos that straggled above the cobble beach. Roofed with tattered sailcloth and crudely chinked with sod, these wretched dwellings did little to inspire confidence in any of the newcomers waiting to go ashore — least of all Marie.

A howl went up from her three stepsons when she suggested they remain on board with her for the nonce. Nicole would not hear of them remaining behind. 'Both you and these boys need to take a turn or two on God's dry land, Madame, and there's an end to it! Do you want your little girl to be born with the gait of a drunken sailor?'

Marie consented to be so led, but first she slipped below to the galley and filled a gunnysack with the last of the hard tack. The ship's company had grown sick of the weevil-infested biscuit during the last weeks of the ocean crossing. *Now Pierre can bake us some real bread. Those poor people stranded on the shore have more need of this than we do.*

When Marie came back on deck, Nicole had already situated herself in the ship's boat. She clutched all four of the children about her like chicks. 'Here's Hugo to hand you down into the boat, Madame. You may sit across from me on this thwart. No need to worry about these children falling overboard. I will make sure that no harm comes their way. Monsieur Sabot, you may row us ashore, if you please.'

Nevertheless, it did not reassure Marie to see Nicole tuck the nymph and satyr into the sleeves of her heavy jacket before hiking up her skirts and leaping ashore. The intrepid maid did not even so much as get her feet wet while helping her and the children reach dry land. Pierre Lazar stayed behind to guard the ship's boat and the captain's gig with his cutlass. *God help any German peasant who gets in our way this day. This cutthroat crew of ours would as soon spit one of these poor devils as look at them.*

The stench of human waste hit them like a wall at the shoreline. Toothless mouths and open sores gave witness that scurvy had taken its toll among the colonists. Many of the hands stretched out to greet them were swathed in rags or missing fingers, reminding Marie of Father Jerome's stories of Jesuit missions to the leper colonies. Even Philippe stayed close behind her trailing skirts as they entered the settlement.

Positioned protectively in the fore of the little party, Hugo halted abruptly and turned upon the sailing master. 'What kind of people be these, Master Sabot?'

'My dear fellow, these be Hanoverian subjects of your German King George.' The brown stain the sailing master spat on a drift of snow passed for commentary on the situation at hand.

139

'These creatures be all a pack of Lutherans, then! Where are the feathered redskins you promised me when I signed on, Master Sabot? I see nothing here but these bloody Lutherans and countless acres of snow!'

'Never fear, you'll have your fill of Indians yet.' The sailing master spun the coxswain round and propelled him forward with a long-practiced shove. 'No doubt the native savages have more sense than to frequent such a pesthole as this.'

Marie shot Nicole a reproachful glance. 'Master Sabot is right! Our children could catch a terrible disease in such a place!'

The maid tossed off her mistress's concerns with a tilt of her Gallic nose. 'Our children have full bellies and stout hearts, Madame, whereas these poor wretches suffer from starvation of body and spirit. People in such straits quickly forget who they once were. Mark their plight well.'

Marie met the blank stare of a woman bending low to exit a log lean-to. 'You need not worry on that score, Nicole. Faces so full of misery as these will be inscribed forever upon my very soul.'

'Bad as it is, Madame, what you see before you is a pale shadow of things as they are in this world.'

'Quite vivid enough for my taste, Nicole! I don't wish to ever see anything worse than this.'

'One must have a cast-iron stomach to get along in this world, Madame! '

'Look, Nicole, that poor woman over there is pregnant!' Marie screwed up her courage and hurried forward before the object of her pity could slink away. 'Pardon me, my good woman, but do you speak English?'

The woman simply stared back as Marie opened her sack of hard tack and repeated herself in French. Scabs and dirt blotched the thin face, and the breath reeked, but Marie would not give over so easily. Mustering what she hoped would pass for a gracious smile, she pointed into her sack and gestured. More blank staring faces drifted in around her as Nicole and the children passed on down the icy path.

The peasant's puzzlement suddenly dissolved. Shaking her head indignantly, she stepped backward and spat, gap-toothed, upon the snow. One by one as if following a ritual, the silent assemblage of Lüneburgers followed her example. 'Where did you go, Nicole? What's the matter with these people?'

'They despise charity, Madame.' The deep gutturally accented voice startled Marie. 'They would rather die to the last babe than accept your free biscuit.'

She spun round and was relieved to see her husband approaching. A dark-featured little man in a shabby frock coat and muddy buckled shoes accompanied him. A magisterial pince-nez straddled the bridge of his aquiline nose. 'Madame Campagna, see you the silver chain this poor wretch wears about her neck? It has doubtless been handed down generation to generation. That small misshapen pendant was very likely a passable Latin cross before Martin Luther came along and spoilt it. Definitely a trace of good metal there or my father — may he rest in peace — was no Frankfurt silversmith.'

It annoyed Marie to be addressed so familiarly by a stranger. Her husband seemed anxious to make the necessary introductions, but his companion was not about to let himself be interrupted. 'This amulet, Madame, 'tis probably the only thing of value the poor wretch still possesses. I mean no offense, Capitaine Campagna, but merchants from Halifax have already sucked these people dry. There's not much left for new men of business to feed upon.'

'I well believe it, Herr Doctor. We stopped over at Halifax before coming here. Smallpox kept us from landing, but I made the acquaintance of a few of the leading citizens who came out to us in boats. They did strike me as an exceptionally avaricious lot — even for merchants.'

'One has to be avaricious to survive in this obscure corner of the world, M. le Capitaine. As for this peasant woman, I'll wager you this good English shilling that she will exchange her silver amulet for the same ship-biscuit she would not let your lady give her.'

Luigi Campagna stared blankly at the silver coin. 'I'm not a gambling man, Herr Doctor!'

'You call yourself not a gambling man, Capitaine Campagna? Surely you jest. Only an inveterate gambler would cross the Atlantic in mid-winter. Madame, I beg you offer to trade this poor wretch your sack of biscuit for the neck-piece.'

'Sir, I can hardly accept a valuable heirloom in exchange for these moldy biscuits!' The sheer effrontery of the man appalled Marie.

'Madame, a commodity is worth what the market will bear, no more, no less.' The stranger palmed his spectacles and fixed a hypnotic gaze upon Marie. 'Can this wretched woman eat silver? Would you rather her unborn child miscarry because you fear her trinket may have sentimental value?'

'Very well, Monsieur.' Still only half-convinced, Marie gestured again with her bag and pointed at the Lüneburger's scrawny neck. The woman scowled back at her and fingered the amulet; then she pulled it off over her head, kissed it and offered it up to Marie, making sure not to let go its chain till the sack of biscuit had been delivered up to her. Clutching the miserable bounty to her bosom, she turned without so much as a parting glance and scurried into the miserable hut.

'Quod erat demonstratum!' The stranger gestured as though he had indeed demonstrated a Euclidean theorem. 'Behold, M. le Capitaine and Madame Campagna, these German peasants are not the complete animals the English take them for. They are quite predictable within their own sphere of logic. As you just saw, the wretch did much value that chain, but she valued her principles more.'

'Is there no way I can return it to her?' Marie stared dolefully at what she took to be her ill-gotten gain.

'None, Madame, unless you wish those hard biscuits thrown in your face.' Isaac Ben Yussuf resumed his pince-nez. 'These poor German clods of mine are proud. Indeed, I fear their pride will be the death of them all.'

'You know them very well, Herr Doctor.' Luigi Campagna pressed on to take advantage of his new friend drawing breath. 'Forgive my rudeness, Madame: permit me to present Herr Doctor Isaac Ben Yussuf, the medical officer appointed to this colony by His Britannic Majesty himself.'

'Tis no great honor, M. le Capitaine. His Highness, the Elector of Hanover and King of England, Scotland, Wales and Ireland appointed me because no God fearing Christian would undertake such a wretched commission.' Ben Yussuf clicked his heels and bent stiffly over Marie's gloved fingers. 'Enchanted, Madame. Pray pardon my clumsy speech; I only learned my poor English from the British officers since coming to this dismal place. And yes, I am a Jew, as you surely presume by now.'

Marie promptly reversed her first impression and decided she was going to like this strange man after all. 'Jew or not, Herr Doctor, you'll save the lives of many Christians if you heal as well as you speak.'

'Madame, you are too kind!'

'Major Sutherland is away, so the good doctor kindly consented to show me around the settlement.' Luigi Campagna coughed gently into his seal-fur cuff before including the assembled throng of Lüneburgers in an expansive sweep of his arms. 'It appears from what I've seen that we face formidable difficulties in getting on with these new neighbors of ours.'

'Formidable is too mild a word for the situation, M. le Capitaine. These dull Teutons are quite reduced to starvation and apathy after three winters in this God-forsaken hole!' Ben Yussuf adjusted his pince-nez, which threatened anew to slip off the end of his nose. 'Unlike my own, these people are not cut from a cloth suitable for all seasons. I tell you, M. le Capitaine: it will take more healing skill than I possess to cure their malaise.'

'Herr Ben Yussuf, I can see we much need your counsel on this matter. What will it profit me to set up a trading post on yonder island if all these people perish?'

'Your point is well taken, M. le Capitaine!' The physician appeared to be warming to the Huguenot as though to a promising disciple. 'However, it quite begs the question whether these displaced peasants will ever give rise to profitable enterprises.'

'Do they hunt?' A glance at her husband gave Marie to fear she was grasping at straws, but obviously something had to be tried. 'We could always use a supply of fresh meat, could we not?'

'The skilled poachers among them were all hanged in the Old Country, Madame. Most of this lot have never so much as handled a musket, let alone fired one. Those who've gone out hunting tend to get lost in the woods or else fall victim to marauding Indians.'

'Marauding Indians?' Marie definitely did not like the sound of that.

'Yes, the local M'ikmaq are in an ugly mood. Their Acadian friends were just kicked out of this land by the British, you see. Quite extraordinary the affection and loyalty these supposed savages are capable of. I don't seem to recall our heathen neighbors in Judea making such a fuss when the Imperial Romans gave us Jews the boot.'

'Don't the British soldiers protect these people, Herr Doctor?'

Isaac Ben Yussuf burst into uproarious laughter. 'Madame, the English robbed this miserable place from the French, so they consider it theirs by right of conquest. Naturally, they resent their own king for gifting some small miserable part of it to these Germans. The English do not fight for glory as you French sometimes do.'

'Still, Herr Ben Yussuf, surely the presence of these redcoats must afford these colonists some measure of security.'

'M. le Capitaine, you must realize that Major Sutherland has only a company of mercenaries to garrison the entire colony. He'll be more than happy when the colonists are all dead of scurvy and he can take himself back to Halifax. His Hessian officers tell me he's terrified of being scalped in his camp-cot by Gilles Leblanc.'

Marie was almost afraid to ask. 'And who is this Gilles Leblanc?'

'An Acadian fish that keeps slipping through the English net, Madame.' The Jew spoke with the spectator-like objectivity peculiar to his race. 'They say his wife and children were among the victims of the recent Expulsion. He has sworn to peddle the scalp of every Englishman in Nova Scotia to the French at Louisbourg. I must say he's off to a promising start. Just yesterday came news that the renegade and his friends have massacred a small detachment of redcoats. Took all their scalps, of course.'

This singular custom of taking scalps horrified Marie. 'Can they not catch this monster, Herr Doctor?'

'It cannot be long till they do so, Madame. Governor Lawrence has posted three hundred pounds bounty on Leblanc's scalp. Well may the Governor worry, for he himself ordered the expulsion of Leblanc's people from this land. I trust that my bald Jewish pate will not tempt the awful renegade.'

Luigi Campagna had remained silent through all this as if thinking of something else. 'Herr Ben Yussuf, we must not succumb to pessimism.'

'My own sentiments exactly, M. le Capitaine! If only our situation warranted more optimism!'

'Let us put our heads together and see if we cannot do something to remedy the situation.' The Huguenot extended his hand to the Jew. 'Please come dine with us aboard *L'Espérance* this evening, Herr Doctor.'

Again the physician bowed and clicked his heels. 'I would accept your gracious invitation with delight, M. le Capitaine, if only I were sure your good lady shares your willingness to tolerate a Jew at her table.'

Marie hastened to speak for herself. 'Herr Doctor, you misjudge me! I have long felt that our two peoples have a great deal in common. We Huguenots are also wandering pariahs, you know. Indeed, I can already see that my husband looks to you to point our way through this wilderness.'

'Madame, like all sons of Judah, I am a student of human nature.' The physician absentmindedly adjusted his periwig; Marie couldn't help noticing that it stood in great need of powdering. 'How else could we have survived? Alas, such knowledge often drives us to painful conclusions, as in the case of this peasant woman.'

'How so?' Marie felt increasingly drawn to the Jewish physician despite all the prejudice against his race so thoroughly ingrained into her.

'Alas, Madame, I greatly fear your good biscuits will serve no useful purpose. The woman with child will share them with her people rather than hoard them for her own need. What might save one will be wasted on many.'

Luigi Campagna was not about to let so auspicious an occasion descend into despair. 'Come, my friend! Let us not stand here amid this squalor and dwell on the negative. I've a bottle or two of good Moselle to share with you.'

'Moselle, did you say? You're not serious, M. le Capitaine! I never thought to breathe the sweet bouquet of Moselle again! I'm told it doesn't travel well.'

'You may judge for yourself, Herr Doctor. I think you may be pleasantly surprised.'

'Madame Campagna, your husband is simply too kind! Believe me, dear lady, I won't mind scraping this infernal mud from my boots for a few hours aboard your lovely ship.'

'She's a mere brigantine, actually, Herr Doctor.' Modesty was a hallmark of Luigi Campagna's religion.

'A brigantine, you say, M. le Capitaine? Well, what would a poor Jewish physician know about such things? My one illustrious countryman to follow the sea was swallowed by a whale: an object lesson the rest of us have much taken to heart.'

Luigi Campagna took comradely hold of Isaac Ben Yussuf's arm. 'You may be a landlubber, Herr Doctor, but I know nautical prudence when I meet up with it.'

'Ah, do not overestimate me, Capitaine Campagna, as some of my poor German clods do. What good are medicinal powders and leeches under conditions such as these? I should become a Christian and perform miracles? I tell you, M. le Capitaine, if ever there was a time and place for loaves and fishes, it is here and now.'

The analogy seemed to catch the Huguenot's fancy. 'Perhaps manna from heaven would suffice, Herr Doctor?'

'No, Capitaine Campagna; these German oafs would toss it out to the wolves and savage Indians!'

'As you say, Herr Doctor, it's a question of what the market will bear, is it not?' Marie had never seen Luigi Campagna so pleased with himself.

Arm in arm, the unlikely companions led the way back to the dock. Feeling somewhat abandoned, Marie gathered up the children, just returned from wandering with Nicole amongst the Lüneburgers.

147

'These people were left here to die, Madame!' The maid spoke with all the cold fury she normally reserved for occasions of committing manslaughter. 'Many women and children have died here already!'

'Yes, Nicole, I know.' It took Marie somewhat aback to see the two men embark in the captain's gig without so much as a backward glance. 'What is needed here is a Saint Francis of Assisi to perform miracles.'

'Madame, I fear these stiff-necked Lutherans would turn your good friar out in the cold.'

'And all those two men can think of right now is sharing a bottle of wine!'

Nicole's cold fury turned to warm merriment in the twinkling of an eye. 'Do not despair, Madame. Two such men can accomplish a great deal while in their cups if only they be managed by women such as us.'

No less than four bottles of Moselle were consumed that night. As Nicole had suggested, the flow of masculine thought was much facilitated by convivial spirits. Marie seconded her maid in making sure the occasion was an auspicious one. To top things off, a bottle of fine Old Malmsey was also sacrificed to the good cause.

'Half a shipload of flour and salt pork should see these people through the winter, Herr Doctor.' Luigi Campagna raised his glass to his newfound friend. 'There are also several kegs of lime juice aboard. That should put an end to the scurvy.'

Isaac Ben Yussuf wrinkled up his nose at the mention of pork. 'Cabbages would serve better, M. le Capitaine!'

'Cabbages, Herr Doctor?'

'Yes, cabbages!' The physician sniffed the splendidly preserved bouquet of his Moselle. 'My Germans normally subsist on pickled cabbage, you know.'

'Make a note of that, Nicole.' The Huguenot might well have been speaking to a private secretary. 'We must make sure to grow plenty of cabbages once we get ourselves set up on Sanctuary Island. Herr Doctor, I'm afraid we brought no pickled cabbage with us.'

'Well, beggars can't be choosers.' The Jew's nose had turned quite red from the effects of the wine. 'Flour and pork will have to do. My Germans shall just have to wait another year for their sauerkraut.'

'But they need something to trade for it, Herr Doctor, since they cannot grow much of it here themselves. Albeit they are Lutherans, such honesty and thrift as you describe are sure to win out in the long run.'

'Their backs may be strong, but their minds are dull.' The physician held up his glass for Marie to refill it. 'Mind you, dullness is most essential to surviving in such a place as this.'

Marie could stand this deepening male debauchery no longer. 'I wish to ask a question, messieurs.'

'Ask away, Madame.' Ben Yussuf inclined his wig graciously. 'Your wife is a true daughter of Eve, my friend. She is a paragon of curiosity about the nature of things.'

'That is very true.' Luigi Campagna sighed as if shifting a burden weighting down his shoulders. 'I am blessed with a woman of most excellent mind, Herr Doctor.'

'A virtue many men have vainly questioned in womankind and the principal reason I intend to remain a bachelor.' The Jew brushed cake crumbs off his waistcoat. 'Be that as it may, pray pose us your question, Madame.'

'Luigi Campagna, what do you know about growing cabbages?'

'Absolutely nothing, Madame.' The Huguenot stifled a hiccup. 'What is there to growing vegetables other than watching them grow?'

His physician friend hastened to agree. 'It's mere peasants' work, Madame, though these German clods try to make a mystery of it. But let us give them their due, M. le Capitaine: one does need a proper peasant's back for clearing land, plowing, weeding and harvesting.'

'Herr Doctor!' Luigi Campagna started up from the table as if he had discovered a pin in his seat. 'I do believe you're on to something!'

'I am indeed, Capitaine Campagna!' Isaac Ben Yussuf raised his glass in toast to his host. 'Never mind it having crossed an ocean, this is a most excellent Moselle! I am forever in your debt, my friend.'

'No, Herr Doctor, it is I who am forever in your debt! You have just presented me with the solutions of our two problems all rolled up in one! Tell me, would these peasants accept credit?'

'Not gracefully, M. le Capitaine, but I might bring them to it if they knew how payment of their debt was bound to occur.'

'Hard manual labor, Herr Doctor! The strong backs of peasants, as you put it so succinctly! And to think I was actually losing sleep worrying how I might induce those lazy sailors of mine to become farmers!'

'M. le Capitaine, do you propose to hire my German peasants to work your island?'

'Exactly so, my friend! What else can they supply in trade at this time? And certainly I have a demand for peasant labor. It's all so beautifully simple, Herr Doctor, but I should never have seen the light if you had not accepted my invitation to dinner!'

'Food for their families is all these people ask, M. le Capitaine!' Marie marveled how instantly the good physician took up the merchant's enthusiasm. 'I hereby undertake to deliver them to you at a bargain.'

'On commission, of course!'

'Of course! A more practical solution than dispensing loaves and fishes, M. le Capitaine, and one for which I deserve to be paid. Ha! Ha! What do you say to ten per cent?'

Luigi Campagna blinked his eyes at the Christly joke, but apparently decided to forgive it. 'Make it eight per cent, Herr Doctor, and you've got yourself a deal! I'll unship the flour and pork tomorrow, and you may apportion it among these good colonists according to their need.'

'What a true Christian you are, M. le Capitaine! I stipulate that each Lüneburger must agree to report for a month of labor on your island in return for receiving food sufficient to feed his family for a month.'

'My friend, I've no wish to fleece these people! I wish them to prosper, not just merely survive. That way, I stand to prosper alongside them. Offer them employment at the rate of a month's rations for two weeks' work and send them to me in staggered crews. I shall make better use of them that way.'

'Capitaine Campagna, you are indeed a gentleman and a scholar! Shall I have the first lot report for duty in a fortnight's time?'

'Better make it three fortnights, Herr Doctor. I've no mind to work sick men in winter. Let them fatten a bit and come to me in full spring. Have them bring their axes, mattocks, shovels and hoes. We shall start by erecting a dock and some proper log cabins for my womenfolk and children.'

'Agreed, M. le Capitaine! My peasants were born grasping such implements. One question, though: how do you propose to employ your sailors?'

'By keeping them busy doing what they do best, of course. We'll be needing to trade with Halifax. I've a mind to start with a cargo of oak cleared from our island. Some of my seamen are fine Basque fishermen, so we'll fetch back some cod from the Grand Banks to go with the sauerkraut.'

'Indeed, that would go down much better than salt pork, M. le Capitaine! Madame, I see why you married this man. He's a genius of industry and commerce!'

151

'Next year, Herr Doctor, we'll send *L'Espérance* with salt fish and timber to the West Indies and bring back a cargo of molasses and rum!' The phlegmatic Huguenot was rapidly becoming a visionary. 'Nicole, another glass of Old Malmsey, if you please.'

'To your good health, M. le Capitaine! I look forward to a mutually profitable partnership. Perhaps you'll permit me to take passage on your brigantine's first run to Halifax.'

'Certainly, Herr Doctor, and may the God of Christians, Lutherans and Jews smile on our enterprise!' Cheeks aglow, the boon companions touched their glasses and solemnly drank.

Nicole chuckled at the thunderclouds gathered on Marie's brow. 'So, Madame, now you see how a woman's best work is done!'

The snores of her inebriated husband kept Marie from sleeping till the wee hours of the morn despite the thick bulkhead between them. Clutching her ring to her bosom, it came almost as a relief to feel the presence settle upon her.

I thought you'd never settle down, Marie of Hohenstaufen. It felt as though her nocturnal visitor were breathing in her ear. *Shame on you carrying on like this over the human flotsam scattered on this forsaken shore! Really, flesh of my flesh, such an exhibition of pathetic sentiment doesn't become someone of your exalted lineage.*

Were you so insensitive to human suffering when the ruler of Christendom, Sire?

Well, we never wore the stigmata like the sainted Francis of Assisi, if that's what you mean. The voice took on a plaintive tone. *We overheard you wishing that he were here to heal the sick. We knew your black robed pet quite well, you know. He stank to high heaven, even after we had him bathed by our eunuchs lest the women of our harem catch some disease.*

152

Did you not respect his virtue, Sire?

In all truth, Your Highness, we didn't at first. If you only knew what a foul assortment of popes and cardinals and priests we came across in our reign!

I'm anxious to hear what changed your mind about Saint Francis, Sire.

He was an obnoxious and obstinate fellow, if truth be told. A prime exponent of pompous humility if we ever met one. Just the sort we enjoy exposing as a fraud. That was the reason we invited him to come pay us a visit at our favorite palace in Benevento.

I trust he did the right thing and refused your invitation.

Hardly, Princess! Accepting an Imperial invitation wasn't an option in those good old days. We would have been forced to hire assassins if he had declined.

So then, Sire, you admit that you were much like King Herod summoning Saint John the Baptist?

Something like that, my dear, except our Salomes had no designs on his head — till we bid them try to turn it.

Ah, so you wished to tempt his virtue! Sire, I've every faith he confounded your evil designs.

Being a woman, you are undoubtedly a better judge of character than us, Princess Mine. The voice betrayed the barest hint of regret. *We stranded him amidst the finest seraglio any monarch ever assembled, every last one of them an excruciatingly lovely creature whom we commanded to satisfy his every whim. Yet all the sanctimonious fool could do was blat like a sheep set among wolves!*

He was indeed set among wolves, Sire!

No doubt our mistake was enticing him with infidel women. That put him in fear for his immortal soul, we suppose. If only we'd taken the trouble to supply good Christian flesh, the bigot would have fallen for it like a ripe plum!

Sire, the virtue of Saint Francis passes your under-standing. Beneath genuine feeling of indignation, Marie couldn't help being amused. *I trust he admonished you properly for your sin in tempting him.*

As we remember, he promptly complained to that old fart Gregory IX that we were Satan incarnate. Of course, His Holiness was most appreciative of his slanders and promptly began excommunicating us for being the Antichrist. Now that we ponder on it, pretty boys might have served our purpose better. There's nothing like a good catamite to test which way a man naturally goes.

I think you are truly an evil man to even suggest such a thing, Sire!

Methinks you judge us too harshly! Do bear in mind that we have seen much more of this world than you. Sleep well, Your Highness!

Chapter XI

SANCTUARY

Mahonne Bay, April 1756

L'Espérance sailed with the dawn. Swathed in patchy fog, Isaac Ben Yussuf's battered tricorne stood out among the waving caps and bonnets of the stolid Lüneburgers. Many of the peasant folk standing on the beach were already contracted to work for Luigi Campagna in the spring. In token of this, they had helped the crew build the driftwood dock and stack it high with the casks and sacks of provisions the settlement so desperately needed.

Heeling far over before a stiff breeze, the half-laden brigantine braved the rough waves rolling in off the Atlantic before slipping deeper into the protected inner waters of the Bay. Below decks, Marie got the morning off to a similarly rough start by trying to teach Euclid's Fourteenth Theorem to her excited stepsons. Exhausted and sore of mind, she brought them on deck to discover *L'Espérance* scudding under a cloudless sky through a chain of jewel-like islands. If anything, her anticipation exceeded that of the liberated children. *Today our long voyage will end. I will finally reach the first true home I have ever known. Here shall be born this stranger's child I carry.*

Chart tucked under his arm, her husband expectantly paced up and down his quarterdeck. He handed her the telescope and pointed. 'There it is, Madame. If the wind holds, we shall lie at anchor there by noon.'

'How can you possibly tell which one is Sanctuary, Monsieur?'

He unscrolled his chart for her. 'See, Madame, it is marked right here. One simply takes a compass bearing *et voila!* We shall know it by its many oak trees when we come a bit closer.'

'Oak trees that your brethren planted, Monsieur?' The question did not require an answer. Marie furrowed her brow as some memory of flames and smoke flitted across the surface of her mind. 'But surely you intend to build our home out of good stone, do you not?'

'I would build our house of solid stone, if I could.' Luigi Campagna's manner and tone were those one might use in speaking to a child. 'Alas, there's no suitable building stone on this island of ours, only some fertile soil. In any case, we lack stonemasons. I fear I must ask you to settle at first for a log cabin, Madame.'

'Luigi Campagna, you need only promise me that someday you will build us a stone house to live in.' Marie restrained an impulse to reach up and stroke his beard into some semblance of order. 'I can never be truly at home in a house that could burn down around us.'

'Very well, Madame. If God be willing, someday we'll fetch proper building stone to the island and build such a house.' For the first time, she felt his touch counted for something more than a fatherly gesture. A current of manly strength flowed from him to her.

'Bien!' His promise was all she had hoped for, but Marie could not let it go at that. 'Does that mean that we may live here as a married couple are meant to live, Monsieur?'

'God willing, Madame.' Luigi Campagna cast down his eyes as though embarrassed by his wife's importunity. 'His ways are mysterious, but perhaps He will discharge us from our special mission after your child is born. Perhaps all He will ask of us is to rear this child as best a loving man and woman can.'

He tried to withdraw his hand, but she would not let go. 'I agree to mother your children if you will father mine, Monsieur. Come, I know we are already married, but let us swear anew by the love of God to do this for one another — if He so wills it, of course.'

Solemnly with hands interlocked, they both swore. 'Sworn companions we are now, Madame.' Luigi Campagna's blue eyes twinkled under his shaggy eyebrows. 'True Huguenots we are become at last.'

'Much more than sworn companions we shall be to one another, Luigi Campagna. As your wife I shall do my best to make you a happy man. That much I swear to you.'

'No, you mustn't swear that.' He put a finger to her lips. 'It's not our lot to be happy in this vale of tears!'

'God at least permits us to try.' Marie stood on tiptoe to kiss his grizzled cheek.

The children burst onto the quarterdeck, even little Guillaume clamoring along with the others. 'Papa, please come show us which one is our island! We want to go ashore and hunt for pirate treasure!'

'You see, Monsieur? Even these boys know what is buried there!'

Obliged to yield up her husband, Marie turned the telescope upon the shallow cove opening up before them. *A fair isle in a beautiful bay at the end of the world. What more could a homeless band of fugitives want for their final refuge?*

Yet the sight of Sanctuary Island made a shiver run down her spine. The Templars had been scheming to bring her to this place even while she was a prisoner praying in the shadow of Father Jerome. Just what had been waiting here so long? She lowered the telescope to find her maid standing beside her. 'So, Madame, there it is at last. I never truly thought I'd live to see this day.'

'Oh come now, Nicole.' Marie handed her the telescope. 'Our voyage wasn't all that bad!'

'You mistake my meaning, Madame. While still a young girl in training, I used to dream of coming here.'

Marie turned to better survey the Dread Maiden, her legs firmly braced against the motion of the sea, her uncoifed dark-blonde hair whipped by the wind about her head. Try as she might, she could make neither head nor tail of what this stranger meant to her. Stranger indeed, for despite their many intimacies, the maid servant had become even more of an enigma to her mistress than she had been at their first meeting in France; Nicole was to her a compass rose full of mysterious signs ranging all the way from the sublime to the ridiculous. 'I'm afraid that no sailors waits for you on this island, Nicole.'

'Alas, Madame, I fear you are right: no sailors are waiting.' Nicole swept the island with the spyglass as if she yet hoped. 'There was a time when hundreds of them would have gathered here to greet such a new arrival as us. Masts once stood so thick in yonder cove that *L'Espérance* would have been obliged to anchor offshore. Think of it, Madame: all those lusty young mariners lie long dead and forgotten, and all those splendid caravels and galleasses they sailed here now rot at the bottom of the sea!'

'As always, Nicole, you lead me where I am quite unable to follow!'

'As always, Madame, you are quite unwilling to let yourself be led!' With a girlish tilt of her head the maid succeeded in training the telescope as purposefully as any man. 'Try and remember why we have come here, Madame.'

'Remember, did you say?' Marie's hands flew to her midriff as though to stifle her belly laugh. 'How can I remember what no one has yet to tell me?'

Hugo led four sailors up the ratlines to strike and furl the great square-rigged sails. *L'Espérance*'s rush across the tranquil bay became a crawl. Others of the crew began shackling the huge double-fluked anchor to its rode. Luigi Campagna relieved Sabot at the helm and sent him forward to pilot the brigantine into the cove.

A warm land breeze wafted the fragrance of the still-slumbering spring to Marie's nostrils. *I have come to like the sea, but it will be good to set foot firmly on land again. I think Nicole is right to insist that my baby not be born on this brigantine. How lucky I am to have her with me even if she is a Dread Maiden! Who else would be as likely to get me through what lies before me as her?*

L'Espérance inched into the cove under a reefed mainsail. At a nod from Sabot, Luigi Campagna spun the wheel and pointed the bowsprit into the wind. The sail luffed and the anchor splashed deep. Hugo released the mains'l halyard, and the brigantine swung to and tugged obediently at her cable. The brigantine's captain did not rest content till a second rode had been run out and made fast to a giant oak standing at the water's edge.

Even when all had been made fast, Luigi Campagna seemed in no hurry to disembark, but Nicole was not one to be denied. Securely seating herself in the gig, the maid crossed her arms in firm resolve upon the high pile of blankets she held in her lap. 'Lower away, Master. I refuse to ever come back aboard this hell-ship, so help me God. And do be sure to bring along a sail on your next run to shore; we shall camp right there on the beach.'

Sighing and shaking his head as men have done since Adam was given Eve, the Huguenot climbed into the gig and prepared to ferry his women and children to the island. It left Marie wondering as he rowed them to shore which one of them was really the servant and which one the master.

Holding her gently in his powerful arms, the Huguenot insisted on wading his protesting wife ashore. Meanwhile, all four children had scampered through the waves onto the beach where they formed up in a ring round the skylarking Nicole. Marie would not have believed a woman could perform such acrobatic feats. The maid seemed quite oblivious of the dark sand encrusting her wet gown as she playfully used it to baptize each of the four children in turn. Luigi Campagna ended the horseplay by setting his burden down rather heavily in their midst. 'This is our home now, my sons. Let us pray to God that we may never need to flee captivity again.'

The boys dutifully bowed their heads, but Nicole did not follow suit. Brows straight and even, she held her mistress's gaze while their lord and master intoned a soulful prayer. Marie felt as though the maid were excusing her from participating in such masculine nonsense. It set her mind to wandering where it had never wandered before. 'Amen! Very well, my hearties, you may explore the island till Pierre pipes you home for your suppers. But first you must promise your mother to be careful of falling from the cliffs, and take care not to stray beyond sight of our masts. As you are the oldest, Philippe, I lay a special charge upon you to look after little Louis and Guillaume.'

The boys promised Marie to be careful and marched off after Philippe as though on a parade ground. By the time they reached the first oak tree, their solemnity had quite melted away. 'After being so long cooped up, your sons badly need to escape us, Monsieur.'

'Ah, Madame, this Sanctuary Island of ours is a perfect paradise for raising these children of ours. Here they can learn to fish and swim and sail.'

That was all the opening Nicole needed. 'Then, Master, we'll be wanting one of the sailors assigned to watch over them. There's no telling what trouble they may get themselves into.'

The Huguenot sighed and shrugged as if bowing to the inevitable. 'Aye aye, Nicole, a sailor ye shall have.'

'It best be Hugo, if you please, Master. When it comes to business other than hauling on sails, I wouldn't give tuppence for the rest of that crew of yours.'

Marie decided that if a serving maid could talk to her husband so, she should at least be able to tease him a little. 'Also, Monsieur, Hugo would be the perfect one for guiding the boys when they go hunting for pirate treasure.'

'I doubt any pirate has set foot on this island in four centuries.' At last catching the smiles and glances passing between the women, Luigi Campagna refused to rise further to the bait. 'Madame, Nicole, please excuse me. I must return to *L'Espérance* and direct the crew, or we'll never make camp tonight. It won't be many more weeks, you know, till Isaac Ben Yussuf descends on us with his army of Huns.'

A few skilful strokes brought the gig under *L'Espérance's* graceful transom. Watching the crew belay the running rigging and stow the sails, the brigantine reminded Marie of a wild bird trapped in a web. Domesticity seemed already to be the order of the day in this New World of theirs.

"I much doubt any pirate has set foot here in four centuries." Luigi Campagna's words kept echoing in Marie's mind. *So this is Sanctuary Island, my refuge from a world gone mad with hatred and intrigue. And yet even here terrible secrets lie hidden. I can feel something more waiting here than these open pastures shaded by majestic oaks, these sandy beaches and bluffs crumbling slowly into the sea.*

It saddened Marie to know this was not a virgin island she stood upon. A swarm of Europeans driven by forces beyond her reckoning had already intruded here. Even this maid of hers walking barefooted along the beach was an extension of some strange powerful force projecting itself across the centuries. 'Take off your shoes, Madame. This warm sand will be good for your poor foot.'

Marie sat down obediently upon a drift-log and began to dreamily unlace her ankle-length shoes. Her ring came to hand as she closed her eyes and wriggled her toes down into the warm sand. *Yes, this does feel good. Thank God I still have one foot that Nicole need not pity. How strange that the young chevalier praised this other one as being the fairest part of me.*

And quite right he was to do so, Marie of Hohenstaufen! Both your feet are surpassing fair. It is many centuries since the feet of a woman so stirred our long-cooled blood.

You overreach yourself, Sire! Marie felt her own blood rushing to her face. *'You claim to be my ancestor, remember?*

And so we are! If it were not so, your mettle would sorely be put to the test, Princess mine.

I'll not countenance your effrontery in the light of day.' Marie tried angrily to rise to her feet but failed.

Take care not to strain yourself, Princess! You have fallen asleep upon the sand.

That's because I do not sleep well at night thanks to you troubling me, Sire.

What an ungrateful child you are! Know you not that we are come to be your comfort amid the trials and tribulations that await you? Think you wild horses could have dragged us into this desolation if we had not sworn to guard your welfare?

I believe nothing of what you say, Sire. Why would so great a king bother with the likes of me?

Emperor of the Romans, if you don't mind.

Whatever you once were, Sire, you seemed to have fared badly in your kingship. Perhaps that harem you boast of kept you from applying yourself.

On the contrary, we applied ourself only too well, both to the harem and to being a great sovereign over diverse people. As a recent English poet so aptly put it: "Be not the first by whom the new is tried nor yet the last to lay the old aside." Our crime was breaking that rule in giving shape to the world you now live in, sweet Princess.

You delude yourself, Sire. Your realms are quite vanished. If you are the same nameless Antichrist the Jesuits spoke of, not even a statue or painting of you remains.

The voice took its time responding as though it had taken her words to heart. *Germany ceased to exist before our time, Highness. As for Jerusalem, it never was. Only Sicily do we pine for.*

Sicily? That little triangle of an island? Sire, you yourself described it as nothing but a heap of ashes.

Indeed, wretched it has become, but that little island, as you call it, was the great breadbasket of the ancient and mediaeval worlds. We loved it more than all the rest of my realms put together! Our Norman ancestors made of it a fair and enlightened kingdom. It became the wonder of the world during our reign.

And you would have me believe that is the sin for which your offspring are hounded from the face of the Earth?

My dear, you must understand that the House of Hohenstaufen stood for reason in an age of madness and dark superstition. We encouraged science and art and learning. Our ultimate sin was extending religious tolerance to all. Can you imagine how we threatened Holy Mother Church's hold on the souls of men?

I think you give yourself airs, Sire. I've heard dark stories about you. Some of them ring with truth.

Oh we admit that we burned heretics and witches on occasion.

Burned them, you say!

Indeed. Smoke from scorching flesh rose from every piazza in Italy. It was a time of burning, my dear. No crowned head could have held his throne without feeding those awful flames.

Enough, monsieur! Marie opened her eyes and shook her head to dispel her unwelcome visitor. She scrambled to her feet and fled to the returning gig. Pierre Lazar looked at her askance as he struggled to carry a folded sail and a galley full of cooking utensils ashore. 'No pot au feu tonight, Madame: I promised the captain *bouillabaisse a la Marseillaise.*'

'Bien!' Marie's fondest childhood memories were associated with an old Provençal cook at the convent. 'But, Pierre Lazar, you must know better than I that one needs fresh fish to make bouillabaise.'

'Don't worry, Madame.' The cook pointed where the ship's boat was being lowered away from the brigantine. 'There go Arnaud and Sebastien. I swear those Basques could catch fish in King Louis' bathtub.'

The two young women set about gathering driftwood for Lazar's bonfire as a way of insinuating themselves into the management of the emerging camp, but the ship's cook politely ignored all their attempts to influence his culinary preparations. Masculine ineptitude notwithstanding, the great copper kettle was hanging from its wrought-iron tripod when the first boatload of provisions and stores landed ashore.

The seamen expended a good deal of salty language contriving a serviceable tent out of the old canvas foresail. Covering her ears, Marie retreated up the beach. 'Surely, those two are doomed to burn in hell, Nicole!'

'Their sins shall be forgiven, Madame — never fear.' As always, Nicole seemed stirred by the presence of such unfettered men. 'As my poor father used to say,

Almighty God would never have created Eve if He had-n't meant for Adam to curse and swear.'

'What a story to tell on us, Nicole! We women are not mere children to be humored by men!'

'Certainly not, Madame, but it always goes best for us to let them think so.' In what struck Marie as a com-plete non sequitur, the maid held up a bramble grow-ing along the edge of the beach. 'This plant is raspber-ry, Madame. Teas made from its roots at this time of year are a good remedy for scurvy.'

'Then let us dig some, Nicole! I should like to keep my teeth yet awhile.'

'Psst!' Every muscle in Nicole's body seemed sud-denly poised for action.

At first Marie assumed this was more of the maid's frolicsome nature asserting itself. 'What is it, Nicole?

'Someone is watching us, Madame!'

Three of the boys broke through the tree cover high above and stood looking down at them as though con-scious of having something to hide. 'Ahoy, Jean, how many pirates did you find up there?'

'We found no pirates, Madame, but Philippe, he found us a whole lot of Indians. He went down to speak to them while the rest of us hid in the bushes.'

'Indians?' Marie looked at her maid aghast. 'Jean, where is Philippe?'

All three boys began to cry at once. 'Madame, they took Philippe off with them in their canoe! Will we never get to see our brother again?'

Chapter XII

WAKSITANOU

Sanctuary Island, April 1756

Neither Marie nor Luigi Campagna slept that night.
Two boatloads of sailors armed with muskets and cutlasses combed the waters around the small island, but
they did not locate the missing boy. Nor did they find
any trace of the "Indians" whom the other children
claimed to have seen. Nicole borrowed sailor's clothing
and a sheathed dirk from Hugo and slipped off into the
oaks. She returned in the first light of morning having
fared no better than the others.

The sun had risen high in the cloud-decked sky
before the lookout sounded a warning from his perch
atop the brigantine's mainmast.

Scarce casting a ripple, more than a dozen canoes
came gliding out of the morning mist. Their paddles
dripped rainbows and suns as they slid into the island
cove. Standing on the beach, Marie feared the worst.
Yet so struck was she by the gossamer craft that she
restrained her husband's arm from leveling his musket.

'Father, it's me, Philippe! I come bringing you many
guests!' Solemn of visage and tremulous of voice, the
youth rose up in the bow of the lead canoe. Without
saying a word, Luigi Campagna handed his wife the

musket and waded out. Knee-deep, he hauled his pro-digal son straight over the prow and dangled him aloft as though searching for lost limbs.

The birch-bark vessels grounded on the sandbar stretching out from the beach at low tide. One of the paddlers vaulted forth and lofted a long staff in stately greeting. 'Ho! Ho! Ho! First Stranger, I welcome you to this land where my people have dwelt since memory began. I am Waksitanou of the M'ikmaq. Your son was kind enough to guide us here to you. We come in peace.'

The Huguenot's red-rimmed eyes widened at hear-ing the strangely accented French. Still holding his son at arm's length, he made haste to shrug his coat over the pistol butts and cutlass hilt jutting from his belt. 'I bid you welcome, Waksitanou of the M'ikmaq. I am Luigi Campagna the trader, and all these you see before you are my people.'

Marie couldn't help comparing these two men: the one wet to the knees of his breeches and armed to the teeth; the other in a beaded tunic worn loosely over leggings of soft deerskin and weaponless except for the baton-like staff. Even the quilled moccasins stayed dry as their wearer advanced along the sandbar and swept the assemblage with his gaze. Marie trembled and moved closer to Nicole as the smoky irises engulfed her.

'First Stranger, you are a fortunate man to have two such fair wives and so many brave sons. You come here in a canoe worthy to bear Glooscap himself across the great water. Truly, you must be a mighty chief among your people.'

'Waksitanou of the M'ikmaq is most gracious.' Marie watched anxiously as her husband warily groped for words. 'I hope such a great chief will pardon us the ungracious manner of our welcome. This son of mine alarmed us greatly by going off without a word.'

Philippe chose that moment to start kicking his feet. 'Father, you're hurting my arms!'

'Son of my loins, you may consider yourself fortunate if only your arms hurt this night!'

'Please, Father, the son of Sachem Waksitanou made me his brother. I slept in a wigwam and ate their food and everything!'

'Gave you no thought to your poor mother, Philippe?' Luigi Campagna shook his son vehemently as he waded back to the beach. 'Did you not think she might be frightened to death on your account?'

'Father, they let me paddle one of their canoes!'

The Huguenot smiled at the M'ikmaq and set his son down on the sand between them. 'Philippe, you must promise me never to do such a thing as this again!'

'Father, I willingly promise it.' The boy rubbed his arms and seemed close to tears. 'Next time I will think of others before doing what pleases me.'

'A worthwhile lesson if you have truly learned it, Philippe.' The Huguenot buttoned up his coat with a magisterial air. 'Waksitanou of the M'ikmaq, I am sorry for this unseemly display.'

'Trader Campagna, it is never unseemly for a father to counsel his son. Forgive my young men for letting him come with them, but my people have learned to be cautious when encountering strangers. Things are no longer as they once were in this land.'

'Your caution is understandable.' The Huguenot looked from Philippe to the scowling seamen still standing to arms on the deck of the brigantine. Having made himself as presentable as possible, he stepped toward the canoes and raised an arm in a rather lame imitation of the M'ikmaq greeting.

Waksitanou gave a nod to those who accompanied him. Unfrozen, a pair of slender youths and a maiden sprang barefooted into the cold surf and beached their canoe. 'These are my sons, Trader Campagna. Their birth-names cannot be spoken till they have earned the names of men.'

Luigi Campagna pretended amazement at this. 'Have the Jesuits not christened them with the names of papist saints?'

'First Stranger, do not imagine that all M'ikmaq follow the Black Robes, although 'tis true that many do so.' Waksitanou sternly grounded his carved staff in saying this, but then broke into a smile. 'There be one thing all my people love to do, and that is parley and haggle with the French for the wondrous goods they bring us from afar.'

Luigi Campagna looked relieved to hear it. 'Then let the trading begin, Waksitanou of the M'ikmaq.'

Trade items were quickly ferried ashore from *L'Espérance*. Still warily gripping his belted cutlass with one hand, Jacques Sabot welcomed the M'ikmaq with the other as they swarmed past him. Hugo had already set up shop behind a ship's plank laid upon two upright casks. He began hawking copper kettle ware, steel axes, mirrors and glass beads. One young brave loudly demanded rum, but the coxswain sadly shook his head. A bit of an altercation ensued till Luigi Campagna stepped forward to explain that he refused to traffic spirits. Waksitanou and the women greeted his announcement with approving nods and smiles.

Marie found her native counterparts fascinating. Unlike the men who went half-naked in the chill spring air, the women wore knee-length tunics of soft pale doeskin decorated with dyed quills and beads. Old or young, each bore a large basket on her back supported by a head strap. Each basket contained a variety of necklaces, earrings and bracelets, even carved figurines of animals and what seemed to be children's toys. Indeed, so diverse were the exotic handicrafts the M'ikmaq offered for trade that Hugo had difficulty determining fair market value. 'Captain Campagna, how many glass beads is this bark carving worth?'

'Doubtless back in London it's worth all the glass beads we have in stock. Haggle hard with them, Hugo, but you must then slowly give way till their faces tell you they are satisfied with the bargain they've struck.' The seaman's expression made it clear that he thought his master had some very strange ideas about trading with savages. 'Only that way will we know what these items are really worth to them, coxswain. Remember, these people love to haggle for the sake of it, but they won't take kindly to being cheated by strangers. We're mainly after the beaver trapped by the men, but it is the women who decide how much return business we get.'

Marie soon confirmed the shrewdness of her husband's business principles. The M'ikmaq men, confused and disappointed by the lack of rum, were reduced to trading prime beaver for copper kettles. These were promptly snatched up and trundled off to the waiting canoes by their beaming womenfolk. To offset this loss of masculine face, Luigi Campagna presented each adult male with a long clay pipe and a generous supply of black pigtail. Hugo even modeled a plaid tobacco pouch as a kind of tam o' shanter, complete with long braided drawstring tassels.

This combination of debonair bonnet and gruesome scar proved rather too much of a good thing. Hugo found himself besieged by a bevy of feminine admirers; so much so that some of the young men hastily emptied their new tobacco pouches and adopted the new fashion in male attire. Even so, the seaman was soon quite overwhelmed by the rising tide of feminine favor.

The sailing master came along and sent a broad wink his way. 'Well, coxswain, do ye be getting' enough Indians comin' yer way for yer liking?'

Marie finally had to rescue the hapless seaman. 'Hugo, let me spell you off for a while. I've always wondered what it would be like to be a shopkeeper.'

The M'ikmaq women mourned Hugo's departure with many sighs and forlorn glances. Not that a European woman failed to interest them. They scrutinized Marie carefully, and the older women fingered her voluminous skirts and patted her tiny waist as though she were a visitor from the moon. Shaking their heads, they stared at her lily-white hands and spread her fingers to expose the tender palms.

When all trading had ended, Luigi Campagna came bustling up, concern written all over his grizzled face. 'Waksitanou, your people are hungry! I fear we can offer but poor hospitality at such short notice to so many.'

'Trader Campagna, you are guests of the M'ikmaq this day.' Waksitanou gave a hand signal to his womenfolk. His wife, Nasqualik, a sturdily handsome woman of middle years, had already lit a fire upon the beach. Younger women began fetching hampers of provisions from the canoes. Still others went gathering along the beach and the marsh that stretched beyond.

Sitting cross-legged on a caribou hide, Waksitanou clearly enjoyed playing host. Marie sat near him in a place of honor on a driftwood log, watching Nasqualik boil a huge basket of soup by immersing hot stones in it. She could not believe that ducks' eggs gathered on the marshes and baked under the coals could taste so good. She savored pounded roots of an aquatic plant seasoned with wild mushrooms and a huge salmon delicately smoked with the wood of some native tree. At first she had been reluctant to partake of such strange food, but who could refuse Waksitanou of the M'ikmaq?

'Sachem, the food your womenfolk have prepared for us is excellent.' Luigi Campagna seemed less sure about the pipe being passed around by the men.

'You French know how to eat well.' The M'ikmaq watched the Huguenot with an expression that bordered on amusement. 'Long did we live and trade in peace with your people, but they are gone from us now.'

'What about these English who have taken their place, Waksitanou? Can you live in peace with them?'

'Trader Campagna, these English do not live to feast and be happy with one another. They have led our friends into captivity.'

'Are there none of the Acadians left in this land?'

A frown furrowed the features of the M'ikmaq. 'Only a small remnant of our friends still remain. A few of them have sworn to fight the English till the death. I fear much blood will flow unless the farms and homes they claimed so arduously from the sea are returned to them.'

'Yes, we heard of this Gilles Leblanc in Lüneburg.' Luigi Campagna shook his head sadly. 'Putting up resistance will do his people no good. The English will hang him high on a gibbet along with those who follow him.'

'The English are an uncivilized people.' Waksitanou thoughtfully savored a wild chanterelle until Marie thought him finished with speaking. 'Why did the French not send the Black Robes to the English instead of us?'

'Even Jesuits find it hard to teach the English anything, Waksitanou.' Luigi Campagna cautiously exhaled tobacco smoke through his nose. 'It has taken nearly two centuries just to teach them how to keep proper track of the days in the year.'[1]

'The English destroy everything before them like a plague of grasshoppers, Trader Campagna. They burn the forests and they slaughter the moose and caribou for

---

1. England adopted the Gregorian calendar in 1752 (170 years after it was proclaimed by the Pope).

nothing more than their hides. How can the M'ikmaq share this land with the English as we did with the Acadians? It is our hope that our friends will someday return to us.'

Luigi Campagna shook his head gravely. 'The English grow stronger day by day, my friend. For every Frenchman in this New World of yours there are forty English. The French are not likely to win this new war.'

'Then I fear for my people, Trader Campagna.' Waksitanou swayed his head from side to side as if already in mourning. 'We made a treaty with the English while the Acadians were still among us. In this shameful treaty we claimed that the land was ours to sell. Now God punishes our foolish pride. Our friends are driven from this land without our consent, and war follows as night follows day. Our peace treaty with the English means nothing.'

'I am only a simple trader, my good friend.' Lost for words, the Huguenot swept his arms about him. 'I am not wise enough to counsel you on such weighty matters.'

The M'ikmaq looked at the Huguenot a long moment as if he thought he was being too modest. Then he turned to Nicole. 'Fortunately, Trader Compagna, you bring us this wife of yours. She is a powerful medicine woman. Many winters ago, one such as her fostered friendship between my people and the First Strangers. With your leave, my friend, I would ask her counsel.'

Nicole did not wait for her master's leave. 'Sachem Waksitanou, my counsel is full of grief and pain.'

'My people are used to grief and pain, Medicine Woman.' The M'ikmaq shrugged his wide shoulders and raised a finger to a livid scar that ran along his jaw line from ear to ear. Marie found it hard to imagine how someone could receive such a wound and still live. 'It is only by accustoming ourselves to such things that my people endure.'

'Your people's pain and grief will be long and difficult, Waksitanou.' Marie thought the maid looked much more at home in Hugo's castoffs than she ever had in a gown. 'Your people will suffer greatly; they will be trodden under foot by these Last Strangers. Only a few will endure the winter of despair that is coming.'

'I see now that is how it must be, Medicine Woman. So let us live well while we may.' With a wave of his hand, Waksitanou swept such unpleasant prospects aside. He turned an inviting smile upon the young woman standing nearby as if he had been reserving her for that moment. 'This is my daughter, Mishikwit. She dreamed a few moons ago that you First Strangers would soon come back to us.'

The young woman made shy gestures linking Marie to the child sleeping in the specially shaped basket she wore on her back. Marie's affirmative nod signifying that she was pregnant occasioned quite a stir among the M'ikmaq women. They plainly doubted that such a fabulous and delicate creature could mother children.

Mishikwit carefully loosed a pouch from about her neck. It was strung with cheap and gaudy glass beads obtained from "the Indian trade," but the M'ikmaq maiden drew forth from it an exquisite stone that shone in the slanting sunlight like a violet star. With eyes downcast, she tendered the stone to Marie as a gift.

'Waksitanou, please tell your daughter for me that such a gift is too precious by far!'

The M'ikmaq shook his head. 'It is amethyst meant for the child you bear, Chosen One.'

'I can't even say your daughter's name properly! How I wish I could talk to her!' Marie lightly touched the hair of the sleeping child. 'She would have much to tell me about how to bear children in this land where the M'ikmaq dwell.'

'Mishikwit does speak a little French, O wife of my new friend. She is only silent because her mother has taught her she must not speak to strangers upon first meeting.'

'Bien, Waksitanou. Please tell your daughter for me that I hope we will meet again. I would like to be her friend some day.'

'Sadly, her husband comes for her.' Waksitanou gazed fondly upon his daughter and his infant grandson. 'He is sachem of a band who live far away on the shores of Glooscap's restless Sea.'

'I have heard of that sea from my son, Jean. He says that its tides are even mightier than those of my homeland.'

'As a young man, I often hunted and fished upon Glooscap's Sea.' The M'ikmaq's eyes glowed with the kindling of old memories. 'When the waters are rushing, no canoe dare pass across that mighty water. Our old men say Glooscap scooped it out in a fit of anger, but how can a mere man know why a great god does such a thing?'

Nicole rose up on her knees like a beast of prey about to pounce. 'Waksitanou, tell me: is not this island also a place of wonder?'

'A place of wonder, yes, Medicine Woman, but not so great as one shaped by a god. Mere men like us built the hidden wonder of this place.'

Luigi Campagna lowered his voice as though he suspected Jesuits of lurking among the surrounding oak trees. 'Waksitanou, will you help us discover the hidden wonder? We come seeking the Guardian of this Isle.'

The M'ikmaq waited to take his turn upon the pipe till the very last. 'The one you seek journeyed to our ancestors many winters ago, Trader Campagna. His son and the son of his son followed after him, but the promise that our people made to the First Strangers has always been kept.'

Looking askance at his own seamen, the Huguenot drew Waksitanou and his sons to the far end of the beach. The sailcloth tent stood pitched there like the cocoon of some great moth. Several of the young M'ikmaq women knelt or squatted before it as though transfixed with awe. Leaning on his carved staff, Waksitanou also examined it with interest. 'This reminds me of the pictures my ancestors drew of the wigwams of the darkskinned men who came with the Templars.'

It seemed to Marie that her husband's ears twitched at hearing this. 'What dark-skinned men?'

Once more Waksitanou took a long while to speak. 'Sarcenes, if I remember rightly, that is what the old men call them in their tales.'

'Saracens? Do you mean to say that the Templars brought Saracens here?'

The M'ikmaq looked at Luigi Campagna as though amazed he had to be told such things. 'Yes, Trader Campagna, men of great skill who knew how to shape stone for building and to dig great holes in the ground. They knew how to do many other things just as well. It was they who prepared the great cache to receive the Templar Treasure.'

The Huguenot could not curb his impatience to know more. 'Does this cache you speak of still lie undisturbed, Waksitanou?'

'Yes, Trader Campagna, the great cache still lies deep within the Place of Dreaming. No Black Robe has found it yet, though they suspect it is somewhere near.'

'They have been searching for it then?'

'Indeed, my friend. That is why my elder brother delivered this staff into my two hands before he went away.'

Luigi Campagna looked anxiously at the M'ikmaq's carved staff. 'God took your brother?'

'No, Trader Campagna, the Black Robes took Sayadana.' The M'ikmaq drew himself up proudly. 'It is my elder brother's birthright to welcome you to this isle, but he is no longer here to see it done.'

'We must accept what God sends, Sachem.' The Huguenot seemed at a loss how to commiserate with his new friend while seeking that which he came for.

Nicole felt no such inhibitions. 'Waksitanou, can you make for us the sign of the Chosen?'

'My own father inscribed it upon me and my brother.' The M'ikmaq exposed his great-bronzed chest. 'Do I speak the truth, Medicine Woman? Am I the true appointed guardian or no?'

Nicole turned burning eyes upon the white scar incised upon the breast of the M'ikmaq. 'Master, this is the Hohenstaufen lion, exact in every detail. Waksitanou is indeed the true guardian of the treasure we come seeking.'

The M'ikmaq carefully scrutinized the young maid as if he also needed to affirm something. Then he spoke to his sons in French. 'This second wife of Trader Campagna is a true Medicine Woman. Long ago when my father's father's father lay dying, he warned us about these terrible creatures. Though they be our friends, they are more witch than woman, so we must beware of them.'

The Huguenot seemed greatly disturbed by these words. 'I would not deceive you, Waksitanou. This Dread Maiden is not my wife, but she occupies a place of honor in my household.'

'It is only meet that such a sacred one not share your bed, Trader Campagna. Such a woman of blood is not meant for men of this world.' Turning to Marie, Waksitanou raised both arms and bent his head. His sons followed suit. 'As for this first wife of yours: welcome home, Bearer of the Chosen Seed.'

Marie had to resist a strong impulse to reach up and touch the M'ikmaq's face. 'How could you possibly know what I am?'

The Guardian of the Isle reached out to trace Marie's brow with a forefinger. 'Here plainly written for those who can see is the mark of the Sleeping King.'

'The Sleeping King? Then it is true that Templars once dwelt on this island?'

'The Templars only sojourned here as priestly guardians of your ancestors and their treasure. Only the Chosen themselves truly lived here.' Thumbs and one index finger folded, the M'ikmaq held up both hands before her. 'For as many generations as you see fingers, your ancestors and mine were kin-friends.'

'Waksitanou, tell me: why then did they leave this place?'

A deep sadness took hold of the M'ikmaq's features. 'Soon after the coming of the First Strangers to Port Royal, the Black Robes cast their long shadow over this land. Just as a lynx scents and stalks its prey, they began searching for our Secret Places and for the Chosen. My people held a council with the Templars deep within the Place of Dreaming. My father's father's father, he was there. His own father brought him, still an unnamed boy, to witness what would be done. It was the judgment of the Council that the First Strangers must return whence they came. So it was that this Staff was entrusted to my forefather's line for safekeeping against this day of your return.'

'Guardian, you must understand that those Chosen went back to an Old World which still was far from safe.' Nicole reached forward and took hold of the M'ikmaq's elbows. Marie saw him noticeably shrink back from her as she went on speaking. 'A new and much deadlier enemy — those Black Robes of whom you speak — cast their shadow over the land. My mistress is the last Bearer of the Chosen Seed left alive. If she fails in her task, no one will remain to fulfill the Promise.'

Again the M'ikmaq traced Marie's brow, and she felt a deep sadness well within him. 'Great danger follows in your footsteps, O Chosen One. Yet hope remains for your seed so long as you do not surrender to your fear.'

'Not even the Societé can defeat God's purpose.'
Luigi Campagna crossed his great arms upon his chest
with an air of serene confidence. 'The French are gone
from this land now, Waksitanou of the M'ikmaq, so we
are come here to be with you again in our time of
greatest need.'

'In the name of my forefathers, I welcome you, for I
know that a trader is not what you truly are, Templar.
You are wise to wear such a mask. The French be gone,
but the Black Robes still stalk this land.'

'Waksitanou, we know only too well that no place is
without danger for such as us.' An extreme urgency
had manifested itself in Nicole. 'You and your forefathers have been made to wait much too long for our
return; you have sacrificed much too much for our
sake. But at last we can relieve you of the burden we
cast upon you, for you have your own perilous fate to
live out. Yet I foresee that someday our debt to you will
be repaid.'

The M'ikmaq passed his long staff to Nicole.
'Behold, the covenant made by my people with yours is
fulfilled, but my people do not keep counting-books
like strangers from across the sea. There is nothing to
repay, Medicine Woman. My forefathers will rest easier
now; that is enough.'

Nicole ran her fingers along the carved ivory of the
staff. 'This is the fabled horn of a unicorn, is it not?'

'Call it what you will. Our old men say that Ice
People, they who hunt the great whales of the Frozen
Sea, guided the First Strangers here.' Waksitanou's eyes
glittered with the telling of the tale as he turned back to
Marie. 'It was they who fashioned this Guardian's staff
from the horn of the beast they call "narwhal".'

'Did my ancestors come with the First Strangers?'

'No, Chosen One, only a few scouts came with the
Ice People to spy out this land.' Waksitanou's eyes
looked afar. 'After more winters than a man can live,

the First Strangers came again in many sea-canoes as large as yours, except that their vessels had great paddles and many rowers as well as sails.'

'Your people welcomed such strangers to this land?'

'Not at first, O Bearer of the Chosen. The strangers took possession of this sacred island without our leave. Much blood would have been shed, but a great shaman of our people and a Medicine Woman such as this sister of yours came together. After three nights of striving with one another, they brought back a pipe of peace from which arose the smoke of understanding and brotherhood. So it was that my people agreed to share this island. Only then did those Templars — for that is what those First Strangers were — fetch their great treasure fleet and your ancestors from across the great sea.'

Trembling inside, Marie met the gaze of the M'ikmaq. 'Bien, Waksitanou. On behalf of all those who went before me, I thank you and your fathers for guarding this place so long and so well.'

Waksitanou acknowledged her gratitude with a slight inclination of his head. 'It is only a moment in the unfolding of the M'ikmaq, O Bearer of the Chosen.'

Nicole remained ever restless. 'Guardian, we will need your guidance to open the Great Cache.'

'Yes, Medicine Woman, but the time for such doing is not now.' At a sign from Waksitanou, all the M'ikmaq detached themselves from the knot of curious seamen and went out to their beached canoes. Again the M'ikmaq touched Marie's brow. 'I will come to you again and share with you all that we remember of your ancestors.'

Marie could find no words, but involuntarily her fingers returned Waksitanou's gesture of farewell. A spasm of pain flared between them. Through tears she saw the steadfast eyes of the M'ikmaq also glisten as if he knew of things too sad to speak of. Then he wheeled on a moccasined heel and was gone.

Silence and stillness fell on the beach till the silver canoes had vanished from the cove into the setting sun. Luigi Campagna began chafing his hands against the cooling air. 'And now, my people, I send you all to your beds, save for the sentries, of course. Tomorrow, we've much work to do.'

The first order of the new day was to build a dock capable of berthing *L'Espérance*. Two great drift-logs were towed into the cove and fastened to stout piles driven deep into the sand. Empty water-casks were lashed to the logs with hemp to buoy the dock. Sailors armed with broadaxes began squaring smaller drift-logs to supply decking. Luigi Campagna himself tried his hand at the strenuous work. His awkward strokes afforded his seamen much merriment; they quickly relieved him of the axe, saying they did not wish to have a one-legged captain.

A tiny spring cascaded from the cliff-face and formed a pool before emptying into the cove. While the children dragged brush and piled it for burning, the two women busied themselves washing clothes. They pummeled and soaped the foul accumulation of an ocean crossing upon the smooth black rocks. The cold water turned a sudsy brown as it rinsed away to the sea. The harsh lye soap reddened Marie's small hands and the heavy work taxed her slender arms, but she was filled with a contentment she had never known while praying.

As good as her word, Nicole refused to return to the brigantine. After regular work had finished for the day, she cajoled Hugo and several other sailors into beginning to lay out her new log cabin.

As for Luigi Campagna, he took his wife and went prospecting sites for their future home. It was pleasant to stroll under the bare oaks and feel life reawakening on the little island.

They soon came upon a pool of salt water, deep and clear, which gave no sign of harboring life. They were pondering the strangeness of the place when they were severely startled. Large birds nesting upon the oak trees rose in great clouds and swirled about them.

Husband and wife stood frozen in wonder till the birds resettled upon the branches. Luigi Campagna bagged a fat brace by simply tossing a few stones at them. 'These brainless creatures are what the English call passenger pigeons. We may have faith that the God who sends us such fine bounty will not permit us to come to harm.'

At last they reached the southern promontory and looked out over the Bay toward the islands guarding its entrance from the Atlantic. A thin wisp of smoke rising up from Lüneburg afforded Marie some sense of connection with the rest of the world. She knelt down alongside her husband to pray. *Dear God, grant that our existence go unnoticed by our enemies in this empty place. Give us peace to prosper and let our children grow to manhood on this island. Let this place by the sea always be their home.*

Praying was not something the young woman could endure for very long. She sprang up excitedly and went running to a little meadow that opened on the cliffs. A vast number of large squared stones lay piled about her in utter abandon. ' Monsieur, I think I have found the place for our stone house!'

'It's very exposed here, Madame.' Her husband knelt down to examine the ground. 'Every wind will catch us here.'

'Luigi Campagna, the good Lüneburgers will build us a stout house of these stones. A good stone house will not care how hard the wind blows. '

'Some large edifice has already stood here.' Luigi Campagna held up a dressed stone. 'See, there are more foundations over there. And what huge stones they are! Marie, here is the spot where your ancestors must have sojourned a long time ago.'

Marie looked round at the spreading oaks and the blue sea. *Is such a thing possible? If so, were they happy here? Did the exiles pine for their homeland across the ocean? What were these people like?*

Marie felt the presence of her dream visitor, but she would not let him intrude upon her at such a propitious moment. She put away her ring and took hold of her husband's arm. 'Then, their spirits will welcome our return, Luigi Campagna. From here your brass telescope can sweep the entire bay. Not even a seagull may light upon these waters unless it be seen from up here.'

'A compelling consideration, Madame, I must admit. We shall build a little hearth inside your bedroom to keep you warm when the wind blows off the sea.'

'This land is much colder than France.' Marie felt bound and determined to get things off to a better start this time. 'A hearth is not enough to keep a proper Frenchwoman warm. I've no mind to sleep alone, my husband.'

Ever cautious, the Huguenot looked round at her. Then he broke into the laugh of a much younger man. It was the first unguarded laughter Marie had ever heard from him. It reverberated under the oak trees and shook the dry acorns. For the first time he enfolded her in his arms, as a husband should, and for the first time he kissed her.

Chapter XIII

KIN-FRIENDS

Sanctuary Island, April 1756

Isaac Ben Yussuf found the island cove buzzing with activity when he came to pay a surprise visit. An official-looking scroll tucked under his arm, he paused for a moment to take it all in. Portly hogsheads of flour, molasses and rum paraded in columns along the beach. Under old sails sheltered kegs of gunpowder, bolts of trade cotton, bales of twist tobacco, crates of axe-heads, several casks of brandy and, last but not least, a half-pipe of port. In the thick of it all, the good physician came upon Madame Campagna and her maid busily delving into a profusion of opened trunks and upended barrels.

'Simply splendid, my dear Captain!' Isaac Ben Yussuf stooped to kiss Marie's hand from which dangled a pair of beribboned wedding slippers. 'Simply splendid! My cup runneth over! Your advent in this wilderness is truly God's answer to an old man's prayers!'

'Herr Doctor, to what do we owe this pleasant surprise?' The Huguenot wore his wire-rimmed spectacles, having just left off making inventory of his cargo to welcome his new business associate.

'This!' The Jew unscrolled his parchment and cleared his throat. 'From Whitehall to all His Britannic Majesty's dominions, under seal broken just yesterday, that being the date of official royal proclamation in London. Major Sutherland let me borrow his copy for your edification.'

'What is it, Herr Doctor?' Marie still had not lost any of her girlish liking for surprises.

'Madame, this is a Declaration of War against His Most Christian Majesty, Louis Quinze, Empress Maria Theresa of Austria, Czarina Elizabeth of all the Russias — not to mention the King of Sweden and the Elector of Saxony.'

Marie found the good physician's reading of the Declaration rather boring despite his stentorian delivery. Countries were always fighting with one another, but she could see from the deliberate way her husband kept straightening his glasses that he was somewhat staggered by the news. 'A fair set of enemies King George has taken upon himself, Herr Doctor. Doesn't His Majesty feel the need for some allies?'

'He's picked some rather piddling ones, if I may say so.' Ben Yussuf sniffed dismissively. 'The upstart Frederick of Prussia and a pack of petty German states including, of course, his own beloved Electorate of Hanover. That rascal Pitt has promised His Majesty an empire on which the sun never sets. Did you ever hear of such colossal gall, Capitaine Campagna?'

'Herr Doctor, what difference can all this cockfighting possibly make to us?' The Huguenot delivered himself of a rather unconvincing Gallic shrug. 'It's not as if the French and English don't tear at each other's throat already.'

'What we have seen to date are mere opening skirmishes, M. le Capitaine.' The physician slipped into the role of Old Testament prophet as readily as he had that of town crier. 'Now the dogs of war shall be unleashed upon us with a vengeance. Don't delude yourself, my friend. The coming struggle will be a long and bitter one. All our lives and fortunes hang in the balance.'

Marie had already learned there was nothing a good Huguenot liked better than a rousing political debate. 'Say what you like about William Pitt, my friend, but he's a formidable war minister. He knows how to pick able generals and admirals. I am a Frenchman, so I know only too well that the French regime is rotten to the core. And besides, the English are spoiling for this fight. Already, they've expelled the Acadians from this land, and I hear they've already taken Fort Beauséjour. Mark my words: the English are bound to win this war in the end.'

'You forget the Indians, M. le Capitaine. The French have won over most of the tribes to their side of the balance, including the M'ikmaq and the Maliseet. As we speak, their priests will be fanning out to every tribe, inciting them to war against us. Lüneburg even Halifax, may be attacked by hordes of savages.'

'Is it fear of Indians that brings you here this fine afternoon, my friend?' Luigi Campagna cast a critical eye upon the leaky pinnace bumping his new dock. Tattered cap in hand, its Lüneburg skipper waited on the strand.

'My friend, you might at least thank me for my trouble! I risked drowning in yon peasant's wretched boat to bring you timely warning!'

'Something tells me you have more on your mind this morning than bringing us a warning, Herr Doctor.'

'Actually, there is another matter I do wish to discuss with you, M. le Capitaine.' As though a switch had been thrown, Isaac Ben Yussuf was suddenly all business. 'Now that war has been declared, I wish to point out to you that your fine brigantine presents us both with a splendid opportunity.'

'Herr Doctor, say no more if you're about to suggest I make *L'Espérance* a privateer. I came here to make my living as a peaceful trader; a peaceful trader I shall die.'

'I am as much a man of peace as you are, M. le Capitaine. These endless Gentile feuds mean no more to a son of Israel than a high-risk investment. However, we do have these poor Germans of ours to consider. There's no way they can prosper let alone survive while farming these cold rocky shores. They must learn to take their living from the sea or die.'

'What in the world has this to do with me, Herr Doctor?' The Huguenot merchant disliked being suspected of harboring altruistic impulses. 'Already your peasants feast on my victuals in exchange for airy promises.'

'They signed a written contract, M. le Capitaine, witnessed by mine own hand and that of Major Sutherland. You may rest assured that the Lüneburgers will fulfill their end of the bargain.' Ben Yussuf drew himself up as though his personal honor had been impugned. 'May I remind you, sir, that I am not the *seigneur* of these Teutonic *habitants* — only their humble physician. I come here today not to seduce you into an act of charity but to apprise you of a lucrative business opportunity.'

'Herr doctor, you missed your true calling. You should have been a solicitor.'

'Capitaine Campagna, this war will increase tenfold the flow of commerce along these shores. Good ships and steady crews will be sorely needed. We have only to apprentice these Lüneburgers as shipwrights and sailors, employ them to build a mercantile empire and thus turn a fortune out of doing good for our fellow man.'

'You expect a broker's share of the profits from this charitable enterprise, of course.'

'I am no Utopian, M. le Capitaine.' The physician emphatically tugged his waistcoat into place. 'I undertake to deliver the Lüneburgers into your hands in return for a third partnership in our joint enterprise.'

'A third partnership! Herr doctor, I confess I did not fully share my wife's appreciation till now as to how much Calvinists and Jews have in common.'

Ben Yussuf chose to take that as a compliment. 'Then you will consider my proposition, M. le Capitaine?'

The Huguenot resolutely folded his arms. 'No, Herr Doctor, one can't make mariners out of swineherds!'

'Capitaine Campagna, the reference is unkind! Most of these Lüneburgers have neither herded swine nor tasted pork in their entire lives!'

The Huguenot was not about to be stampeded. 'Forgive my indelicate choice of metaphors, Herr Doctor, but I'm sure you take my point.'

'Not at all, my dear Captain! I myself belong to a tribe of pastoral desert-dwellers who were forced by dire circumstances to become urbane moneylenders. I assure you these kraut-eaters are just as determined to survive as any son of Judah!'

'But they're not nearly so adaptable as sons of Judah, Herr Doctor. I remember you saying so yourself. Stubbornness is nothing but a mess of potage if it isn't leavened with adaptability. I much doubt we can persuade these dyed-in-the-wool Lutherans to take to the sea.'

'Look at him, my dear Campagnas!' Ben Yussuf swung round and pointed dramatically at his unprepossessing boatman. 'Groping blindly, but nonetheless determined to find his way! M. le Capitaine, this man will survive with or without us. Look at his pathetic travesty of a vessel; he doesn't know it yet, but I promise you his sons will someday build and sail famous ships. The question is whether you and I have the vision to profit by guiding his struggle to survive.'

'Hmmm, well, when you put it like that, Herr Doctor, I begin to see things in a somewhat different light.'

The Huguenot abruptly took his friend's arm in his as though he had been expecting this outcome to their conversation all along.

Isaac Ben Yussuf dismissed his boatman with a half shilling for his trouble. After supping on roasted passenger pigeons, the two entrepreneurs quaffed the last of the Moselle and plotted how best to lure the poor Lüneburgers into their web. 'Madame Campagna, did I ever tell you that you're married to a brilliant man!'

'Yes, Herr Doctor, several times!'

'Well, it bears repeating, Madame. Your husband's a man of parts who sees clearly the future of this barbaric land. Someday, an entire fleet shall proudly fly the Campagna pennant from their masthead. Their home port of Lüneburg shall be known throughout the Seven Seas.'

'Lüneburg, is it?' Luigi Campagna winked surreptitiously at his wife. 'I'm surprised you don't wish to see a Star of David flying from their mastheads.'

'Captain, a Jewish symbol associated with our fleet is the last thing we need in this bigoted world of ours. A Huguenot association is bad enough. As for their home port, our Lüneburgers will determine the outcome, whatever we emblazon upon our ships' backsides. Mark my words, the day will come when we'll want a better home port for our great fleet than this little cove.'

'Herr Doctor, you are descended from a race of prophets, but I lack your foresight of things to come — not to mention your ambition to make them happen.' The Huguenot put his arm around his wife's waist as though she were a delicate piece of china. 'God willing, there'll be no more long sea voyages for me! I'm willing to make a small beginning, but I'm content to let our sons fulfill your vision. You see before you a man who stands ready to make his final peace with his Maker. Till that day is upon me, let me stick close to hearth and home.'

'Well spoken, M. le Capitaine!' Isaac Ben Yussuf raised his glass of port. 'Madame Campagna, I drink to your health! May your next child prove to be a son as brilliant as his father.'

Marie almost blurted out that her child was going to be a little girl. She blushed to the roots of her dark hair. 'Thank you, Herr Doctor. I confess that the prospect of giving birth in this wild land fills me with some trepidation.'

'How thoughtless of me not to have volunteered my services before! Madame, I don't anticipate any difficulties since you've already proven your mettle as a mother. Still, a wise physician assumes nothing where a female of the species is concerned. With your husband's leave, I shall conduct a thorough examination before returning to Lüneburg.'

Luigi Campagna rushed quickly into the breach. 'Your concern is much appreciated, Herr Doctor. However, you should know that we come prepared for such exigencies. Madame's maid-servant is a skilled mid-wife.'

'Capitaine Campagna, the delivery of children into the world is no longer the province of village wise-women!' Marie could see that Ben Yussuf was determined to be patient in explaining such matters to her husband. 'You mustn't be old-fashioned, my friend. Far better to place your precious consort in these trained hands of science than those of a superstitious mid-wife.'

'You're situated too far away from us, my friend! I fear we must manage as best we can without you.'

'Nonsense, M. le Capitaine! You have only to fire your ship's gun, and I'll straight across the bay to your good Frau as fast as yon Lüneburger can sail me.'

Luigi Campagna failed to dissuade his friend from conducting an obstetrical examination in the first light of dawn. The physician also insisted that Nicole be present. He expressed the hope she might learn something about assisting him in the scientific birthing of babies. The only one he did not consult on the matter was Marie herself.

'My dear lady, you are the picture of health!' Ben Yussuf withdrew his head from the modesty tent erected over Marie's abdomen. 'A trifle inclined to the phlegmatic humor, which is good, but I'd not believe you've thrice given birth before, were it not for the living proof.'

'Madame is a natural mother, Herr Doctor.' After so much prodding and poking, Nicole quickly intervened to cover off Marie's confusion. 'Her babies come of themselves.'

The physician carefully adjusted his pince-nez. 'Fraulein, there is no such thing as a 'natural mother' amongst our species. Such innocence was lost by Eve in the Garden of Eden. You are all condemned to bear your offspring in pain and suffering. Read the Book of Genesis if you require documentation. All of you need science to offset the dire curse which Lucifer laid upon your sex.'

'So good of you to explain these scientific matters, Herr Doctor!' The maid affected a winsomely grateful air. 'Someone should have set us silly women straight before. I see now that neither my mistress nor myself have taken this birthing of babies seriously enough.'

'Ah, how I wish I had time to devote myself to obstetrics, dear Fraulein, but yon Germans keep me busy lancing boils and pulling teeth.' Ben Yussuf turned back owlishly to Marie and fixed his eyepiece on her amulet. 'That poor peasant's bauble, Madame: why do you insist on wearing it on the same chain as that magnificent signet ring?'

'So I won't forget to find an honorable way of returning it. Indeed, Herr Doctor, I call upon you to advise me: perhaps a baptismal gift to that poor woman's child would serve the trick?'

'A kind and gracious thought, Madame. Unfortunately, it comes too late. Yesterday the little girl entered the world stillborn.'

'Oh, that poor woman! Luigi Campagna, I must go to her at once!'

'Madame, rest easy! Merciful God took both mother and child. They are both to be buried tomorrow in a common grave.'

'That can't be!' Marie's lip began to quiver. 'Was not the biscuit sufficient?'

'To quote a fellow Jew, Madame: "One does not live by bread alone." Perhaps if there had been a bit of cabbage she and her child might have survived.'

'Or if I had found some means of aiding her, Herr Doctor!'

'Madame, it is irrational to blame yourself! Think you I should beat myself about the head and shoulders each time one of my patients dies?'

'Forgive my outburst, Herr Doctor. I know you did everything in your power to save her.' Marie's tears had begun to freely flow as she detached the ring from the necklace. 'At least now I may return this amulet to the woman's little girl. Will you do that much for me?'

The Jew accepted the silver necklace and undertook to see it buried with the child. 'Dear lady, I know how you feel. I myself sometimes wonder whether I do more harm than good.'

Still pensive, Isaac Ben Yussuf boarded *L'Espérance* with Jacques Sabot and the crew who were off to fetch the first contingent of Lüneburgers to the island. The brigantine's sails were still silhouetted on the horizon when a lone canoe paddled into the cove.

Taking Marie by the hand, Luigi Campagna went down quickly to meet the M'ikmaq as they beached their canoe. It somewhat pained Marie how little time her husband allowed for greeting their new friends. 'Waksitanou, I have been thinking since you were last here. I fear much harm may come of what we have a mind to do this day. Perhaps the Treasure should remain unopened till the Black Robes have all been driven from this land.'

'Our fate is sealed by the promise our ancestors made one another, Templar.' Waksitanou's gray eyes shifted to the rudely crafted door of Nicole's new cabin. 'There is one among us who will not set either of us free from that sworn promise till it be fulfilled.'

'Then should we not at least wait for the morrow? It is already well past noon.'

'Where we are going, my friend, it makes no difference whether it be night or day.'

Nicole chose that moment to emerge from her cabin. Marie stifled a little gasp at seeing the maid had decked herself out in a tunic almost identical to that worn by Nasqualik. At the sight of the Dread Maiden holding his ivory staff, the light fled from Waksitanou's gray eyes. 'We are come here to do your bidding, O Medicine Woman of the Sleeping King.'

'I have waited long for this day as I'm sure you have, O Guardian.' Coming forward, Nicole handed Waksitanou back his staff. 'How is it that only one of your sons accompanies you?'

'As is his right, my first-born son wishes no part of covenanting with strangers from across the sea.' Waksitanou turned to the Huguenot and placed his hands on both his shoulders. 'Templar, I myself will rest easier when our covenant is fulfilled and we can go our separate ways.'

'Then let us proceed, Sachem. Nicole is right. We owe it to you to remove this burden from your shoulders as quickly as possible.' Now that the long anticipated moment had finally overtaken him, Luigi Campagna seemed to gravely resign himself to what lay in store.

Nasqualik and her younger son pulled the magnificent jacket over Waksitanou's head and draped it carefully upon the sand. Clad only in leggings and breechclout and holding his ivory staff in the crook of his arm, the M'ikmaq framed Marie's face in both his hands. 'Long have my people waited for your coming, O Bearer of the Chosen. Now the brother of Sayadana, True Guardian, will guide you into the Place of Dreaming.'

the kin-friends arrive
on Sanctuary Island

Chapter XIV

PLACE OF DREAMING

Sanctuary Island, April 1756

The M'ikmaq unwound a protective boot of leather from the staff, holding up for all to see the heraldic lion of the Hohenstaufen deeply etched in the ivory footprint. Slender torso gleaming like burnished copper; he transformed the leather strap into a headband, the hardened boot projecting from his forehead like a miner's lantern. Then slinging the staff across his back, he immersed himself to the waist in the ice-cold water and stood gazing upward at the high bluff.

Nasqualik signaled the other members of the party to remain upon the beach. She and her youngest son waded past Waksitanou till they stood with their bodies braced against the cliff-face. Coming behind them, the M'ikmaq placed a hand on each of their heads and vaulted lightly to their shoulders. Balancing precariously, he stretched out against the sheer wall of rock as though about to scale it. Then he freed the ivory staff and thrust it upward at an angle into the solid rock till it almost disappeared. Nodding and grunting at those who bore him, he grasped the vertical rock face with both hands and fitted the boot projecting from his headband over the protruding butt of the staff. Watching his muscles strain,

Marie fancied that he was struggling in some strange way to maneuver the staff into place as one might fit a key into a lock.

A resonating click followed by the sound of stone grinding against stone echoed across the cove. After a moment of sustained effort, Waksitanou extracted the staff from the shaft with his teeth until he could grasp and pull it free. Then he leapt down and drew Nasqualik and his son back from the rock face. Almost immediately, long jets of water began spewing forth from several crevices.

Waksitanou slid into his jacket without a word and started gliding up the path. Only when he reached the first oak trees did he turn round and address the mystified people still waiting on the beach. 'The way is now open, First Strangers! Come, the Place of Dreaming awaits us.'

Feeling heavy with child for the first time, Marie moaned her gratitude when Waksitanou finally halted their short trek. The party rested for a time near the salt pond where she and her husband had lingered one fine evening. Luigi Campagna expressed amazement at discovering the deep depression drained of all its water. Following the other members of the party, he helped his wife descend a stepped formation into the still damp rock-basin.

Marie sat down to rest before looking round with a growing sense of fearful wonder. She found herself perched upon a raised bench ringing the center of the natural amphitheatre. Little Louis edged close to her in search of maternal comfort. His older brothers joined their father in examining the slimy monolith standing upright inside the circle of dressed stone.

Nicole carried her sleeping child straddled upon her hip. 'This has been a place of power for a long time.'

Waksitanou uttered a grunt of affirmation. 'Our old men tell the tale of how the Deer People fashioned the

Circle of Meeting around this great stone long before the coming of the M'ikmaq.'

The prosaic Huguenot took out his sheath knife and began scraping its edge along the black and pitted surface of the rock. 'I have never before seen a meteorite as large as this.'

'There are no other stones in this land like it, Templar.' Waksitanou put a restraining hand on the Huguenot's shoulder. 'The sacred talisman beneath your feet is the gift Glooscap sent down from the sky when he first came to this land. He struck the water with it and caused this whole island to rise up from the sea.'

Nicole turned to face the M'ikmaq. Despite her womanly burden, she looked perfectly at home in her costume. Marie wished that she had chosen to wear something as suitable for hiking and climbing over this rugged island. 'The origin of this stone does not concern us, O Guardian.'

Waksitanou did not seem at all surprised to hear these brusque words from the Dread Maiden. He merely nodded his head and turned to brace his shoulder against the rock that towered pulpit-like above the circular bench. His son joined him in straining against the rock, both their slim sinewy bodies arching like strung bows.

'Can I help?' Philippe Campagna rose up expectantly, but the pulpit-stone had already begun sliding back from the circle with a screeching sound. It moved as though mounted on wheels, exposing a shaft in the rock floor. Their guide inserted the carved end of the staff, driving it down as before until no more than a handhold of ivory shaft protruded. Prostrating himself on the slick surface, Waksitanou took hold of crevices cut in the rock and again applied his odd headband to the butt of the staff.

Marie was reminded of someone trying to open a lock in the dark. The M'ikmaq apparently required direct contact with his forehead to guide the key into its proper place. Ever so slowly he drove the ivory staff home until a resonating click sounded as before.

Rushing water echoed beneath them. Waksitanou rose to a crouch, and once more retrieved the staff with his teeth before rising to his feet. 'Now the sea shall lower us down into the Place of Dreaming. All who would go there must join with me inside the circle of stone.'

Fervently wishing she had remained behind with Nasqualik on the beach, Marie rose to her feet and stepped into the circle forming round the M'ikmaq. Little Louis clung to her hand, frightened by the roar resounding from deep within the Earth. The noise crescendoed till she could no longer hear Philippe and Jean excitedly asking questions of their father. She felt rather than heard rock grinding ponderously against rock beneath them. She watched aghast as the stone bench began to rise up around them. It took several moments before her petrified mind realized that she was the victim of an illusion. It was the great stone they stood upon that was sinking straight down into the bowels of the Earth.

Except for Guillaume whimpering, the gathering on the descending monolith kept silent. They stood facing inward toward Waksitanou, as though afraid of what might be sliding past them in the deepening gloom. The sensation of being transported by such vast alien power utterly terrified Marie. She suffered a seizure of vertigo and clutched frantically at the strong arm of her husband. Nauseous, she held on tightly to him while a wave of images swept over her. *You will never build us a stone house on this bewitched island. How could I have ever been so foolish as to believe that the outside world would leave us in peace?*

The roar faded. Marie became sufficiently accustomed to the dim light to make out the pale faces of her companions. The group had clustered tightly around the Guardian, who had taken Nicole's crying child in his arms. Inexplicably, the protective tenderness of the M'ikmaq brought tears to Marie's eyes. She staggered and would have fallen if not for the steadying grip of her husband and youngest stepson. The broken images flashed across her mind so swiftly that she was left with little more than a profound sense of foreboding as she stared into Waksitanou's gray eyes. 'It is accomplished, O Bearer of the Chosen. We stand deep inside the Place of Dreaming.'

Jean peered into the gloom and sniffed the faint breeze wafting through the cavern. 'I can smell the sea!'

'This place is so arranged that both the stone and the air are moved about by harnessing the hydraulic power of the tide.' Nicole recited these words as if reading them from a book. Indeed, the Dread Maiden seemed frozen in a kind of trance as though totally absorbed with bringing to mind what she already knew of this place.

Waksitanou gently rocked the sleeping child until the members of the party dared of their own accord to unlink their hands and face outward. Philippe was the first to venture beyond the circle, much to his cautious father's chagrin. 'Stay with us, my son! Let the Guardian show us the way.'

Marie looked straight up and saw a small circular patch of dark sky and stars shining high above. How she regretted leaving that last vestige of her world behind! Nicole showed not the slightest sign of sharing her trepidation. But then, the Dread Maiden was never afraid of anything. 'Which way, Guardian?'

'That depends where in the Place of Dreaming you want to go, Medicine Woman.' The M'ikmaq's deep voice echoed off the bare stone walls.

'Please take us first to the Archives. I should know the way, but this strange light confuses me.'

201

'Indeed, these walls themselves give off light!' The Huguenot looked around in astonishment. 'Does some luminous lichen coat them?'

'That which shines is the wall itself, Templar. Our old men tell the tale that this shining rock was spewed up from the bowels of the earth when the great stone struck it. The Saracens slaves who burrowed here for your people eventually died from bathing in this light.'

Marie cried out at hearing this and clutched little Louis tightly to her bosom as if to shield him. Nicole hushed her. 'Do not worry, Madame: according to the chronicle of this place, one must spend many months down here for the poison to take effect.'

'Where do all these other passages lead?' Philippe indicated wrought iron grates guarding archways branching off to both left and right from the main corridor.

'Some lead to the Saracen lodges, son of my kin-friend. It is now a place of tombs where only their spirits dwell.' The M'ikmaq gave the gates a shake to indicate that they were safely locked. 'Still others lead to the main storage magazines.'

Philippe joined him in rattling one of the locked grates. 'Yes, but where do these two other barred passages lead?'

'To the left lies the vault of silver and to the right lies the vault of Templar gold.'

'I thought so! I'd much rather go there than to some dusty old library.' Philippe made as if to turn aside. 'Can you open these gates with your staff, Sachem?'

'No, son of my kin-friend. My people would have nothing to do with keys to the treasure vaults.'

'Come, Philippe.' Nicole took the unwilling boy by the hand and hurried onward. ''Tis true there are many tons of precious metal hoarded here, but the Archive is the true treasure of this place.'

Philippe allowed himself to be half-dragged along. 'I still do not understand, Sachem. Why did your people refuse to accept the keys to the treasure vaults?'

Waksitanou fell into step beside the boy. 'Son of my kin-friend, look not so disappointed. The old tales tell that the metal so precious to the First Strangers is dull stuff to look upon.'

'But why did your people refuse to ward those particular keys?'

'Lusting after silver and gold is the bane of your people, son of my kin-friend. We were afraid that the curse might spread to us.'

'I think you miss the mark, Waksitanou. Our lust for riches is what makes us go seeking. My people would be as nothing without such hunger.'

Waksitanou sent the boy a beatific smile. 'You stand thoughts on their heads, son of my kin-friend. Awareness that you have become shadows of what you were meant to be, that is what makes you go seeking. Some day, God willing, you will discover that the luster of silver and gold is a poor substitute for the shining spirit that lies buried within all living things.'

Abruptly, the narrow passageway opened onto a circular gallery overlooking a high-domed cavern. Luigi Campagna took a step backward at sight of it. 'Praise be given the Lord of Hosts! It would take a brace of seraphim a thousand years to carve all this out of living rock!'

'After the star fell, the great god Glooscap forged this island around the smoldering star-stone with fire and lightning.' The M'ikmaq liked nothing so much as to tell his mythical tales. 'With sea and tide he scoured it clean. And all this island he gave into the keeping of the Deer People, who passed the mystery on to us when their time here was done. We promised them we would wait here beside the Great Water till the bearded ones should come to us. And so we waited many winters till they finally came. And when we recognized them for what they were, we shared with them this sacred Place of Dreaming. So it was that the Saracen slaves came here and built for the Templars a secret hiding place for their greatest treasures.'

As if grown weary of the M'ikmaq's tales, the Dread Maiden wandered on ahead. 'As I recall, this next cavern is the antechamber to the Central Archive. But as you can see, it is much more than that. Come, Madame, and look at these walls!'

Marie gasped in amazement, for the circular wall of the great cavern was covered with huge paintings.

'These look as fresh as the day they were painted!' Nicole examined a flatly styled mosaic of an emaciated Hermit wandering wild-eyed in the desert. 'Madame, the Saracen slaves carved out these galleries to preserve these treasures of the Ancient World until the seed of your body shall come for them.'

Luigi Campagna spoke up before his wife could ask about this coming of the Chosen One. 'Saracens wouldn't preserve this kind of pagan art, Nicole. Like good Calvinists, they consider such black magic the work of the Devil.'

'Nay, Master! Enlightened Moslems considered the destruction of pagan art a sacrilege, just as there were many Christians who tried to preserve it. At the risk of their lives, they helped preserve these relics and spirit them here to sanctuary.'

The Huguenot skeptically eyed the Coptic Hermit staring back at him out of the painted desert. 'Well, Nicole, I grant you someone must have thought all this worth preserving.'

The M'ikmaq smiled at the simple Huguenot's perplexity. 'They who brought all this to pass await us at the other end of this cavern.'

The Dread Maiden showed reluctance to quit the chamber of wonders, but the Guardian of the Isle led off without a single backward glance. Nor did he halt till his little group stood clustered before great bronze doors, each bearing a magnificently carved relief of a Hohenstaufen lion. Yet it was the huge gilt-framed painting crowning the archway that claimed everyone's attention.

Nicole let out a gasp of recognition and went down on her knees. 'Mistress, these are your ancestors! Yolande the Prophetess and her husband Frederick!'

The entire party joined in staring up at the huge painting. Stiff with damask and brocade, heavily laden with precious stones, the Emperor sat staring out of the painting in tawny-bearded splendor. The dark-haired girl in the painting stood transfixed in the act of placing a diadem upon her husband's head. Marie's hand flew to her ring at sight of this pair. *So you are the ones who brought us here. Dead, you still reach out across five centuries and twist our lives.*

At last we meet face to face, Marie of Hohenstaufen. Does your ancestor not look every inch a Holy Roman Emperor?

Thank God you are only a painting, Sire!

Be not too sure of that, Princess mine! You are no longer dreaming in your sleep, are you? Look carefully! Is not your own resemblance to Yolande striking?

It is dark in this place, Sire. Dark enough to cloak an overbold impostor!

Impostor? How sad that you of all people should call us that!

Marie couldn't take her eyes off the young woman in the painting. It was indeed something like looking into a mirror. *Sire, why is Yolande pictured as bestowing that crown upon you?*

Because she was the legitimate Christian heiress to the lost kingdom of Jerusalem. Yet her title remained virtually empty so long as Jerusalem was held by the Sultan of Egypt. Her father went to war with us over what this painting signifies.

What did Yolande herself think of all this.

Oh she bridled at first, but we soon convinced her that crowning the husband who restored her kingdom and made her an Empress was not too much to ask.

Frankly, Sire, it shames me to think of the awful things you did to Yolande! According to the Jesuit books I read, you seduced her maid-in-waiting on your wedding day.

It seemed to Marie that the Emperor in the painting bowed his head. *It grieves us that the Jesuits told you that story, Princess Mine. You must understand what it is to be a hot impetuous youth as full of ourself as any Hohenstaufen ever was. Your ancestress forgave us quick enough when she discovered we had gotten her with child.*

And you abandoned her even so! You left her, still a girl of sixteen, to die alone in childbirth!

That is a vicious calumny served up by our enemies, though we admit it served our purposes well to have the world think so. The news of her death long kept her safe. Thanks to being thought already dead, Yolande survived not only us but her son Conrad and grandson Conradin as well. How else do you think the Chosen Seed have survived this long? If she had not been there to forge the Dread Maidens and seal our bond with the Templars, you would never have been given this chance to live.

Would it were so, Sire! Would it were so! Your arrogance and defiance of your world sealed the fate of all who came after you!

Do you think we do not regret our impetuous nature, Princess Mine? Thinking back on it now, it does seem a bit overbold having ourself crowned King of Jerusalem on the very site of Solomon's Temple, but it seemed such a fitting touch at the time. The Ayyubid sultan, worthy successor of the great Saladin, had just become our friend and ally. Like a brother, he gave freely into our hands the city of Jerusalem and the towns of Bethlehem and Nazareth. In return, we gave him our solemn promise that Moslems might worship freely at the Mosque of Omar and Jews might wail at their wretched Wall.

What arrogance, Sire! You permitted infidels to worship in the Christian Holy Places? No wonder the Pope excommunicated you!

You disappoint us, Princess Mine. We expect more from one with Hohenstaufen blood flowing in her veins. Those who follow after us would do well to heed our example. Who else has ever restored peace to the Holy Land and extended freedom of worship and tolerance to all?

Marie could not forbear laughing. *But where did it get you in the end, Sire?*

Certainly that pompous ass Gregory did not share your amusement, Princess Mine! Yet it seemed to Marie that the stern face in the portrait deigned to smile. *Never mind that we had recovered the holy places according to our Crusader's oath without a single drop of Christian blood being shed. His Holiness summarily excommunicated us a second time — Holy Roman Emperor and King thrice over that we were — because we made peace with the infidels instead of slaughtering them.*

At that moment, Nicole turned Marie to face yet another huge painting. A mounted paladin armed with a lance was battling a dragon so black that its features were barely visible save for its fiery nostrils. 'Yet another likeness of your forefather, Madame. He spent his life battling the dragons of darkness.'

'Did not the Pope excommunicate him for his pains?'

'Three times, Madame, and he died excommunicate. All such works as this are supposed to have been destroyed. Imagine, Madame, what the Black Pope would do if he were here to see this!'

Marie shivered at the mere thought of the General whom all Jesuits obeyed. She turned to the little boy standing transfixed in front of the magnificent tableau. 'What do you think of this, Louis?'

'Some day, I shall paint like this, Madame!' Holding the boy's trembling hand, Marie tried to gaze within the shining knight who sat so confidently astride his magnificent white charger. A colossal upheaval began inside her breast as her fingers flew again to the cameo ring she wore around her neck. *I was taught to think of you not as God's knight but as the vanquished dragon with Saint Michael's foot resting upon your head. Yet I pitied you, even though Father Jerome called you the Church's greatest enemy, the Antichrist. Sire, somehow I have always known you were my ancestor.*

Indeed, Princess Mine, you have always known.

The voice receded as Waksitanou handed the staff to his son. The youth looked from it to his father in surprise before inserting it into the medallion sealing the entrance. Again Marie heard the metallic click of a lock mechanism. The great bronze doors swung inward with a gong-like roar.

Unadorned, the Archive was simply a vast catacomb of dusty stelae, eroding tablets, papyrus scrolls, vellum manuscripts and parchment codices. Once more Luigi Campagna went down on his knees. 'Praise the Lord! It would take a full-rigged ship to carry all this across the sea!'

'A fleet of ships, Master.' The Dread Maiden took up again her task of reciting. 'In 1307, Anno Domini, the last Templar fleet left La Rochelle forever and carried here this entire treasure trove.'

But Waksitanou would not keep silent with his part of the tale. 'Already, newborn babes had aged and died since the First Strangers came. The first Saracen slaves had all joined their ancestors, but still their sons and grandsons labored on to build this Great Cache. Some of my people labored alongside them, for we understood what was coming would change our way of life forever.'

The M'ikmaq permitted Nicole to once more take up the story. 'Frederick and Yolande were long dead, their dominions shattered and all traces of them erased from Europe by the Church. Since the Christians would not heed the Emperor's way, the Holy Land had once again been lost to the Saracens, but the Templars had prospered well enough. Their trading fleets dominated the Mediterranean Sea, and fabulous had grown their wealth of gold and silver and precious jewels. For half a century, they kept safe the forbidden treasure entrusted to them by the sultan and emperor. They also sought out and gathered new riches from many other hiding places. Most carefully of all, the Templars joined with Yolande's Dread Maidens in safeguarding the seed of her union with Frederick.'

'Father, it's just a collection of musty old scrolls!' Philippe lowered himself from the lip of a giant urn. He was becoming more and more impatient with the fuss the adults were making. 'Let's go find the real treasure!'

'Young master, you see before you the greatest treasure trove ever!' Nicole seemed not to take into account that she was addressing a child. 'The Great Libraries of Alexandria were once home to many of these manuscripts.'

Marie had been taught otherwise. 'That cannot be, Nicole. The Great Libraries were utterly destroyed by the fanatics and barbarians who swept over the land.'

'The Libraries, yes, Madame. But their greatest treasures were saved from the flames.'

'Let's go find the gold and silver, Papa! A proper treasure should also have emeralds and rubies!'

It was the M'ikmaq who took the time to explain things to the boy. 'Son of my kin-friend, you know well that my own people have now entered upon the darkest time they have ever faced. Here lies much of what was lost when the dark times swept over your people.'

Marie was glad that Philippe chose to ask the obvious question. 'If that is true, why not give all this back to the world that lost it?'

'Not so long as the world remains unready to receive it, Philippe.' A fierce flame burned ever brighter within Nicole. 'A whole section of the Archive is filled with works condemned to the flames just because their authors were women!'

'Even the sacred writings of our brothers far to the south have been brought here.' Waksitanou pointed at the immense array of stelae that seemed to go off into the dim recesses of the Great Archive. 'Within these stone tablets is all that remains of what long lost peoples learned in their Golden Age.'

Marie felt she already had more than her share of secrets. 'Philippe is right! All this must be returned to the light of day. How else will the world ever shed its ignorance and hate?'

'Your parents paid dearly the last time that we made that judgment of the world, Madame.' The Dread Maiden came face to face with Marie, gripping her two arms in steel fingers. 'Just as Yolande foresaw, the Societé has driven us to our last refuge here. They are still out there seeking both the Chosen Seed and these forbidden relics. No, this Place Of Dreaming must preserve these treasures till the Chosen One rises up and calls for them.'

'That's all very well, Nicole, but what if this Chosen One never comes?'

'Then, Madame, all this shall remain hidden here forever. True to the prophecy of Yolande, so runs the will of the Sultan and Emperor who gave these things into our care and keeping.'

Marie knew not why lightning streaked across the inside of her skull. She reeled and would have fallen to her knees if Luigi Campagna and his youngest son had not steadied her. 'That is why you have come here, isn't it, Nicole? Your real mission is not to protect me or the seed I carry but to seal up forever this Place Of Dreaming!'

'Your husband and I have been given both tasks to perform, Madame. We must seal this mirror up so that only a world grown ready to look within itself may ever reopen it.'

'What right have any of us to judge such things, Nicole?'

'The right bequeathed us by Yolande and Frederick, the royal pair who kept a light burning in the world at the time of its greatest darkness. Even more than I, it is you, Madame, who is the inheritor of that right and duty, for you are the Bearer of the Chosen Seed.'

So powerful was the maid's grip upon her mistress's mind and body that she could think of nothing to say in reply. As if sensing one battle won, Nicole moved on to the next.

Indeed, the Dread Maiden moved so quickly that Marie never did see where the young M'ikmaq brave came from. Waksitanou's elder son stood revealed with both arms pinned behind him! Yet with harsh gestures and anger resounding in his voice, he somehow made it seem as though he and his father stood alone in that Place of Dreaming. After a few moments of listening, Waksitanou reduced him to silence with a gesture and signaled Nicole to let him go. The youth spun on his heel and was gone into the shadows as swiftly as he had come.

Marie thought for a moment that Nicole would spring after him and bring the young brave down. It did not escape Marie that she stood ready to kill. 'How did your son get in here, Guardian? There must be a second entrance. Is that so?'

'I am not the intended Guardian.' The M'ikmaq seemed to age before Marie's eyes. 'Many things are hidden from me.'

'Waksitanou, what other things are you hiding from me?' Nicole came close to the M'ikmaq, her killing fury still upon her. She seemed quite small, a puny woman beside the tall muscular warrior. Marie shuddered, knowing how misleading that appearance was. She could only hope Waksitanou sensed the danger as well as she did.

Yet there was no fear in the M'ikmaq as he met the Dread Maiden eye to eye. 'Many winters ago when I was not yet a man, I came here with my uncle to dream my name. My eldest son also comes here seeking his name, but my brother Sayadana is not here to show him the path to becoming a true man.'

With a gesture Nicole made it clear she was not interested in M'ikmaq manhood rites. 'Your son did not enter the Saracen way, did he? Show me that other way.'

'It was agreed when the First Strangers came that the People should keep secret their ancient path to the Place of Dreaming.' The M'ikmaq moved on past the Dread Maiden, beyond their wondering circle, the darkness receding before him as he lit a torch with tinder and flint. More wall-bracketed torches flared till Marie found herself in yet another cavern, its space smaller and unshaped by human hands excepting the decoration covering the sinuously curved walls.

Yet the murals were everything.

The small group of humans stood amid an immense panorama of painted figures: humans, animals and what Marie took to be fantastic spirit forms. Occupying a central place overhead was a bear-like figure with feminine attributes and human face. Conditioned reflexes pulled at her, but Marie could not tear her gaze away from the naked pagan deity. Young and full of life, yet worn with age and experience, the Goddess personified the eternal female principle giving substance to the world. Even Glooscap and his brethren gods, tiny beneath her bulk, drew sustenance from her breasts, for the whole world was her womb, a matrix within her.

'Guardian, why does the Great Goddess preside over a chamber reserved for the initiation of young men?' As if on sudden impulse, Nicole took Guillaume protectively in her arms.

'How should it be otherwise, Medicine Woman? There is in each male child a rage against life, for men are set adrift in birth from partaking of the Goddess. If the rage be not stilled, if we are not reconciled to becoming men in our own right, we are driven to destroy or possess all that She has made in Her image.'

'You possess odd notions, Kin-Friend.' The Huguenot shook his head and made a sign that might almost have been a cross to ward off evil spirits. 'Jean Calvin would definitely not approve of this.'

Marie decided that her husband and her maid were missing the point. 'She looks like she might come alive and step down from the wall at any moment! That hulking bear with her cubs, how formidable she is! Luigi Campagna, this is so wonderful! Little Louis, what do you think of all this?'

The boy shook his head dolefully. 'Mother, even if I should paint till I'm a hundred, I shall never be able to make the things I paint come alive like this!'

Never before had anyone freely given Marie that title. She tightened her grip on Louis' fingers, wondering what the boy-child was feeling as the Goddess pressed down on them with her eternal gaze.

Suddenly Marie began trembling uncontrollably. 'What am I saying? We should never have come into this place! I am afraid of all this!'

'Bearer of the Chosen, you need no longer be afraid.' Waksitanou took her hand in his, and his cool palm felt hard and smooth as the stone surrounding them. 'You have been kept long in darkness, you have still far to travel and will see terrible things, but you will never again be afraid of the darkness after today.'

She dared to meet his eyes. Neither fear nor darkness could she find in their depths, only the same unfathomable sadness that already filled her with wonder. He put his hand to her brow as he began to speak. 'A great evil befalls both your people and mine. They will both wander long in darkness.'

Marie heard echoes of suffering and dying. Discordant, torn bits of noise imploded in her head. And she saw the forces of injustice, inhumanity, bitterness and cruelty sweeping over the land. She stepped back from the M'ikmaq, horrified by the visions he poured over her. 'Waksitanou, your people should never have welcomed the Strangers from over the sea! You should have driven my people forth when they tried to take their first step upon these shores!'

'It was our destiny as a people to welcome you to this land, O Bearer of the Chosen, just as the Deer People welcomed us. Your people have much to learn through us. As for the M'ikmaq, we may journey no farther without the company of their brothers from across the sea. Long ago, a great shaman foretold that a leader born of your Seed will someday guide your people down that path we must travel together. For that reason we have waited long by this sea to welcome you.'

Marie could not credit what the M'ikmaq said. 'Waksitanou, I fear you deceive yourself. You should have driven us back into the sea! Think how much grief, suffering and dying it would have saved your own people!'

The M'ikmaq's face became suddenly hard and stern. 'We could have done so, and we may do so yet if the prophecy be not fulfilled. If your people continue to walk their paths of death, we shall one day unleash the living power that dwells in this land upon them. It is a power your people do not understand. Your people have known terrible days, but that day of unleashing will be the most terrible day ever to fall upon them.'

Marie shuddered at the glimpse his eyes gave her of things to come. She put her head to his shoulder. 'Till then, Waksitanou of the M'ikmaq, let us remain the best of kin-friends.'

Chapter XV

CATACLYSM

Sanctuary Island, May 1756

Jacques Sabot lowered *L'Espérance's* gangplank, and two score Lüneburgers came marching ashore to a fife and drum. They sang Lutheran thanksgivings as they set to work with a will. One old carpenter made a point of telling the Huguenot just how it was. 'Our families have made it through the winter thanks to ye, Herr Campagna. Ye be a good man, even if ye be an addled Frenchman what follows the teachings of that rascal Calvin. Tis a pity our Lord and Savior prepares for ye no place in heaven.'

The Germans broke the spell cast by the M'ikmaq upon the island. Their relentless axes violated its brooding tranquility. They cleared a large plot of land near the cove for the trading post and the little settlement's first garden. They dug a deep cellar high on the southern promontory for the Campagna's seigneury of stone and oak. Much to Marie's chagrin, the forest surrounding her chosen site gave way to stumpy fields and piles of squared timbers.

Isaac Ben Yussuf came back with the Lüneburgers, cajoling them to even greater efforts and meddling everywhere with a critical eye. He did approve of the observatory being framed over the house. 'That's it, that's it! We must keep an eye peeled for the frogs. Sooner or later they'll be coming for us. I'd put a brace of cannon up here as well, Capitaine Campagna.'

The crew's tales of 'feathered Indians' led Ben Yussuf to infer their age-old occupation of the island. Poking about, the amateur archaeologist discovered deep middens of clamshells near the beach. He persuaded his Huguenot friend to use the lime to mortar stone foundations under each of the new buildings. The Campagnas didn't dare ask whether he had noticed any evidence of European occupation.

The physician also subjected Marie to regular examinations, which gave him occasion to further instruct Nicole in the scientific mysteries of childbirth. Amity prevailed between them only because his attention often strayed elsewhere. A man for all seasons, he displayed particular interest in the plantation of cabbages that Marie and her stepsons had sown in the harrowed spaces between the oak stumps. 'Madame, you've the making of a good hausfrau. One might even suspect there's Jewish blood in your veins. If ye were not already a wedded woman, I would consider proposing marriage to you myself.'

Marie enjoyed giving the physician as good as she got. 'Herr Doctor, this is a French garden. See? I am growing beans and romaine for my husband's health. I shall soon have onions and peas as well. These cabbages are planted solely for the sake of yon Lüneburgers.'

'When winter comes again, Madame Campagna, you will discover in these cabbages virtues which outweigh all the other vegetables put together. Cabbage is the wherefore my Lüneburgers will inherit this wilderness.'

Marie saucily wrinkled her nose at him. 'Herr Doctor, I'm sorry to inform you that I find even the thought of cabbage quite disgusting.'

'Ah, Madame, if only my dear dead mother were here to make pickled cabbage for you! Served with sauerbraten, rye bread and beer, sauerkraut is a dish fit for Talmudic scholars. Have you never tasted it?'

'Never, Herr Doctor. But I fancy I can still smell it from our stroll in Lüneburg.'

In three weeks time, Jacques Sabot returned from the Banks with the brigantine's hold chock full of salted cod. Meanwhile, so much surplus timber had accumulated that Luigi Campagna decided to ship it as deck-cargo along with most of the fish to Halifax. Isaac Ben Yussuf went along as sole passenger on this inaugural voyage. 'Herr Doctor, I fear your Germans will miss you. Who's to tend their ills if you're not here?'

'That's a very good question, M. le Capitaine. Now there's a war going on, I've had to prescribe a sleeping potion for Major Sutherland. He fears the Germans will riot if you continue to feed them so well. He thinks it would be better to shoot them, and he bids you do so if they give you any trouble.'

'Herr Doctor, I have no intention of shooting anyone.' Luigi Campagna drew his frock coat about his broad chest indignantly. 'Least of all would I shoot these good workers you've brought me.'

'Yes, Captain, good people but they've been brought very low by these stiff-necked Britishers! That is why I'm off to Halifax. Finding ways for my Lüneburgers to put bread in their mouths and roofs over their heads is better medicine than dispensing powders or letting blood, wouldn't you agree!'

A dozen green-gilled Hanoverian peasants also shipped before the mast on this second outbound voyage. Ben Yussuf prophesied that his Lüneburgers would soon become intrepid seafarers, but the sailing master was somewhat less sanguine upon first inspection of the new recruits. 'I'd as soon go to sea with a crew of Barbary apes, M. le Capitaine Campagna!'

True to his word, the Huguenot stuck close to his new home, as though Marie and his children were all that mattered to him. In the long evenings, the couple would often climb to the summit of the hill where the posts and beams of their new house rose up starkly from the stumps of the oak trees. The merchant insisted on carrying his pregnant wife up the steepest leg of the path. 'Shouldn't you be putting on more flesh, Madame?'

'Nicole says I'm doing just fine, Monsieur. She believes a woman with child should stay fit and trim.'

'What says our good Jewish physician to that?'

'Herr Doctor Ben Yussuf bids me spread out like yon tent down there.' Marie kicked her feet peremptorily. 'There, the hill is behind us. You may set me down now, Monsieur. I shouldn't want to tire you out. You're not as young as you used to be, you know.'

'Madame, perhaps you should obey Doctor Ben Yussuf. Our maid is not the gentlest of creatures. I shouldn't want to lose you. My Eloise died in childbirth, you know.'

'Was she a bigger woman than me, Monsieur?'

'Eloise was of a somewhat heavier build. I was much younger then, but I should have had difficulty carrying her up this hill. You are such a tiny slip of a thing, Madame!'

'Nicole says I'm quite big enough to bear this child. You are not to worry about me, Monsieur. All shall unfold according to God's will, as my dear husband so often reminds me.'

'Which doesn't excuse us from acting responsibly, Madame. Let us be careful lest we put Him to the test.' It pleased Marie to feel emotion stirring powerfully within her husband as he rather breathlessly lowered her to the ground. They stood leaning against one another, transfixed by a magnificent sunset spreading like molten wax across the Bay.

'There are worse places to live out our lives, Luigi Campagna. I only wish we could forget what lies beneath our feet.'

'That will come to pass all in good time, Madame! I just hope Nicole finds the second entrance before Isaac Ben Yussuf does.'

'Once she has broken the staff and the Place of Dreaming has been sealed, perhaps both your brethren and the Societé will forget we are here.' Despite those hopeful words, Marie's old familiar panic rose in her throat as she gazed southward across the Bay. *Is this churning in my stomach just the idle fancy of a pregnant woman? Or does something lurk out there like a coiled snake waiting to strike?*

Certainly Nicole gave no sign that she shared her mistress's misgivings. She kept herself so busy poring over diaries and logs retrieved from the Great Cache that Marie felt somewhat neglected. Yet the maid found time to make eyes at the young workmen, luring one or two of them to the rude cabin erected for her and Guillaume alongside the burgeoning trading post. It made Marie blush trying not to imagine what went on there. Nor did it avail Luigi Campagna to fulminate against such lewdness. The Dread Maiden possessed an indefinable assurance that neither her mistress nor her master could overawe. She confided in Marie with a wink. 'The Jew is right, Madame. These German lads are going to make excellent sailors.'

Marie's chief care remained the classical education of her stepsons. Excepting only the Sabbath, each morning found the foursome immersed in Latin and Greek texts from the Place of Dreaming. She had insisted on "borrowing" several of the extra codices despite objections raised by her husband and Nicole. In the end, they had been unable to deny the Bearer of the Chosen Seed access to these long lost treasures.

Philippe for one was not appreciative of the efforts she made on his behalf. 'Madame, this play is about dead Greeks growing corn. Why must we read it?'

Jean's lower lip trembled with shock and indignation. '*Triptolemus* is a supreme literary masterpiece, Philippe!'

'I call it a supreme literary bore! What a blessing it's been lost for a thousand years! What a shame that we have found it!'

'Madame, forbid Philippe to talk so!' Jean hefted his slate as though he were considering throwing it at his older brother. 'Father will whip him if he hears such talk!'

'Nay, Jean, Father agrees with me. He says a good Protestant requires no more than Holy Scripture to illumine his life. I heard him say Sophocles was a heathen fool!'

'That's enough!' Marie prevented Jean from actually hurling the slate. 'Philippe, you're deliberately provoking your brother. I'm sure your father never said any such thing. Apologize to Jean this instant!'

Deprived of his weapon, the younger brother assumed a lofty mien. 'It is not I, Madame, but the greatest of tragedians who rates Philippe's apology.'

'Utter nonsense! Father says that God commands us to let the dead bury the dead. Jean, didn't you see all the gold and silver glittering down there? Vaults full of it just beyond our reach. I saw coffers of rubies as big as hen's eggs!'

'Big brother, you shame us all.' This reproof from the mouth of a babe silenced Philippe. He glowered at little Louis, but resumed his painful translation of *Triptolemus* into English.

Out of the thousands of long lost books in the Archive, Marie had selected for her own edification a Latin translation of Sappho's complete love poems. Once or twice at the seminary, she had read snatches of Sapphic verse quoted by other writers of antiquity: all that the world retained of its first great lyric poet. It did disturb her to realize that the love-verses were addressed to another young woman. Still, she was filled with pride by the power of the Lesbian poet to evoke the deepest and most profound of emotions. She had always assumed the doing of this to be the exclusive province of men. *In fact, it was Sappho who first taught us all — men and women alike — that it is human to feel such things. To think I am possibly the first woman in a thousand years to read her poems! How can it be after her early example that we women have come to think ourselves incapable of this?*

She also had retrieved original lost manuscripts by Froissart and Joinville from the times of the later Crusades. It astounded her to discover how much Frederick II had dominated his era. Even Saint Louis had described the Hohenstaufen emperor as *Stupor Mundi,* the wonder of the world. A titanic struggle unfolding over centuries between church and state had culminated during the reign of this last of the true Holy Roman Emperors. She came to feel a deep respect for him and Yolande. She came to see his death as marking the early defeat of the principle that all men should be free to worship as they please.

Louis gave himself over to sketching and painting a full-length study of Nicole confronting Waksitanou in the Place of Dreaming. The faces were rendered with a promising assurance, but it was the animal-like bodies that delighted Marie. The Dread Maiden crouched panther-like. The M'ikmaq stood a stag at bay, his arms outstretched like antlers guarding the painted cavern walls behind him. Marie couldn't repress a twinge of envy. *How wonderful to be a man and have people expect you to do such things, whereas we women must rest content with bearing babies!*

She made the mistake of rubbing her ring; Frederick Hohenstaufen whispered solicitously in her ear. *Don't feel sorry for yourself, Princess Mine. You give rise to far more than you know.*

I am expected to feel privileged that I bear your progeny, Sire?

Certainly the women of our experience always accounted it so. Even when we were yet a homeless waif roaming the docks and streets of Palermo, they thanked us courteously for making them happy. It must have been our red hair and powerful build.

Such arrogance quite took Marie's breath away. *Your Majesty was born with a golden spoon in his mouth. Those poor women thanked you because they did not dare deny a prince of the royal blood anything!*

A golden spoon, you say? Our mad father expired soon after we were born. So vicious and cruel had he proven that all Italy rose up against us. To save our life, our Sicilian mother was forced to renounce our claim to the German throne. Before she died when we were four, she appointed Innocent III our guardian. His Holiness doubtless expected the Hohenstaufen orphan to die from neglect, but we fooled him. The King of Sicily grew up diving for sponges and pearls, even picking the occasional pocket for enough to eat.

Why tell me all this, Sire?

Because you seem to have strange ideas about us, Marie of Hohenstaufen. We foresee that the Chosen Seed must again pass through difficult times. If you're to make it through such tribulation, we best get to know one another.

But Marie had already chosen the one she wished to lean on. *Enough, Sire! I've a good husband now. I no longer need you, if indeed I ever did.*

The Templar is mere flesh and blood, Princess Mine.

Flesh and blood, Marie decided, was exactly what she wanted — not echoes of troubles long since dead. *Get thee hence, Sire! I prefer to live my life without you!*

There came the day when the trading post stood ready for business. The workmen celebrated by returning home for the Sabbath. Rumors had reached them of growing unrest in Lüneburg, and the men were anxious to look to the welfare of their families.

As a precaution during the crew's absence, the merchant had already moved Marie and the children from the sail-tent into the stoutly built trading post. For the first time the Huguenot shared his wife's bed, albeit her pregnancy dictated sexual abstinence. His wife welcomed these changes, although Nicole made her blush by noticing that her master did not spring so eagerly from bed as was his former wont.

It was not yet dawn when the couple awakened to the pounding of booted feet. Marie's first thoughts were that *L'Espérance* had returned, that Pierre Sabot was hurrying to bring them news of their successful voyage. Luigi Campagna rose quickly from her arms, turned up the pilot-lit ship's lantern and pulled on his breeches. 'What is it, my husband?'

'Our Germans run amuck.' Still groggy, the Huguenot unbarred the massive oaken doors. 'They've been drinking and have come back for more rum. The good doctor warned me this might happen.'

It did not reassure Marie to see her husband take down his musket. 'You mustn't shoot any of them, Luigi Campagna!'

'Don't worry, Madame. I only mean to scare them off before some damage is done.'

'Nicole!' Marie rose up in her nightgown to check the sleeping children. 'She might kill someone!'

'She's more likely to invite that someone into her bed. Here, Madame, hold this light for me, if you please.'

Raising the ship's lantern above her husband's head, Marie glimpsed shadows fleeting through the murky darkness. A man's low-pitched scream reached her ears, punctuated by the deafening report and blinding flash of Luigi Campagna's musket. More fleeing shadows and the pounding of booted feet. A figure emerged from the dark and stumbled toward them. It sank to its knees before her husband.

The Huguenot stepped forward and leaned over the kneeling figure. 'Hugo!' Where's Nicole?'

'Indians, Master! Many Indians!'

Crazily, Marie wondered what the maid thought of the red tobacco pouch the coxswain wore as a night-cap. Then she realized that the sailor's shock of black hair was gone, that she beheld his raw bleeding scalp.

Her scream echoed from the bluffs as Luigi Campagna caught the wounded sailor in his arms. Shadows congealed out of the darkness. Her husband drew a pistol from his belt as he dragged Hugo toward the doorway. 'Stand, or I'll shoot!'

Red fire lit the night. Smashing glass. Something hard smashed into the wall beside her. She heard the sickening thud of musket balls against flesh. The world erupted in a ragged roar. The two huddled men collapsed upon one another. The echoes of gunfire were swept away by a savage chorusing yell.

The shattered lantern guttered out. Hardly knowing what she did, Marie pulled her husband from beneath Hugo's riddled body and began dragging him across their threshold. Philippe came to her aid.

An immense, howling figure came at them, toma-hawk raised.

Like a genie, Nicole came out of nowhere. The satyr's muzzle flash lit a dark savage face as it blew apart. The nymph shot a second warrior in the naked breast as he charged down. Somehow the slender maid deflected the hurtling body into the darkness. Still reel-ing from the impact, she rallied to meet a third attack-er. The Dread Maiden's thrusting hand choked off the blood-curdling yell as the tomahawk struck.

The Moorish tent burst into flames. Silhouettes danced toward them. Nicole sank to her knees beneath the weight of her dying assailant. Defiant, she raised her head to face a fourth charging form that came at her swinging a musket. A pistol discharged close to Marie's ear. When the smoke cleared, Philippe's hands still supported Luigi Campagna's wrist. The smoking weapon dropped from his limp fingers.

The attackers drew back, leaving several of their number struggling in pools of blood. Nicole thrust bodies aside with one good arm and helped Philippe drag his father inside the trading post. The yells rose again as Marie flung the massive doors shut and dropped the heavy oak beam into place.

A sobbing Jean found the tinderbox and brought it to Marie. Her hands ice-cold but rock-steady, she struck the tinder and blew on the flame. The tinder fizzled, then blazed up again. Her anger flared along with the stub of candle at the sight of the wounded Dread Maiden bending over her husband.

The Huguenot struggled to speak. 'You were right, Nicole. They did find us.'

'The Societé is everywhere, Master.' Blood pulsed between the maid's widespread fingers. 'But they shall not get what they come for. This very day I sealed the Place of Dreaming forever. Both entrances. No one shall penetrate there.'

A cough rattled in Luigi Campagna's throat. 'You are also wounded, Nicole? Badly, from the look of you.'

'Aye, Master, I will not follow long behind thee.' The Dreadmaiden's touch left a trace of blood on the Huguenot's balding brow.

Luigi Campagna cast his eyes about the darkened room. 'Let me speak to my sons.'

Philippe brought his brothers forward by the hand. Their father extended blood-smeared fingers to them. 'I fear I must leave you, my children.'

Little Louis began sobbing. 'Father, what have these devils done to you?'

227

'They have killed me and many more besides. Yet, my little Louis, you must be a man like Philippe. He will lead you now. Jean, do you hear what I tell you?'

'Father, we will follow our brother.' Jean's lip trembled to see blood trickling from his father's mouth.

'You will make a good man, Jean. And you, Philippe, there is one thing you must promise me.'

'Father, you need only ask it.'

Luigi Campagna convulsed in a fit of coughing, the words rattling in his throat.

'I know what you would ask of me, Father.' Philippe shook his head in shaking off the tears. 'Rest assured that we will guard our mother whatever comes, for we know she is more precious to you than life itself.'

The heavy brows lifted and the blue eyes flashed as the stiff fingers reached for Marie. 'Madame, I beg your forgiveness for bringing you to this.'

'Don't leave me, my husband!'

The Huguenot summoned one last effort, trying in vain to focus his eyes. 'Ma chere Marie, I feel my heart growing cold.'

Chapter XVI

BESIEGED

Sanctuary Island, May 1756

Pencil beams of sunlight pierced the unchinked walls, forcing those within to see what they had tried so hard not to see. Marie went on gently rocking Luigi Campagna's head in her lap till Philippe shuttered his father's blank stare. Then gathering Jean and Louis to her breast, she led them in murmuring a Calvinist prayer. Even so, she could not bear to leave off caring for her husband so summarily. All that kept her from signing the cross was Nicole's grim presence.

The Dread Maiden's left arm dangled uselessly from a shattered shoulder. Her sleeve and the front of her smock were soaked with drying blood, but she would not let Marie tend her terrible wound. Instead, she held her body together with a leather belt she had somehow strapped round herself. 'Disturbing me will only make matters worse, Madame. Even the Jew could not avail me now.'

'Guillaume!' Marie held her breath listening to the din their attackers made as they plundered the stores down at the dock. Once or twice she thought she heard a scream. 'Where is Guillaume, Nicole?'

'I left him with Hugo, Madame. Let us pray he is already dead!'

The maid's invocation rang hollow in Marie's ears; she had never known the Dread Maiden to resort to prayer. 'How can you even think such a thing? Is he not your son, Nicole?'

'Yes, Guillaume is my son.' Yet still the maid's face failed to register emotion of any kind. 'Madame Campagna, please compose yourself. We must decide what is best for you to do now that your husband is dead.'

'How now, Nicole? Is your grand design not unfolding as it should?' Marie felt herself teetering on the brink of hysteria as she pressed both hands to her throbbing midriff. 'Did you not anticipate this would happen, just as you did all else?'

'Madame, our grand design, as you call it, was thwarted by the Societé long ago. If that were not so, think you that we would have brought the Chosen Seed back to this island? Your Templar husband and I sought no more than to keep you and the child you carry alive. All might have gone as we hoped, if we had not been betrayed.'

'Betrayed?' Marie looked behind her as if she feared the traitor might be lurking amongst the trade goods stacked to the low ceiling. The image of Waksitanou streaked across her tortured mind. She thrust it away. 'Betrayed by whom?'

'By someone who knows the secret of this island. That same one guided strangers here in search of the Templar treasure — and of you, Madame.'

'Strangers looking for me, you say? They are not M'ikmaq, then?'

'No, Madame, these raiders are of the tribe the French call Maliseet.'

'Nicole, how did you come to know all this?'

'I could not sleep, Madame, so I went out searching for the secret M'ikmaq entrance.'

'At night?'

'I thought I might stand a better chance of finding what I sought if there was no daylight to distract my other senses. I found much more than I meant to find, Madame.'

'You came across these Indians before the attack?'

'Yes, Madame. I heard their clumsy French boots trundling ashore from their canoes long before I smelled the bear grease. Moccasins would have better served their purpose. Their vanity has cost them dear this night.'

Marie could do nothing more than stare at her maid. 'You stalked a party of Indians by sound and smell on a moonless night!'

'There was some phosphorescence off the sea, Madame. I could not think what else to do lest I mistake what they came for! For a while the party stayed near the canoes speaking in broken French as if they were unsure what to do. Some wanted to attack our camp immediately, but the Black Robe who came with them insisted they go first to the Place of Dreaming. Then a few went off with him along the shore away from our camp. I followed them, thinking that they might lead me to the M'ikmaq entrance.'

An old anger smoldering deep within Marie burst into flame. 'And did they?'

'Yes, Madame. I followed them along the beach till we came to a great rock seated against the base of the cliff. It took all of them to roll it up and away from the cavern mouth that lies beneath. Then the Black Robe and all his companions went down inside leaving only one sentry to guard the entrance. That same one told me all I needed to know.'

'And then you killed him?'

'Of course, Madame. What else was I to do with him? He knew the location of the entrance.'

'What difference? You said the others went inside. By now, they've discovered all the doors to the Templar treasures.'

'Those doors are safely locked, Madame. It would take special tools to force their way in. As for the entrance itself, I resealed it by tumbling the great rock back down into its place. They are buried alive inside.'

Marie might have been more appalled if her slain husband were not lying near. 'Can they not push the rock away just as they did before?'

'No, Madame. I noticed another great rock high on the cliff above. With the Templar staff I was able to lever it down. The Guardians must have prepared against a need such as mine by setting that rock there, for it brought the whole cliff-face down with it. It almost buried me along with the others. I broke the Staff in vaulting to safety. The Key itself lies buried in the rubble. The hilt of the staff I hurled far out into the sea.'

Marie could scarcely contain herself from screaming at hearing all this. 'Far better if you had forgotten all that, Nicole! How is it you only thought to protect the Templar trove? You should have thought of your son and these children. You should have hurried back to us and given Luigi Campagna time to prepare our defense!'

'I am truly sorry, Madame. I thought they would wait for the Jesuit to rejoin them. I deceived myself there was time to both seal the Place of Dreaming and thwart the attack.' The Dread Maiden raised her chin to meet her mistress's gaze. 'And so it would have turned out if poor foolish Hugo had not left Guillaume alone and gone out in search of me.'

Marie's thoughts ranged back to the scar faced coxswain. Once again she relived her husband bending over the scalpless sailor kneeling in the light of her lantern. Next moment, a volley of musket fire changed her life forever. 'Oh Nicole, what have you done?'

The Dread Maiden stared back at her unblinking. 'I heard him call my name. I came running, but he must have stumbled upon the Maliseet waiting on the beach and provoked their attack.' Despite her pain, Nicole threw back her head and stared past Marie. 'And so the last of the Dread Maidens proved unworthy of her charge. Pray forgive me, O Bearer of the Chosen Seed, if you can find it in your heart to do so.'

All the anger went out of Marie as she turned to watch Philippe priming the nymph. 'What is there to forgive? It is not as though you broke faith with us, Nicole. Let us not quarrel now that it only remains for us to die. Let us try to do it well.'

'No, Madame, hope still remains for you and these children!' Nicole turned her intense gaze upon Jean and Louis who lay huddled against their father's body. For a moment, Marie fancied that she espied some vestige of maternal feeling in the Dread Maiden. 'Already, it is dawn. These raiders dare not dally here for fear of the redcoats at Lüneburg. The Chosen Seed may yet survive this night!'

'Let the Chosen Seed be damned!'

As if to punctuate Marie's words, a heavy weight crashed against the thick oak doors. Again and again the blows shook the trading post. Marie and the two younger children shrank back against the walls. Philippe struggled to hold his father's great pistol cocked and ready, but Nicole only smiled. 'Do not despair, Madame. They lack the time for getting at us that way. Neither will the chimney and the windows serve their foul purpose.'

Only the day before, Marie remembered having teasingly accused her husband of building a fort instead of a trading post. The windows, heavily shuttered on the inside, were slit-like embrasures designed to permit an outward field of fire through the thick oak walls. The Huguenot had even caused wrought-iron rods to be mortised between the inner stones of the fireplace flue. Yet Marie could see little enough reason for taking heart. 'That only means they must burn us out. How Luigi Campagna laughed at me when I begged him to build our habitations out of stone!'

'This oak is green, Madame. It will not burn easily. In any case, I expect these Maliseet will rate an extra bounty from the Black Robes if you are brought back to them alive.'

Marie picked up the satyr and pressed his howling mouth to her breast. 'Then I will die with the rest of you.'

'You blaspheme, Madame! Would you leave Luigi Campagna's children alone to face whatever comes? I am witness to the oath you swore before the dying father of your child. You swore to preserve the Chosen Seed, remember?'

'Nicole, I am not a Dread Maiden like you! I cannot face what lies before us!'

'You may lack our special skills, but royal blood flows in your veins, not mine. I am only your hand-maiden, Marie of Hohenstaufen.'

'No, Nicole, I will not let myself believe in that! I care nothing for the fables that have lured you and Luigi Campagna to your deaths!'

'How well the Societé does its evil work, Madame!' Nicole's eyes grew feverish with dying. 'You were still no more than a small child when they burned your mother as a witch.'

'Burned her?'

'That is why you so fear the fire, Madame. They made you watch the spectacle from the Capitole over-looking the Place de Toulouse. What you heard and saw that day made you throw yourself headlong from the tower. The long chain shackled to your ankle was all that saved you from falling to your death.'

Dark flickering memories. A fair white city basking under blue skies. A great wide plaza overflowing with people chanting, their uplifted faces gone hideous under a rising pall of smoke. A slender figure writhing and twisting as flames lick up around her. More a wail than a scream burning skull-deep with unbearable white heat. Leaping high on flashing nimble feet over the parapet and plummeting a long way down to awful wrenching pain. Then came merciful darkness.

The world outside had grown deathly still. No more dying screams or drunken cries. Jean and Louis drowsed fitfully against their father's bloodstained chest, the elder holding his father's big cutlass in both small hands. In a kind of stupor, Philippe crouched on his knees, the ship's pistol resting on a keg. Marie eased forward the satyr's hammer and laid him on the broad axed floor.

With painful effort, Nicole managed an approving nod at seeing this. 'Indeed, Madame, there is still hope for you and these children. Just remember one thing: if it comes down to it, you alone among us all are not expendable.'

'It is you who are the witch! How dare you say such things to me!'

'You name me well, Madame.' The Dread Maiden's whole body began shaking as the palsy of death crept over her. 'But now is not the time to bandy such words between us. Hush, two of these killers come to parley.'

Booted feet crunched on the crushed clamshells strewn outside. 'Ho! Ho! Ho! You there inside the house! My compliments to Madame Campagna!'

'Answer him, Madame!'

'He's drunk, Nicole!'

'What do you expect, Madame? They've been drinking the Master's brandy all night.'

Jerked awake, Jean and Louis sheltered like two fledglings beneath their mother's wings. She pressed the boys close. *How does a widow address those who murdered her husband and the father of these children? How does one speak to savage beasts?* 'I am Madame

Campagna, wife of the peaceful trader you came here to murder and rob. What manner of men are you anyway?'

'Ah, Madame, among my Maliseet people I am called Teiskaret, sagamo of many warriors. Black Robes christened me Jean Baptiste by the Grace of God, and Louis Quinze himself has given me this medal, making me Captain over his armies. On behalf of His Most Christian Majesty I offer you condolences upon the death of your French husband.'

'He is probing.' The Dread Maiden struggled closer to whisper in her mistress's ear. 'He is not certain who is alive with you inside this trading post, Madame. Question him as a subtle woman questions a stupid man.'

Marie had to fight hard to keep her shrill voice from breaking. 'Was it King Louis who sent you here to slay innocent women and children?'

'In war, Madame, there are no innocents.' The Maliseet's powerful bass resounded through the thick oak walls. 'Teiskaret comes to slay all enemies of the Maliseet people. In the name of His Most Christian Majesty, Louis Quinze, I demand your immediate surrender.'

'He's unsure what to do without his Black Robe to counsel him.' Nicole's breath burned Marie's ear. 'Tell him you will not surrender. Tell him too few of his men have died to quench a widow's thirst for vengeance.'

Not without misgiving, Marie voiced the Dread Maiden's message. The Maliseet could be heard conversing in their native tongue, their tones rising and falling angrily. 'Madame, I slew your husband in honorable combat after he himself slew several of my bravest men. Yet I have only this scalp of his slave to show for my valor in battle. Open these doors and deliver to us his body, else I cannot answer for the wrath of my warriors.'

Marie did not need to have words placed in her mouth this time. 'Bid your warriors feel shame rather than anger, O great chief of the Maliseet. My husband killed no one! You treacherously struck him down when he went to the aid of his wounded servant! It was my handmaiden and my child who together slew your brave warriors.'

Philippe sent his stepmother a cross-eyed stare from behind his great pistol. Clearly, he no longer wished to be thought of as a child. Nicole gurgled out something that sounded like a laugh. 'Well done, Madame! Hohenstaufen blood flows in your veins, indeed!'

'I begin to understand this world of yours, Nicole.' Marie listened to the buzz of angry voices. More booted feet pounded close followed by absolute silence. And then came the frightened scream of a child.

Nicole stifled Marie's exclamation with a touch of her hand. 'Madame, steel yourself to learn more about this world than you can yet imagine.'

'Mamam, are you there?' The plaintive cry stabbed deep into Marie's vitals. 'Where is my mamam?'

'Guillaume, I am here with Madame! You must be brave!' The Dread Maiden's facial muscles spasmed with the pain of shouting. 'I am busy serving Madame Campagna, but soon enough I shall surely come to you, my dear son. I shall never leave you again, Guillaume: I promise you!'

The child's crying ended abruptly; Nicole slumped back against the wall. 'At least now these bastards know Guillaume is only the child of a servant.'

In the throes of dying, the Dread Maiden did not falter. Yet through that impregnable wall of courage, Marie reached out for the first time and grasped some vestige of what the woman beside her was suffering. Never before had she touched on pain that so far transcended physical agony as this. In the dim light, she glimpsed the trembling of the maid's cracked, parched lips. *Her life runs out like sand in a broken hourglass, yet all I do is reproach her. I do not even think how to ease her pain.* 'Quick, Jean, bring Nicole the water gourd!'

The Dread Maiden sipped the water gratefully, all the while watching as Philippe handed Marie the double-primed nymph. Marie stared at the pistol, its contoured beauty so unlike the grotesqueness of its mate. Always before, she had rejected the notion of using these paired weapons to kill. Could she bring herself to do so now? Even with the lives of these children at stake, could she actually do it?

If I have to!

And then it began: the ring of a hammer striking iron followed by the high-pitched shriek of a child. More pounding punctuated again and again by the heart stopping shrieks. 'Ho! Ho! Ho! Madame Campagna!' How like melted butter the rich male voice oozed through the thick oak walls. 'Captain Jean Baptiste Teiskaret would speak with you again.'

'Does the King of France bid his captain torture children, Monsieur?'

'It is you yourself who tortures this child, Madame. Look and see what you do! You have insulted Teiskaret, sagamo of the Maliseet. You deny him the trophies of his victory, but even so he would show you mercy, if only you will let him. You have but to open your doors and surrender. Do this one good thing, and I give you my word of honor that the child will suffer no more.'

Marie looked to Nicole. The cold anger in the Dread Maiden's gray eyes had given way to weary resignation. 'Tell him his word of honor is worthless to us. Tell him that before you open the door, he must swear on his hope of escaping hellfire to let all your people go.'

The sound of easy laughter riffled through the walls at this. 'Surely, Madame, you jest at the expense of the

great Teiskaret. Do you take him for an ignorant savage? He has studied with the Black Robes at the great
fortress-city of Quebec.'

'What terms do you offer me, Monsieur?'

'Terms? I offer no terms.' The Maliseet's voice took
on a note of command. 'You are all Teiskaret's prisoners to do with as his mercy wills. Think you a great war
chief allows his warriors to die in vain?'

Marie could hear Guillaume mewing like a kitten.
Caked with her husband's blood, she rose stiffly from
her place on the floor and shuffled on wooden legs to
the wide trading window beside the barred double
doors. Steeling herself, she slid open the shutter's peephole.

Through smoke, Marie saw the Maliseet piling broken casks and other combustibles around an upright
stake set in front of the trading post. From a crossbeam
dangled a tiny naked body. Spikes had been driven
through the child's wrists.

'Do you see, Madame Campagna, what you have
done to this child? When the sun rises, my people must
be gone from this place. No choice remains to us but to
set a great fire. Then must all your children die a terrible death. Madame, you would be wise to throw yourself on the mercy of Teiskaret before it be too late!'

Nicole tried to stand, but she had lost too much
blood. 'What have they done to my son, Madame?'

'They have nailed him like Christ to a cross, Nicole.
Under him and against the wall of the trading post they
have built a great pile of wood. They intend to burn us
all alive unless we surrender.'

'We will never surrender!' Philippe calmly cocked
one hammer of his father's great boarding pistol. So
heavy was the weapon that he needed both hands to
steady it.

Despite her own suffering, Marie could not help but
marvel how the Dread Maiden managed to hold on to a

world of darkness and pain. 'Guillaume's fate is sealed, Madame. They have crucified him in plain view of us, have they not?'

'Yes, Nicole. They have hung him up directly outside the trading-window.'

'Help me up, Madame. Take my good arm over your shoulder and lead me to the window. Philippe, stand ready to hand me your pistol.'

'You cannot get up, Nicole! Listen to me, for I am your mistress!'

'He suffers needlessly, Madame!' Though badly broken, the Dread Maiden remained a weapon forged of the finest steel. 'There was so much I did not know how to do for my son, but this is one thing I can do!'

'No, Nicole, I will not let you do it!'

'It's a small enough indulgence for a faithful servant to ask, Madame.' Somehow Nicole managed to pull herself onto her knees. 'Listen to me, for I am Guillaume's mother!'

'That is why I cannot allow it, Dread Maiden.' A flood of unspeakable thoughts flowed between the two women as Marie picked up the nymph from the floor. 'It is not given a mother to slay her own child.'

'But the friend of such a mother could.' Nicole drew back her lips into what passed for a smile. 'You were good at hitting the clay ducks with the little pistols, Madame. Will you do this one last kindness for your handmaiden?'

'I will do it for Guillaume.' Marie raised the pistol and stumbled to the window. The peephole was too small to take both the nymph's pitcher and a line of sighting. She struck the shutter's bolt loose with the heel of her hand and slid the slab of oak into its recess between the squared timbers. Bright dawning light invaded the dark room, blinding her.

Men dove to shelter as she thrust the nymph's muzzle outward. Close-up, she spied a squat, pock-scarred figure in a tall military hat with a great crucifix and a gold medal dangling from a chain upon his broad naked chest. He stared back at her, blocking her view of the wailing child. Marie cocked the hammer, but it came as no relief to see the stranger duck aside, to look into the familiar blue eyes of Guillaume. *He does very well for a child just learning to speak. How proud Nicole will be of him one day!*

'Madame, is that you?' The child called out to her gladly and smiled through his tears. 'Where is Mamam?'

'Your mother is here with me, Guillaume.' Marie ignored the leveling firearms of the Maliseet. 'She asks me to help you go to sleep.'

From angles too wide, leveled muskets fired, the balls thudding round her in the solid oak. 'Yes, Madame, make them stop hurting me!'

The nymph's report deafened her. Gun smoke filled the aperture, choking her with acridness. Her blood running cold, she willed herself to witness what she had done, but all she saw was a huge Maliseet swing his musket. The impact tore the hanging child loose from the crossbeam and batted him beyond her field of vision. She slid the shutter home and staggered back from the window. Retching a thin stream of bile, she stared down at Nicole through drifting clouds of smoke.

'It is done, Madame?'

'It is done, Nicole.'

'Thank you, Madame.' The Dread Maiden sought out the hand of her mistress. 'There is one more thing I need ask you to forgive me.'

'Nay, Nicole, it is my place to ask your forgiveness. No one has ever done more for me than you have done, and I have repaid you with nothing but bitter words.'

'Madame, you must hear me out! I have grievously sinned against you from the day we first met! What befalls me this day is my just punishment. You once told me that Guillaume's father was no sailor. Do you remember?'

'I remember, Nicole. What matters it now?'

Nicole closed her eyes and clenched Marie's small hand in a powerful grip. 'Madame, I dare not die without telling you: Luigi Campagna is the father of my poor dead child.'

The confession failed to surprise Marie. *After all is said and done, why should this sad tale require anything from me? Certainly not my forgiveness! I was never the Huguenot's true wife. I only bore his name, not his child.* 'Bien, Nicole, I am glad you told me. My husband's remaining sons and I shall join in mourning their brother.' The fingers of the two women remained interlocked till the one felt the other let go.

The last of the Dread Maidens was no more.

The three children gathered round quickly in response to the sobs racking their stepmother's shoulders. Little Louis stared down soberly at the diminutive rag doll lying on the floor. 'Mother, is Guillaume really our brother?'

'Yes, Louis.' For a moment Marie forgot that she was the widow of a Huguenot. But then, there was no one left to care any longer that she made the sign of the cross. Even Philippe had not yet learned to worry about such things. 'Your little brother has gone to be with his mother and your father. Let us pray for them.'

The widow and orphans knelt in prayer over their dead amid the sounds of timber and brush being heaped against the wall. Marie took up the signet ring hanging around her neck and looked at the rampant red lion of the Hohenstaufen. *How many more do you require to die for the sake of this, Sire?*

A familiar voice spoke musingly in her ear. *This Dread Maiden has indeed proved worthy to be the last of her kind, Marie of Hohenstaufen.*

Because she killed so many before she died, Sire?

Do not be rude, Princess Mine. Do you not want to know a little of what she was?

A trained assassin, what else is there to tell?

Indeed, the Dread Maidens began serving the Fatimid sultans of Egypt as harem guards against the assassins sent to murder them in their beds. For centuries, they were weaned as babes from their mother's milk soon after birth so that they might not drink in feminine tenderness. They were trained in their dreadful mysteries as only young females of our species can be trained.

Marie felt almost grateful to be so distracted from her woes. *How then did they come into your hands, Sire?*

As a gift from our friend the Sultan, of course. We think he meant them for a brotherly joke, having himself found them, shall we say, rather too much to handle. And so did we, if the truth be told. We thought at first to include them in our harem as body-guards and dancers par excellence, for they were wondrously trained in such skills. But they could kill a man with a single stroke, which made them rather too dangerous for pleasant dalliance. To put the matter succinctly, they were too much hardened by their discipline to please a man of our cultivated taste. It is hard for a man to be amorous with such a creature, Princess Mine.

So what did you do with them?

I let Yolande filch them from me. It was she who saw them trained to be something much more than mere guards and assassins. Like exquisite falcons that sit upon one's wrist, she had only to slip off their jesses to launch them at their prey. Seldom did they fail her.

An interesting story, Sire. If memory serves me right, you had much experience of hawking.

No doubt they taught you that we wrote the first and best manual on falconry, De arte venandi cum avibus.

Too bad Nicole was not born one of your falcons, Sire. It would have spared her from dying full of womanly regrets.

How else should a Dread Maiden die? Your sex is capable of all things, Princess Mine, but the toll to be paid is terrible indeed if you bend too far from your true nature.

Please leave me now, Sire, and let me prepare these children to meet our end. Already, Marie could smell smoke sifting through the squared timbers of the trading post.

What talk is this of dying, Princess Mine? How often must you be reminded that the blood of the Hohenstaufen flows in your veins? Think you your forebears could have survived so long were they so faint of heart as this? Many are the times we ourselves talked our way out of far worse affairs than this one.

Marie fought to keep from succumbing to hysteria as she looked down upon the bloody bodies of her husband and maid. *Do you laugh at us, Princess Mine? When the Golden Horde destroyed the Poles and our Teutonic Knights at Leignitz, we knew no force on earth could stay the hand of their great khan from destroying all Christendom if he chose to come. All that was left to us was a wing and a prayer, so we persuaded Batu Khan with fair words and gifts to send his Mongol hordes elsewhere. So Christendom was saved and Islam ravaged; that is why you are able to still talk with us in French.*

Sire, I fail to see what your obscure history lesson has to do with the doom that looms before me and these children now!

Isn't it obvious? You must save yourself like a true Hohenstaufen.

What about these children? Is it only your precious Seed that you care about, Sire?

Marie sat waiting for a reply that never came. Jean had dispelled the Emperor's presence from her mind by abruptly standing up and climbing down the ladder into the open cellar. Without a single word, he began digging up the hard-packed clay floor with his father's cutlass.

'What are you doing, Jean?'

'The lost books from the Place of Dreaming must be given a safe hiding place, Mother.' The boy braced himself as though expecting his older brother to laugh at him. 'I will not let the savages destroy *Triptolemus!*'

Without a word both Philippe and little Louis climbed down the ladder and joined their brother in the cellar. They worked silently together, burying the sail-cloth-wrapped codices a foot beneath the cellar floor of the trading post. As they packed the dirt back in place, the space above them began filling with smoke from the roaring bonfire outside.

'Ho! Ho! Ho! Madame Campagna!' If anything, the voice sounded even friendlier than before. 'Teiskaret would speak to you one last time.'

'I attend your words, O great chief of the Maliseet.' Cold and weary, the widow gripped her ring and called upon the Emperor to come save her, but he was nowhere to be found. She searched the recesses of her mind in vain for him. *I can't do this thing without you, Sire! Yolande's Dread Maiden is dead. How can I beguile this savage and save these children without one such as you or her to guide me?*

And still the Hohenstaufen did not come. 'Already the sun rises in the east, Madame. Already my warriors ready their canoes to be gone from this place. They are wroth that you should delay us so.'

'Great chief, hear me! Angels from God have come to tell me that we are meant, you and I, to cause each other grief to the very end.'

'What you say must be so, Madame Campagna, for even now the flames climb up the walls of your pitiful refuge. I see them lick up under the eaves of the roof. I am a civilized man, Madame. It will indeed grieve me greatly to watch you and your children burn alive.'

'Your fair words would console me, Teiskaret of the Maliseet, if I were not full of Christian grief for you!'

'Madame, save your grieving for yourself and your children! This great bonfire only warms my back against the chill morning air.'

'Open your eyes and see what comes upon you, Teiskaret! Already, the redcoats in Lüneburg will have seen your great pillar of black smoke rising over the island. Your great bonfire beckons them to come. As we speak, they file aboard their ship of many cannon. Soon they will come racing under their white sails across the Bay faster than any canoe can paddle. The British commander is a great friend of my husband. How Major Sutherland's rage will kindle against you when he sees what your warriors have done to his good friend.'

'He! He! He! The English dog will dance and curse in helpless rage!' The Maliseet laughed aloud at his vision of things to come.

'Nay, Teiskaret, it is you who shall dance and curse! These English shall hook you from your canoes like so many fish. As we speak, God sends me a vision of you and your men swinging from the yardarm of the English ship. Great hemp collars are wound around your necks. Terrible indeed is what passes before my eyes, great chief. When your mouth no longer curses and your feet no longer dance, not only your scalps but your heads as well shall be cut off and taken as trophy to Governor Lawrence in Halifax. He shall spit them upon pointed stakes and have his redcoats throw stones and spit upon them. Then shall your wives wail for their husbands just as I now wail for mine.'

It took Teiskaret some time to review Marie's vision. 'The redcoats are many, Madame Campagna, but they are clumsy and we are agile. They can never catch Teiskaret and his Maliseet.'

'Not unless the Maliseet wait around like passenger pigeons to be struck down.' The widow of Luigi

Campagna clutched desperately at what little she knew of this dark land. 'Long will people tell their grandchildren tales of how foolish Teiskaret let the clumsy British net his brave warriors like fish in an Acadian's weir.'

Smoke thickened the air of the trading post. Marie made her three sons lie on the moist cellar floor. Holding a wet neckerchief to her mouth and nose, she stayed just inside the barred doors, listening to the Maliseet harangue one another in their strange tongue.

She heard boots crushing the clamshells. 'Ho! Ho! Ho! Madame Campagna is brave for a woman. But she is too wise to let herself be roasted alive with her children.'

'Chief Teiskaret is gracious.' The widow stifled her choking cough with the neckerchief. The fire which she had feared all her life was hard upon her.

'To take such a brave captive would do Teiskaret great honor. Surrender now, and I shall take you and your son's captive. Louis Quinze and the Black Robes will praise Teiskaret for the mercy he has shown you.'

'Great chief, do you swear to do my children no harm?'

'On my honor, Madame, I swear to see your children safely home to the land of the Maliseet.'

'No, you must swear on your hope of the Christian heaven and by your fear of the Christian hell, Captain Jean Baptiste Teiskaret. You must stand where I can see and hear you swear it, holding your crucifix before you in both hands.'

'Madame Campagna, first you yourself must swear not to shoot me with that witch-pistol of yours!'

'I gladly swear it by all that's holy!' The widow could hardly speak for choking into the neckerchief. Sparks were singeing her hair as Teiskaret, sagamo of the Maliseet, stood before Luigi Campagna's trading-window and solemnly swore.

Then together Marie and Philippe lifted the great oak bar from its rack and opened the doors.

Chapter XVII

VOYAGEUR

Sanctuary Island, May 1756

Gasping for air, Marie sank to her knees on the threshold. Howling bodies shoved past her into the trading post. Through billows of smoke, she watched first her husband and then her maid dragged clear, saw them lifted by the hair to meet the curved blades of the scalping knives. As she cast about for Philippe, a powerful hand seized her own thick braid. Compelled, she looked up at a tomahawk poised beyond the flapless right ear of a horribly scarred and shaven head. She stared into a face of fiendish madness. *How foolish to think I could bargain with you savages! How Nicole would laugh if she could see her silly goose of a mistress now! Far better to have let smoke and fire do their work.*

A plume of bronzed hair danced past, the torn scalp dripping blood. Screams rose from the cellar. Philippe scrambled up the ladder, clutching the nymph to his chest. Marie closed her eyes and prayed. *Oh God, be swift and merciful to them. I accept whatever else you hold in store.*

She let herself be dragged past Hugo's sprawled body. The cruel hand thrust her head down, and she kept watch for her brains to bespatter her bloody knees.

A pair of heavy unmated boots invaded her field of vision. 'Ho! Ho! Ho! Madame Campagna!'

The war chief barked in his native tongue, and the hold upon her hair relaxed. She looked up at folded arms and widespread legs. The squat muscular figure loomed familiar in contrast with all else around her. 'You swore by your hope as a Christian to spare us, Teiskaret of the Maliseet.'

'The Black Robes would say my swearing was not an act done of free will.' The Maliseet stroked his medal fondly. 'They count as nothing an oath sworn under duress.'

Air whooshed from lungs as two small bodies were dumped around Marie like so many bags of sand. 'You will burn in hell for what you've done to these innocent children, Teiskaret.'

The Maliseet frowned and wagged a finger at her. 'It is never wise to joke about such serious matters, Madame. One of my old believers might think you are casting a witch's spell. As for the good Christians among us, we know full well that the priests will give us absolution for all our sins this very day.'

'Somehow I don't think so.' Marie pointed downward with both her thumbs. 'Your Black Robe will be waiting for you when you get to hell.'

'There are plenty more Black Robes where ours came from, Madame Campagna.' Teiskaret managed to cut a majestic figure despite his short stature and tall hat. 'As for Father Antoine, I warned him that devils would be waiting for him down there in that M'ikmaq cave!'

The two smaller children were clinging to her now. Marie gathered them in her arms. Dropping to his knees, Philippe leveled the nymph at the warrior who held Marie by the hair. 'Let go my mother, you earless dog!'

'You have brought brave sons into the world, Madame Campagna!' Teiskaret threw back his massive shoulders and laughed to see such sport. 'This one would have made a splendid warrior one day.'

Should I tell him I am carrying a child? Will that make him value me more and spare me from what is surely to come? Or will it only anger him that his captive bears the seed of another man?

'You grow big with child, Madame.' The Maliseet nodded wisely as if he did indeed know what she was thinking. He fingered the fresh scalp hanging from his belt. 'In more ways than one, your husband must have been a great warrior despite his gray hairs.'

'Sagamo of the Maliseet, tell this savage of yours to take his filthy hands off my mother!' The cocking of the nymph's flintlock punctuated Philippe's words. 'Do it now, else I swear by Jesus Christ our Savior that I will blow you straight to hell!'

Teiskaret raised an eyebrow and nodded to the warrior. As Marie pitched forward onto her chin, the Maliseet chief snatched the pistol with a swipe of his hand that knocked Philippe sprawling. He sniffed at the barrel and priming pan in mock surprise. 'Madame, I see you keep your witch-pistol loaded and ready to fire! A good French mother should not entrust her nameless child with so dangerous a weapon.'

'My name is Philippe!' The youth rose to his feet and dusted himself off, the gravity of his bearing a match for that of the Maliseet chief. 'I slew one of your savages with my father's pistol, O Sagamo of the Maliseet. If I had lived but a fortnight more, I should have been thirteen years old.'

Teiskaret kept his features stern as he uncocked the nymph and held her out by the barrel. 'Then you will need this witch-pistol, Philippe. I shall warn my men that a true warrior guards his mother with his life.'

The boy looked from the extended pistol to Teiskaret as though expecting a trick of some kind. 'Attend me well, Philippe Campagna: indeed you guard your mother with your life. Her scalp and those of your brothers are forfeit if you have need to fire the pistol.'

The youth nodded and squared his thin shoulders as he took hold of the weapon. A moment later, he turned deathly pale and again sighted the nymph upon Teiskaret. Marie reached out for him with both hands. 'No, Philippe!'

'My prize is fairly taken.' With a lordly air, the Maliseet went on securing the grizzled scalp to his belt. 'Teiskaret is a mighty warrior. It brings your father great honor to be numbered among his slain.'

The Maliseet turned away, barking at his men as he strode off. Philippe lowered the nymph till her pitcher pointed at the ground. Convulsive sobs wracked the stripling's frame.

Behind them, the trading post had become an inferno. The green oak had finally caught fire; it blazed straight up through the slab-board roof into a heavy pall of smoke. The Maliseet swarmed about like ants, torching the piles of timber and the supplies stored on the beach.

A final blow for Marie was the pillar of fire she saw rising high upon the brow of the island. A warrior came running down the path from the half-built house, brandishing the brass cylinder of Luigi Campagna's great telescope. He dashed the instrument to pieces against the butt of an oak tree, delighting in the shattering of glass and rending of metal.

The raiders methodically destroyed everything shaped by the hand of man. They plundered only what they valued most, for they came from afar and must travel lightly: just a few bales of twist tobacco, several small kegs of brandy and gunpowder, a half dozen muskets and a gunny sack crammed with glass beads.

They heaped their prisoners on the beach with the other spoils. The huge, battle-scarred warrior rigged a hemp cord round all their necks and gathered up both ends in one hand like reins. His other hand wielded a tomahawk ready to do slaughter at the slightest provocation. A vicious tug on the coffle leash dropped Marie onto her knees.

Philippe reached down for her. 'Mother, pray give me your leave to kill this earless brute!'

Marie scrambled to her feet. 'No, Philippe! We must bide our time till God sends us a sign!'

'We are forsaken, Mother!' The boy sighted the nymph square at the chest of the leering warrior. 'These devils intend to murder us anyway. Why not get our suffering over with?'

'No, Philippe, put the gun down! We know not what God wills! That He has spared our lives for the moment gives us some cause to hope!'

'I hope only for revenge!' Yet Philippe nodded his head and brought the nymph to rest against his thigh. 'You are right, Mother; it does not suffice our vengeance to kill Old No Ears. We must wait for a chance to kill many of these brutes!'

Down to the canoes two Maliseet led another prisoner, cold and wet. Marie gasped a little scream at seeing a familiar face, but the wide gray eyes coldly passed her over, dashing her slim hope. The youth let himself be shoved along till he stood before the war chief. 'Ho! Ho! Ho! Son of Waksitanou!'

The young M'ikmaq only stared back at the Maliseet chieftain.

'Tell me, nameless boy, where did you abandon Father Antoine and my three warriors?'

'It pleased me to leave the Black Robe buried alive in the Place of Dreaming.' The youth's fluent French took Marie by surprise. 'I remembered his face last night in the light of the torches. It was he who lured my uncle onto a sea-canoe never to return. My only regret is that I did not cut the priest's throat and lift his scalp before taking my leave of him.'

253

'He-he, nameless boy, you are not the first who has thought to kill the Black Robe.' Arms akimbo, Teiskaret bobbed his head disdainfully. 'Their scalps decorate the crosses of the churches Father Antoine builds among the Maliseet villages. He is formidable when driven to anger.'

'Be that as it may, he dies a poor death for a holy man. He pleaded with me to find a way out if I could and bring you back to find him. When last I saw him, he was down on his knees crying out to his god to save him from evil spirits.'

Teiskaret folded his massive arms across his chest as if conceding that the ways of priests passed all understanding. 'Did not the Black Robe give you a message for me, son of Waksitanou?'

'Only some words concerning this Frenchwoman whose husband you slew, Sagamo. The priest bade me tell you not to harm her, that she must be taken to Quebec. His Black Robe brethren will generously reward you for your trouble.'

'He! He! You Black Robes do not ask much of your friends, do you?' The Maliseet's powerful voice cast echoes off the surrounding cliffs as though he were indeed speaking to the buried priest and not his messenger. 'You are as good as dead, Father Antoine, and Quebec is many days canoe journey from here. It is not Teiskaret's pleasure to voyage so far.'

'A Black Robe awaits you at the first portage, great Teiskaret.' The young M'ikmaq's gray eyes flickered to Philippe. 'You are to give the Frenchwoman and her children into his keeping.'

'Father Gabriel is a young fool.' The Maliseet mimed a priest at his prayers complete with supplicating hands and pious upturned expression. 'Without Father Antoine, he is good for nothing! He will not know what to do with our prisoner.'

The youth looked again to Philippe as if to say he had done all he could. 'Great Teiskaret will do what pleases him.'

The Maliseet grunted as if to affirm that this was indeed so. 'My three warriors, what can you tell me of them, nameless boy?'

'Only that their death-dance disturbs Father Antoine's prayers.' Marie saw that the young M'ikmaq was trembling with cold and pain. A great swelling bruise stood out upon his shoulder and neck. 'Your Maliseet wail like women!'

'Father Antoine lacks Christian tolerance. He should know that a Maliseet warrior must meet his fate in his own way.' Yet Teiskaret sighed as if something deeply troubled him. 'Tell me, nameless boy, why do they wail like women?'

The youth curled his lip at the chieftain. 'Because, great Teiskaret, it shames them to die at the hands of a woman.'

The Maliseet took hold of the youth's arms. 'What is this?'

'Our father warned us of her.' The youth pointed to the young Maliseet sporting the plume of golden hair. 'Evil spirit or not, it was the Dread Maiden who trapped us inside the Place of Dreaming. We heard our sentry call out, for his pain at her hands was great indeed.'

'It is not given a woman to slay warriors!' Teiskaret gave a fearsome shake of his head. 'Unless like my wife Deborah, she possesses magic.'

'My father often told us stories of the Dread Maidens.' The M'ikmaq youth clearly delighted in the Maliseet's discomfiture. 'Since a child this one delved in all manner of magic. She killed men with her bare hands. It was she who sealed us in the cave.'

Teiskaret regarded the boy suspiciously. 'If that is so, how did you escape to come tell me so fine a tale?'

'I squeezed through a small crack in the cavern entrance before she brought the whole cliff down upon it, but she caught and bound me, saying that she only spared my life for the sake of my Father.'

The Maliseet war chief laughed his disdain. 'Would even a nameless boy let a timid woman treat him so?'

Marie could not let it pass. 'Teiskaret, my hand-maiden slew two of your warriors over the body of my dying husband.'

'Silence, Frenchwoman! Here is the scalp of the man who slew Teiskaret's warriors!'

The youth's eyes followed the Maliseet's gesture to the dangling scalps. 'This First Stranger was my father's friend. He will mourn him.'

Marie could not be still. 'Son of Waksitanou, you betrayed them both! Why?'

'For the sake of my people, Frenchwoman.' The boy drew himself up in pale imitation of his father. 'Like the rats who came to us in your ships, your people defile this land. The M'ikmaq and Maliseet must learn to trust each other. We must come together and drive out both the English and the French. Even foolish old men like my father will someday understand I speak words of truth.'

Teiskaret drew his scalping knife from his belt of many beads. ''Tis too late for your father to repent his sins, Son of Waksitanou. The Black Robes will have him burning in hell by now.'

Shock and anger flashed in the young M'ikmaq's eyes. He drew back to stare at the second fresh scalp that Teiskaret drew out from his belt with the curved blade. 'Maliseet dog, you promised me my father's life if I guided you here! The Black Robes are my witness.'

'Nameless boy, you misunderstood the words of Teiskaret. I promised the Black Robes to bring them back the scalp of Waksitanou, not to spare him.'

'Did you also kill my brother?' In the chill voice, Marie felt the boy's acceptance that he also was about to die.

'He escaped us by a hair. No matter, it will better please me to give him a place on my belt when there's a man's name to go with it. Your mother we spared so that her wailing might drive your ancestors to gnash their teeth at what her son has done this day.'

Without warning lunged the son of Waksitanou, but the Maliseet stood ready. His knife plunged hilt-deep into the youth's heaving breast. A twist of the powerful wrist spouted a fountain of dark blood. The blazing light had not yet faded from the gray eyes when Teiskaret lifted up the young head by its long hair. 'Do not scream so, Madame. His father should have schooled him with Jesuits.'

The Maliseet burned their dead among the splintered casks and timbers heaped upon the dock. Teiskaret had some trouble explaining to his warriors that such unchristian rites were necessary. He promised them a special mass to assuage divine anger.

Teiskaret left Waksitanou's son sprawled on the beach under a cloud of flies. He strutted down to the canoes, conscious of Marie's eyes upon him. 'There is no honor in taking the scalp of an unnamed boy. Let the redcoats blame the M'ikmaq for this night of blood. Father Antoine would have been well pleased to have it so.'

The raiders stowed as much booty as they dared in six war-canoes. The seventh, paddled by the war chief and his earless henchman, bore the four captives. Flames licked skyward as the Maliseet canoed from the cove into the gentle swells of Mahonne Bay.

The Campagna's sat in stunned silence staring back at their burning home till they rounded the western tip of Sanctuary Island and turned north. Suddenly Jean pointed at the horizon. '*L'Espérance!*'

'I am in your debt, Madame. Behold, your true vision has saved us!' The Maliseet exulted even as he quickened the stroke of his paddle at sight of the white

257

sails. 'Teiskaret shall pass beyond the salt water before the sea-canoe of many cannon reaches the island.'

Marie could only grieve for what might have been. *If only the brigantine had returned a day earlier. These few Maliseet would not dare attack so many. Luigi Campagna, Nicole and Hugo would still be alive. Isaac Ben Yussuf, you will be standing on the quarterdeck by now, my husband's spyglass pressed to your eye, trying to make sense of the smoke rising over the island! Your dreams have all been shattered, Herr Doctor. Jacques Sabot, you will be cracking on more sail. There is no need. You shall find only ashes and mutilated corpses. Little Guillaume! Dear God, forgive me! I didn't think to look for him!*

Marie felt the dark forested mainland looming closer. Once under that canopy of trees, she knew that the Maliseet would be safe from all possible pursuit. The wilderness would swallow them up.

The raiders joined their war chief in chanting a wild and jubilant song. Marie felt the throbbing beat capture the stroke of their paddles. The canoes streaked across the water, leaving Sanctuary Island far behind. *L'Espérance* slowly receded into the gathering mists despite a fair breeze from the southwest. The widow's despair grew overwhelming as she rocked to and fro among her dozing stepchildren. She put her hand upon the ring hanging round her neck.

You follow my counsel well, Marie of Hohenstaufen.

You mock me, Sire! Marie did not know whether to feel grateful for the Emperor's return or not. *Did you not see how I caused my only friends and faithful servants to be slain?*

I understand your pain, Princess Mine. We also once had a friend and faithful servant.

Surely you did not stand by and let him die for you?

Worse, we betrayed him!

You are a King and Emperor! How could you betray a faithful friend and servant?

Papal agents suborned so many around our throne that we grew suspicious of all, even those who most loved us. Seeing this, the priests set us a clever trap. They deceived us with false evidence that our right hand, Chancellor Piero, had turned traitor.

What happened to Piero?

We imprisoned him — ah, if only that had been all we did! But no, we gave him over to our minions to question. In their zeal they put him to the torture and plucked out his eyes. Even so, they failed to obtain the confession we commanded of them. And so it came to pass that being led in chains down a stairwell, he tore loose from his guards and hurtled his skull against a wall of stone.

Oh Sire, what wretched despair that poor man must have known before he died!

No greater than that of his king and emperor when we discovered the truth. Much better we had lost both arms than lose our only faithful friend! Our vengeance felled many a priest and agent of the Curia. Doubtless many innocents fell victim to our rage as well, but the killing did not bring our Piero back.

You still mourn for him, Sire!

Yea, we still search for him but find him not. O Princess Mine, now comes the time of your greatest test. Do not lose your way as we have done!

The ululating song went on till the canoes reached the nearest point of land. The party passed from sight of the brigantine into the quiet northwestern arm of the Bay. A majestic moose idled out of the forest and stood on a headland to watch them pass. Old No Ears, as Philippe had dubbed him, raised his paddle in salutation.

The sun had climbed overhead when they reached the mouth of a small river screened by a tidal *barrachois*. Holding a musket at the ready, Teiskaret signaled the second canoe forward. The others waited a safe distance from shore while a young Maliseet in the lead canoe warbled the call of some wild bird.

Almost immediately the notes echoed back across the water. Two figures emerged from the trees and greeted the raiding party with hand signals. Teiskaret dipped his paddle in the water and led his little flotilla through the sandbars.

The two Maliseet met the canoes on the inner beach of the *barrachois*. Teiskaret conversed briefly with them in Maliseet using many fierce gestures. The scouts gleefully examined the booty and prisoners, but great was their grief and rage at the loss of several warriors.

Old No Ears quickly enacted the story of the raid on the island, often turning a baleful eye on Philippe. So much did he inflame the passions of the young scouts that Teiskaret had to calm them down. Marie could not make out his words, but his theatrical gestures seemed to be praising the boy's courage.

The widow of Luigi Campagna still felt no hunger when Old No Ears finally brought them something to eat. Having gone without eating since the previous day, the children were ravenous, but they spat out the Maliseet food. His mouth crammed full, Teiskaret came to stand over his prisoners. 'Madame, you must eat. This *sagamite* is very good for voyaging fast and light.'

'Monsieur, it smells to me like the fish in it is rotten!'

'That is what makes it good to eat, Madame!' The Maliseet treated her to a gap-toothed grin. 'Think of it as being much like the rotted milk of animals. You French call it *la fromage*, do you not? Eat, Frenchwoman, you will need all your strength before this voyage is through.'

Marie gagged on the *sagamite,* but her protruding abdomen and persistent backache kept her eating. Another life than her own was in her keeping. Yet her efforts went for naught; she vomited over the side of the canoe, much to Old No Ears' amusement.

Teiskaret took advantage of the brief halt to remove his footwear. The rest of the Maliseet had already done so. He groaned with pleasure and wriggled his sore toes in the cold running water, but he did not forsake the French instruments of torture. The war chief slung the boots by their leather thongs around his neck, for they were gifts of honor, given to him and his warriors by Father Antoine for raiding deep into enemy territory.

The Maliseet wasted no time over their meal. Soon the two young scouts loped off along either bank of the river to safeguard the main party from ambush. The canoes followed closely, skimming effortlessly across the quiet pools of the lower river, skillfully shooting the narrow rapids that occasionally barred their passage. More moose snorted and bolted away from the river's edge as they moved rapidly north. An osprey swooped low overhead and seized a great fish in its talons. A troupe of otters cavorted on the muddy bank, indifferent to their passing.

Marie's despair grew ever deeper as she became aware of the incredible speed at which the canoes bore her and the children away from Sanctuary Island. She turned and glanced back along the stream unwinding between stands of tall evergreen forest. *My vision is fulfilled. Luigi Campagna and Nicole and Sanctuary Island are gone forever. Waksitanou and Guillaume cruelly murdered as well. We waited for this like lambs helpless to avert our fate.*

The sun was sinking in the west when the raiders reached the headwaters of the river. Graceful stands of hackmatack and pine descended to the edge of a serene lake. Somewhat winded by their long and strenuous trek, the two scouts came aboard the canoes and immediately took up paddles. The Maliseet gave a wild cheer and picked up the pace across the mirror-smooth lake.

The canoes were racing each other now, their tireless crews in high spirits. Even Teiskaret took leave of his dignity and entered into the spirit of the mad dash. Flocks of ducks, coots and geese took wing at their frenzied passage, nor did the pace slacken when the sandy marge of the lake drew near. A loud-chorused cry rang out as the Maliseet drove their canoes aground in a final burst of speed.

Breathless from such novel sensations, Marie looked up through the reeds at hearing the familiar litany of a Latin prayer. She beheld a black-robed figure coming down the grassy knoll to meet them. The dark-haired priest kissed his silver crucifix and held it up to the newcomers with outstretched arms.

Chapter XVIII

PORTAGE

Indian Hill Portage, May 1756

A stiff moccasin nudged Marie awake. She opened her
eyes and stared up unbelieving at white birch trees.
She willed the dawning nightmare to go away, but the
Maliseet encampment persisted around her: the armed
sentry perched on a rock; his naked comrades splashing below him in the lake; the canoes overturned amid
their plundered cargo upon the cobbled beach; the
Black Robe bending over the fur-blanketed bodies of
the sleeping children.

He prays to excess even for a priest, but then, he has
much to pray for: his Jesuit brother ekes out a slow
death even now; the Maliseet buried alive with him;
those other warriors killed slaughtering innocents in the
service of his cross; and last but not least, the hell-bent
souls of these Huguenot children.

Full of aches, Marie struggled up from the hard
ground. Oblivious of the priest, the three orphans went
on sleeping the sleep of the dead: Philippe with the
nymph clutched to his chest; Jean with dirty tears
crusted upon his cheek; little Louis with a thumb
tucked in the corner of his mouth.

Hunkering on his heels, Old No Ears looked up from his breakfast of *sagamite* and grinned malevolently at the widow of Luigi Campagna. Fresh rivulets of water still veined the Maliseet's war paint and beaded his pewter crucifix, the cold-shrunken genitals spilling from the flat, hard muscles of his belly. She caught herself recoiling upon the Jesuit for protection. *I am shameless! This papist priest will not even speak to me. In any case, far better to be violated and torn apart by these savages than to seek help from my husband's true murderers.*

The Jesuit rose to his feet and signaled with an upraised crucifix. The Maliseet expectantly thronged about the priest as he prepared to say mass. Old No Ears put on his breechclout and tethered his captives to a large birch tree. Drawing his fingers suggestively across his forehead, the warrior hurried off to join his kneeling comrades.

Marie withdrew herself into a clump of alders. It was the first privacy afforded her since surrendering the trading post. Her ripening body had somehow endured the whole night without bursting. The tenor strains of the Roman mass rising to the treetops, she deposited her body waste in the cool deep moss.

One by one, she awakened the children and helped them prepare themselves for the day to come. One by one, the Maliseet came forward to receive communion. Each in turn tasted the chaliced Blood of Christ with reverential awe and received His bannock-crusted Body on their penitential tongues.

When the mass had run its course, Teiskaret led the Black Robe to the birch tree and solemnly handed over his captives' leash.

'My children, I am Father Gabriel. Let me lift this heavy yoke from your necks.' The mild benevolence of that priestly gaze affronted Marie. Nevertheless, she lowered her head so that he might free her neck from the noose. 'First, my daughter, you must swear before God not to attempt escape.'

The widow of Luigi Campagna took a backward step. 'I cannot do that, Jesuit.'

Almost playfully, Teiskaret cuffed her with an open hand. 'Heretic woman, you had best learn to address our priest with respect!'

Philippe sprang up and leveled the nymph at the war chief. 'Strike my mother one more time, Maliseet dog, and I swear by Jean Calvin I will kill you.'

Too quick for the eye to follow, Teiskaret knocked the boy sprawling. 'I should like to take this braveheart for my own son, Father Gabriel.'

Philippe gathered himself up. 'Sagamo, this Black Robe is no priest of ours!'

The Maliseet would have struck the boy again if Father Gabriel had not intervened. 'The child speaks the truth, Great Teiskaret. Madame Campagna, I cannot intercede with God for your souls unless you give me your free consent.'

Marie's ears were still ringing. 'My dead husband was a Huguenot, Monsieur. He would not wish me to swear papist oaths.'

'My child, we all pray to the same Savior, our Lord Jesus Christ. You have but to swear on his name not to attempt escape, and I shall remove this cord from your neck.'

'To do so would be the end of all our hope, Monsieur Priest.'

'What hope is there for heretics?' The Jesuit heaved a heavy sigh and tugged at their leash. Shouldering his pack, he led them up the meadowy hill without a backward glance, his long cassock dragging stiffly behind him through the grass and shrubbery.

The portage began. Maliseet warriors dogtrotted past the priest and his prisoners up the long incline. Each precariously balanced an enormous shoulder-pack of Luigi

Campagna's trade goods. An equal burden was carried on their backs slung from a tumpline. Limping along, Marie guessed that each porter was carrying almost twice his own weight. Even Philippe had to admire such prodigious strength and endurance.

The Jesuit called a halt on the crest of the hill. Marie sank gratefully into the tall grass beside the worn trail. The anxious children gathered around her. Jean shaded his eyes against the rising sun. 'Now we should be able to get some idea where they are taking us.'

The hilltop offered a splendid vista in either direction along their canoe route. To the south lay the narrow lake they had ascended. It gleamed somber and steel-gray under shape-shifting clouds. Mahonne Bay and Sanctuary Island lay beyond that dim horizon. Was that a smudge of smoke still hanging there? Marie reached for her ring only to find its chain gone from round her neck. Even so, she fancied she could see *L'Espérance* riding at anchor in the cove. Heads bowed, Jacques Sabot and the crew sifted through the ashes, sorting out the mutilated bodies. Kneeling on a makeshift carpet, the yarmulke-capped Jew prayed for his friend.

It goes best to put all that behind you, Princess Mine. It profits us little in this world to grieve over spilt wine.

Easy for you to say, Sire. You are no longer of this world.

True, but our spirit still lingers here. So much we left undone. Our reign had nearly finished before we so much as suspected the existence of this New World! Feuding with Popes and Guelphs over bits and pieces of Italy, we overlooked a boundless empire till too late.

Is building empires all Your Majesty can think of? Did your sojourn here in this world teach you so little wisdom?

As for that, Princess Mine, be warned that the Hohenstaufen are all born to Empire, whether they will it or no.

I care nothing for such things. Marie dissolved into tears for the first time since the ordeal began. *I only wish we were all still living on the island.*

The Emperor sighed again, and Marie felt warmth envelop her. *We have felt what you are feeling, my dear. All our children were hunted down and slain or left to rot in prison. That is why you and the seed you carry are so precious to us.*

Your dynasty has fallen on evil times indeed, Sire, if all your hopes depend on me. See you not that I am being led to my doom by this foul priest?

Certainly the beggar stinks to high heaven. One of my many failures on this earth was trying to persuade the clergy that cleanliness is next to godliness. They gloried in their filth. They even condemned us for bathing, citing it as proof we had become no better than an infidel. We would have done better to humor them!

I refused to humor this Jesuit, Sire!

Think again, Princess Mine. It behooves you to cultivate yon green Jesuit for the sake of these children.

For the sake of the Chosen Seed, I think you mean!

That goes without saying, Marie of Hohenstaufen. Try to make the best of it. This too will end, we promise you.

Marie's eyelids squeezed shut on the tears. She looked north where an expanse of water shimmered under a rising sun. She wondered aloud if it might be an arm of the sea. 'This is Panuke Lake, my child. It is a canoe route much used by the savages. It will carry us down to the Saint Croix and the tides of La Baie Francoise.'

So we are being taken far from here. At least that augurs well for our survival. Surely they would not drag us so far just to kill us.

Marie's unsettled mind alighted on the message sent by Father Antoine to Teiskaret. *This Father Gabriel must suspect who we are. Perhaps the full truth is not yet clear to him, but he is a Jesuit. As deadly in his way as*

Nicole was in hers. Yes, I know what you are, priest. You cannot fool me with your pious prayers.

The Maliseet piled their booty near the prisoners and trotted back down the hill for more. Old No Ears and another battle-scarred warrior stood guard over the *pose* with ready muskets. The *portageurs* soon reappeared in the distance, bearing canoes over their heads. Others followed with more of the trading post spoils. Teiskaret himself brought up the rear, bearing a load on his back and shoulders that dwarfed all those gone before.

The Jesuit stood up and aroused his drowsing captives with a flick of his wrist. At the head of the line, Philippe bared his teeth like a cur not trained to the leash. Heads lolling from side to side with fatigue, his brothers fell into step behind him.

The broad descending trail made for easy passage, but Marie's knees began to ache painfully. It seemed to her their journey would never end. Finally, her stomach growled so loudly that the young priest turned round and stared at her. 'Have they not fed you, my child?'

'They offered us *sagamite,* but it makes us ill.'

'*Sagamite* is an acquired taste, Madame. Perhaps I can provide something more to your liking. I left instruction here that a meal was to be prepared for the arrival of Father Antoine.' The Jesuit led them to the edge of the lake where stood a guardian cross. Not far from its base burned a smokeless and untended fire of glowing coals. Marie sank to her knees before it. The children formed up in a half-circle as if to protect her from the papist symbol.

The priest genuflected before the cross before taking up a stick and raking back the smoldering embers from the center of the rock-bound fire-pit. His efforts soon uncovered a blackened copper kettle. Unlidded, a heavenly aroma wafted from the pot. The priest poked a skewered hunk of meat at Marie. 'What is this?'

'Beaver tail, my child.' The Jesuit burned his fingers raising a morsel to his lips as though to reassure Marie that she and the children were not to be poisoned. 'It's delicious and quite tender when slowly stewed under an open fire. You are unlikely to be offered better fare on this journey. Come, help yourself or go hungry.'

Marie gingerly accepted the burnt offering. 'How is it that a papist priest devours meat on a Friday?'

'You are mistaken on both counts, my child.' The Black Robe kept busy forking out more morsels for the children. 'Today is Tuesday.'

'It can't be Tuesday!' Marie reluctantly tasted her bit of beaver tail. 'Your savages attacked us yesterday, and the previous day was a Wednesday. I distinctly remember my husband saying so.'

'It is only four years since the English adopted the reformed calendar of our blessed Pope Gregory XIII, Madame Campagna. Inasmuch as your sinful husband was a lackey of that benighted nation, I expect your household still adhered to the old Julian calendar.'

'Give me none of your Jesuitry, Monsieur Priest. Today is Friday.' And with that categorical pronouncement, Marie set herself to chewing the beaver tail. She found it as rich and delicious as it smelled, but she could not leave the hungry priest to eat his meal in peace. 'You are committing the papist sin of eating meat on fish day.'

'Even if it were Friday, my child, our bishop has decreed that beaver is a fish.'

'What utter nonsense is that! Beaver is no more a fish than I am!'

Father Gabriel seemed to enjoy the sophistry. 'This beast I am eating swims as does a fish, my child; therefore for the holy purposes of true religion, it is a fish!'

'This beast I am speaking to argues as does a Jesuit, Monsieur; therefore for the foul purposes of papistry it must be a true Jesuit!' Marie bit her tongue too late.

'So, Madame, I take it you are familiar with the Society of Jesus.'

'Black Robe, the Societé's infamy spreads every-where.' Marie chose her words carefully lest this Jesuit entrap her just as Father Jerome had so often done.

'It is our mission to save erring souls and to drive back the forces of Satan from this world.' Father Gabriel rearranged the flesh-colored cap that covered all but a fringe of his black skull-clinging hair. Marie did not reply, fearing her words might betray her. The Jesuit sadly shook his head and turned to the children. 'So then, my sons, I see you find the beaver tails agreeable. Unfortunately, I've no more to give you.'

Louis and Jean both looked hungry still. Without lowering the nymph, Philippe passed most of his por-tion to his brothers. 'Black Robe, was it you who brought these savages here to kill my father?'

'Your father was an outlaw, my son.' The priest made a condemnatory gesture with long black-nailed fingers. 'He was proscribed for fleeing France and exposing his children's tender souls to the risk of eter-nal damnation.'

'Answer my question, Monsieur Jesuit.' Philippe waved the nymph at the priest. 'Did you bring these Indians here to kill my father?'

'Madame, this child of yours has the makings of a good Jesuit!'

'He has posed you a fair question, has he not, Monsieur?'

'Madame, I do not answer to the accusations of a child steeped in heresy.' The Jesuit drew himself up commandingly. 'Better you give thanks to God that Holy Church now may be able to save your children from eternal perdition.'

'What of little Guillaume's salvation? Your savages nailed the child of our handmaid to just such a pagan cross as this one you worship.'

'Madame, I have it on good authority from these Maliseet that it was your own hardheartedness that slew the child.' The Jesuit conferred the sign of the cross upon Marie. 'I shall pray that your soul does not tarry overlong in Purgatory for committing so heinous a sin.'

'Black Robe, God is my witness that I slew the child to save him from a horrible torture!'

'The Holy Father himself is not empowered to spare us the agony of death.' The Jesuit began trickling rosary beads through his fingers as though to ward off evil. 'You have committed murder in the eyes of God, my child; your soul needs the intercession of God's priest lest you burn forever in hell.'

'Certainly you are quick enough to offer these Maliseet forgiveness.' The widow of Luigi Campagna spoke with spirit, but deep inside, she felt herself slowly sinking under an immense and dreadful guilt.

'I pray that the child Guillaume is now safe in purgatory.' Sensing Marie's doubt, the Jesuit rose to the full height of his religious enthusiasm. 'No doubt his original sin has been much expiated by his earthly suffering. I deem the souls of these miserable Maliseet to be in much greater need of my priestly offices. They try to be good Catholics, but they do not yet fully understand Christian charity.'

Father Gabriel turned aside from Marie, greeting Teiskaret with a silent benediction. The perspiring war chief lowered his triple pack and returned the Jesuit's salutation. He spared only a passing glance for the prisoners before signaling his warriors to embark upon Lake Panuke.

The raiders carefully restowed their plunder in the fragile birch bark canoes. As before, their perfect teamwork filled Marie with amazement. It was still morning, but already the heavily encumbered Maliseet had portaged more than a league overland.

Father Gabriel led his cue of prisoners to a curious pile of brush and uncovered a huge canoe. Marie and the children soon found themselves seated on its midthwart between the Jesuit and Old No Ears. Three other warriors completed their crew. 'Today, we travel all the way to Pesiquid.' The priest took up a paddle. 'Prepare yourselves accordingly, my children.'

'Pesiquid? Hah, you daren't go to Pesiquid!' Jean expressed himself with boyish certainty. 'The British keep a fort there to guard the back door to Halifax.'

'Fear not, my children. God willing, we shall slip past the English under cover of night.' The priest spoke as though he were taking fellow conspirators into his confidence.

'And where do we go from there, Father Gabriel?' The calculatingly pleasant tone of Jean's voice betrayed his underlying intent.

The priest cocked his head at the boy. 'My son, it would be folly to attempt escape. These Maliseet would track you down. As you have seen, my influence over them is tenuous at best. When their blood is up, there's no telling what they might do to you and your mother.'

Marie sought to distract the priest lest he further bind them with fear. ' 'This Lake Panuke looks more like a great man-made canal than a natural waterway.'

'According to the M'ikmaq, it was dug by their pagan god Glooscap.' Father Gabriel treated his captive to a condescending smile. 'His friend, Beaver, wished to float some giant logs across the land to build a great dam, so the god obliged by gouging out this straight and narrow lake with his tomahawk.'

'Did he really?' Little Louis gazed with wondering eyes from the priest to the smooth rock cliffs bounding the lake.

'Of course not, silly!' Jean turned a patronizing gaze upon his little brother. 'The story is rather crude, I think, but otherwise it puts me in mind of the Greek myths.'

The Jesuit gave the boy an approving accolade with his crucifix. 'Madame, your second son has the making of a scholar.'

It shocked Marie how quickly a kind of normality had insinuated itself among them. Barely a day had passed since this priest and these Indians massacred their loved ones, but already their canoe journey had taken on aspects of an excursion. Breathing deeply, she drew back into her innermost being.

Only Philippe remained totally immune to the Jesuit's natural charm. Not for an instant did he relent from loathing his captors. Marie felt herself drawing strength from his hate. She summoned her own memories of the massacre, and they recharged her defenses by flooding back. Disgruntled by her sudden coldness, Father Gabriel ceased fingering his rosary. 'My children, let us make the best of it. I understand your pain, but God brings us together for some good purpose.'

'Do not blame God for your crimes, Monsieur Priest.' Marie's outrage raced outward at the Jesuit. 'What dreadful blasphemy you utter!'

'Take care, Madame!' Stung by her fury the priest visibly recoiled. 'Where we go, many are not so forgiving of heretics as I am.'

'You dare speak of forgiving us, Black Robe?' Marie's anger became a thing of wonder. 'It is for these children to forgive you the murder of their father!'

'Madame, discretion on your part is well advised for the sake of these children.' The priest rallied courageously, but he was quickly learning that logical thought was a poor shield against the fury of a woman. 'Do not tempt the Lord thy God.'

'Do not quote His Scriptures to me, Black Robe! I know your devilish kind too well for that.'

Father Gabriel seemed to marvel as he looked back at Marie. 'Indeed, my child, it is plain to me that your mind was shaped by the Society of Jesus.'

'A Jesuitical woman?' It frightened Marie that he guessed so much, but she was still quite beside herself with anger. 'Would that not be a paradox?'

'Just so!' Father Gabriel bolted upright, his eyes gleaming. 'I'm convinced of it now! Judging by your accent, you attended one of the seminaries we oversee for young Huguenot women in Languedoc. The cursed Huguenots abducted you from us, didn't they?'

'No one abducted me till yesterday, Jesuit. I accompanied my husband to this wilderness of my own free will. We hoped to make a home here for our children. But for you and your savages, we would have done so!'

'Huguenots may not immigrate to the colonies.' Father Gabriel waxed indignant at the mere thought of what Marie and her husband had in mind to do. 'His Most Christian Majesty has heeded our General's advice that heresy should not be allowed to spread here.'

'My husband was a British subject, Monsieur. You and these savages murdered him inside British territory.'

'You must understand, my child: c'est la petite guerre. God wills that we drive the English heretics into the sea.'

'You delude yourself.' Marie remembered the words of Luigi Campagna. 'The English are too many. In the end, it is they who shall drive the French into the sea.'

'No, Madame, God wills His work be done in mysterious ways. These simple Indian children will help us drive out the English. We shall return L'Acadie to France and true religion.'

Teiskaret turned his canoe aside and awaited them. Marie was startled to notice her gold ring on the Maliseet's little finger. Her hand sprang to the empty place between her breasts. 'Father Gabriel, we make too good time. We must take care not to reach the River of the Cross too soon.'

'Why?' The priest precariously rose to his feet and stretched. 'Gilles Leblanc keeps watch for us, does he not?'

'So will the English.' Teiskaret did not bother to hide his amused contempt for the Jesuit. 'Their shadow spreads over the land since the Acadians have left us. It will be best to slip down the river under cover of night.'

'No, my son. Speed is our best ally. We must reach the English fort before nightfall. Let us trust in God to see us through.'

'Then you best pray for us, Father. I trust in God well enough, but not this Acadian renegade of yours.'

Satisfied, Teiskaret paddled once more into the lead, a stiff boot flapping against his shoulder blade. The dutiful priest took up his rosary. 'He did wrong to take your ring, my child.'

'Teiskaret is an ignorant savage, is he not?' A great bitterness welled up in Marie. 'He tries to be a good Catholic, so we must make allowances for him.'

'You mock me, Madame. Nevertheless, I shall return good for evil as our lord and Savior taught us.'

The Jesuit resumed mumbling his *Hail Marys*. The three boys drowsed fitfully. The rocky shoreline slid past while the sun blazed down upon them. Marie felt her cheeks burning and her lips blistering from the glare reflected off the water. A pair of white-headed eagles soared overhead. From time to time, monstrous fish leaped clear of the lake.

Not even for *sagamite* did motion cease. This time Marie forced herself to consume the foul mixture. Nauseous, she cupped her hands together and scooped lake water into her parched throat. The buckskin pouch swung down from its hiding place inside her gown. Old No Ears snatched it up and broke the leather thong.

'It's only amethyst. It's a gift to my unborn baby.' Marie tried to snatch the pouch away from the

Maliseet. He regarded her quizzically as though measuring her desire for the object. Then he laughed and tossed the unopened pouch into the lake.

The sun had begun to sink in the west before they came to the far end of Lake Panuke. Here it poured over its natural brim and began its short river journey to the Bassin des Mines. Teiskaret stepped ashore long enough to urinate in a lordly manner. Blushing furiously on the end of her leash, Marie sought partial privacy behind a bush. Father Gabriel politely directed his attention elsewhere.

Then they were off again, the river current sweeping them onward. Even the refreshed children grew infected with the expectancy of the Maliseet. They had traveled only a short time when the two scouts broke from cover on the riverbank.

Teiskaret called a halt and paddled forward. After conversing briefly with the scouts, he turned and gave a signal. Old No Ears deftly plucked the nymph from Philippe's limp fingers. Marie felt the cold steel of his scalping knife scrape across her throat. Her two youngest stepsons uttered small stifled cries as Father Gabriel pulled them close. 'Calm yourselves, my children, lest your mother die. English redcoats guard the old Acadian bridge.'

Chapter XIX

RENEGADE

Saint Croix River, May 1756

Marie lay forever with her face pressed against the frame of the canoe. Old No Ears neither relented his hold upon her hair nor eased the knife from her throat. Small snufflings were all that reassured her that Luigi Campagna's sons still lived. Countless 'Our Fathers' poured over her as Father Gabriel whispered his rosary. Once, she imagined that she heard someone cry out in pain.

Marie focused all her attention on the canoe's cedar lining. Its incorruptible fragrance comforted her. The outside world ceased to matter as she followed the warp of each thin strake through the seamless woof of it all. She fancied she inhabited a warm sanctuary crafted specially for her by some fatherly person. Water splashed into the canoe and baptized her, sealing her safe from all the evil lurking outside.

Her thought passed from her stolen ring to the painting of the Hohenstaufen coronation. *Tell me, Sire, what manner of woman was Yolande?*

Too ambitious and ruthless and intelligent to be truly beautiful as you are, Princess Mine, but it was that inner lust for power that drove us to madly desire her. We both knew from the first time we met that we were meant for each other.

Meant for each other, Sire? You condescended to share your destiny with a mere woman? I should have thought that impossible for such a man as you!

You have such a Hohenstaufen way of putting things, Princess Mine. Let us simply say that each of us was a mirror of destiny for the other. Our fates are star-crossed forever.

Star-crossed forever, Sire? May I take it that Yolande is with you even now?

She never leaves us, Princess Mine.

Am I not her descendant as well as yours? Why does she not join with you in chastising me?

Because we judge you are not yet ready for so painful an epiphany, Princess Mine.

Marie thought it over before replying. *Or is it Yolande who is not yet ready, Sire? Perhaps she holds back because her own experience of this world is not yet complete.*

The Emperor also took an unusually long time to respond as if reluctant to follow Marie's line of reasoning. *In a manner of speaking, I think you understand the situation only too well, Marie of Hohenstaufen.*

But if that be true for her, Sire, it follows that it must also be true for you. You are not yet through with living in this world, are you?

Methinks yon breast beating Jesuit is right, Princess Mine. His brethren have indeed shaped your mind in their own image.

Sire, I but follow your favorite maxim: "To defeat one's enemy, one must tread in his footsteps."

We don't recall ever saying any such thing! The Pope's minions delighted in putting evil words in our mouth, you know.

Old No Ears yanked Marie upright before releasing her. She blinked painfully at him through sunspots and detected a certain grudging respect in his painted leer.

Tell me, Sire: How shall I go about defeating my present enemy?

You have already quoted us on that subject, Princess Mine. Walk in this savage's footsteps. The way he man-handles women reminds us of an Ethiop eunuch we once owned. Yolande had him subjected to a second opera-tion, more drastic than the first. You'll soon enough take the measure of this brute.

Jean and Louis clung to Marie's waist as they shot forth upon the rushing stream. The canoe swerved around a sharp bend to a narrows spanned by a bridge. A huge raven circled overhead on widespread wings.

A small blockhouse flying the Union Jack guarded the bridge, but Marie saw no sign of red-coated sentries. Instead, a figure clad in buckskins and homespun occu-pied the span. He beckoned to them with an upraised crossbow before vanishing from view.

Old No Ears cried out eerily as the canoe slid under the low bridge. Marie felt warm wetness splash her hand, but her dazzled eyes saw nothing in the shadows. The Maliseet paddlers grasped at overhanging bushes and drew themselves close to the riverbank. A sack like object fell heavily into the canoe, nearly capsizing it. Another dead weight landed on top of the first as little Louis whimpered and cringed against her.

Then they drifted clear of the bridge.

Amid budding willows dappled by sunlight, Marie stared into unblinking blue eyes. The young man's scalped head lay at her feet, blood dripping from his mouth and nose. Marie felt something oozing along her fingers, heard the Jesuit's muttered prayer take on a more fervent tone.

Another body dropped into place behind her. No dead weight this, for she felt the man move to balance the precarious equilibrium of the heavily laden canoe. A blended aroma of twist tobacco and rawhide assailed her nostrils.

They began drifting down on the swift-flowing stream. Old No Ears took up his paddle and resumed his short powerful strokes. Jean looked up at her through his tears. 'Mamam, your hand is bleeding!'

'Certes, boy, it is only the blood of these redcoats.' Fingers of steel gripped her forearm and thrust her hand into the clear cold water. Her mind reeling, she watched the red smear dissolve and swirl away. Philippe reared up between her knees and glared angrily over her shoulder. 'Stand easy, young man. I'm not about to hurt your mother.'

The banks of the rushing stream were no longer clothed with trees and bushes. Its mud flats grew more naked with each twist and turn. Great flocks of shorebirds milled and swirled about them. Flies buzzed over the uniformed bodies. Marie fought to keep from fainting amid the heat and the stench of death. *I must overcome this. I must somehow endure all this for the sake of these children.*

As if applauding her resolution, the unborn child began to kick. *Especially for your sake, my beloved. Whatever you are and whatever you will become, I can do no less than see you safely into this world. In spite of all our enemies may do, I will see you through this!*

Marie looked to the praying Jesuit. *Pious wretch, do you expect to absolve your conscience so easily? Do you think God will credit your soul for trembling over these bodies with affected pity? Do you expect Him to forgive you for sanctioning the slaughter of innocents in His name? How you deceive yourself, Black Robe!*

Father Gabriel looked up at her and reflexively signed the cross. Their eyes met for an instant. Then the priest's inner agony burst its bonds and deluged her before she wrenched loose of him. *So, I see what you are clearly now! You envy rather than pity this dead soldier boy. You wish to be canonized among the martyrs of New France. Brébeuf and Lalement and Gabriel! That is what you pray for, isn't it? But I tell you this, Black Robe: evil such as yours is the blackest evil of all. Divine grace will forever elude you, I fear.*

Teiskaret turned aside his slim canoe. His dark eyes flashed. He had cast off the French boots. Marie sensed the tremendous power building in him. *You have learned how to suck life from death, you murderer. I pray this war will prove your undoing!*

Teiskaret barked in the Maliseet tongue at the stranger seated behind her. Marie could feel his hatred, could almost see the lines of conflict stabbing outward from him. Then the Maliseet paddled on, his piercing eyes scanning the mud dunes that cradled the brown indolent river. The body behind her stirred and leaned forward. 'We've come far enough from the bridge, *mes amis*. Let us be rid of this carrion.'

Grinning horribly, Old No Ears laid up his paddle and reached behind him. He tugged the topmost redcoat into an upright position, but the stiffening corpse refused to disembark gracefully. The exertions of the huge warrior threatened to capsize the canoe. 'You best help him, Madame.' The stranger spoke French with an accent Marie had never heard before. 'Quickly, take up the wretch by his belt and cast him over the side.'

Marie could not will her limbs to move. It was left to Philippe to topple the redcoat into the river. The dead body drifted after them till at last it sank beneath the lapping waves.

Philippe proved unable to dislodge the second, heavier body from the bottom of the canoe. Old No Ears grinned wickedly to see the boy slip and slide in the pooling blood. Marie looked into the dark mustached face of the chevroned soldier and witnessed his final terror. Little Louis cried out and hid his eyes in her skirt. Gagging, she reached out and heaved with all her might. Crucifix upraised, Father Gabriel consigned yet another soul to the muddy deep.

Old No Ears daintily dipped a finger in the pool of blood. Grave of countenance, he glossed long red streaks across his hideous features. Then he handed back the nymph to Philippe as though he were making a bounteous gift.

'Let us hurry, my good friends.' The faceless stranger dipped a paddle in the river for the first time. 'We need to reach Pesiquid before the turning of the tide.'

Marie welcomed the cool breeze sweeping in off the sea. Yet the Saint Croix still meandered on aimlessly through the mud flats. On the nearest bank, a shaggy black she-bear reared up and stared at them. Two cubs romped playfully in a tidal pool. Old No Ears raised his paddle high and saluted them without missing a stroke.

The sun began to sink upon the horizon. The current no longer hurried them onward. The river became still and swollen as though dammed into a lake. Far ahead, Marie caught a glimpse of Teiskaret's canoe leading the way, his paddle flashing in the slanting sunlight.

'The tide is turning! We must paddle faster!' The man behind Marie added his determined stroke. His hot breath violated her neck, but she could not force herself to look at him. Who was he? Surely no true Frenchman would speak his mother tongue in so bizarre a fashion. All that she could sense of him was that he hated the British and was a familiar of violent death.

The lightened canoe was fairly racing now. Yet another bend unfolded before them. The stranger pointed with his paddle at a low ridge of grassy dunes. 'There it is, Madame! Behold the dike my people built to hold back the tide.'

The stranger behind me is the Acadian Isaac Ben Yussuf told us of! The notorious renegade who vengefully murders the British!

Teiskaret's canoe had disappeared, but Marie's eye caught something that glittered and undulated across the water. She thought for a moment that some monstrous serpent was rushing headlong toward them. Again the Acadian raised his paddle and pointed. 'The tidal bore! Hurry, my friends! Paddle ashore!'

The big canoe turned and hurtled straight to the muddy bank. The others followed close behind like so many ducklings. They had scarcely grounded when a wall of water surged over them, tumbling the Maliseet about as they struggled to haul their precious cargoes and prisoners ashore. Last to make it onto dry land was the soaked and miserable Jesuit, still holding grimly to the long tether despite his evident fear of drowning.

Already the water had risen the height of a tall man, but the sea kept pushing the river back upon itself. What Marie had seen of tidal power on the coasts of Normandy paled by comparison. Father Gabriel scuffed at the thick mud caking his laced boots. 'How bad is it, my son?'

'Not bad at all, Reverend Father.' The Acadian wiped water and mud from the black metal of his crossbow as though thoroughly enjoying their situation. 'We have only to portage across the neck of this oxbow. Teiskaret will be waiting for us just over the way.'

Old No Ears roundly vented his disgust at the prospect of making yet another portage. But soon he and his brethren were trotting up the muddy slope bearing their enormous packs. The Acadian took up a vigil on the highest dune, and the Jesuit knelt to pray.

Marie ministered to the needs of the children. They had not eaten or relieved their bodies since morning. Indeed, little Louis' failure to control his bladder added much to his distress. His stepmother had to leave him go wet and disgraced. *He suffers more than his brothers. I fear he will never be the same little boy again.*

283

The children refused to consume the loathsome *sagamite*. Marie interrupted the priest's devotions to demand better sustenance for the children. 'The Lord will provide our needs in His own good time, Madame.'

Philippe swore under his breath as Father Gabriel began leading them across the mud dunes. Yet they had not gone far before the Jesuit's faith was vindicated. As the pitiful little procession wended its way past the Acadian, he drew forth a leather pouch from his pack and offered it to Marie. 'Madame, a little something for your children.'

Marie drew back, expecting nothing good from the Acadian renegade. 'What is this?'

'Dried caribou meat, Madame. A *coureur de bois* can subsist on it for months if need be. My own children liked it better than molasses taffy.'

Marie thanked the man, although his inquiring brown eyes made her even more keenly aware of her pathetic condition. She had neither bathed nor combed her hair for days. She became suddenly aware that she still wore her long-suffering riding gown, that her half boots were caked with drying mud.

She blushed and would have quickly passed on, but the Jesuit reined the little procession to a halt. 'Monsieur Leblanc, I pray you forgive my rudeness in not introducing you to this lady. I fear I am a bit distracted today. As we speak, Father Antoine is suffering martyrdom for the greater glory of God.'

The Acadian doffed his loose wool toque and bowed his head respectfully. 'God's will be done, Father.'

'Monsieur Gilles Leblanc, allow me to present Madame Campagna, widow of the late Luigi Campagna.' The priest spoke as though performing introductions in some Parisian salon. *Here we all stand surrounded by murdering savages in the wilderness, yet this Jesuit expects me to enact some civilized charade with this awful man who murders the English for the sport of it!*

'Bonjour, Madame.'

Marie's laughter had a high wailing pitch to it.

'Pray pardon her incivility, my son, but she is still in a state of mourning. These savage Maliseet slew Madame Campagna's husband a bare two days ago.'

'Nay, Black Robe, these Maliseet were but your marionettes!' Again Marie broke into a peal of high-pitched laughter. 'God in heaven knows who is responsible for the cowardly murder of my husband!'

Her hysterical outburst caused the young Jesuit to give ground. The Acadian only shrugged and shouldered his crossbow. 'Father Gabriel, I fear this woman's mind is close to coming unhinged. What will you do with her?'

'Fortunately, my duty in this matter is clear, Monsieur Leblanc. Madame Campagna is a runaway heretic. She remains intransigent despite my constant prayers and admonitions. So she must be handed over to the proper ecclesiastical authorities. I've more hope for her children once they've been removed from her influence. Given some care by good Catholics, their souls may yet be capable of Christian salvation.'

'It's a long way to your order's nearest mission, Father.'

'Alas, too true!' The priest permitted himself a knowing smile. 'Perhaps you yourself are looking for a wife, my son. This young widow would be a formidable challenge to take on, but you have always been a man who likes challenges.'

'Father Gabriel, I'm already a married man, as you know!'

'True, my son, but the British have carried away your wife and children. Who knows what evil has befallen them? We can only pray they are already mercifully gone from this world.'

'They still live, Father Gabriel! That much I do know!'

'Perhaps so, but they are as good as dead for you, Gilles Leblanc.' Father Gabriel held up his cross to the

285

last rays of the sun. 'In its mercy, Holy Church may make special dispensation for those who uphold the True Faith in spite of having lost so much. Who knows? It might be the will of God that you should lead this woman to salvation.'

'I already have my vocation, Father.' The Acadian settled his metal crossbow on his hip. 'So long as one English breathes Acadian air, I shall need none other.'

The priest crossed himself. 'What has got into you, Gilles Leblanc? You Acadians were never a vindictive people! Vengeance belongs to God alone. Your soul stands in mortal danger till you free it of such a burden. Be sure you perform the penance I set you this very night. Helping save this woman's soul may be the redemption you seek.'

'Certes, Father, I fear my soul must remain in danger for the nonce. I am quite impenitent. As for taking another wife, Claudine is the only woman I shall ever know in this world. I do not doubt I shall find her keeping watch for me, should I ever make it to the Gates of Heaven.'

'Celibacy is only worthy of a priest, my son! By denying your true nature, you give aid and comfort to God's enemies. They multiply like rabbits in this New Land!'

'Enough, father, speak no more to me of this!' Gilles Leblanc turned away from the priest and strode on along the grassy dune.

Angry and humiliated, Marie watched the Acadian's long springing strides leave them far behind. Tall and slender with narrow shoulders for a man, he looked harmless enough, but she remembered the terror etched in the face of the dead redcoat. *Even that black toque pulled low over his long black hair bespeaks his murderous resolve. He carries his crossbow like a scythe. That tomahawk in his belt has scalped how many men? I daresay he would be capable of slaying even women and children.*

Father Gabriel followed her gaze and thoughts. 'You could do far worse, Madame. Many a sinful woman has achieved salvation here on Earth and in Heaven through judicious choice of a husband. Gilles Leblanc is a God-fearing Catholic.'

'A proper butcher, don't you mean? Black Robe, I'm perfectly certain that the Societé's plans for me do not include giving me away in marriage.'

'Why do you fear me so, my child?' The priest lapsed into the pastoral tone he reserved for the faithful. 'My sole concern is to see you and these children of God delivered from evil!'

'Into the hands of your brethren waiting at Quebec, Father?' Marie could not forbear laughing deep in her throat. 'For us, that will hardly constitute deliverance from evil.'

'I shall urge merciful consideration of your case, Madame.' The cleric slung the leash over his shoulder. 'You have only to help us understand why you were domiciled on that accursed island.'

'Surely you can answer such questions far better than I, Monsieur Priest.'

'My child, that is not the sort of answer your holy inquisitors will be seeking.' The Jesuit was at pains to be long-suffering. 'You must tell us all you know of your husband's heretical conspiracy against Holy Church.'

'Luigi Campagna was a devout Huguenot, Black Robe.' Marie felt her heart congealing inside her. 'What more is there to tell? I was only his wife. I was never privy to his affairs.'

'What can you tell us of this serving maid of yours?'

'Nicole? What of her?'

'She was no ordinary handmaiden, my child.'

'It's too bad your savages murdered her, Black Robe. You, yourself, could have put these questions to her.'

'God's will be done, I am only a poor scholastic!'

The priest turned and started walking down the grassy slope. 'It seems you give me no choice but to deliver you into the keeping of my wiser brethren. There are those among them who know well how to deal with heretics.'

Philippe leveled the nymph at the Jesuit's back, but the long rawhide leash jerked the boy into motion. Jean and Louis fell into step behind their brother, gnawing hungrily at their strips of dried caribou as they half-trotted along.

The sea had drowned the river and was swamping the surrounding marshland as the priest led his coffle to the canoes. The Maliseet had already reloaded them in certain expectation that the rising tide would float them off. Teiskaret and Leblanc were gesticulating at each other again. Called to give judgment between them, Father Gabriel listened attentively, cupping his beardless chin in the palm of his right hand.

Finally, the priest uttered a single word and returned to his waiting charges. 'It has been decided, Madame. Teiskaret would have us camp here till tomorrow night, but the Acadian rightly insists that we pass the British fort before the alarm is sounded.'

'Black Robe, these children can journey no further this day.'

'Do not let Teiskaret hear you say that, my child. It could be the death of them. Soon we shall be behind French lines. Indeed, our forces may be much nearer than we know. Perhaps Fort Beauséjour has already been recaptured. His Most Christian Majesty has sent us a *marechal de camp*. The noble Marquis de Montcalm is a brilliant general by all accounts. By the grace of God, where we stand shall soon again be French soil.'

'Father Gabriel, these children need to rest!'

'Then let them rest, Madame.' The priest turned his back to her and opened his breviary. 'We must bide here several hours till the tide begins to ebb.'

Marie bedded the boys down as best she could on the flattened marsh grass. They fell asleep instantly, their faces pinched and haggard. Marie sat down among them and began to massage her aching foot. The insistent pain made her despair of getting any rest, but the drone of the praying Jesuit soon lulled her to sleep.

It was quite dark when she awakened to a stranger's touch. She started upright and glanced quickly round at the children, their small forms barely visible in the dim starlight. Once again, the odor of twist tobacco and rawhide filled her nostrils. 'Time to go, Madame Campagna.'

'You frightened me, Monsieur!' Marie looked quickly where the Jesuit lay sleeping.

'You may rest easy, Madame. I shall keep you from coming to harm.'

Remembering what kind of man the Acadian was, Marie was hardly reassured. She recoiled from his touch upon her shoulder. 'And why should you care about us, Monsieur?'

'For the sake of Claudine and our children, Madame. If I help you, perhaps God will listen to my prayers for them.'

'Then find us more food, Monsieur! These growing boys are starving.'

'Madame, today we have only fresh *sagamite*. We shall fare better tomorrow in the land of the Acadians.'

The renegade vanished into the darkness. Father Gabriel sat up wearily and crossed himself. Marie began rousing the children. Still tired and hungry, they ate the soft cakes of *sagamite* flung to them by Old No Ears.

The old warrior pushed off the canoe and leapt among them, his war paint luminous in the darkness. He cared nothing for Marie's concern at being separated from the two oldest children. Paddles dipped into water that rippled like quicksilver, and the ghostly canoes drifted down the resurgent Saint Croix till it joined a broader river.

Soon the lights of Fort Edward glimmered ahead. Inside the silhouetted blockhouse she knew redcoats were standing guard, British soldiers who would gladly rescue them. *Perhaps these children can still be saved. I shall cry out as we pass! I shall fling myself into the water!*

Old No Ears' painted face grinned back at them. He pivoted on the forward thwart and brought the stink of his bear grease close.

'I ask your pardon, my children.' Little Louis uttered a muffled squeak as the Jesuit's hands enfolded him. Old No Ears gathered her tangled hair, thrusting her head roughly against the gunwale. Again the scalping knife grazed her throat.

Chapter XX

LEVIATHAN

Bassin des Mines, May 1756

Marie's hopes flickered out along with the lights of Fort Edward. Grim despair seized upon her and would not let go throughout that long night in the big canoe. Even after Philippe and Jean were restored to her keeping, she displayed a fortitude more feigned than real. Little Louis awakened screaming from a nightmare. Jean would not let go her hand after that. Even Philippe snuggled against her for warmth. Sea spray rinsed their dirty faces clean as the canoes dashed headlong through the breaking tidal waves.

Cold and powerful, the Bassin des Mines pulled them onward.

Dawn found the canoes hugging the coastline. Gray fatigue lined the faces of the Maliseet warriors, but Teiskaret drove them on. Marie gazed upon the fire-blackened chimneys of the ruined Acadian homesteads scattered along the shore. Amid scenes of such total desolation, she caught herself looking to the war chief to keep her and Luigi Campagna's children safe.

The morning unveiled itself fine and clear. A calm sea bore the fragile birch barks safely onward. Even so, little Louis lost his portion of *sagamite* to the undulating motion of the swells. His anxious stepmother persuaded him to drink some water from Father Gabriel's canteen. She tore a strip of cloth from her underclothing and wiped up his vomit. In vain did she try to wash away the horror stamped upon the tiny pinched face.

Jean pointed out the red sandstone cliffs of Glooscap's Mountain, radiant and majestic in the morning sunshine. Marie thought it a fit abode for the god and his boon companions. *Did they welcome the first Acadians here? Waksitanou said that they did. Do they sit up there brooding over these emptied meadows? How could they? The Black Robes would have chased them away by now, exorcised them like evil spirits from their land. It must be so, or else they would have prevented ships flying the Union Jack from anchoring here. Redcoats herding thousands of miserable Acadians on board those miserable prison hulks! Ah, shameless creature that I am! What I would give if one such ship were here now to block our way!*

Teiskaret grudgingly relied on Gilles Leblanc to guide the raiding party along the tidal shore. It was as though he tacitly acknowledged that the Acadian rightfully belonged in this land. Marie kept vigil for the solitary renegade as he ranged far ahead in his small covered canoe. *Which one of these ruined farms did Claudine and your children call home? What must it feel like to be welcomed by the ghosts of your departed people?*

Dawn had broken when the Acadian finally led the Maliseet canoes into the marshy estuary of a small stream. The tide was going out, but a hidden *aboiteau* held the water of the small creek dammed behind a skillfully engineered system of locks. Soon the Maliseet canoes floated securely upon a fine freshwater pond.

Tireless, Teiskaret posted Old No Ears as sentry and went off with his young scouts to reconnoiter. The other Maliseet flung themselves down and slept where they fell. Father Gabriel and his prisoners were willing enough to follow their example, but Gilles Leblanc insisted on taking them to an Acadian homestead nestled among poplar trees.

Half the roof had been burned away. The hearthroom gave signs of occupation by wild animals, and a carved wooden crucifix had been thrown down from the mantle. The priest shouldered the fallen cross like Christ on the road to Calvary. Restoring it to its rightful place, he knelt before it and began to pray. Marie looked up and was struck by the ecstasy of the wooden Christ figure. She hastily signed the cross, noticed by none save the cold-faced Gilles Leblanc.

'I inherited this farm from Lucien Deschamps, uncle to my mother.' The Acadian looked to Marie as if expecting her alone to understand. 'None of my family shall come this way again, so feel free to make yourselves as comfortable as you can.'

Father Gabriel chivalrously billeted his prisoners in the privacy of the one surviving bedchamber. The whitewashed room had been stripped bare except for a tattered picture of the Madonna with Child and some old bedding. Marie and the three boys collapsed on the musty pallets of straw. Hearing the priest bolt the door, she got up and set about exercising her cramped foot.

Thus she came upon a pair of white-ribboned wedding shoes lying abandoned in a heap of rubble. Remembering the Acadian's words, she picked them up and hid them inside her shawl. In doing so, she groped for the ring that should have been hanging round her neck. *These must be Claudine's wedding shoes. Now she and her children are scattered God knows where. Was ever there such a crime as this expelling of an entire people?*

Crimes more heinous beyond counting, Marie of Hohenstaufen. In truth, these English grow soft; else they would not have left these papist peasants so much as their lives. They destroyed the Irish root and branch, just as they are about to destroy the M'ikmaq.

There are still many Irish left in Ireland, Sire.

Through no charity of the English, Princess Mine, we assure you.

We Huguenots fare no better at the hands of our French-Catholic compatriots, Sire.

Indeed, the French have done still worse in their time. During our reign, whole towns and villages were raped and plundered from the face of Southern France by French knights wearing the Cross. Crusaders licensed by the Church to burn alive thousands of women and children. Even many good Catholics were slain, lest any Cathars escape. "Burn them all, for God will know his own" was their battle cry. From beyond the Alps we did pity the poor wretches.

You were Holy Roman Emperor, Aire! How could you stand by and let this happen?

As some Frenchman aptly put it, a Holy Roman Emperor is neither holy, Roman nor an emperor. In vain did we remonstrate with young Louis Capet to halt the massacre. He was not the sharpest pike in the stack, you understand, but a good enough king of France for all that.

You refer to good Saint Louis, I presume, Sire.

Hah! The popes canonized him not for his saintly ways but for leading his people to die by the thousands on two futile Crusades!

Saint Louis was a great crusader! Louis IX of France had been a favorite hero of Marie's childhood. Father Jerome had even allowed her to read a book about the mediaeval French king. *Too bad you did not profit by his example, Sire!*

Princess Mine, did the Jesuits not teach you that it was Saint Louis who countenanced the creation of the Catholic Inquisition? He concurred after the fact with our own guardian, Pope Innocent III, in proclaiming the

Albigensian crusade, and it was he who sanctioned our nemesis, Pope Gregory IX, in ordaining the Holy Office to perpetuate the massacre of innocents over most of southern France. The fires he permitted to be set burned so-called heretics in Carcassone and Toulouse for centuries.

Why are you telling me all this, Sire?

The voice would not speak, but Marie felt a wind race howling through the corridors of her mind. *That is how my mother died in Toulouse, isn't it?*

Yes, Marie, your mother was one of the last to burn there. How we wish it had been possible to spare her that ordeal!

Your Majesty wishes to be excused for standing by and watching the Bearer of your Chosen Seed writhe and scream amid the flames?

Princess Mine, all that remains to us is to whisper in her ear as we do in yours. The Emperor kept his voice impassive, but Marie felt anguish welling within him. *Believe me, Princess Mine: your mother died as a Hohenstaufen should.*

No doubt you speak from experience of such things. Did Your Majesty also burn heretics alive?

We loathed treason, and what is heresy but a kind of treason to the established system of things? Even while we protected Saracens and Jews from the priests, we roasted heretics on spits lest Christendom be overturned by them. We considered it our duty to do so. After all, our people believed that the Christian God had chosen us his ruler over all the world.

But you did not believe that, Sire! I didn't think you even believed in God! What ironic justice that you are made to watch your seed be punished for your godless sins!

Indeed, Princess Mine! What more exquisite torment could there be than to witness your seed hunted down and exterminated? Dante the Guelf makes us inhabit the Tenth Circle of his Hell, but that would be a kinder fate than to wander this miserable earth as we do now. Dante was wrong: there is no Hell or Heaven where the evil and good can be brought to justice.

You are worse than a heretic, Sire! How can you claim to be a Christian monarch if you don't believe in Heaven and Hell?

We believe only what we discover by scientific investigation to be the truth, Princess Mine.

Yes, Sire, I read about some of your so-called experiments in Father Jerome's books. You once sealed a condemned man in a lead-lined cask and left him to die for want of air.

Actually, it was deemed a rather brilliant experiment at the time. We even had learned doctors on hand to bear witness to what transpired when we opened the cask. They found no evidence of an escaping spirit, Princess Mine: only a stinking corpse. We realized then and there that the notion of an immortal soul was nothing more than a priestly fiction.

Your experiment was flawed, Sire! Your presence here proves as much!

Then you must believe in us, Marie of Hohenstaufen. That is at least something! Do not despair. We shall come to you soon again.

Wait, Your Majesty, you haven't yet told me what to do!

My dear, you are as much a Jesuit at heart as is this priest! And you are a woman to boot. You'll know what to do without being told.

Sire, one small piece of advice is all I ask!

Look to the Acadian renegade, Marie of Hohenstaufen.

Marie and the children were disturbed by a priestly knock on the door. 'My children, the sun is setting. Rise up quickly now, for we must be gone from here as soon as darkness falls!'

Little Louis lay folded in her arms. Philippe and Jean clung to one another in a tight embrace. Marie roused them and opened the door to find a cheerful fire blazing on the hearth. The priest was turning something on a spit. The aroma made her head spin. 'The Acadian found this smoked pork hidden in his cold cellar. Come quickly and eat, my children, lest Teiskaret drag us forth from this place with nothing but the fragrance for our pains.'

The prisoners greedily consumed strips of the fat bacon till none remained. The Acadian also obliged them to drink spruce beer, vouching for its medicinal qualities. He even gave Marie a few small cabbages found moldering in the cold cellar. Thinking of Isaac Ben Yussuf, she gathered them up in her shawl with the wedding-shoes. *Someday we shall come back here. We shall forget Sanctuary Island with its blood and ghosts ever existed. Someday I will take this bountiful place to be a home for my children. The soul of this man has been lost beyond hope, but Claudine and his children shall not have lived here in vain if I can help it.*

Teiskaret cut short the widow's pleasant reverie. He spoke harshly to the Acadian in Maliseet while the Jesuit girded the cord tightly round his black-garbed loins. 'A British ship has entered the Bassin. We must be gone from here quickly, mes amis.'

The Bassin des Mines was barely high enough to float off the heavily laden canoes as they issued through the locks of the *aboiteau*. The Jesuit and his coffle waded out through the surf while two young Maliseet held the canoe steady. The priest stumbled; his cassock became so waterlogged that he had to be lifted into the big canoe.

Although offended by the Acadian's rude stare, Marie stayed relatively dry by drawing up her skirts to her thighs. From the corner of her eye, she watched him sign a last farewell to his ancestral home. Then he drew forth a strange covered canoe from its hiding place beside the *aboiteau* and paddled away to the north along the coast of the Bassin.

297

Quickly warming to the task at hand, the half-naked Maliseet dipped their paddles and took up again the short swift rhythm of the wilderness voyageur. Their passengers huddled wretchedly under furs on the middle thwarts of the canoe. A ghostly half-moon lighted their misty way from headland to headland.

From time to time, Marie sighted Gilles Leblanc scouting far ahead, driving through whitecaps with his strange double-bladed paddle. *What is he to me and these children? Why does he fill me with both fear and hope?*

Teiskaret led the raiding party along the western shore of the Bassin. Naked to the waist like his men, eyes and teeth flashing amid the tossing spray, the war chief had entered his proper element. Marie observed him making some strange gesture of obeisance to the brooding mass of Glooscap's Mountain. *Are his ancestral gods the same as those of the M'ikmaq? Could it be that in this one special place their power endures. Certainly the Black Robe fumbles his beads and stammers his Latin as though warding off evil spirits here.*

The two younger boys became caught up in the mad dash of the Maliseet across the inland sea. Hunched alone sat their elder brother, keeping the nymph's powder dry inside his jacket, listening to Old No Ear's eerie chant. *Like Frederick Hohenstaufen, Philippe seeks to understand his enemies. In his mind, he stalks the Maliseet, hoping to take vengeance upon them and escape. He cannot see that we have passed beyond hope of deliverance.*

They canoed onward till the moon and stars faded. The cliffs of Glooscap's mountain loomed as a dark shadow high above. The tide had poured its waters into the Bassin till it seemed it could hold no more. Seabirds were calling, and Marie once heard the hoot of an owl.

The canoes rushed on till the Acadian came gliding out of the morning mist. 'The British ship guards the strait. We must wait here for a chance to slip past.'

The gentle cliffs and beaches of red sandstone receded. In their place, steep bluffs of dark forbidding rock reared up over beaches of boulders and cobblestones. The waves also grew more restive as they entered the narrow strait connecting the Bassin des Mines with the Sea of Glooscap. Marie sensed that they were now in a place never truly at rest, a place where the very elements were locked forever in an unrelenting struggle.

It was all the Maliseet could do to bring their fragile craft safely to shore. The Jesuit and his prisoners struggled through the breakers, slipping on seaweed, straining to lift themselves over jagged boulders and driftlogs. The entire party, complete with canoes and baggage, took refuge behind giant fragments of cliff lying on the beach.

The rising sun was burning off the morning mist. Marie watched a sloop-rigged vessel emerge from the banks of fog shrouding the opposite shore. Under a billowing jib sail, the small warship rode the ebbing tide, its blue-capped lookout visible high in the rigging, red ensign whipping at the backstay in the fresh breeze. *What if they should spot us? Should I call out and bring them down upon us?*

The ship vanished in the fog. Marie felt an odd relief. She harbored a growing hostility for the British. Was it not they who had expelled the Acadians, a people who only wished to live in peace and speak their strange French? If not for the English ambitions of world empire, she and Luigi Campagna might have lived out their lives in peace. Waksitanou and his son would still be alive. Nicole would still share her cottage with Hugo and Guillaume. She felt in her heart that these British did not belong in this land.

It was all she could do to shake off such perverse reasoning. *It was not the English who murdered Luigi Campagna. Even now, they would rescue us if they could!*

A waterfall cascaded down the face of the bluff. Scrawny bushes struggled here and there against the ranging tides of the Sea that Glooscap made. Fine glistening spray from the waterfall coated the surrounding rock with moss and lichens. Marie let the jetting plumes of water tempt her. *Do the M'ikmaq goddesses still come here to bathe? Of course, you silly goose, all goddesses love to bathe!*

In vain did Father Gabriel ignore Marie's interruption of his *matins*. 'Hear me, Black Robe: I want to wash our clothes!'

'Madame, we are in the wilderness and we have no change of clothes for you or these children.' The resolute Jesuit resumed his attitude of contrition. 'You had best learn to curb your penchant for cleanliness.'

Marie set her arms akimbo upon her hips. 'Cleanliness is next to godliness, Black Robe, or do you not heed Sacred Scripture?'

'Holy Church does not deem a vow of cleanliness essential, Madame. It's no part of my vow of poverty and perpetual penance to bathe!'

'More's the pity, Monsieur Priest! That is why you stink worse than a farrow of swine.'

Father Gabriel drew his coarse black habit about his thin shoulders indignantly. 'In the manner of the sainted Thomas à Beckett, I have worn a shirt of horsehair since the day of my ordination as a priest of God.'

'To what end, Black Robe?'

'To mortify my body and soul, of course! To purge all thought of sin from my being.'

'That's utterly appalling, Monsieur! You must be covered in lice and sores!'

'A small enough burden to bear for the love of God. I assure you, Madame, that my bodily discomfort pales in comparison with the anguish you heap upon my soul.'

Marie shifted to a wheedling tack. 'Father Gabriel, there's a pool at the base of the waterfall just beyond these rocks. We can wash our clothes and lay them out to dry in the sun while these savages of yours are all sleeping.'

'Madame, go and bathe your iniquitous body, I pray you!'

'Bien, Monsieur! Relieve us of these nooses so we can remove our clothing. '

'I will gladly do so, but first you must swear by our Lord and Savior not to attempt escape or to harm yourselves.'

'Clearly you need not fear us fleeing a spot so surrounded by high cliffs and the sea, Monsieur!'

'You must swear, Madame!'

Realizing it was useless to argue, Marie solemnly placed her right hand across her breast. 'For the duration of our stay in this place, I hereby swear by our Lord and Savior, Jesus Christ, not to attempt to escape. Now, Black Robe, I call upon you to insure our privacy while we are bathing.'

'Madame, no one will disturb you. The Maliseet find the nakedness of white women disgusting.'

The priest's words piqued Marie after spending the last two days fearing the inevitable. 'There are also the Acadian and yourself to consider, Monsieur.'

It was Father Gabriel's turn to be insulted. 'Madame, you sorely try my good nature by making such an insinuation. As for the Acadian, he is off hunting. He shall not disturb you. In any case, you have only to call out and I shall come to your assistance.'

It raised Marie's spirits to be free of the hemp cord. Dragging exhausted children and halting often to rub her foot, the young widow hobbled through the huge stones to the small freshwater basin. Already old enough to stand in manly awe of feminine nudity, Philippe stood guard with his back turned on a rock high above them. She and Jean and Louis undressed and immersed themselves in the chill water. Their pale skin glistening, they showered beneath the waterfall. The morning sunlight slanted there, making the moment idyllic despite the lice she pursued and cracked in each of the children's hair.

They lacked soap, but Marie put to good use a foamy substance she found floating on the surface of the little pond. Their clothes she pounded pitilessly on a flat rock and hung them to dry in the sun. Resuming her wet chemise, she eventually cajoled Philippe into putting down the nymph and joining his brothers in the pool. For a few precious moments the three boys forgot their misfortune and became mere cavorting animals. *How thin their limbs! How utterly defenseless they truly are! I promise you, Luigi Campagna, to see them through this. I promise you: your seed at least will endure.*

And what of this other seed? Bien, Guy de Bouillion, I hope you are pleased how your seed slowly takes over my body. A girl-child, you promised me. And Nicole promised this as well. Certainly a girl-child would be a better thing to bring forth. My dear dead lover, I promise you to make this happen if only God be willing!

In truth, Marie loathed and feared her inexorable body. Already her breasts were growing pendulous. Extra flesh padded her thighs despite her world having ended when the Maliseet came down like a wolf on the fold. *How could my belly so betray me as to continue thickening and swelling after the death of my husband and the loss of my home? Nicole would say that it was feminine nature to endure in spite of everything. But I do not want to endure. I want to sink through the clear waters of this rock pool into oblivion.*

Looking up, Marie spied someone perched high on the brow of Glooscap's Mountain. She froze, a doe startled by her stalker. The Acadian did not attempt concealment; so apparently captivated was he by the tableau set before him. Her throat shaped a cry of alarm, but the sounds would not come. She had no wish to be saved by Father Gabriel.

Instead, she gathered her thick skein of long black hair in both hands and slowly wrung it dry. *A woman must survive as best she can with what God has given her. What little is left to me must be used to good effect. Gilles Leblanc, I shall follow the emperor's advice if I can. Though heavy with another man's child, I am desirable in your eyes, yes? Perhaps I remind you of your Claudine. Bien, Acadian, your lust for me will cost you dear!*

Philippe's pile of dirty clothing still awaited her attention. Kneeling, she began to soak and pound the wool and linen fabrics. And still the Acadian maintained his vigil high above.

Jean came to his stepmother with a thorn festering in the palm of his hand. She caught herself expecting Isaac Ben Yussuf or Nicole to attend to the child. Screwing up her courage, she carefully prised out the splinter with her white even teeth. Calming the anxious child, she sucked the wound with chapped lips. Gathering some salt crystals from the top of a large flat rock, she cleansed the raw flesh and bound it with another strip of linen torn from her chemise. When she looked up, Gilles Leblanc had vanished from the cliff.

A gentle spring breeze dried their clothes. Their bodies warmed by the sun, Marie and her stepsons dozed on the smooth black rock. For the first time she felt them to be her own children despite their lingering memories of a mother supplanted. His head propped on an elbow, little Louis touched her swollen abdomen and smiled down at her. 'I am to have a brother even littler than me?'

'Perhaps it will be a little sister, Louis.'

The boy looked up at her in innocent surprise. 'Girls can be born in our family? Why has it not been tried before?'

As if suddenly uneasy, Philippe rose to his feet. He put on his damp clothes and reprimed the nymph from his father's powder horn. Somehow he had filched it from the canoes. 'Mamam, we must plan our escape. Each passing day it becomes more difficult to do.'

'No, Philippe, Father Gabriel is right.' Jean looked to his stepmother for support. 'If we escape, Teiskaret will hunt us down and kill us for sure.'

'That is the Black Robe's way of frightening us.' Philippe gave a fair impression of Luigi Campagna's fatalistic shrug. 'Better they do kill us than let ourselves become their slaves. We must save Mamam and her unborn child from these papist savages. Either that or die honorably in the attempt!'

Marie felt acute alarm. *How much do these children know? As it once was for me, their only defense against the Societé is ignorance.* 'My sons, we must be careful what we say to the Jesuit. Give him no reason to suspect I am not your natural mother.'

Jean's puzzlement somewhat reassured her. 'Madame, we are all the family of the Huguenot merchant, Luigi Campagna. What more is there to say?'

Philippe snorted at his brother's simplicity. 'That is enough to hang us all!'

His younger brother looked back at him calmly. 'Father Gabriel assures me that the sins of children are never mortal. Even Mamam can hope for forgiveness by the Roman Church.'

'Father Gabriel can join Father Antoine in hell!' Philippe's cold retort forced Marie's unwilling mind back to the entombed Jesuit. She shuddered, fervently wishing him and his Maliseet companions had passed beyond suffering. Not even upon Father Jerome would she have wished such a lingering death.

'Sometimes, one must bend in order not to be broken.' There was a religious fervor to the way Jean bespoke himself. 'We must deceive the Jesuit into thinking that we can be won over to his papist faith.'

'That sounds like a good plan to me!' Despite her enthusiasm, Marie was somewhat taken aback by the child's calculating shrewdness.

'I shall leave deception to you and Jean, Mamam.' Philippe glowered up suspiciously at the cliff high above them. Marie wondered if he also had seen the Acadian.

Their stomachs began growling. Marie unwrapped a shriveled cabbage and divided it among the children. Reluctant to leave the pleasant spot, they put on their clothes and wended their way back toward the Maliseet camp. The Jesuit, breviary in hand, hemp leash slung over his shoulder, met them on the way

With a little smile, the widow of Luigi Campagna bared her neck to him.

A full moon prevented their departure that night. The white sails of the English sloop-of-war ghosted on the treacherous strait that separated Glooscap's Mountain from Chignecto. Thankful for small mercies, Marie settled her children in a nest hollowed from fine gravel among the huge fallen rocks.

Next morning, the sloop had disappeared from the Bassin des Mines. Teiskaret rose from his place near the small driftwood fire and summoned Marie to him. He wore only a breechclout, his broad chest a bronze shield in front of him. 'Madame, I give you back this spoil of war.'

He pulled the signet ring from his finger and held it out to her. Surprised, Marie looked from the priest to the war chief and back again. 'As I promised you, my child, I have persuaded Great Teiskaret to return your family heirloom.'

The Maliseet's bloodstained hands slid the ring upon Marie's middle finger. 'I thank you, Chief Teiskaret. The ring belonged to my father.'

She bit her tongue too late. The Jesuit's eyebrow rose quizzically. 'So, Madame, the portrait is of your mother! I did think it strange that you would carry your own image around with you.'

'She died when I was still a baby.' Marie quelled with a trembling hand the terror welling within her bosom. 'This cameo portrait is all I retain of her.'

'Indeed, the likeness to yourself is remarkable.' The Jesuit thoughtfully rubbed his finely stubbled chin. 'Was she also a Huguenot, my child?'

'To her dying breath, Monsieur!'

'How sad that such beauty burns in fire even as we speak.' The priest smiled sadly and signed the cross. 'My child, it is within your power to redeem your mother from Purgatory.'

Seeking escape from the indefatigable priest, Marie turned to the Maliseet chief. *What does he think of all this? What strange creatures we must seem to him despite his pretension to being a Frenchman. Is there something behind this savage mask he wears that I can use as a weapon?*

Teiskaret met her troubled gaze. 'Madame Campagna, our crossing of this narrow sea will be hard and long. Eat of the fresh meat and see that your children sleep well.'

Old No Ears offered them dripping gouts of raw liver, but Marie and the boys settled for strips of venison roasted over the open fire by Father Gabriel. She avoided his knowing stare as he poked her portion at her. *Have I betrayed vital knowledge to him? What does he mean to do with these children and me?*

The Acadian rejoined the party, carrying yet another deer haunch upon his shoulders. This time he ignored her eyes as if shamed. *You will not look at me because I am clothed now? Nicole said that most women do not fully know what they do to men, but I think we all know well enough what we do. Bien, I can play your game, Acadian. What other remedy do I have?*

Marie led the children to a sheltered place, and the Jesuit was obliged to follow after. She detected a fear in him that she had not seen before. 'Tonight without fail, Madame, we must cross over to Chignecto and pass through the British lines.'

Night had already fallen when the Acadian awakened them. Father Gabriel could be heard praying aloud in a roofless cell set among the fallen rocks. 'Come, it is time to move quickly, Madame. We must cross Minas Channel before the tide begins to ebb.'

Already the tides of Glooscap's Sea were cresting again; already Teiskaret's tiny fleet was bobbing inside a natural breakwater formed where the bluff had spilled into the sea. Marie hiked up her skirts, but the high-spirited war chief snatched her up and deposited her, dry-shod but protesting, in the big canoe. Even the young priest he carried on his shoulders into the waiting arms of his earless henchman. Gilles Leblanc similarly ferried Jean and Louis. Philippe alone insisted upon wading out to the canoe, holding the nymph high above his head.

Then Teiskaret gave a gesture of command, and a score of ashen paddles dipped into the choppy waves. The canoes darted straight out from the bluffs toward a distant coastline invisible in the darkness. Accompanied by a young scout, the Acadian took the lead. Sometimes his tiny craft disappeared beneath the swelling waves.

'We have only a league to go, my children. All shall go well if we reach the farther shore before God empties these waters.' Father Gabriel's tremulous voice pumped new strength through Marie's limbs. *Bien, this Jesuit is not so fearless after all. He craves martyrdom, but these churning waters terrify him. Jean says this is no ordinary place. Through this narrow channel course the greatest tides on earth. Twice a day, the sea rises and falls as much as fifty feet: forever breathing like a great*

307

pair of lungs and holding its breath only for an instant. How powerfully the current must surge here! These birch bark canoes are not made for such places. Rocks and reefs and whirlpools are lurking ahead to pull us down in the dark.

Marie looked over her shoulder, but Glooscap had hidden his Mountain in a veil of fog and night. The cockleshell canoes were plunging through a black universe, and the tempo of the Jesuit's prayer kept on mounting. She heard the rosary beads clicking through his fingers. A spasm of nausea knotted tightly inside her. The unborn child gave a kick that rocked her forward onto her knees. She smelled the children's fear as they clung to her. She thought of calling upon Frederick Hohenstaufen for reassurance but reminded herself that he was only a figment of her overtaxed mind. *Dear God, I pray you: spare our lives. Do this for me, and I promise to pass this way again and plant the seeds I carry in this land.*

She waited for a sign amid the throb of the paddles. A light misting rain was falling, smoothing the waves and spreading an absolute calm about the canoes. Yet the tide was irresistibly swelling, gathering again for a wild career. She felt it pull upon the waters within her, lulling her sea-child, filling her to bursting. She half-imagined a wild mournful sound rippling faintly around them. The tightening clutch of Jean and Louis told her they heard it as well, that the sound must be real. Then it came across the waves again: louder, closer, powerful beyond imagining and born of the sea itself.

'My children, be careful how you pray to God!' The Jesuit half-rose to his feet in the canoe. 'Do not remind Him there are heretics among us!' And then it came, a great black shadow rearing beside the canoe, a gigantic monster geysering straight up from the sea.

Chapter XXI

PURSUED

Chignecto, May 1756

'Satan's Leviathan!' The Jesuit clutched at Marie desperately. 'He has sent it to drag us down to hell!'

The young widow gasped for breath, so tightly did the priest cling to her as the great black shadow pitched upward from the sea. The dense glistening body drenched them with spray. The silent darkness exploded in an orange plume of light and a clap of thunder. She felt a great fin pass over them, saw a huge staring eye and gaping maw, smelled the suffocating stench of it, heard its piercing cry as it plunged deep, almost swamping them with the luminous wave of its passing. *Is this the sign I prayed for?*

The priest loosed his stranglehold upon Marie as Teiskaret swung round his canoe. Old No Ears bailed water furiously from the stern and barked responses to the war chief's questions as the two canoes bumped together. The moon broke from behind a cloud upon angry faces. The telltale smoke of gunpowder drifted over them.

Teiskaret snatched the smoking nymph from Philippe. 'Black Robe, this boy attacked the sea-god!'

In the tight quarters of the canoe, Marie could feel the Jesuit struggling manfully to regain his composure. 'My son, I call upon you to remember you are a baptized Christian. Do you forget there is only one true God? This boy merely shot at a whale.'

The Maliseet grunted, his eyes flashing in the dim phosphorescence. 'Pray that the great one does not come back and make you eat those words, Black Robe. This foolish boy knew the price to be paid if he fired the witch-pistol.'

'Great Teiskaret, this boy fought off a monster of the deep!' The priest warded off the upraised tomahawks with his crucifix. 'He may have saved our lives for aught we know. As a priest of God, I cannot stand by and let him come to grief for performing an act of Christian courage!'

The Maliseet war-chief scented the salt air and peered warily into the gloom before turning away. 'It would seem the Father of the Sea bears us no malice. As for the English, they are not so forgiving. You best pray they did not hear that shot, Black Robe.'

Teiskaret's canoe darted off into the gloom. Much to Marie's relief, Old No Ears and the other warriors put down their tomahawks and resumed paddling. The Jesuit heaved a sigh and crossed himself once more. 'A proper Christian should know better than to travel the sea by night in the company of savages. He is certain to encounter some monster of Satan.'

As for Philippe, he seemed not the least bit grateful to have gotten off so easily. 'Black Robe, your savage stole my pistol!'

'It goes just as well, my son.' Father Gabriel passed in an instant from sincere thanksgiving to his habitual sententiousness. 'This way you shall not be tempted to place all our lives in jeopardy again.'

Neither was Marie inclined to sympathize with her indignant stepson. 'Keep still, Philippe! This is hardly the time to make difficulties. Just be thankful you are still alive.'

A cannon thundered brazenly across the water. The Jesuit resumed rattling his beads. 'The British are signaling each other! They know now we are trying to slip past them in the darkness and fog.'

Marie's flagging spirits revived a little at hearing this. *Is there hope of rescue after all? Isaac Ben Yussuf must be out there, driving on the British to find us. Certainly no one else would care what happens to the family of a dead Huguenot. Even if rescued, I shall be a friendless stepmother of four fatherless children.*

Little Louis watched the Maliseet drive the canoe onward with great soulful eyes. He had passed a tolerable night and day, but Marie remained anxious on his account. 'Are you all right, my little one?'

'Mamam, the whale is a truly magnificent creature, is he not?'

'*Mais oui*, Louis! After us, he is God's most magnificent creature.'

'I think Teiskaret was right to be angry with Philippe. Did he kill the whale, Mamam?'

Marie reasoned that the pistol ball could be no more than a bee sting to such a huge beast. Yet she had distinctly felt a sensitive consciousness recoiling from Philippe's hostile act. It reminded her of Luigi Campagna's pain and incomprehension when the Maliseet struck. 'I believe the whale will live, Little Louis, but I fear he is no longer our good friend.'

The boy nodded sorrowfully. 'I would much rather be him than one of us, Mamam. If God can create such wondrous beings, why did he bother to create hateful creatures like us?'

Mindful of uttering some terrible blasphemy, Marie did not even try to answer Louis' question, but she could not so easily sweep her own mind clear of doubt. *This pathetic priest makes no better sense than these*

Indians. His beliefs explain nothing worth explaining. Like my ancestor, I need to bear witness with my own eyes. I must learn to distinguish what is real from what is illusion. I must discover what role I am truly meant to play in this life.

Thick fog drifted over them. Marie heard angry waves crash against the invisible bluffs. She felt the canoe being pulled relentlessly down the Channel into Glooscap's Sea. She sensed the mounting desperation of the paddlers as they struggled against the monster. *Where on so hostile a shore do they mean to land? We are caught between this whirlpool tide and those rock-bound beaches. What chance have we of surviving such a savage sea as this?*

Some wild beast howled from the invisible shore. Old No Ears echoed the call and swung the canoe to the right. Marie remembered with a sense of relief that the young scout and the Acadian had gone ahead as pathfinders, but the tide was racing now, sweeping up the canoes as it rushed landward.

The wild cry reached them again, faint this time and much too far to their right. The Maliseet drove on till the running sea became a foaming maelstrom, clutching at them, sucking them down into a churning vortex of green water. Rosary beads flowed like spray droplets through the fingers of the Jesuit.

Then without warning, the sea let go of them. The choppy waves vanished, letting the canoes glide close under cliffs that reared up like black icebergs from the drifting fog. The Maliseet scout perched high above them on a rock. Out of the dark swells swept Gilles Leblanc with his double-bladed paddle. 'Hurry yourselves, you Maliseet! The English will spot us for sure if the fog lifts. We must ascend this small stream before we lose the tide.'

Marie espied the scarlet uniform of a British marine floating in the tidal pool. She caught the flash of a pale upturned face. *That boy must have been posted here as sentry. Yet another scalp lost for the sake of the madness that brings us here. This Acadian is as good as his word; soon there will be no redcoats left in this forsaken land!*

A boatswain's whistle shrilled loud and near. Gilles Leblanc whirled about and took off in a flurry of paddle-strokes. 'Make haste, my friends! Many accursed English will soon be upon us!'

In single file, the canoes rode the tidewater into the fastness of Chignecto. Again and again the cannon boomed behind them, but still no redcoats barred their way. Marie caught occasional glimpses of the two young Maliseet scouting far ahead along both banks of the stream. The pent-up river began to flood down, its current slowly turning the tide, but powerful Maliseet muscles drove them on till the breaking of dawn.

The fog lifted, but the sky still hung low and heavy when they reached the first rapids. Teiskaret would not spare the time needed to portage. Elbows locked together, the Maliseet waded waist-deep in white water, threading their canoes one by one through the fang-like rocks. Even Philippe cringed to see his enemies suffer such heavy blows.

Then the lulling paddle-rhythm resumed, driving them onward. Marie took out the ring and strung it once more between her swelling breasts.

These birch bark canoes are simply amazing, Marie of Hohenstaufen! A remarkably swift and pleasant way to travel, is it not?

I could wish myself spared the experience, Sire! You should try it yourself some time!

Ah, Princess Mine, if only we could! Alas, a monarch is obliged to spend most of his waking life in the saddle. We learned to sleep astride a horse before we were twelve years old. You can't begin to imagine how much pain and fatigue we suffered from the need to travel during our lifetime. Piles are an occupational hazard of kingship, you know. That's why we preferred to stay in Italy as much as we could. But just feel how comfortable and cozy you are! In this canoe we could have traveled across Germany in a fortnight. It used to take us months to accomplish such a journey!

Somehow, Sire, I cannot imagine you traveling in a canoe!

I take your point, Princess Mine! A monarch dare not let his people look down upon him. Say what you like against the horse: its rider occupies a commanding position in the eyes of the rabble. Still, we envy yon Acadian his freedom to roam at will.'

Envy him? He is a cold-blooded murderer, Sire. Why did you ever recommend him to me?

You'll find there's more to the man than meets the eye, Princess Mine. Think of him as being somewhat akin to the crossbow he carries. Always cocked and ready to fire. All he needs is a Hohenstaufen to aim him.

Crossbows are dangerous weapons, Sire. The Pope banned their use against Christians, did he not?

His Holiness might just as well have forbidden the tide to come in. What the Church has done for peace over the centuries could be inscribed on the head of a pin.

And what did Your Majesty accomplish? Your grand empire perished soon after your death, did it not?

Yea, Princess Mine, after all those centuries of travail, you carry in your belly all that is left of the Hohenstaufen.

Then nothing remains to us when all is said and done, Sire. This will be just another poor babe crying out in this endless wilderness.

A note of urgency arose in the Emperor's voice. *The Chosen Seed must endure, Princess Mine. There comes a time when the world will sorely need us again.*

You deceive yourself, Sire. The Hohenstaufen dream of a universal empire is dead. All that remains to us are empty legends. Your grandfather Barbarossa will not rise up again from his mountain nor will you!

You are as stubborn as he was, Marie of Hohenstaufen! The Emperor chuckled to convey his admiration. *Indeed, your irrepressible spirit renews our faith that the prophecy will come to pass. We shall go now and bide our time till you have need of us again.*

The widow of Luigi Campagna drowsed till she dimly sensed the Maliseet shipping the paddles aboard and swinging themselves one by one into waist-deep water. Muscles of spring steel lifted her from the canoe and deposited her on dry land. The three groggy boys clustered around her while Father Gabriel refastened his tether about their necks.

The prisoners were forced to carry burdens, for there would be only one crossing of this long portage. Wary of pursuit, Teiskaret cached what remained of his booty. Lame and pregnant, Marie was made to bear only the boxed set of pewter cutlery that her dead husband had purchased as a gift for her in Plymouth.

'We dare not loiter here lest these English heretics catch up with us, my children.' Father Gabriel hoisted his pack and gave a tug on their leash. 'This moose trail runs all the way to the headwaters of the next river. We must prepare ourselves for a long and arduous portage.'

Yet the priest himself was not prepared for what awaited them on the other side of that first ridge. Marie dragged her bad foot into the trampled clearing and lowered the pewter case to the ground. Teiskaret responded contemptuously when the Jesuit questioned him. 'These are only wigwams of the M'ikmaq! We must have frightened them away.'

Both men braced themselves warily as a party of native women emerged from the forest. The scouts and Gilles Leblanc followed after them. 'English rangers passed here looking for us yesterday. We found these esqua burying their dead.'

The priest took alarm at hearing this. 'Christ's blood, are none of their menfolk left alive?'

The renegade shook his head, his face expressionless as he singled out the one older woman in the group. 'Father Gabriel, this one survived by hiding inside a hollow log. She overheard the rangers laughing and talking about the fat bounty Governor Lawrence has promised to set on M'ikmaq scalps. It seems your raid on the Huguenot settlement has not gone unnoticed.'

At first the widow of Luigi Campagna did not know what to make of the glances exchanged between Teiskaret and the Jesuit. It finally dawned on her that yet another objective of their raid into Nova Scotia had been achieved: the M'ikmaq were being blamed for the massacre on Sanctuary Island. Their very survival as a people was now at risk. No choice was left to them but to ally with the French in their great war against the British.

Impassive with grief and shock, the M'ikmaq widows and orphans huddled together. They seemed utterly resigned to whatever might next befall them. Crucifix upraised, Father Gabriel passed among them dispensing benedictions and drawing forth bits and pieces of their story. 'See what your English heretics have done, Madame? First they struck down all the men from ambush. Then they killed and scalped all the rest save these young women and girls.'

Marie fought to keep from screaming. *God in heaven, listen to this man who pretends to be your priest! He pretends that what the English have done here shocks him! He pretends he cannot understand why they have expelled the Acadians! He pretends he cannot grasp why the native people are hunted down or why these women have been spared. He pretends it grieves him that my husband and his servants lie murdered! He pretends he does not know who brought such a curse upon this land!*

The Acadian came forward with his crossbow riding on his hip. 'The rangers have only spared these women and girls because they plan to return here on their way back to Chebucto. An esqua's scalp is worth as much as that of a man in Halifax.'

One of the M'ikmaq shuffled forward to face Marie. The widow of Luigi Campagna did not at first recognize the woman. Her raven braids of hair were shot through with streaks of white and there was no longer an infant strapped to her back.

Smiling the same shy smile, the daughter of Waksitanou slipped the hemp noose from Marie's neck. The Jesuit started to object to this freeing of his prisoner but seemed to think better of it. Instead, he began to remonstrate with Teiskaret and Gilles Leblanc in the Algonquin tongue. So it was that the widow of Luigi Campagna muffled her sobs in the M'ikmaq's fur mantle. Shame at her own weakness stifled her tears as her friend held her out to arm's length and gravely studied her face.

The older woman guided the Jesuit and Marie to the freshly dug mass grave. The priest fashioned a rude cross and quickly performed the last rites over the M'ikmaq dead in the prescribed Catholic manner. Numbly the women and girls nibbled at the crumbs of bannock and sipped from the silver wine flask. Their expectations of the Huguenot widow were not nearly so clear. Yet somehow Marie was made to feel that they were deriving more comfort from her silent presence than they did from Father Gabriel's beautiful tenor.

Apprehensive at the strange way the M'ikmaq women treated her, Marie dared question the Jesuit as they retraced their steps to the wigwams. 'They think you are a virgin mother, Madame. They whisper among themselves that the child you bear is God's Chosen One!'

'I'm sure you set them straight, Black Robe.'

'It is hardly worth my trouble to disabuse them, Madame. Nor would it matter in the scheme of things if Teiskaret would only leave these people here. The Maliseet is a fool!'

'So we shall be taking them with us!' It relieved Marie that it should be so.

'Teiskaret says we must.' The priest seethed with impotence. 'Since when have the Maliseet ever cared what happens to M'ikmaq?'

'What about you, Black Robe? Do you not care what happens to them? They are good Catholics, are they not?'

'Their souls are safe enough now that they have had the benefit of a priest.'

Marie shuddered at this insight into the mind of the Jesuit. *How ironic that it should be up to a savage to save them! Certainly it is not the souls of these women that Teiskaret values. Their bodies are serviceable as beasts of burden, as concubines and childbearers. The children will augment the ranks of the Maliseet nation, decimated as it is by disease and war. Could any woman doubt the meaning of the gaze the war chief casts upon my friend?*

'Father Gabriel, what can you tell me about this young woman, Mishikwit. What will happen to her?'

'That is hardly for me to say, Madame. Ask your question of Teiskaret.' Father Gabriel shouldered his burdens and gave a firm tug on the boys' leash.

Marie relapsed into silent grief as she retrieved her pewterware. The pain rose again in her stiff leg as she fought to keep pace with the portage. Alongside her walked Jean and Louis, bearing burdens that staggered them. Philippe trotted ahead of his family, sullenly bearing a man's half-load up the steep trail.

The stands of rough spruce gave way to lofty pine trees. The little valleys echoed with the bird-song of spring. The hilltops hummed with squadrons of dragonflies, affording some relief from the hordes of whining mosquitoes.

Marie caught sight of Gilles Leblanc and a young scout carrying the Acadian's strange canoe atop their huge shoulder-packs. The other young Maliseet returned from scouting and traded places with his fellow, but the Acadian remained in the lead, trotting along with his crossbow slung under his arm. It annoyed her to catch herself waiting for what the renegade would do. *Why should I assume he means to help us? Why do women everlastingly expect men to determine what will be?*

Marie's breath came in short wheezing gasps by the time they reached the next river. The Acadian and the Maliseet scout had already launched their canoe upon its narrow stream. In company with the children, she lowered the pewter case, heavy as lead, to the grassy riverbank and collapsed on her side. Teeth gritted against the pain, she massaged the knotted, spasming muscles of her ankle and calf. *How much more of this can my beloved survive? No matter what comes, I mustn't let go of her. Surely, it cannot get worse. Surely, we cannot be far from wherever they are taking us. Or do we journey on forever?*

Jean anxiously drew near. 'Are you all right, Mamam?'

'I am all right, Jean. I only need to rest a while.' Marie's guilt lay heavy upon her. *Why is this child less precious to me than his brothers? His face is full of freckles and his teeth grow crooked. He is neither so pretty as Louis nor so intense as Philippe, but his is the best mind of all three. Do I slight him because he most resembles his father, Luigi Campagna?*

Little Louis dropped like a sack of wheat against Marie's curled back. She looked for Philippe and found him standing over them, still bearing his heavy load. *Why is this one always the center of your concern? Why do you fret so over him?* 'Sit down, Philippe. Come, you must rest. Jean, help him lower his pack.'

The M'ikmaq women, each bent double under man-sized burdens, caught up with them. Marie witnessed

Teiskaret's eyes burn as they boldly appraised Mishikwit's crouching form. *Yes, there can be no doubt he means to take her for his own.*

The Jesuit had again reduced his world to breviary and beads. His consummate ability to shut out all around him angered the widow of Luigi Campagna. *Why does God let him cause so much suffering without sharing in it himself?* 'Black Robe, these children require food.'

'The Maliseet will see to it, Madame.' The priest unhooked a small scrivener's case from his waist-cord and began writing with a short black quill.

The Acadian and his young companion returned to camp dragging a white-tailed buck between them. The M'ikmaq women soon had the gutted animal roasting over a smokeless fire. They offered choice portions of raw viscera skewered on sticks to the Maliseet warriors. Despite their strict observance of wilderness protocol, Marie sensed that the M'ikmaq women were subtly taking charge of the raiding party.

Teiskaret bade Mishikwit present the roasted heart of the deer to the Jesuit, but he waved away the peace offering to the famished boys. So it was that Marie came face to face with her friend in the flickering glow of the campfire. Their fingertips silently told each other of the loss of husbands and children. That strange pooling of misery afforded Marie the strength to make it through another night.

Watched over by sentries, the starlit camp had grown still when a shadow crept close to Marie. She smelled rawhide and tobacco before hard fingers sealed her lips.

Chapter XXII

PRECIPICE

Chignecto Bay, May 1756

The shadow pressed close to whisper in Marie's ear. 'Do not be afraid, Madame! Gilles Leblanc has come to place himself at your service!'

Marie struggled to reply through the hard fingers bridling her lips. 'It is not well done to taunt a poor widow, Monsieur. As you can plainly see, I am beyond hope. My fatherless children and I are prisoners of this papist priest.'

The Acadian shifted his gaze to Father Gabriel. Silhouetted against the dying campfire, the slack-jawed Jesuit lay with both ends of the rawhide tether fastened to his waist-cord. 'There is a saying among my people that only fools and demons dare rush in where Black Robes tread. Be that as it may, Madame, you may rest assured that I consider you well worth my risk.'

Marie recalled how this man had lurked high upon the cliffs of Glooscap's Mountain. *I saw you up there spying upon my nakedness, Gilles Leblanc! What a fool you are to lust after this misshapen flesh of mine!* 'You are a married man, Monsieur. Have you forgotten Claudine?'

A grimace tugged at the deeply etched lines of the renegade's gaunt face. He let go her jaw and recoiled from her touch. 'You mistake me, Madame. I wish only to deliver you from your enemies.'

Marie felt hot blood rush to her cheeks. Grateful for the near-darkness, she arced up at him onto both elbows, her whisper fierce. 'Who sent you to test me, Monsieur? Was it this priest?'

The Acadian scanned the inert forms scattered around them like so many logs. 'Sent me, Madame? You should know by now that no one sends Gilles Leblanc on errands. I place myself at your service because I cannot abide to see women and children torn from their homes and harmed.'

She did not believe him. She thought of what the Emperor had told her and her legs began shaking. *Will it never end? Am I no more than a bone to be fought over by vicious dogs?* 'Then I shall put *you* to the test, Monsieur. Tell me, can you help us escape from all of this?'

'Not for the moment, Madame. But soon we pass behind the French lines. Closer to home, the Maliseet will grow careless. I shall seize my first opportunity to steal you away.'

'And what then, Gilles Leblanc? What about my children? Even if we were to escape, where could you take us that would be safe for them? For their sake, I fear I must accept once and for all that the Societé has won.'

A muscular contraction convulsed the lean body of the Acadian. Marie felt him throw all caution to the winds. 'Listen to me, Marie de Noquet: the Societé has not won so long as the Seed you bear endures.'

'So I was right, Monsieur! You *are* indeed much more than you seem. Tell me, how is it you know my mother's name? Are you a Templar?'

'Many generations ago, Madame, a small band of us were planted among the Acadians to keep watch over this land.'

'What talk is this of generations, Monsieur? Templars take vows of celibacy, do they not?'

The renegade nodded his head regretfully. 'Some sacred things have been lost to us due to the need to perpetuate ourselves. So long have we waited for your coming that we had almost forgotten who and what we are.'

Marie thought to further test the Acadian. 'Tell me, Templar: what do you know of the Dread Maidens?'

'Only that my own great grandmère was one of them. Waksitanou told me that your handmaiden Nicole was the last.'

'Waksitanou told you of her? Why then didn't Nicole tell me of you as she lay dying?'

'Your Dread Maiden knew little more of us than that we existed, Madame, but it was she who gave Waksitanou a message summoning me.'

'But you were too busy slaying English to heed her call?'

The Acadian could only hang his head. 'After my people were taken away, I ceased believing you would ever come.'

'Tell me about Waksitanou, Monsieur. He must have known who you were.'

'But yes, Madame! He taught me much long forgotten Templar lore. We called each other friend until I swore revenge on the English. He came to doubt that I could still be trusted.'

'No wonder he doubted you, Monsieur! How is it you are brought so low that you guide the one who took your friend's scalp?'

'I came too late to save either him or your husband.' The Acadian's hand slid down to the huge knife belted at his waist. 'Shall I slaughter the dog where he lies sleeping, Madame? I thought to bide my time, but you have but to say the word, and certes, his scalp is forfeit this very night. God willing, I might be able to slay them all in their sleep.'

'Nay, Monsieur, I do not want even a savage's blood on my hands! Leave me now or I shall call out! My conscience bids me not to trust a man who slaughters others so easily!'

'Madame, you must understand that we long believed ourselves abandoned. One or two messages delivered over more than a century could not keep us from becoming Acadian. And now these English have dragged my wife and children I know not where. This land will be utterly raped if they win this war. Already they burn its forests and slaughter its wild creatures. Even the fish are not safe from them. We must drive them back into the sea if we and the M'ikmaq are to live here in peace again.'

'I am only a simple woman, Monsieur!' Marie pulled back from the renegade till their bodies were no longer in contact. 'It is not the English I have cause to fear. Far from it! They would help me if they could for the sake of my poor dead husband. Tell me, where is Father Gabriel taking us?'

'Why, to Quebec, of course! Where else would he take you?'

'Quebec? I thought he was only telling me that to frighten me. Quebec is hundreds of leagues away!'

'Tis a mere fortnight's hard journey in a fast canoe, Madame.' The Acadian uttered a laugh from deep in his throat. 'Father Gabriel has asked me to escort him there. The priest of God trusts me because I slaughter the English.'

'But why, Monsieur? Why drag a pregnant woman and these young children so far?'

'The Black Pope's own deputy, Gaspar de Gérard himself, will be waiting for you there.'

'Mon Dieu, then they do know who we are!' Blood began congealing in Marie's veins. 'Monsieur, if what you say be so, these children are as good as dead.'

'Nay, Madame. The Societé does not worry unduly about the seed of a mere Huguenot. Given time, some

Jesuit will make good enough Catholics out of these boys. It is you and the babe you carry who are in great peril.'

Marie rose to a crouch as if about to bolt into the surrounding forest. 'I pray to God not to abandon us in this wilderness!'

Quick as the strike of a snake, the Acadian reached out and grasped her wrist. 'Madame, I beg you to consider that it is He who has send me to deliver you!'

Marie pulled free and cradled her head in her arms as though to keep it from exploding. 'What would you do with us if I were to deliver us into your hands, Gilles Leblanc?'

'I shall take you where no Black Robe shall ever find you, Madame; I swear it by the memory of Claudine and my three children. More than that I dare not say.'

'Swear to return us to Mahonne Bay, Monsieur. We have friends there who will protect us.'

'Madame, even if the English win the war and break the hold of the Black Robes on this land, it would not be wise for you to go back to your island. For now, all I can promise you is sanctuary from the Black Robes.'

It became suddenly crystal clear to the widow of Luigi Campagna what she must do. *One must make haste slowly, as my infamous ancestor would say. Take one step at a time, Marie of Hohenstaufen. Use this renegade to free the children. Thread your way through the conflicting wills of all these warring men. If you think like a true woman, the next step will present itself soon enough.* 'So be it, Monsieur. I commit our fate into your hands.'

'I swear I will not disappoint you, Madame.' Marie let the Acadian touch her shoulder as though sealing the bond between them. 'One more thing: do not underestimate Father Gabriel because he is young and untried. He is a true Jesuit for all that. Therefore do not tell your children of our covenant. Let the priest go on seeing that I am as much hated by you as are the Maliseet and him.'

'Monsieur, you may depend upon me to treat you with all the disdain a cold-blooded manslayer deserves!' Marie's mocking whisper went unheard; Gilles Leblanc had already vanished into the night.

She groped for her signet ring with both her hands. *So, Sire, think you your Chosen Seed can safely pass through the fires of hell raging inside this renegade? Dare I entrust Luigi Campagna's children into such bloody hands?*

Indeed, Marie of Hohenstaufen, you must! This Gilles Leblanc spoke only the truth. Long ago the Templars planted several of their brethren among the Acadians who first came to this land. Dread Maidens were given those knights to be their wives.

Why were they put here, Sire?

As he told you, Princess Mine: to maintain perpetual vigil over the Chosen Seed. The Black Robes based at Port Royal were a constant menace to the Templar refuge on your island. It was foreseen that one day the Bearer of the Chosen Seed would need to come back here.

Nay, Sire, you cannot hide the truth from me any longer! This renegade also carries your blood in his veins. In truth your Chosen Seed never left this land, did it, Sire?

You are clever even for a Hohenstaufen, Princess Mine. It was a saying of my namesake grandfather that one should always keep more than one arrow notched to one's bow.

Of course! I see it all now! The Acadian is collateral breeding stock in case of need. That is why Nicole permitted Guy de Bouillion to die! His death was a diversion. If I had not proved with child or if I were to lose it, she would have put this bloodthirsty frontiersman to stud! That is why she contacted him, isn't it?

Why must you women always make things so difficult? You simply refuse to be practical about the disposition of your bodies! Yolande even accused us of wedding her in order to become King of Jerusalem!

Fie on you, Frederick of Hohenstaufen! Just as she did, I grow tired of being used by you!

Princess Mine, we are just an echo in your mind, remember? The Emperor reached out and made as if to touch her hair.

Old No Ears was shaking her awake by his favorite handle. Marie sat up, kneading her hips with both hands to relieve the horrific backache. Suppliant in the torchlight, Father Gabriel knelt at his *matins.*

Squatting behind a tree, Marie's rancor passed from the long dead Emperor to the living and breathing priest. *Still praying for Father Antoine, Jesuit? Surely he and his pagan escorts are dead by now within the Place of Dreaming. Who knows? Perhaps they tore each other apart. Yea, you do well to pray for your brother's soul, Black Robe. His stint in Purgatory will be long indeed.*

The canoes awaited them upon the swampy headwaters of the north-flowing stream. By the flare of a burning pine-pitch torch, Old No Ears tossed each of the prisoners a cake of ripe *sagamite* before taking up his paddle. No one took the trouble to complain this time. Even little Louis managed to swallow his portion with no more than a few murmurs. His eyes great dark circles, he palmed up clear cold water from the river and slaked his thirst.

Six canoes paddled by M'ikmaq women and girls joined them. Mishikwit wore her shoulder-basket filled to overflowing with roots, dried fiddleheads and other fruits of gathering. The eyes of the two women met as their canoes passed in the dawning light. *How different we truly are from one another, ma chere sauvage! Things you accept without question as part of life drive me to despair.*

The swift current caught them up and swept them down from the lake through a deep-vaulted valley. The Acadian and the Maliseet scouts pushed rocks aside with their paddles or used brute strength and tomahawks to clear fallen trees. Finally, confluence with a tributary formed a truly navigable river.

The spring morning unfolded bright and clear. Flashing in the sun, the canoes rode the ebbing tide to the sea. Ever wary, Teiskaret sent off his two young Maliseet and the Acadian to scout the estuary. Jean shaded his eyes to look afar as Chignecto Bay opened before them. 'Mamam, look!'

Marie could have wished she had been spared that vision. Yet her heart leapt as though it could no longer stay inside her chest at sight of full white sails reaching across the blue sea. Straining, she recognized portly Isaac Ben Yussuf on the brigantine's quarterdeck. Praying, she watched him raise a telescope to his eye and scan the Chignecto coastline. *Let him spy us out despite these cedar boughs. Dear God, they are so close and yet so far!*

Clad in blue beret and red bandanna, Jacques Sabot joined the physician on deck. The scarlet uniforms of several Royal Marines were also visible. Jean leapt to his feet. 'They have sailed all the way around Nova Scotia to rescue us, Mamam!'

Old No Ears toppled the boy between the thwarts with a backhand swipe. Frozen with horror, Marie waited for the poised tomahawk to strike, but Philippe braced his stripling limbs against the Maliseet's thick, copper-bound wrist. The warrior's awful frown transformed to an approving grin as he settled back into the canoe. The Jesuit belatedly held up his crucifix. 'My children, be careful! This savage Maliseet will slay you all if one of you should try to betray us.'

Jean's heart pounding against hers, Marie gazed longingly upon the transom portholes of the brigantine. Inside them lay the master cabin that she knew so well.

How difficult life aboard that ship often seemed! If only it were in our power to put all back the way it was! Oh, see how loyally our husband's friend and crew search for us! How bravely that ugly British flag flies from the taffrail!

Ebbing tide and fair wind bore *L'Espérance* swiftly down the Bay. Father Gabriel wished it good riddance. 'Thanks be to God we need not wait for night! The seas are calm and shall be clear of all our enemies as soon as yonder vessel is gone. We shall cross this little bay in broad daylight. Once up the Petitcodiac, the British will not dare pursue us.'

Teiskaret waited till the brigantine's sails patched the horizon before paddling forth upon Chignecto Bay. The M'ikmaq women shrieked aloud as the spray broke over the prows of their canoes. Curious seagulls swooped low overhead and lighted nearby to the delight of the children.

The Maliseet began chanting their songs. Marie had expected to see the M'ikmaq women and girls fall rapidly behind, but their paddling technique proved no less accomplished than that of the men. She looked where Mishikwit worked the stern of her canoe like a true voyageur. Behind her, the lofty cliffs of Chignecto receded into a bank of fog. A subtle calm fell upon the Bay marking the momentary quiescence of the tidal flow.

Marie turned her attention to the farther shore. She watched an immense flight of birds funnel down like smoke into the low-lying marshlands. *What awaits us in that wilderness? What will Gilles Leblanc do when we get there?*

A porpoise surfaced and began sporting with them. Even Teiskaret broke stroke to salute the sea-mammal with his paddle, seemingly overjoyed at such a favorable omen. Old No Ears tossed the creature a small fish, provoking the Jesuit to deplore such a waste of good food.

Cats' paws tiptoed across the Bay to them, and it began to softly rain amid the sunshine. Marie looked up and saw a single dark cloud hovering overhead. *What will they make of that? Bien, it makes our Jesuit anxious; he speeds up the counting of his beads.*

Some Maliseet held up gaping mouths to catch the large raindrops. Their chant became a deep, majestic hymn to the god of that sea. Long wet hair silver-streaked in the sunlight, the Jesuit darted his anger about but stopped short of rebuking his backsliding parishioners. Marie saw wisps of steam rising off his wet cassock, smelled the foul stench of him.

Teiskaret stood up abruptly in his war canoe and shaded his eyes. Shouting, he pointed, and every head aboard the fifteen canoes turned to look. It was left to Philippe to state the obvious. *'L'Espérance!* She's come about! She's coming after us.'

Two score paddles conjured flashing rainbows from the sun. Marie remembered that the M'ikmaq women had no more reason to welcome the brigantine's return than did the Maliseet warriors. Behind them, L'Espérance's great sheets of white canvas unfolded on a splendid quarter reach. *Can they possibly catch us? If they do, the Maliseet will cut our throats and take our scalps for sure. The good doctor will have nothing for his trouble but our grisly remains.*

Between long capes of marshland, the wide mud-washed estuary of the Petitcodiac opened before them. Birds milled there in their tens of thousands. Sea lions and seals thronged the beaches, their barking audible over the screams of whirling seagulls. The sluggish current of the river, a mere trickle amidst vast meadows of brown silt, washed over them and slowed their progress. Onward and upward the drenched voyageurs struggled, tired now, strain contorting their faces under the blistering sun.

The paddles seemed almost to lift the canoes clear of the water. Marie stole a backward glance that was both hopeful and forlorn. Her heart leaped to see that

the distance separating pursuer and pursued had nearly halved. Urine staining the cloth between his thighs,
little Louis fairly danced in her embrace. Philippe sat
back and crossed his arms. 'Prepare yourself, Mamam.
The brigantine's bow chasers have the range of us by
now! Soon it begins!'

'Jacques Sabot wouldn't dare fire those awful guns
at us, Philippe! They might hit us — or these poor
M'ikmaq women! Why, even a near miss would swamp
us!'

A cannonball whooshed down among the canoes.
The boom of the brigantine's gun thundered across the
narrowing waters. Countless seabirds took flight on
flashing wings. *What made me think my husband's crew
would care what happened to the M'ikmaq? Perhaps
they think it better to kill us than to leave us in the hands
of the Maliseet. Perhaps they intend to pluck us from the
water before we drown! That might be our best chance.
If only I had learned to swim! At least these boys can
swim!*

Again, Marie looked over her shoulder at the pursuing brigantine. Coat and hat flapping madly in the
wind, Isaac Ben Yussuf stood ready with several armed
marines in the bow. He raised his arm and waved a cutlass. *He sees us! Only save us, Isaac Ben Yussuf, and I
shall take you up on your offer of marriage, even if you
are a circumcised Jew!*

Then the fleeing canoes were overtaken, lifted up
and carried high on the crest of a boundless wave. The
native people of the land simply surrendered to the
irresistible power sweeping them onward, but Father
Gabriel emitted a giddy squawk of thanksgiving. 'My
prayers have been answered! God has sent the incom-
ing tide to save us from the heretics!'

Hull sheered round as though her keel were scraping the silted bottom of the river, *L'Espérance's* sails
flapped into irons. One last cannonball splashed down

and skipped across the waves. Teiskaret cocked his ear and waited for the roar of the gun. Then he threw his head back and ululated amid the cheers of his warriors.

The chant of the Maliseet became a paean of savage joy as the tide swiftly carried them inland. Marie gasped sobbingly for breath and gazed longingly at the receding brigantine. It was then that she finally accepted that her life as the wife of Luigi Campagna was over. She lost herself in comforting the weeping children. *It is over, my beloved. Our last hope of rescue is gone. Only this bloodthirsty Acadian can save us now.*

The sun was sinking low when the flood tide let go of them. Weary but exultant, the Maliseet paddled their canoes ashore upon a long sandbar formed by confluence of a tributary stream with the broad river. Stiff and sore, Marie and her stepsons disembarked upon the pebbled strand. The Jesuit removed the hated nooses with a sign of the cross for each prisoner. The solemnity of the occasion was somewhat marred by' running off to relieve themselves.

The M'ikmaq quickly unloaded the canoes and beached them. Marie offered to help, but Mishikwit shook her head. Chattering mirthfully, the women nursed what babies were left to them and set up camp for the night. They seemed to take it for granted that the hunters would provide game. *Our despair is their salvation. Mishikwit and the M'ikmaq are better off in the hands of the Maliseet than at the mercy of the English. Perhaps God does know what He is doing after all!*

With water and sand, the Maliseet raiders soon scrubbed the war paint from their faces and torsos. If not for the odd missing ear and other mutilations, Marie would not have recognized any of them. Watching one young brave romp with the M'ikmaq children, she had to remind herself that these carefree, good-natured men had recently slaughtered women and babies. In her confusion, she looked around for the Acadian, but he had vanished once more into the trackless wilderness.

Maliseet hunters soon returned to an enthusiastic welcome. The M'ikmaq women carved one hindquarter of a moose into huge roasts. They wrapped the meat in the animal's hide and buried it beneath the glowing bed of coals. The older girls were put to work preparing shellfish and edible roots for the improvised feast.

The younger children played with sticks and stones. The sons of Luigi Campagna looked on like visitors from another world, quite unable to understand games lacking provision for winning or losing. Marie stumbled across a large circle of blackened stones and a huge open midden of clamshells. *Perhaps it is the custom of warriors raiding across the isthmus to halt in this place. How many lives have been ended or ruined that there should be something to celebrate here? How many prisoners made to witness this? How many men put to death and women violated where I stand?*

Father Gabriel kept aloof from the council of senior warriors. After praying longer than usual, he opened his scrivener's case and dipped his quill. Marie suspected him of preparing reports on his prisoners for his superiors at Quebec. It made her uneasy that he halted from time to time to observe her intently, as though sketching her likeness.

Jean spoke to the priest in schoolboy Latin. The cleric put down his writing materials and responded pleasantly enough. Their budding friendship much perplexed Marie. *Jean deceives himself if he thinks a mere boy can beguile this Jesuit. The boy is bound to fall under the serpent's spell, but what can I do?*

The stars were shining when Gilles Leblanc returned. His hunger drew him to the steaming joints retrieved from the glowing ashes and scorched moosehide. He waited patiently while the women served the tongue and inner organs to Teiskaret and his council of warriors. The Jesuit's beautiful tenor voice beseeched God's grace, but he dined apart from the others on a modest portion of roast moose and boiled clams.

The hungry M'ikmaq girls waited silently with their mothers. There was enough food for everyone this night, but Marie wondered what winter might bring for these refugees. She began to understand the good spirits and industry exhibited by these women. Each strove desperately to establish her market value in the eyes of these men before the journey ended.

The young warriors basked in so much feminine attention, but the members of the council wore inscrutable masks, as though awaiting further proofs of value. Even Teiskaret affected disinterest as Mishikwit fussed over him. *Do these M'ikmaq women hope to cement relations with these men before their waiting wives can reassert themselves? If so, where will it end tonight? Will the Jesuit maintain decorum? Or will he grant absolution in the morning as he did after the massacre?*

Such was Marie's state of mind when Mishikwit returned. Flushed and fatigued after the long arduous day, the young M'ikmaq knelt before her friend and bowed her head. Long hair cascaded upon the wet wool jerkin covering her milk-heavy breasts. 'Can you not yet speak to me, *ma pauvre sauvage?* '

'Kin-friend, I have a little French.'

'Mush-quick! Oh but your French *is* very good compared to my M'ikmaq! I cannot even say your name properly. Mush-quack. Ho, do not laugh at me! Why did you not speak to me before?'

'Kin-friend, a proper woman of my people does not speak with strangers in their own tongue.' Mishikwit's head sank even lower. 'No need to worry more. I am no longer a proper woman.'

'Neither of us are what we were before, Mush-quick.'

'I know well enough who you are, Madame Marie. I know why the Black Robes take you to the Stone City on the Great River. They will try to keep you from birthing the child who is meant one day to lead both our peoples to peace and happiness.'

'Hush, Mishquick, the Black Robes murdered my husband! My children and I are prisoners! This babe I bear is like any other babe. I am no more chosen than you are!'

'A proper M'ikmaq woman may not betray her friend.' The M'ikmaq gravely lofted her head. 'I will never betray you, Kin-Friend! '

'I know that, Mishquick, but we've better things to talk about than me. Now you must tell me what they have done to you!'

Mishikwit lowered her head to stare at the hands folded upon her lap. 'Madame Marie, the English blame the M'ikmaq for slaying your husband and his people at the Isle of Kin-Friends. Many English Rangers from Pisiquid come yesterday morning. They lay in ambush for our men when they returned from fishing for cod.'

My God! Teiskaret has slain her father and brother, and now the English have killed her husband and son —
and all because my poor dead husband brought me here! 'Your little boy was only a baby!'

'He was son of a long line of great M'ikmaq chiefs.' Mishikwit drew herself up proudly. 'The rangers dare not let such a one live to take a warrior's vengeance upon them.'

As though all this killing were in the nature of things.
As though the status and honor of her husband and child demanded that they be sacrificed! 'Yes, go on!'

'After killing our men, the rangers drink rum and kill all the old people who do not hide in the woods. As for us young women, we do not struggle. We let them come into us to save our children, but they killed and scalped all the male children anyway. Afterwards, they take or burn everything we have.'

C'est la guerre. Tis the sport of men to murder and destroy. We women are left to live on and to try to make our world right again. 'My friend, let us help one another.'

The M'ikmaq shook her face free from her long straight hair. 'Madame Marie, what I can do for you and your children, I will do.'

'Tell me, my friend, what can I do for you?'

'Madame Marie, you can do nothing for me.'

A presence loomed heavily over the campfire. Marie looked up at Teiskaret and smelled the stink of rum. 'Esqua, come to my bed now! Tomorrow we travel far.'

Marie rose from her squatting position. *My friend has been raped! To spare her what is to come is the least I can do for her.* 'I come, great chief.'

Teiskaret recoiled from Marie as though she had struck him. 'White woman, I gave you to the Jesuit to do with as he wills. It is this M'ikmaq esqua Teiskaret takes for his own this night.'

The Maliseet seized his prize by the wrist. Mishikwit met Marie's glance before being drawn into the night.

Chapter XXIII

OO-LAHS-TOOK

Kennebacasis River, May 1756

The voyageurs canoed onward till the broad Petitcodiac
diverged from their path. The M'ikmaq women proved
as sturdy and enduring as the Maliseet men in making
yet another long portage. Lame and worried that she
might miscarry, Marie finally let Old No Ears bear her
on his shoulders. She seized hold of his greasy scalp
lock as though it were a rein. Father Gabriel blessed
her as the makeshift camel trotted past. 'Have courage,
my child. This is the last time we must do this before
we reach La Pointe de Sainte Anne.'

Marie tried to picture their destination from what
little she had gleaned from Father Gabriel. Since the
fall of Fort Beauséjour, the village had become the
main bulwark of New France against English expan-
sion westward. The French actively supported the war
bands based there with firearms and other supplies.
The Jesuit mission had been turned into the *de facto*
capital of a loose Maliseet confederacy. But Jean
explained to his stepmother that Teiskaret's stronghold
endured on borrowed time. 'Our liberation from these
savages may come sooner than we think, Mamam. God

help all those who think to find refuge from the English at La Pointe de Sainte Anne!'

The flotilla of canoes journeyed swiftly along the westward-flowing Kennebacasis. Moose, deer, beaver and muskrat flourished along its wooded banks. Great flocks of waterfowl thronged its waters. Jean wheedled scraps of paper and a stub of pencil from Father Gabriel, which he used to record a log of their journey along the serene river. Little Louis contributed a series of "charcoal on birch bark" sketches of the wildlife they encountered.

The hours spent in the big canoe were long, but the rhythm of the paddles eased once British territory had been left safely behind. Marie found herself resting and recovering from their many ordeals. She came to almost enjoy Jean's Latin discussions with Father Gabriel. Even the spectacle of Old No Ears teaching Philippe to shoot a fowling piece plundered from his father's trading post ceased to alarm her.

It was the behavior of the war chief that kept the young widow from succumbing to the spell of the Kennebacasis. That first night on the Petiticodiac, stifled screams had disturbed the darkness. Next morning, the only indication Mishikwit had given Marie of her troubles was to murmur that Teiskaret was not like M'ikmaq men. *Is he more like the English Rangers? The ones who raped you and murdered your husband and son? How can you possibly forget that this man murdered your father? But perhaps I make molehills out of mountains. Certainly the other women take these Maliseet in their stride. Unlike you, they seem little the worse for wear each morning. Why doesn't the priest do something?*

Yet Marie had to admit that the Jesuit did show courage at times in standing up to Teiskaret. Their heated discussions sometimes lapsed into French, enabling Marie to dimly apprehend the complexities of maintaining a far-flung alliance of Indian tribes. Father Gabriel feared that Teiskaret's taking of a concubine might jeopardize important political alliances. He had officiated at the wedding of the Maliseet war chief to Deborah, daughter of a powerful Ottawa chieftain. So it was that Marie began to appreciate the critical and often difficult role Jesuits played in knitting together a New France larger than all of Europe.

Yet the priest's efforts availed him little. Teiskaret rode the current of the river more like a conquering hero each day. Certainly he treated Mishikwit more brutally each passing night. She developed a limp and began to have difficulty paddling her canoe. The widow of Luigi Campagna became convinced that Teiskaret was slowly and methodically beating her to death. In despair, she took her fears to the priest.

Father Gabriel barely looked up from his breviary. 'Madame, surely you realize Teiskaret dare not bring this M'ikmaq esqua home. Deborah is every bit as formidable as her Biblical namesake.'

Marie had trouble conceiving of Teiskaret as a henpecked husband. 'Then why did he take Miskquick to his bed in the first place?'

'Her proper Christian name is Hagar, Madame. I suggest you employ a name you are capable of pronouncing.'

'She prefers her M'ikmaq name, Monsieur Priest.'

'*Mishikwit* is actually an Ottawa word, Madame. It means "clear sky." Not that it matters what one unbeliever calls another. What does matter is that the esqua is the daughter of a famous line of *sachems*. Stories are still told around M'ikmaq campfires of how her forefathers raided the Maliseet. Waksitanou himself was a mighty warrior in his youth. He took many scalps and women before my Jesuit brethren taught his people the error of their ways. Indeed, Mishikwit herself is the offspring of a woman he took captive on such a raid.'

'Father Gabriel, are you trying to tell me Teiskaret's honor demands that he kill Waksitanou's daughter? I thought you were sent here to make Christians out of these people?'

'One cannot understand the behavior of these savages in civilized terms, Madame Campagna. Teiskaret's honor is assuaged by despoiling the daughter of Waksitanou, not by the killing of her. But soon he must rid himself of the esqua. Agamemnon dare not sleep soundly at night if he take Cassandra home to share Clytemnestra's bed.'

Marie's fears were not assuaged by the classical allusion. 'Father, what shall we do? We cannot simply stand by and let a savage kill this woman!'

The priest sighed and threw up his hands. 'What I can do I have already done, my child. Better that the esqua die swiftly from abuse by Teiskaret than suffer prolonged mercy at the hands of his wife. In this wilderness, God sends many trials to test a Christian's faith. However, as Teiskaret's confessor, there is one thing I do promise you.'

'And what pray is that, Black Robe?'

'A heavy penance shall be exacted for his heinous sins!'

'Father Gabriel, a priest of God cannot so easily wash his hands of such a crime as this! It is our Christian duty to save her!'

The Jesuit closed his eyes as though counseling himself to be patient. 'My child, I'm only Christ's humble vicar! Teiskaret listens to no one on a matter so touching his pride as this. I fear there is no hope for the woman unless....'

'Unless, Father?'

'Unless the Acadian were disposed to buy her, Madame. After all, a healthy young woman is a valuable commodity among these savages. Rather than kill her, Teiskaret would lose face with his warriors if he did not accept a reasonable offer.'

'Father, what would Gilles Leblanc do with a M'ikmaq woman? For that matter, what has the renegade to give in exchange for her?'

'My child, I leave it to you to resolve such questions.' Father Gabriel resumed reading his breviary.

That night, the Maliseet made camp on an island in the middle of the broadening river. Since their escape was no longer a matter of great concern, the Campagnas found themselves increasingly left to their own devices. Thus, they sought out a secluded nook and bathed in the clear cold water. They washed and hung their tattered clothes to dry in the waning sunlight.

Marie began to consider the difficulties inherent in following the Jesuit's counsel. *Why should Gilles Leblanc care what happens to an M'ikmaq esqua? He thinks nothing of taking many lives, so why should he care about saving this one?*

As though drawn by her thoughts, a covered canoe rounded the point of the island. Marie pulled on her long-suffering shift and held up the riding outfit to screen her nakedness. Stick-body jerking with anger, Philippe confronted the Acadian on the wet strand as he beached his canoe. 'Keep off, renegade! You disturb our mother's toilet!'

The Acadian took a step backward into ankle-deep water. 'Certes, Master Campagna, you do right to chastise me! I shall come no closer. My apologies to your mother.'

'It's all right, Philippe!' The boy's brash courage heartened Marie despite the sense of misgiving that had begun gnawing at her vitals. 'I need to ask a favor of this good man.'

Glowering, Philippe folded his arms and held his ground, wavelets lapping his toes. 'Very well, Mamam, you may speak to him, but he mustn't stare at you or come a step closer!'

Gilles Leblanc obediently averted his eyes to the crossbow he carried in his left hand. 'I am at your command, Madame Campagna.'

'Do you truly mean that, Acadian?'

'Certes, Madame, ask of me whatever I may do for you, and it is as good as done. I swear it by the memory of my Claudine.'

'Then I shall take you at your word, Monsieur. The favor I would ask of you concerns the M'ikmaq woman Mush-quick.'

'Teiskaret's esqua? She of the beautiful hands and feet, Madame? A fair daughter of my friend Waksitanou before first the English and then the Maliseet brought her to ruin.'

The Acadian's manifest regret afforded Marie the courage to proceed with her bizarre request. 'Monsieur Leblanc, I implore you to save her!'

'Save her, Madame? Certes, the esqua is beyond saving!' The renegade gave a shrug as if there were no more to be said on the matter.

'Gilles Leblanc, hear me out! The Black Robe says Teiskaret will kill the woman before we reach Sainte Anne. I beg you to buy her from him before it be too late.'

'Let the Black Robe buy her!' The Acadian hawked a stream of brown tobacco juice into the river. 'It is his calling to be saving souls, not mine. Besides, I am not Teiskaret to be needing many women. What would I do with an esqua?'

Marie felt a flush spread across her face. 'Gilles Leblanc, you swore to serve me, remember?'

'Forgive me, Madame, but I fail to see how purchasing this esqua would be of any service to you!'

'She is my friend, Monsieur. What more can I say?'

'A friend? Madame, she is a M'ikmaq esqua — nothing more.'

'You told me Waksitanou was your friend, Monsieur. Will you not save his daughter?'

Heavy lids veiled Gilles Leblanc's dark-flecked eyes. 'If I do as you ask, what would I do with her?'

Marie put her hand to her swelling abdomen. 'I am in need of a handmaiden, Monsieur.'

The Acadian cradled his chin between forefinger and thumb as though to suppress a smile. 'I am sure that the esqua could teach you much about giving birth, Madame. However, I much doubt you would care to learn such things as she would teach you!'

Marie flared up hotly at hearing this. 'You speak of womanly matters that need not concern you, Monsieur!'

'How right you are, Madame! Certes, I've no wish to midwife a babe in the wilderness. Besides, the esqua can paddle a canoe as good as any man. Perhaps, Madame, there is some merit to your proposal.'

Saluting Philippe, the renegade slipped back into his strange canoe. Careful of the fresh kill lashed across the covered prow, he took up his paddle and pushed off. Marie let her shift slip down upon her breast. 'You will do it, Monsieur?'

'I will think upon it.' The Acadian hastily averted his eyes. 'The Jesuits taught you well, Madame.'

Marie looked round at her stepsons. *How your eyes reproach me, Philippe! They accuse me of dishonoring the memory of your father. Oh, to be a child again and have all my choices so black or white as yours are!*

The Acadian's fresh-killed venison was baking beneath the coals when the Campagnas returned to camp. Marie sensed a tribal spirit forging itself among her aboriginal companions: the young M'ikmaq women were clearly busy attaching themselves to specific Maliseet men, who were plainly basking in so much attention. While still critical of his ragtag flock's moral lapses, the Jesuit was gradually setting into the role of shepherd.

Mishikwit scurried past Marie without speaking for reasons that were painfully obvious: a dark swelling had closed one eye; bruises and wounds covered her exposed skin; her limp had worsened to the point of disabling her.

Father Gabriel celebrated mass that evening. Most of the Maliseet and M'ikmaq bowed down together before his crucifix and received communion from his hand. As had become her habit during these religious observances, Marie watched disdainfully, albeit somewhat longingly, from a thicket while combing the snarls from her hair. *So, Black Robe, what bread and wine hold you in store for these children and me? You must suspect by now what the coming of the Black Pope's Deputy signifies for this child I carry. Is that the reason for cultivating friendship with Jean? It is not just the communion of two minds that love learning, is it? It will not be easy to stop you from seizing hold of him, I know. So many spiritual scalps you Jesuits have taken these last two centuries! How is it you failed to claim mine while you had it in your power?*

Lying in a pool of cold perspiration that night, Marie again endured Mishikwit's muffled screams. Finally, she had recourse to her pendant ring. *Tell me, Sire: what penance could repay such bestiality as this?*

We humans are capable of anything our imagination can conceive, both good and bad, Marie of Hohenstaufen. We ourself are a case in point. God knows our own fancies were oft inspired by the Devil.

Pray do not tell me that you yourself tortured women like this, Sire!

For a purpose we deemed high enough, Princess Mine, we were quite capable of torturing the Pope himself. We once kidnapped and imprisoned a gross of cardinals. Yet such tortured screams as these were never music to our ears.

Are you saying that Teiskaret actually enjoys doing this?

He deludes himself that he thus appeases his departed ancestors. In truth their shades pity him.

Pity him?

Yes, they pity him because this Maliseet is a slave to what he takes to be his honor. It is a failing of most kings.

It would seem that you feel a kinship of sorts with this savage, Sire!

Indeed, Princess Mine! Our time and place differ, but the inner realities we face are much the same: Frederick II Hohenstaufen came too soon to the age he lived in; Jean-Baptiste Teiskaret comes too late to his.

The least you could do is show some remorse, Sire! It might win you a reprieve from the purgatory you dwell in.

Remorse is the most hypocritical of all emotions, Princess Mine! What point in that? Our purgatory, as you put it, is our need to discover the meaning of our past existence — if indeed it had any meaning.

Ah, so after all these centuries Your Majesty is still prey to doubt!

We are the quintessential doubter, Princess Mine. No man was ever more filled with doubt while alive than we were. Doubting all things made the popes and priests hate us.

I greatly fear I have inherited your doubt, Sire!

How could it be otherwise? The Hohenstaufen blood runs true. Perhaps in time, Princess Mine, we shall pass beyond doubt to some new certainty.

In the morning, Mishikwit could barely crawl to her canoe. Watching her, Marie and the Acadian exchanged a fleeting glance behind Father Gabriel's back. The priest sat oblivious to all around him, engrossed with Jean in a discussion of Aristotle's influence upon the Fathers of the Church.

A rather bedraggled feather adorning his knotted hair, the war chief assumed his place of honor in the lead canoe. His hawkish profile and august bearing struck some vestigial chord in Marie. *So must Caesar,*

345

crowned with laurel and riding in a chariot at the head of his legions and captives, have appeared when staging a triumph at Rome.

Far behind, Mishikwit struggled to keep pace with the M'ikmaq canoes. It heartened Marie to see the Acadian hovering near her friend. *Even so calloused a soul as his cannot stomach such senseless brutality. He must intervene tonight. Something tells me that tomorrow will be too late for my friend.*

Borne along by the Kennebacasis, Marie turned her mind back to Frederick II Hohenstaufen. She wondered whether there could ever be an end to doubt so great as hers.

Teiskaret in the lead canoe pointed out a great white-headed eagle standing sentinel in the crown of a tall pine overhanging the river. Suddenly the bird spread enormous wings and dove. Screeching, it soared and swooped above them. Marie watched charcoal streak across little Louis' scrap of birch bark. 'Mamam, do you see him? Isn't he magnificent?'

A firearm discharged deafeningly in Marie's ear. The eagle plummeted into the river. Old No Ears' fowling piece smoked in Philippe's outstretched hands. Little Louis cried out and turned to pound his brother with his fists. 'You murderer! Philippe, you are no better than these Maliseet!'

Teiskaret plucked the bird from the water. Marie watched him weave a spray of blood and jubilant language upon thin air. *Is that some kind of accolade he bestows upon our son? He thinks it a good omen — this gracing of his triumph with eagle feathers! Ah, ignoble savage, you are hopelessly lost between worlds! As for you, Philippe, I fear we lose you to something far worse than death.*

Jean resumed his Latin conversation with Father Gabriel as if nothing had happened. *I am losing your second son as well, Luigi Campagna. Thank God it was*

346

not I who brought these boys into the world. They are becoming men much too soon. How unbearable to watch your own gentle offspring become hardened in the space of a few days! I pray my lover's prophecy comes true. May the baby kicking beneath my heart be a girl!

Little Louis finally pulled loose from sobbing in her arms. Pale and composed, he took up his charcoal sketches and cast them upon the river. A long silence ensued before he spoke. 'Mamam, I will neither draw nor paint ever again.'

Marie crushed him to her. 'Louis, your father would want you to be strong in spite of all!'

'That is why I shall not make pictures anymore. I wish to stand as strong as he did against this cruel world. I will not let it touch me deeply anymore!'

'Louis, your father would not want you and your brothers to become as cruel and heartless as the savages who murdered him!'

'Philippe is already one of them, Mamam! It was foolish of me to paint pretty pictures in a land so savage as this!'

'If you do not paint pictures, what is there left for you, Louis?' Amid her despair, Marie felt a wave of relief pass over her. *Why should this little boy persist in suffering so much pain? Louis must grow tough skin like yonder sunning turtle to survive in this wilderness.*

'I shall follow in my father's footsteps, Mamam. I shall become a merchant.'

The image made the bereaved widow smile in spite of herself. *It may well come to pass, Marie Campagna. Is this not how little boys lose their dreams and grow into men? Is this not how their budding promise is misshaped and pruned to fit this world?*

As the afternoon shadows grew longer, Louis' inner silence rippled outward and engulfed the voyaging canoes. Teiskaret's ebullience quickly subsided. The Jesuit abruptly ended his conversation with Jean and furtively resumed his prayers. Old No Ears had snatched the blunderbuss away from Philippe as if deeply offended by the killing of the eagle. He bent to his paddle as if he alone were responsible for getting them to La Pointe de Sainte Anne. Even the young Maliseet braves ceased calling out to the M'ikmaq women following close behind.

Mishikwit paddled on despite the pain her face manifested at every stroke. As though fatigued, the Acadian let his canoe idle back till he could mutter something in the M'ikmaq's ear. The words brought no light to the woman's drawn face, but her paddle picked up its rhythm.

It was mid-afternoon when the voyageurs arrived where the clear Kennebacasis pours into an inland sea. Teiskaret pointed westward as a ragged cheer went up from the Maliseet. 'Oo-lahs-took!'

The Jesuit waved his crucifix about in a vain attempt to stem the pagan Maliseet chant. 'Samuel de Champlain named this river in honor of your name-saint, Jean!'

The boy shaded his eyes and looked afar. 'It's too big to be a river, Father! I can hardly see its further shore!'

'This water is called Long Reach, my son! This is where the great Saint Jean backs up into a kind of lake before emptying into the tides of La Baie Francoise.'

Teiskaret grounded his canoe upon the first grassy sandbar they encountered. He posted sentries and ordered the women to gather shellfish and prepare a feast. The Maliseet had come home to Oo-lahs-took.

The sons of Luigi Campagna helped Mishikwit crawl ashore from her canoe. She tried to join in making camp, but Marie made her lie down upon a trade blanket that Jean and Louis spread upon the sand. Abrasions, welts and bruises covered her. Spittle bubbled forth upon her cracked lips. The other women averted their gaze as they hurried past.

Several curious young warriors drew near. Philippe bared his teeth at them and put up his fists. They laughed at him but soon went about their business of preparing to play some native game.

Teiskaret himself gave no heed to Mishikwit's plight. He squatted down in the waning sun and lit a pipe. Soon he was passing it among his senior warriors along with a flagon of rum.

Marie looked about anxiously for Gilles Leblanc. *Renegade, where are you? Mishikwit will not endure another night such as the last one. We draw close to La Pointe de Sainte Anne. This is no time for you to be gone off hunting!*

The young woman began coughing uncontrollably. Blood stained the saliva drooling upon her chin. The priest drew near and sank to his knees. 'Some of her ribs are cracked or broken, I fear.'

'Do something to comfort her, Father!'

Signing the cross, Father Gabriel spoke to Mishikwit in her native tongue. The young woman responded with a vigorous nod of her head. The priest held out his crucifix to be kissed before unfolding sacred items from the sacramental pouch slung from his waist. His fine tenor took up the familiar litany. Tiny droplets of holy water sprinkled Marie's hand.

A wave of nausea swept over the widow of Luigi Campagna. *Black Robe, you administer last rites as though the death of this woman had been ordained by God. As though there is nothing to be done. Dear God, is there not one true man among us?*

Then it struck the widow of Luigi Campagna that the Acadian had gone absent by design. *Gilles Leblanc, you condone this murder! You will remain out of sight and out of mind till the evil deed is done. Tonight, you canoe across tranquil waters to slaughter some doe with these same dark eyes. Come morning, you will have nothing to show me but an empty stare and bloody hands!*

The Maliseet commenced their games upon the long strip of grass-tufted sand. The M'ikmaq women and girls excitedly congregated about them. Marie's stepsons wondered aloud what the commotion was all about. Even Mishikwit raised her head to gaze beyond the chanting priest.

Naked save their breechclouts, six young braves raced out to where the two rivers mingled. Splashing through knee-deep water, the lead runner snatched up a flat case from the sentinel rock before being dragged down in an explosion of spray. The object they fought over changed hands many times before one of the youths twisted clear of the mêlée. With a high-pitched scream of triumph, he dashed into the squatting circle of warriors and flung his token of victory down before the war chief.

With an awful pang of shock, Marie recognized her one and only gift to her husband. Teiskaret held the shaving case on high before returning it as a trophy to the champion. She watched the young scout open his wondrous prize and raise Luigi Campagna's razor to flash in the sun. In waving it about, he slashed his forearm with the honed steel blade. It amazed Marie how the trifling accident occasioned the M'ikmaq women to break into gales of laughter.

Next came the portage event. Seven stout warriors, again clad only in immodest breechclouts, hoisted enormous packs upon tumplines and dogtrotted down the beach through a gauntlet of shouting women and girls. The war chief quickly broke into the lead, bare feet kicking up spurts of sand. Old No Ears trailed distantly till Teiskaret stepped in a hole and tripped. Tortoise-like, the old warrior trudged past his fallen leader to the finish line. A rather muted cheer rose from the spectators.

Teiskaret drank deeply of his rum before presenting Old No Ears with the satyr pistol. Marie had not seen the weapon since the morning of the massacre. *How small you are in the hand of this big warrior. Who could believe that you have claimed several lives? Ah, goat-man, something tells me you will kill again ere long.*

As if attracted by Marie's anger, the war chief turned his eyes upon her. His gaze took in the knot of people kneeling protectively around the M'ikmaq woman he had taken for his own. He yelled and came striding drunkenly up the beach. The widow of Luigi Campagna felt her throat tighten, but she did not let Mishikwit push her away. She felt only contempt for the Jesuit's prudence when he stood aside.

'Do not be afraid, Mishquick! I'll not let this monster hurt you ever again!' Marie arched herself across the heaving bosom of her friend in time to be yanked up by the hair, Teiskaret brought her face to face with his awful frown. A smart slap made her ears ring, but she held her warding position with all her might. All that remained to her was a forlorn hope that the priest would say a prayer for them both.

The discharge of a firearm reverberated across the beach. Still holding Marie by the hair, the Maliseet war chief gave a startled yell and spun about on his heel. She caught sight of the Acadian sitting sedately in his canoe a dozen strides offshore. Telltale smoke wafted up from the musket he held lofted in his right hand.

For a long moment Teiskaret stood as if struck dumb. 'Ho! Ho! Ho! Acadian! Did one of my warriors finally teach you how to fire that musket?'

Gilles Leblanc curled a thin lip and tossed the smoking weapon overboard. 'Certes, Teiskaret, many things can be learned in the company of so great a teacher as you are. Behold how the great sagamo of the Maliseet teaches his young braves the fine warrior's art of abusing women! He teaches them that this be a safer and more honorable way of counting coup than scalping men!'

The Maliseet let go of Marie and folded his powerful arms upon his bull chest. 'Gilles Leblanc, you grow more impudent each day. I think the time has come to teach you which of us is the better warrior!'

'Great Teiskaret, you may find that fighting a man is not so pleasant a sport as beating a woman. Let your warriors hear you tell what shall be my prize for teaching you so needed a lesson.'

The war chief pounded his chest. 'The fame of the warrior who defeats Teiskaret is sufficient prize for any man, let alone a renegade Acadian!'

'Certes, what you say is true enough, great Teiskaret, but I shall need some trophy of my victory, lest jealous tongues waggle that my boasts are empty.'

Teiskaret threw back his thick-necked head and laughed. 'Whatever you desire of mine shall be yours, Gilles Leblanc. All you need do to win your prize is best me — if you think you can.'

'All these Maliseet and M'ikmaq are your witness, Teiskaret. The tale of your generosity and great honor will live forever!' Gilles Leblanc raised an arm in token of accepting the Maliseet's terms. 'In accordance with your words, I pick for my prize the daughter of my old friend Waksitanou.'

A look of cunning swept the pockmarked face of the Maliseet. 'Acadian, you have forgotten something! Tell us, what will be Teiskaret's prize when he lays you groveling in the dust!'

'Myself!' The renegade raised both arms and bowed his head in mocking token of submission. 'If you defeat me, O Sagamo of the Maliseet, I shall become your bondservant to do with as you will for a year.'

'He! He! Gilles Leblanc! To hold as slave such a scalper of the English would bring me much honor! He! He! He! Let our contest begin!'

Chapter XXIV

CHIVALRY

Oo-lahs-took, May 1756

When questioned by Jean, Father Gabriel clearly stated what his mission to the New World entailed. 'We must thoroughly Christianize these pagan savages and secure their souls from hell. This we shall do by using them to drive the Anglo-Saxons into the sea. We must prise the heretics loose from their pernicious toehold upon the Atlantic seaboard of this great continent. One can only begin to imagine what an evil contagion would arise if we were to let this infection linger here. Every means must be seized upon to realize an end worthy of Saint Ignatius himself.'

The Jesuit brought that same clarity of vision to the task Teiskaret set him of arranging his "affaire d'honneur" with Gilles Leblanc. It challenged the classical scholar in the priest to reshape a wilderness brawl into the classic pentathlon of antiquity. No fight to the finish would this be but rather a chivalrous contest of skill. First, throw a tomahawk at a target. Second, race in canoes across the river. Third, climb to the top of a dead sentinel pine to retrieve strips of a dead redcoat's tunic. Fourth, swim back across the river. Finally, test marksmanship at thirty paces with the contestant's weapon of choice. First man to hit three targets wins the contest.

Marie suffered pangs of contrition at witnessing what her meddling had wrought. Stripped to the waist, Gilles Leblanc's spare build and pallid skin contrasted poorly with the coppery musculature of the war chief. She trembled with terror as the formidable barbarian took off the belt from which hung her husband's scalp. A single cast of his outsized tomahawk might well be enough to end all hope of saving Mishikwit. To heighten the sense of all things hinging on one another, Father Gabriel had stipulated that the loser of the throwing match must launch the winner's canoe upon the river before fetching his own.

The Jesuit set a brandy-jug swinging to and fro from a tree limb at twelve paces. Teiskaret threw first, but his cast went wide of the mark. The Acadian waited till the Maliseet had retrieved his weapon and stood clear before making his throw. The whirling tomahawk grazed the jug and sent it spinning. A gasp rose among the spectators.

Teiskaret's second throw cracked the jug and restored its oscillation. Again Leblanc narrowly missed the swinging target. The assembled throng murmured excitedly as the two men retrieved their weapons and returned to their throwing positions. In virtual unison, they cast their tomahawks a third time.

The jug shattered. The Maliseet's tomahawk affixed itself in the tree trunk; the Acadian's fell among the pottery shards. Amid a howl of protest, the Jesuit summarily lofted his crucifix and awarded the first event to Gilles Leblanc.

Daring to hope for the first time, Marie squeezed the hand of her M'ikmaq friend. Not that Teiskaret seemed the least discomfited by losing the first round of the contest. The cunning Maliseet stranded the rene-gade's sealskin kayak among the rocks guarding the beach. While his opponent wasted precious time extricating himself, the war chief trotted his birch bark craft down to the water's edge. A moment later, he shot out cleanly from shore. Yet the Acadian so skillfully plied his double-bladed paddle that he actually increased his lead during the crossing. He scrambled up the steep riverbank and raced for the giant pine.

Teiskaret plowed ashore and crashed his way through the bushes to the foot of the dead tree. He launched himself hand over hand through the branches in pursuit of the Acadian. Lacking his opponent's phenomenal upper body strength, Gilles Leblanc depended on his leg muscles to propel himself upward. Lunging awkwardly across empty space, he snatched up a scarlet rag. Marie held her breath as she watched her champion dangle from his legs.

Teiskaret was almost upon him, but the Acadian dropped down and seized the second strip of scarlet cloth. The Maliseet was left with no choice but to take his trophy by force. Risking everything, he caught hold of his opponent's wrist and twisted. From across the river, Marie watched their silent struggle transfix itself against the sky.

The renegade tightened his leg-hold on a branch and simply waited for his opponent to release his tenuous hold. Instead, the Maliseet let himself fall, seizing the trailing ends of both pennants. He dangled for a moment below his rival, suspended by the two scarlet ribbons. From far across the river, Marie imagined she heard the tearing sound as both pieces of cloth ripped apart.

Teiskaret crashed straight down through the dead branches. Somehow, he landed on his feet, a snatch of cloth fluttering brightly in either hand. A dozen broad leaps carried him plunging into the river.

Gilles Leblanc let himself fall outward into a living pine. He curled up into a ball and tumbled down through the green boughs till he hit the ground running. Without breaking stride he dove headfirst into the muddied water.

The war chief ranged far ahead, powerful breast-strokes lifting him clear of the swirling stream. The Acadian's efforts appeared puny to Marie by comparison, but his long body coursed gracefully across the current. She told herself that he gained upon the Maliseet as they drew closer.

Teiskaret came up out of the water like a raging bear. Old No Ears thrust into his hand the silver-engraved musket of Luigi Campagna. He shouldered it and fired. One of the five clay targets exploded.

Blood dripped from a dozen wounds upon the Maliseet. His hands shook as he tipped his powder horn. He glowered fiercely as he tore the strip of cloth with his teeth and wadded the charge home. Again he fired.

All the remaining clay bowls survived. The war chief's profanity provoked the Jesuit to ward off demons with his crucifix. Marie hated both men fiercely in that moment. *Yes, Teiskaret, 'tis time to repent yet another of your countless mortal sins! You will end the life of an innocent woman tonight, but this priest considers this blasphemy a heavier weight upon your black soul.*

Marie's fading hope swept ashore. Philippe handed him his crossbow. He raised it and pulled the trigger in one smooth motion. One clay pot disintegrated into a cloud of dust.

Then Teiskaret smashed his second target. Marie was down on her knees beseeching God when the Acadian evened the score.

A last clay pot survived. Teiskaret glanced sideways at the renegade reloading the double crossbow. He reaffirmed his need to do penance as he rammed the powder home and leveled his musket. Marie's heart soared to see him fail to load his gun with shot and wadding.

A vast cloud of smoke erupted from the muzzle. The ramrod waggled snakelike across the beach and dashed the last target into a thousand pieces.

Amid the ensuing silence, the Acadian shouldered his weapon and went down on one knee. Then the beach erupted in a medley of hoots and howls. Triumphant, Teiskaret raised his smoking musket high above the clamoring crowd.

Marie looked down at her friend's stoic face. The sons of Luigi Campagna closed up around them, but she waved them back. Father Gabriel drew near and resumed his sorrowful litany.

Serene and majestic, the Sagamo of the Maliseet wiped blood from his chest and approached his defeated opponent. He manacled both the Acadian's wrists with his great fingers and swung his arms high. 'Gilles Leblanc, you are mine to do with as I will for a year!'

The slump-shouldered renegade hung his head in token of submission. Utter despair filled Marie. *I am death itself, Acadian. Our last hope is gone, for Teiskaret hates you. I have marked you out for certain death by making you do this.*

The war chief grew somber and a terrible light glittered in his little dark eyes. 'Perhaps, Acadian, I shall give you over to the women to do with as they wish. How they will laugh at you and torment you as one who has lost his manhood! They will make you their beast of burden for unclean things no proper man would touch.'

Unflinching, the Acadian stared back at him as if willing the Maliseet to do his worst.

Then Teiskaret let out a mighty howl. 'Gilles Leblanc, have no fear! Think you I would so demean such a mighty slayer of mine own enemies?'

And still, the renegade said nothing.

357

'Nay, Acadian, the Black Robes would have me burn forever in their hell if I stayed your hand while there are yet English to be scalped in this land.' The Maliseet laughed, grasping the thin shoulders of the renegade. 'I would have us together take the war path against the enemies of both our peoples.'

And still, the Acadian spoke not a word.

'None of my warriors shall enjoy greater honor in my council.' The war chief placed the captive's hands on his own shoulders and gazed fiercely into his bonds-man's eyes. 'What say you, Gilles Leblanc?'

And still, the Acadian stood as if waiting for the other shoe to fall.

The war chief's brow furled as though seeking to find whatever was still missing from his largesse. Suddenly, he turned with an expansive sweep of both arms to glower upon his warriors. 'As for this M'ikmaq esqua, what more have I to do with her? Have I not brought her to bed and taken full revenge upon her forefathers? Does not Waksitanou's ghost gnash its teeth to see what I have done to his daughter? I did not know this Acadian desired her, or I would have gifted her to him long before. I warn him truly as my friend: this esqua lacks the strength to bear the weight of such men as we two are!'

Freeing his captive's wrists, Teiskaret stepped back and extended his right hand. Gilles Leblanc smiled and grasped the thick forearm. 'The black blood between us has been used up, Acadian. We have fought one another like brothers, have we not? Take the esqua you desire as my gift. Now come, let us eat and be merry. Together we have done things this day that our sons' sons will tell tales of!'

Gilles Leblanc looked neither right nor left as he followed his master into the circle of warriors. Disbelieving what her senses had witnessed, Marie gazed after the two men. The Jesuit came up to stand beside her as though he too shared her incredulity. 'As always, Madame, God works his wonders in devious ways. See how merciful Teiskaret is today? It is an item I will reckon up when accounting a proper penance for his sins.'

Marie almost forgot the role Gilles Leblanc had given her to play. 'They are both butchers, Father!'

The musing priest smiled to himself and folded his arms within the loose sleeves of his filthy cassock. 'True, my child, but let us be happy Hagar yet lives. You must try to see how God shapes events to suit His high purpose. Let this evidence of His merciful hand at work make you more accepting of His divine will.'

The Jesuit knelt down beside the prostrate woman and spoke to her in M'ikmaq. 'Hagar no longer requires extreme unction of me, Madame. See that she rests easy till morning.'

Marie slumped down among the sons of Luigi Campagna. They huddled together in their dirty blankets and watched the M'ikmaq women cheerfully dispense food to the Maliseet men. Even Mishikwit had become a stranger to her now. She felt shocked and confused by all that she surveyed.

Teiskaret celebrates his bounty tonight, but what will the morrow bring? The widow of Luigi Campagna dreaded what waited for them at La Pointe de Sainte Anne. The fierce but easygoing warriors valued their prisoners as tokens of wealth and prestige, but they were susceptible to the womanly wiles of their captives as only men could be. Marie knew in her bones that their wives would take a rather different view of the trophies their husbands were bringing home.

The Maliseet turned to dancing and singing. Two M'ikmaq women brought the prisoners a skewer of steaming meat and a basket of hot tea. Marie could not help marveling afresh as she assisted Mishikwit to eat. *How can a basket be woven so tight as this? The tea tastes of the hot dunking stones, but the makers of such wondrous things are far removed from savagery. It is my sons who are the savages. Their father would admonish me for permitting them to eat like wolves. But he is not here to see it, and they are hungry children.*

The last Maliseet celebrant was snoring before his shadow uncoupled herself and drifted across the moon-lit beach to join the other M'ikmaq. Work-hardened hands stroked Mishikwit's hair. Broad high-cheeked faces smiled their thanksgiving at Marie. Together, the women observed a silent communion under the stars.

It was dawn when Marie finally settled into her blankets, clutching her ring to her breasts. *So these women do care. They gave up Mishikwit for dead, but they honor me for working to save her. Did the notion of gainsaying these arrogant men never enter their own heads? Why do we women always place ourselves at the mercy of such brutes? What would it be like to be free of the pain and suffering they bring us?*

Marie felt a familiar shadow pass over her. *So, Marie of Hohenstaufen, you think the world reflects sole-ly the nature of men, do you?*

Women are buried alive in this world, Sire. We are shunted about from pillar to post at the whim of our lords and masters!

Look again, Princess Mine. No truth is learned so long as we blame others for what stems from our own nature.

Your victims should blame themselves that you broiled them alive, Sire? Does it comfort Your Majesty to be so facile at excusing your monstrous crimes?

Dear Princess Mine, we are here to comfort you in your time of travail! This respite from the void is given us to ponder our past and discover its meaning. Does not our very presence convince you that reason is at work in the universe?

Nay, Sire! I think only that I have conjured you out of nothing to help me bear the unbearable. You will pass

*like a gallstone when I am feeling better. Be gone back to
the void!* Marie turned on her side and closed her eyes.

The Jesuit was already pouring out his agony to
God when Marie awoke. Fumes of stale rum hung in
the air. Teiskaret and his warriors had overindulged
and were sleeping late. The Acadian and his canoe had
vanished on the shimmering surface of Long Reach.

The widow of Luigi Campagna threaded her way
past naked bodies sprawled on the ground in every
conceivable aftermath of coupling. *That coarse dark
face lying abandoned there was last night a luminous
half-moon pressed against Mishikwit's forehead. That
callused hand lightly clasped mine and offered friendship. That hanging breast offered suck to a hungry
child. Alas, these people live on borrowed time. Some
great tidal wave overtakes them all, and nothing in this
land shall ever be the same again.*

Bathing, Marie studied her reflected self in the quiet
pool. *Princess Mine, indeed! I am definitely of peasant
stock regardless of what Frederick Hohenstaufen says.
No proper lady would survive, let alone thrive, under
these conditions as I do. So much for being the Bearer of
Chosen Seed!*

The camp was in upheaval when Marie returned.
Teiskaret was striding up and down, barking orders.
Bent double under heavy burdens, M'ikmaq women
were scurrying hither and yon. The Maliseet were lazi-
ly launching their canoes. The sons of Luigi Campagna
were solemnly urinating into the bushes in company
with the two young scouts.

The blue discoloration around Mishikwit's eyes had
darkened alarmingly. She ate some moose meat, but she
still had difficulty gaining her feet, even with Marie's
help. 'Madame Marie, where has my master gone?'

'The Acadian? I think he's gone off scouting for
Teiskaret.'

'Why did you not leave me die, Madame Marie!' Mishikwit limped off dismally.

The widow of Luigi Campagna joined the priest in launching the big canoe. 'Father Gabriel, what is wrong with Hagar this morning?'

'Many things, my child.' The priest hiked up the skirts of his cassock and waded into the water as though it might dissolve him. 'First and foremost, the esqua is ashamed that Teiskaret has handed her off to his slave after bedding her. Second, even the slave does not value her enough to let her share his bed. Both men have made her feel she is worthless.'

'Is that all?' Marie watched her friend crawl forlornly into her canoe. 'She will soon get over it.'

'I would not be too sure of that.' The Jesuit signed the cross before letting himself be picked up by Old No Ears. 'Indian women have been known to simply die if they are deeply shamed, and they know no deeper shame than to be considered worthless by their men.'

'A woman cannot simply will herself to die, Father!'

'Hah, I have seen even baptized men do it!' The Jesuit clinically studied the grinning Maliseet who bore him in his arms like a child. 'You will appreciate that such volitional death poses theological problems for a priest of God. Is it a kind of suicide? If so, is it sacrilege in such a case to administer last rites? Is there any hope of God's mercy for such a lost soul?'

'Father, let us avoid such questions by keeping Hagar alive!' Marie followed the priest into the water and let herself be picked up in her turn. 'I pray you, let me paddle her canoe today.'

'Certainly not, Madame!' The Jesuit settled himself resolutely on his favorite thwart. 'You're much too close to your appointed time for such heavy work.'

Philippe came up to stand thigh-deep in the sluggish current. He placed both hands on the gunwale of the canoe to steady it for Marie's descent. 'Then let me paddle her canoe, Black Robe.'

'Philippe, you lack the strength to paddle all day!'

'No wonder Plato insisted that males be taken from their mothers at an early age!' The priest crossed himself as though to ward off a witch. 'Madame, let your son paddle Hagar's canoe.'

Marie looked to her suffering friend and back again to the eager stripling. 'Very well, Philippe, you may go to her.'

'Wait, my son!' The Jesuit grabbed hold of the boy as he started to splash away. 'Tell Hagar that Gilles Leblanc sent you to paddle her canoe whilst she heals.'

'Father Gabriel, you are asking this child to lie!'

'Madame, must you always speak before you consider things as they are? Think you she'll let this boy paddle her canoe otherwise? A discreet falsehood often averts evil.'

Teiskaret spread the canoes in a broad crescent upon Long Reach. Slowly they turned and swept north till it narrowed and became a discernible river. Marie had never seen so great a stream before. *How can all this water come down from rain? Jean calls this river the Indian highway to the City of Quebec. If the priest has his way, we shall be made to journey its entire length. Dear God, spare me from giving birth in this canoe!*

Marie kept turning round to check on Philippe. The youth's face exhibited a fierce pride. He and Mishikwit's companion were holding their place in Teiskaret's triumphal procession. The widow of Luigi Campagna suffered a pang of loss at seeing him thus. *I think Plato may be right. Women do dread their sons becoming men. Considering what manhood entails, it is no wonder!*

Mishikwit dozed sullenly in her canoe. The spirit was visibly draining from the M'ikmaq, even while her body recuperated from its ordeal. 'Father, I think you're right about Hagar. Tell me, what must we do to make her want to go on living?'

The Jesuit arched a brow without so much as lifting his eyes from his breviary. 'My child, surely you can see that neither of us can further help the woman. All we can do is pray to God that the Acadian decides to meet her need before it be too late.'

'What need is that, Father?'

'Madame, you ask questions like a child!' The priest stirred uncomfortably. 'It is not meet for us to discuss these matters. The ways of the flesh are abhorrent to a priest of God. You would do better to consider your own fate and that of your children.'

'What fate, Father? How can I possibly consider what you keep secret from me?'

'My child, I cannot foretell what the ecclesiastical judges will decide in your case. I pray to the Son of God that your sin is judged to be redeemable.'

Marie felt herself turning cold inside. 'Save your prayers for those who need them, Father!'

'Do not demean the power of our Savior to forgive, my child! The Pharisee Saul, though he martyred Saint Stephen, became the Apostle Paul on the road to Damascus. I am hopeful that at least one of your sons can be saved by my prayers.'

As though to give example, Father Gabriel turned away and began conversing with Jean in Latin. The boy seemed to become more fluent in the language each day — much to Marie's chagrin. *I am glad his father cannot hear his son being treated to a homily on the life of Saint Ignatius. Slowly everything is slipping away. The further we travel, the more I am alone. Even little Louis no longer clings, and my beloved kicks inside me, already impatient to be born.*

Philippe paddled all that day without so much as a whimper, but he had to be literally lifted from the canoe that night by Old No Ears. The big Maliseet gently laid him to rest upon the strand selected by Teiskaret for a campsite. Mishikwit crawled ashore and seated herself upright against a stone. She would not speak to Marie, nor did she offer to help with making camp.

Father Gabriel crossed himself as though washing his hands of the M'ikmaq woman. But the widow of Luigi Campagna could not so easily turn aside from her friend. *The Jesuit thinks she has surrendered her soul to Satan and is eager to go to him. Though she was baptized Hagar as a child, it is doubtful he will even perform the last rites for her, if it should come down to that. Dear God, pardon me for being so stubborn! Is it your will that Mishikwit must die?*

Dusk had settled when the Acadian reached camp. Marie hastened down to meet him as he dragged his canoe ashore. 'Monsieur Leblanc, permit me to thank you for saving my friend.'

The renegade nodded his acknowledgement of her gratitude. A bruise sustained in falling from the pine tree gave a sinister cast to his eyes.

Marie was not quite sure what to say to such a strange man. 'I am sorry you've been made to pay such a terrible price for my whims, Monsieur. Forgive me for drawing you into this.'

The Acadian ran his eyes all over Marie as if marveling at what he beheld. Not for the first time he made her feel that she was being stripped naked. 'There is nothing to forgive, Madame. As I told you, I came here to deliver you from evil.'

Marie could not explain even to herself why she chose to take exception to his words. 'I think it is you yourself who needs such deliverance, Gilles Leblanc!'

'I seek no deliverance, Madame.' The Acadian shrugged off his pack. 'The esqua will have been worth all my trouble if she can help you safely deliver the Chosen Seed into this world.'

This was the opening Marie had been waiting for. Gladly, she let the tears come to her eyes. 'Monsieur, the priest says that Mishikwit is willing herself to die!'

Gilles Leblanc shrugged and stepped cautiously to one side. 'She is a M'ikmaq esqua, Madame! Who can say what demons hold sway over her?'

'Mishikwit's life is in your hands, Monsieur! Father Gabriel says it is in your power to relieve her shame. She is the daughter of Waksitanou and a beautiful young woman to boot.'

The renegade stopped dead and looked at her. 'Madame, you ask too much! Think you I would so betray my Claudine?'

'Monsieur, from what you have told me of her, I doubt Claudine would begrudge an act of Christian charity. What compares so little a sin with what you've done to avenge your wife and children upon the English?'

Gilles Leblanc laughed mirthlessly, his moccasins sloshing water as he resumed his progress. 'That's easy enough for you to say, Madame. Would you give yourself to Teiskaret if I should ask such a favor?'

'Certainly not!' Marie bridled indignantly. 'Monsieur, you insult me by even suggesting such a thing!'

'Do I, Madame? Then let me hear no more talk of this esqua.'

He made to move past her, but she stopped him with a small hand on the homespun wool covering his thin chest. 'Monsieur, I would give myself to Teiskaret to save my children.'

'I believe you, Madame.' The flecks in the Acadian's eyes were dancing. 'And I would gladly bed your esqua to have mine returned to me.'

'I would also do such a loathsome thing to save Mishikwit.' Marie took a deep breath. 'Monsieur, I would even do it to save you.'

The Acadian laughed again. 'Beware what you promise, Madame! I may hold you to it before our race is run.'

Again he tried to move on. 'Monsieur, what I ask of you is of great importance to the Chosen Seed. An inner voice tells me that I am going to need Mishikwit before my course is run.'

'Madame, you will be the death of me!' Marie felt a chill run along her spine as Gilles Leblanc removed her hand from his chest. 'Look, the moon rises! It is time to seek our beds.'

Sleep did not come easily to Marie that night, for she was prey to conflicting thoughts. *Have I sunk so low as to become a panderer of sin? If a M'ikmaq woman wishes to die, and God knows she has good cause for it, who am I to stand in her way? Little Louis is right: one cannot hope to survive in this wilderness if one wears one's heart on one's sleeve. Yet I cannot desert her. I know Nicole would not have deserted me.*

The sun already had risen high when the raiders began the last leg of their return journey to La Pointe de Sainte Anne. Teiskaret put on his French boots, the bronze medallion given him by Louis Quinze and his tall cavalry busby decorated with new eagle feathers. Old No Ears bedecked himself with Luigi Campagna's beaver hat. The other Maliseet warriors sported a bizarre range of items taken in the plunder of the trading post.

It relieved Marie to see Philippe once again paddling Mishikwit's canoe. As for the M'ikmaq herself, she had taken her rightful place in the Acadian's kayak. She held her chin high and gripped her paddle firmly as she matched her stroke to his rhythm. A telltale sheen of renewed vitality graced her eyes and skin. Her new master kept his face averted as he glided past Marie and the Jesuit.

Trust Father Gabriel not to let sleeping dogs lie. 'You have done extremely well for a heretic, my child.'

Long shadows were creeping across the river before welcoming canoes hove in sight. Soon, hundreds of Maliseet clustered around them. Hoots, war cries and the discharge of firearms disturbed the broad meadows surrounding La Pointe de Saint Anne. A terrible dread resurfaced in Marie as she watched women and children gathering at the water's edge to meet them.

More than one Maliseet found herself a widow that day. These keening women were pushed into the background as the crowd pressed forward to share the spoils of war. Hard eyes passed over Marie. Hard fingers punched her swollen belly and pulled at her hair. She wilted at the thought of being delivered into those groping hands.

Then Marie felt the presence she had dreaded most of all. The crowd parted, and a tall, wide-shouldered woman clad in white doeskin swept through. Her long hair was streaked with silver, and she flourished a scabbarded saber like a cane.

'Ho! Ho! Ho! Deborah, my wife!'

The matron gave no more than a nod to her husband before turning to survey the spoils of war. The war chief seemed to shrink before the gaze his wife fixed on Marie. He turned to the Jesuit as if needing him to tell the story of her capture. The imperious woman grunted at the priest's words and continued her inspection of the prisoners.

It took Mishikwit's rainbow of bruises to turn Deborah's baleful stare on her husband. She half-drew her saber to free it from its scabbard. Teiskaret tried to vindicate himself, stammering in his Maliseet tongue and pointing at Gilles Leblanc. 'Acadian, my husband tells me that this esqua is yours.'

'Yes, O honorable wife of Teiskaret, this esqua Mishikwit belongs to me.'

A light dawned in the closed darkness of Deborah's eyes. 'Mishikwit? Is that your name, esqua?'

'Yes, O wife of Teiskaret. Mishikwit is my name.'

'How came you by an Ottawa name, esqua?'

'My father, Waksitanou, raided far as a young man. My mother was an Ottawa prisoner among the Maliseet. He took her from them and brought her home to be his first and only wife.'

Deborah turned imperiously to address her husband. 'Does this M'ikmaq who steals women from the Maliseet still live?'

Teiskaret fingered one of the fresh scalps dangling from his beaded belt.

'My husband, you have done well for a Maliseet.' Deborah deigned to smile as she eased her saber back into its scabbard. Then she turned to the children cowering in the far end of the big canoe. Almost tenderly she lifted Philippe up by the armpits and ferried him ashore. 'This fine boy will requite us for the son we mourn.'

Gilles Le Blanc and Mishikwit

Chapter XXV

EXCOMMUNICATION

La Pointe de Sainte Anne, September 1756

The square-timbered church stood guard under a brilliant canopy of autumn leaves. The tall steeple served more as watchtower against enemies than as belfry summoning the faithful. In witness thereto, its bronze bell hung cracked and chipped from the last English attack. That same cannonade from the river had tilted its rough-hewn cross, lending the rude structure an air of impending doom. Yet still, a brooding power emanating from within drew the Huguenot widow ever closer along the warren of pathways.

Persistent rains were slowly swamping the huts and wigwams of La Pointe de Sainte Anne. A barefoot toddler, still shy of the Frenchwoman, broke off splashing mud puddles to take cover in a wigwam. Beyond the rolled-back entrance flap, an old warrior hunkered, staring out at Marie with rheumy eyes.

Grey skies and the chill in the air threatened the coming of winter. Each day, canoes arrived at the village to offload quarters of caribou and moose. Marie passed Maliseet matrons filleting fish from the great river. They kept their daughters busy hanging the strips to dry in lean-to shelters open to the sun.

Marie's waddling walk occasioned much mirth among the native women she passed. They seemed to take bearing children in their stride, whereas the captive Huguenot spent all her waking and sleeping hours trying to strike a balance between her own delicate form and its burgeoning intruder. She felt herself an overripe melon fit only for bursting.

Yet she did not yearn for deliverance. *I am not ready for what comes. I lack the strength and courage of these native women. Without Isaac Ben Yussuf or Nicole to guide me, I shall surely die giving birth in this Godforsaken wilderness. Mishikwit may be skilled enough at Indian ways, but I am a Frenchwoman!*

Nor could she help resenting the ease with which the M'ikmaq refugees had adapted to their new surroundings. Already it grew hard to pick them out from the native population of La Pointe de Sainte Anne. To a woman, they seemed to have forgotten the crazed hostility that greeted their arrival in the Maliseet village.

But Marie had not forgotten being dragged from the canoe. The women had stripped her pregnant body naked and herded her through the settlement with pointed sticks. Children armed with hissing switches had lined the way. Pitiless jeers and a flurry of stinging lashes had repaid each gasp or grimace of pain. She had quickly learned to stifle her sobs and keep her eyes fixed on the path ahead.

Neither she nor little Louis would have survived that day if Father Gabriel had not walked beside them, his lofted crucifix shielding them. The chanting Jesuit deflected many of the meaner blows with his arms. One vicious swipe aimed at Marie opened a bloody stripe across his cheek. The priest walked on unflinching as though approaching martyrdom, as though the widow and child of Luigi Campagna were helping him bear a cross along the road to Calvary. *Should I feel grateful, Black Robe? Should I forget who it was that brought us to this?*

372

Her other two stepsons had fared little better. Philippe's sudden adoption by Teiskaret and Deborah obliged him to take the lead in opening a passage through the mob for the others. Jean had fallen down twice trying to follow him. He had crouched on the ground beneath the raining blows and covered his head. Tears and dust had streaked his cheeks. Strange noises had poured from his throat. Each time, his brother had dragged him along the path till he regained his feet. The blizzard raging in the older boy's eyes had thrust the inflamed crowd back. Marie remembered Deborah towering over that gauntlet of pain like a schoolmistress. *So, she-bear, this is how you make boys into men, is it? This is how you shape a manslayer. This one will become another Gilles Leblanc if he be left to your care and keeping.*

The Acadian had not been there for the young woman who shared his canoe and bed. How Marie had cursed him as Mishikwit led the phalanx of M'ikmaq refugees through a sea of torment. Her full body, already a patchwork of vivid bruises, had attracted more than its share of slashing willows. Long crimson weals had crisscrossed her belly, breasts and thighs. So many blows had fallen upon her buttocks that blood coated them.

The M'ikmaq had neither bowed nor flinched before her assailants. She had walked straight ahead, as though nothing unusual were befalling her. *Ma pauvre sauvage, something tells me that you have seen such things before. As a young girl, did you yourself line the way for Maliseet prisoners? Did you offer them the same mercy that they offered us?*

'Be sure to wear your sealskin, Madame Marie. Winter is coming.' That very morning, Mishikwit had mumbled those words through the strips of ash held ready in her mouth as she wove a new baby basket. Her own father, husband and child were dead, but each day the M'ikmaq's will to live reasserted itself more strongly.

Marie faltered to a halt in front of the church. This symbol of faith, hope and charity had formed no part of their reception by the village. *He who now prays inside permitted it to be omitted from our itinerary that day. How carefully he divides his world into two opposing spheres. How can he be both capable of great kindness and this terrible thing he has done to me?*

Marie shivered and knocked upon the stout oak door. Kneeling there, she fancied herself once more a flat-chested girl. Magically, the leaf-strewn ground crusted over with snow, and her plump knees turned skinny again. When the portal finally opened, it framed a cowled face that darkened the world. 'Lost sinner, you do well to pray for God's mercy and forgiveness!'

'Father, I beg you hear me out! I must speak with you!'

'My child, nothing you can say will change the verdict of the ecclesiastical court. We leave for Quebec tomorrow.'

'Father, I will willingly go with you. But do not make me abandon my children here!'

'Madame, the sentence of excommunication stands. My brethren and I carefully tried your case. We all concurred in judging you an unrepentant heretic.'

'Surely my trial could have waited till Quebec. The deputy of the Black Pope himself awaits us there.'

'You will refer to our general as His Reverend Excellency, Madame.' The Jesuit withdrew himself further within his voluminous robe. 'His Apostolic Delegate has more pressing matters to attend to than one wayward Huguenot widow.'

'Father, I pray you to show me mercy for the sake of my fatherless children!'

'Madame, it is precisely for their sake that your excommunication was deemed necessary. Innocent souls cannot be left in the care of a heretic.'

'Instead, you would give away my sons to savages? You believe this conducive to their salvation, Father? This very morning they were taken away from me for some pagan initiation into the Maliseet tribe!'

'Captain Jean Baptiste Teiskaret and his good wife Deborah are both baptized Catholics. I grant you they have not yet attained a perfect Christian sensibility, but at least with them your sons will receive an upbringing within Holy Church. You may rest assured that what we have done is for the good of their souls, Madame.'

Marie despaired of obtaining mercy. 'For the good of their souls? Concern for their souls is not why you have done this thing, is it, Black Robe?'

'Madame?'

'You and your unholy brethren wish to appease your mercenary and his Ottawa esqua. You sacrifice my children to further the Societé's political ends.'

'How you try me, Madame! Would that our hold over the minds and hearts of these savages were as complete as you deem it to be! Jean Baptiste and Deborah lost a son and a daughter in the recent English raid on this settlement. They are in no mood to be denied compensation, even by a Black Robe.'

'Father Gabriel, you are still a Frenchman for all you are a Jesuit. Do not abandon the sons of your countryman to uncivilized savages!'

The priest clearly found it a struggle fending off Marie's appeal to his patriotism. 'Madame, I find your posturing quite absurd. This so-called countryman of mine has been proscribed an outlaw in France. Furthermore, it is not as though you are the natural mother of these children.'

Marie felt the ground give way before her. 'What Jesuit ruse is this, Monsieur?'

'Lost child, your innocent face cannot conceal your lying heart!' The cleric drew forth a scroll from the sleeves of his cassock. Marie recognized one of the unfurling documents as that given her by Sir Yves Le Masson. 'Luigi Campagna was a traitor. He swore allegiance to the heretic German pretender to the throne of Great Britain. In return, he obtained an English grant to stolen French land. Do not further expose your soul to the fires of damnation by denying it, Madame. These three incriminating documents were retrieved from your late husband's trading post.'

Marie stared dumbly at the fire-scorched parchments. *I am no match for him. I delude myself that I can sway him to mercy, but he plays with me the way a cat toys with a wounded sparrow.*

'I have questioned each of the children in turn, Madame. Despite their attempts to deceive me, I have concluded that their true mother is dead, that you are Luigi Campagna's second wife. I confess your counterfeit of maternal affection nearly fooled me. My own step-mother was not so convincing an actress as you are.'

'Father Gabriel, I confess much of what you say is true. But it is not true that I lack a mother's affection. I beseech you: do not give my late husband's sons over to savage strangers!'

'Campagna abducted both you and those children from France. Holy Church never joined you in wedlock. How dare you live in sin with a heretic, Madame?'

'There was no carnal sin, Father! Our marital union was never consummated!'

Too late Marie clamped her teeth on her tongue. The Jesuit's glance had fixed triumphantly on her distended belly. 'I thought so!'

'You tricked me, Monsieur Priest! I will say no more!'

'You have said enough already, Madame.' Father Gabriel cast up his eyes to heaven. 'You were never Campagna's wife in more than name. Now God has shown me why you were on that Accursed Isle!'

Marie's eyes narrowed with hatred and fear. If there had been a weapon to hand, the Jesuit's life would have been at risk. 'You disgust me, Monsieur!'

'Such a nose the reverend Abbé Le Loutre has for evil! It was he who smelled Satan's minions stirring again at Mahonne Bay! Before returning to France, he charged us to cast them out, root and branch! Ah woman, you are a creature more sinister in the eyes of Holy Church than a mere breeder of heretics could ever be!'

The widow of Luigi Campagna lowered her eyes to the leaves swirling at her feet. The priest thrust forth his rosary and fervently signed the cross. 'Now I know what you are, woman! Even my most reverend brothers speak of you in whispers. You are the bearer of the Antichrist's seed!'

'It's not true, Monsieur! I am innocent of all your charges!'

Marie might as well have been talking to the log wall. 'For centuries we have labored to cast out the Devil from the garden of God! Confess, woman: did you let Satan himself lie with you? You let him impregnate you with his devilish seed, didn't you?'

'No! No! Father Gabriel, I swear it's not true!' Marie flung herself down and grasped the priest's cassock.

He took a step back all the while wielding his cross as though exorcising a demon. 'Get thee behind me, ye whore of Satan!'

Marie cowered among the fallen leaves, lest in his magnifying horror he unleash some unearthly power against her.

'Get thee gone from here, harlot!' He shook his skirts at her as if to drive off vermin. 'This is a sanctified place of God!'

She turned on her knees and fled. She had almost reached the inner ring of Maliseet dwellings when Father Gabriel's voice brought her to a halt. 'Prepare yourself well, my child! Tomorrow we leave for Quebec! My brothers in Christ await you there!'

Marie tried not to run for the sake of her beloved. Sliding in the treacherous mud, she slipped and fell heavily. Her ring looped up around her chin and caught in her mouth. *Pay no mind to this raving priest, Marie of Hohenstaufen. We ourselves were excommunicated thrice and survived to tell the tale.*

Your Majesty was Holy Roman Emperor! I am only a weak and defenseless widow!

Our royalty signified little in the scheme of things, Princess Mine. Wherever we turned, we found the minds of men shackled with chains.

Sire, I much doubt you were ever brought to wallow in mud as I do now!

It might surprise you what we were reduced to doing upon occasion, Princess Mine. As for all that they do to you, we see you grow stronger each day.

Marie laughed and struggled to her knees. *Your Imperial Majesty thinks me endowed with Barbarossa's strength, I suppose?*

Truly spoken, but there are times such as this when even a Hohenstaufen needs a resolute ally. We have foreseen your need, Princess Mine.

Marie's hysterical laughter rose up against the blanketing stillness. *Do you expect me to thank Your Majesty for sending me a boorish Acadian to be my knight in shining armor?*

Suddenly Marie sensed that the hand grasping her shoulder was not that of the Hohenstaufen Emperor. She startled, looking up into the flat-featured face. 'Pray pardon me, Madame! I mean no offense.'

'Ah, the damned Frenchwoman! I thought it was you!' Deborah lifted Marie up from the mud as though she were a small child. 'Come with me. I would speak with you in private.'

Not without trepidation, Marie followed Teiskaret's consort into her smoky dwelling. War trophies and ceremonial gifts festooned its fur-draped walls, but a palpable emptiness pervaded the single room. 'Welcome to the lodge of Deborah, O birth mother of my two sons.'

'Three sons you have taken from me, Madame.'

'Your youngest get is not fit to be son of a chief, damned Frenchwoman, but do not worry about him. Some other empty wigwam will be found to take him soon enough. Many of my husband's people are in great need of children to replace those butchered by the English.'

'Little Louis is what we call an artist, Madame. He is a true seeker after beauty. There is no place here among the Maliseet for such as him.'

'It is more a question of making each of them fit their place, I think. I am loath to confess it, but there are such cowardly ones to be found even among my own people.' Deborah waved her hand dismissively. 'Would Madame care for some tea?'

The invitation brought tears to Marie's eyes. *This woman has also attended a seminary. How did she end up here in this miserable wigwam?* 'Thank you, O wife of Teiskaret, I would very much like a cup of tea.'

'I am called Deborah by those I offer tea.' Her hostess poured an amber stream from the lidless kettle suspended over the open fire. 'My brother Pontiac is a great chief among the Ottawa, but I am deemed worthy of honor in my own right.'

Both Gilles Leblanc and Mishikwit had told Marie the story of how Deborah had saved the village. English Rangers had attacked under cover of night, thinking to find easy prey during Teiskaret's absence with most of his warriors. Standing astride the bodies of her two children, the Ottawa had killed the commander of the Rangers with his own saber. Then the Fury had gone forth to ring the church bell and rally the old men and boys. A dozen mutilated corpses had marked her passing. The surprised English and their renegade scouts had fled in panic from La Pointe de Sainte Anne. 'Alas, Deborah, I am only the widow of a poor Huguenot.'

'Why pretend you belong to a dead heretic, Madame Campagna? I know very well it is not his seed you carry.'

The bitter tea scalded Marie, but she went on sipping it. Unbidden, she sank down before the fire and stared at the Ottawa matron. *No wonder her husband fears her. She has indeed the spirit of a warrior trapped within her. Nicole would be as a young sister to her.* 'Tell me, Deborah, what makes you think my husband did not father my child?'

'My husband told me how you did not wail for him as a woman should. A woman with child does not turn away lightly from the bleeding corpse of the man who filled her with life.'

Marie inhaled the reek of her tea. A saying of Father Jerome came to mind as she stared at her hostess. 'It's a wise man who knows his own children, Deborah.'

The wife of Teiskaret smiled secretively and sipped her tea. 'You perceive things clearly, Madame. My husband is a mighty warrior, but he could not fill me with life. I would never have conceived at all if he were not easily deceived. But then, it often happens that men wish to be deceived about such things, do they not?'

Marie's muddled mind needed time to think through the Ottawa's words. 'If this is true, why take my sons? Why not bear more children of your own?'

'My Black Robe confessor tells me that the loss of my children is the Virgin's punishment for my sin in conceiving them out of wedlock. Perhaps he is right, but a true woman draws life whence it springs most strongly.'

'Bien, Deborah! You have confessed your sins and done penance for them. Now I bid you bear more sons and leave mine to me.'

'I shed much blood avenging the death of my children, damned Frenchwoman. See you now how the Maliseet fear me? Amongst them, a warrior may not bear seed. Their men are incapable of impregnating such women. They quail before me as if I would cut off their manhood.'

'A woman such as you is not so easily thwarted! Deborah, I beg you: let me take my sons with me to Quebec.'

'You wish to give them to the Black Robes? Are you mad, Madame? They are safer with Deborah among the Maliseet.'

'But Deborah, they will never become Maliseet!'

'Nor will they ever again be what they once were, damned Frenchwoman. Their new mother will see to that. She shall shape them into something new in this land.'

'Deborah, they will not survive here! Your own children were not safe! The English will destroy all who remain here in the end!'

'We were slow to defend ourselves, Madame. That time is long past. My husband is a mighty chief now like my brother. Many warriors follow him. The French King provides muskets and powder in exchange for our alliance. Let the English come this way again if they dare.'

'They will come, Deborah! That much you can be sure of! They will keep coming till this village is a heap of ashes!'

'Madame, I think perhaps you are a true prophet. Perhaps even the great fortress at Louisbourg will not long be safe from the English. Even Quebec itself may fall in the end. Yet I think the Goddess will give us time enough for our sons to grow into men.'

Marie did not know what to say to such a woman. 'Not enough time for little Louis. At least let me take him with me!'

'Nay, Madame Marie. Yet for your sake I shall take even the runt of the litter to be mine own.'

'For my sake?' Marie suspected the big woman of mocking her. 'Why should you care about me, Deborah?'

'The Black Robes are afraid of you, damned Frenchwoman. They are not easily made afraid, but they harbor much fear of the seed you bear.'

'They've no need to fear me! My unborn babe is not Satan's Seed!'

'Tell me, damned Frenchwoman, what is it like to lie with the Devil?' Laughter folded the planes of Deborah's face. 'Does he come as a young buck comes into you, hard and overflowing with the vigor of manhood? Did he have horns, a tail and hoofed feet as in the pictures the black nuns love to tremble over. A mere man must be poor fare indeed after such a feast of riches!'

Marie blushed to the roots of her hair. She stifled the doubt lingering within her. 'The father of my child was no Devil, Deborah.'

'Pray pardon me, Madame. I did not mean to laugh at you; I laugh at the priests.'

'I do not laugh. I find them much too dangerous for that.'

'Indeed, Madame Marie, too late I come to see that you are right. They spread sickness of spirit among my people. They drive us on to destruction in their incessant wars. They invoke the love of Christ, but they think of us as merely a weapon shaped to their hand. Wherever they pass among us, we are wiped from the Great Mother's face.'

'So you believe in the Goddess despite that crucifix you wear!'

'Do not all women believe in Her deep down in the depths of their souls? But we best not speak of Her. These days men grow frightened at the mere mention of the Great Mother. Let us speak of you and your unborn child.'

'We are being taken to Quebec. Such is the will of the Jesuits. What more is there to say?'

'You must know that certain death awaits you there, damned Frenchwoman. Either a quick death or it will be slow and lingering in one of their dark dungeons. You must escape the Black Robe.'

'How should a pregnant stranger manage such a thing? I am caged about by wild beasts!'

'Get one of the wild beasts to help you.' Deborah looked Marie up and down. 'You are passing fair for a Frenchwoman. I have seen how my husband's bonds-man looks at you despite your big belly. He escorts you to Quebec, does he not?'

She is trying to entrap me. Father Gabriel asked her to do this thing. If I am not careful, I will cost us all our lives. 'Madame, I fear Gilles Leblanc more than I fear Teiskaret. He is a cruel and heartless man. I fear him almost as much as I fear the Black Robes.'

'And well you might, Madame Marie. Your Acadian knows no limits, and he kills for the sake of killing.'

'Why do you call him my Acadian? He has sworn to serve your husband for a year.'

'A white man's word always has a price.' The Ottawa laughed gaily and spat on the mud-packed floor. 'Discover that which such a man craves, and he will sell his soul to get it from you.'

'I am afraid it is too late to follow your advice, Deborah.' Marie rose to her feet. 'We leave for Quebec tomorrow. Thank you for the tea.'

The Ottawa drowned Marie in more laughter. 'Yes, it is well that you go now. The priests forbid us to talk with the damned Frenchwoman.'

Marie walked to the doorway and pushed the cari-bou skin aside. Fresh air came as a welcome relief from the smoke inside the Maliseet hut. 'What will become of my sons, Deborah?'

'They are mine now.' The Ottawa came to stand behind Marie. 'Best you let go of them, damned Frenchwoman. The seed you bear will be sufficient care where you are going. I shall be a truer mother to them than you could ever be.'

The widow of Luigi Campagna let herself be driven out into the pelting rain. She was grateful that the tell-tale signs of her weakness were thus hidden from the formidable woman. 'So be it, Deborah. Care for my children well, and may the Great Mother be with us both.'

Deborah closed the outer doors to her lodge.

Mishikwit was putting the finishing touches on the new basket when Marie returned to their lean-to shelter. 'Alas, Madame Marie, I have bad news for you. Your dead handmaiden was right. The easy way this ash bends into place tells me the child it will shelter will be a girl.'

'Why should I grieve about that? Are not esquas such as ourselves needed in this world?'

'Yes, but what honor does a woman gain from bearing esquas? Waksitanou loved my mother more than words can express, but she bore him only daughters. So he took Nasqualik to get strong sons.'

'You told Deborah that Waksitanou only took one wife!'

'Only one that he loved!'

Marie threw up her hands as though to say she would never understand the working of the native mind. 'Anyway, my friend, I have three sons already. So I am glad this child will be a girl. I shall have someone to care for me in my old age.'

'Look to the wives of your sons for that, Madame Marie.' Mishikwit indulged herself in a knowing little chuckle. 'In this land, a daughter follows her husband and looks for a place in the lodge of her mother-in-law.'

As if already faced by the desertion of her nonexistent daughter, Marie began to sniffle. The M'ikmaq set her basketry aside. 'Hi-yah, Madame Marie, you make sounds like a child fallen among thorns.'

'Frenchwomen often weep, Mishikwit. '

'What good does it do them? Should we shed tears to delight our enemies? Some things we must yield them, but never our tears.'

My friend, you give good counsel. I will not weep. Instead I will make my dead husband a promise. Luigi Campagna: I will regain your sons in spite of Deborah and the Jesuit. I shall see them brought to full manhood. They shall inherit the land claimed for them with your blood. 'What news of your master, Mishikwit?'

A strange expression sealed the perfect face. 'He went with Teiskaret and some warriors in canoes. They were wearing the black paint of initiation. They took your three sons with them.'

Marie hung a battered copper pot over the fire. 'Will the Maliseet harm them, Mishikwit? Is there danger in what they do?'

'Hi-yah, Madame Marie, you must know by now that going into danger is what God made men to do.'

'But my sons are not yet men, Mishikwit!'

The M'ikmaq picked up her basket again and held it out to Marie. 'Do you wish them to become men, Madame, or do you wish them to remain babes?'

A good question, whether or no I have choice in the matter. Things move too swiftly for me. The sons of Luigi Campagna must join an alien people, whereas I am likely to spend the rest of my days in some Jesuit prison — if they dare even to let me live.

Marie squatted and brooded over her pot of water till it boiled. She took off her ragged riding-gown and began to bathe herself. She lathered her armpits sparingly with the small cake of lye soap given her by Gilles Leblanc.

Sure enough, the renegade appeared in the doorway the minute she fully exposed herself. Yet so inured had Marie become to his invasions of her privacy that she only drew a blanket-smock about her shoulders and went on sponging herself with soapy water.

Mishikwit set out food for her master. The renegade ignored her attentions. In hunkering down, he nearly overturned Marie's pot of hot water. 'Madame, I must speak with you.'

A strange odor clinging to the man disturbed Marie. She noticed thin streaks of blood upon his face and forearms. 'What did you do with my sons, renegade?'

'Madame, listen to me! I left Teiskaret and his warriors drunk with the drugs of initiation. Now is the time for us to flee from here quickly.'

'My sons, where are they?' Marie huddled inside her blanket. 'I will not leave here without them.'

The Acadian rocked back on his haunches, making a visible effort to be patient with the Frenchwoman. 'Most of the Maliseet are asleep from the drugs. I was able to steal your sons away from them. I left them waiting for us in a safe place upstream from here.'

'Upstream? Upstream leads to Quebec! Our way lies downstream till we reach la Baie de Francoise.'

'We would never make it.' The renegade shook his head in wonder at her simplicity. 'They will look for us that way for sure. Our only hope is to go upstream till we leave the land of the Maliseet far behind.'

Marie stood up and drew the smock over her swollen breasts and belly. 'Then let us go. Tell us what we need to bring.'

'All we need is in my *kayak*. We take only this esqua to paddle more swiftly.'

Wise in the ways of women, Mishikwit seemed to know already that they were going on a long journey. She shouldered her heavy pack and handed Marie the tiny baby basket. 'Put this on your back, Madame Marie. Your time is soon upon you.'

The sun still glowed dully in the West when three shadows slipped down to the bank of the river. Marie recognized the young Maliseet scout lying among the beached canoes. The youth wore Luigi Campagna's shaving case fastened to his belt. His scalped head reposed at an improbable angle. *So it is already too late to turn back. Neither the war chief nor the Jesuit will forgive us this. Renegade, this boy was your friend, was he not?*

Marie sank gratefully into the strange kayak. Its skin covering had been stripped off to make sufficient room for the three of them. As she watched, the Acadian wrecked each of the birch bark hulls lying upon the beach with his tomahawk. Moments later, he and the M'ikmaq were paddling upstream.

'I thought Teiskaret was your master, Acadian.'

'I serve no master but the Seed you carry, Madame.'

A full moon had risen before Marie put the specter of the dead scout behind her. 'Gilles Leblanc, this canoe is too small! There's no place for my sons!'

'There is another canoe for them.' The renegade spoke soothingly as though to a child. 'They must paddle it themselves.'

The prospect of that gave Marie pause for thought. *How can he possibly expect mere boys to paddle hundreds of miles? Philippe perhaps, but neither Jean nor Louis is up to it. You cannot be serious, Acadian.* 'Mishikwit will have to help them, Monsieur. I also can paddle if I must. If only you would go downstream, it would be so much easier!'

Gilles Leblanc said nothing. Marie felt his paddle quicken as he headed the canoe out into the middle of the great river. Mishikwit matched him stroke for stroke. The widow of Luigi Campagna could only sit and look upon the river fleeting past. She searched the banks of the river for the pale faces of her children waiting in the moonlight.

Finally Marie looked again into the Acadian's ravaged face. She read there the truth. She could think of

nothing to say. Instead, she screamed and rocked sideways, trying to fall out of the canoe. Steel fingers
gripped her neck and pulled her down. 'You lied to me,
Monsieur!'

Gilles Leblanc locked an arm round her throat and
whispered fiercely in her ear. 'Calm yourself, Madame,
or I will be forced to bind you!'

'You made me desert my children!' Marie's fury
turned cold as ice as she stared at her friend's back.
'Mishikwit, you knew all along what this renegade was
doing!'

'My line was put here to preserve the Chosen Seed.'
The Acadian tightened his grip. 'And serve the Chosen
Seed I shall! No one shall thwart my purpose, Madame
— not even you!'

Chapter XXVI

FLIGHT

Oo-lahs-took, September 1756

Night after moonless night, the fugitives canoed up the river. Day after Indian summer day, they hid along its banks. Marie felt herself swallowed up and carried away, felt herself drawn ever closer to the black-robed menace waiting to engulf her at Quebec. Grey-faced, she kept silent vigil while her captors slept the sleep of sheer exhaustion.

Not that Gilles Leblanc ever let down his guard. Night and day, the double crossbow lay within easy reach. Paddling or resting, the tomahawk and the curve-bladed knife stayed belted at his side. Any unusual sound or movement roused him, weapons at the ready.

The third morning after leaving La Pointe de Sainte Anne, Marie was startled awake by a vast honking overhead. She watched the Acadian rear up from sleep to bring down a goose in flight. It all happened in a flow of reflexive action too swift and smooth for the eye to follow. 'Gilles Leblanc, why do you favor so antiquated a weapon as this crossbow?'

'Old Bernard Comeau of Grand Pré wrought *L'Amanita* to my father's design, Madame.' The Acadian stroked the worn oaken stock lovingly. 'Certes, she is more accurate than any musket in skilled hands. Better still, she shoots twice and reloads far more quickly. And best of all, she kills without making a sound.'

Such incidental discourse did not signify any resumption of amity among the three voyageurs. The widow of Luigi Campagna had reconciled herself to her plight, but her trust in Gilles Leblanc had been nipped in the bud. *He cares only for his Templar mission. Mishikwit means nothing to him. What will he do with her when he no longer needs her to paddle this canoe or to deliver me of this child? She must know he will cut her throat and leave her floating in the river if it serves his purpose. Yet she lives only to please him. She accepts his right to dispose of her as he wishes. She even betrayed my children and me for his sake.*

Such thoughts passed through Marie's head even while watching Mishikwit fashion swaddling clothes from the fur of rabbits. The exquisite little garments made her yearn to hold her baby in her arms, but the Acadian's presence saved her from wholly succumbing to these intense maternal feelings. *Why does he stare at me like this? Surely such a man cannot take a maimed and pregnant widow for the object of his lust! Whence comes this shadow lurking behind his eyes?*

Marie would not forgive how the renegade had forced her to abandon her stepsons. She shuddered each time she thought of them. *Philippe will never stop fighting back. His life will be brutal, but sheer courage and stubbornness will see him through, God willing. Even Jean may survive life among the Maliseet, for Deborah is bound to mark his cleverness. It is Louis who needs my prayers. Little Louis. She will thrust him aside, and he will shrivel up and die. Dear God in heaven, have mercy on the sons of Luigi Campagna!*

The great stream coiled down from the West and North forever. Marie watched and waited; knowing the peace of the river would not long endure. *Where is Teiskaret? By now, he will surely have scoured the Saint Jean to its mouth. Already, fast warrior-driven canoes will be racing upstream. We dare travel only at night, while our pursuers spell each other without halting to rest. A hundred leagues is nothing to them. Out there, somewhere, our enemies are fast overtaking us. God help us all!*

She could feel Gilles Leblanc also waiting. Each evening as he scanned the river before launching his canoe, she studied him for signs of what was to come. *When the Maliseet finally catch up with us, he will greet them with this same strange smile. He will take L'Amanita in his arms and crouch down into the killer that he is. How many of Teiskaret's hounds will die before this lone wolf be brought to bay?*

Mishikwit made a point of repriming the musket each morning, but somehow Marie could not imagine the M'ikmaq defending herself. *Yet there's no telling what she is capable of doing for her lord and master. I believe she will die for him without a whimper if it comes to that. See how she can no longer meet my eyes?*

And still Oo-lahs-took lolled on past their hiding places, its tree-lined banks aflame with every color Marie had ever imagined. On the night of the full moon rising, she looked over her shoulder and shivered. Winter dogged their heels. Large flakes of snow pelted them as they canoed onward. Marie muffled herself in Leblanc's caribou robe, although it galled her to accept the smallest favor from her captor. Near morning, an icy wind blew up, cutting to the quick, forcing even the paddlers to cover themselves with fur.

On the morning of the fifth day, they took refuge in a small marshy creek. The Acadian went off to hunt waterfowl and other small game. Mishikwit quickly roasted a brace of fat rabbits over a smokeless fire. Marie paced back and forth till the chill was gone from her limbs. She felt new life stirring inside her. The fetus became so animated that she judged it prudent to lie down on the caribou robe beside Mishikwit.

A dull spasm of pain gathered deep within. Her sphincter slowly tightened, threatening worse to come. *Dear God, keep this cup from me yet a while! I know I must drink it soon, but withhold it from my lips till we are safe under a Christian roof!*

Agony deluged her like a tidal wave. She opened her mouth but could not cry out till the pain broke over her. Then she lay very still, not daring to move or breathe. Again, her womb constricted, and fear surged upward to her heart. She took a deep breath and licked her dry lips.

The spasms ebbed away as Marie lay on her side, talon-like fingers clutching dry stalks of grass. *It is a harbinger of things to come. Dear God, help me bring this life into Your world. I know my little travail is as nothing in Your eyes, but I am full of fear!*

Mishikwit rolled over and sat up. 'Rest easy, Madame.'

'Easy for you to say, Esqua! It is I who am about to give birth — not you!' Perhaps Mishikwit knew all about false labor pains, but Marie no longer trusted her former friend. *Her fear is not like mine. She lives in a state of savage nature where it is no great thing to be raped or suffer one's children to be brained with a toma- hawk.*

The widow of Luigi Campagna looked where the Acadian lay gently snoring on his side. His tomahawk gleamed wickedly upon his thigh. *Deborah is right: you are worse than the painted Maliseet. Your mother taught you a civilized tongue, even if it be that awful Acadian dialect. Claudine and the children are no excuse for what you do, Gilles Leblanc.*

Suddenly, Mishikwit cocked her head like a bird at Marie. 'What is it, Sauvage?'

The daughter of Waksitanou sealed Marie's parted lips with a raised finger. Then she rose up and glided away through the trees. Loath to remain alone with the sleeping renegade, Marie followed after her.

She came up with the M'ikmaq in a pine thicket. The young woman stood stock-still gazing out over the river. So tranquil was the scene that Marie fancied for a moment that the canoes drifting on the morning mist belonged to fishermen. Then a painted warrior stood up and shaded his eyes against the shimmering sun. Mishikwit unceremoniously pulled her down. 'They search for us, Madame!'

They crawled back on hands and knees from the riverbank. Mishikwit halted her progress abruptly and stared up at the leggings of the Acadian. 'What is it, Esqua?'

'Maliseet canoes on the river, Master.'

Gilles Leblanc grounded his crossbow and used the clever foot lever to cock both its strings. 'How many warriors?'

The M'ikmaq held up four fingers and two thumbs. 'Teiskaret?'

'He is not with them, Master.'

'Certes, he follows close behind them!' The Acadian turned his attention to Marie. 'Get up off the ground, Madame. It is not fitting that the Bearer of the Chosen Seed grovel at the feet of such as me.'

Clad in pine needles, the M'ikmaq also rose to stand with downcast eyes and braided pigtails before her master. He looked over her comely form and shook his head. 'An esqua such as this one can alter a man into a beast, Madame. It was not well done of you to make her mine.'

'I see that now, Acadian. Set her free before it be too late for both of you.'

'It is too late already, Madame. The only way to set her free would be to cut her throat.'

'Then give her to me!' Marie claimed the other woman's attention by seizing both her hands. 'Would you like to belong to me, Mishikwit?'

'Madame Marie is my friend, but ....' The M'ikmaq broke off speaking to glance furtively from the French-woman to the Acadian.

The widow of Luigi Campagna gave voice to Mishikwit's unspoken words. '... but Gilles Leblanc is my master.'

'Yes, Madame Marie.' Dog-like devotion suffused the beautiful face as the M'ikmaq gazed upon the Acadian.

'Then let us pray he proves worthy of such loyalty.'

Marie shot a warding glance at the Acadian. It was as if she could feel a slow transformation stealing over him, as if he were growing fangs and claws before her eyes. 'Madame, you had best get some sleep. The Maliseet will likely move on by nightfall. Then we shall slip past them up the river.'

Marie bristled at him. 'What are you up to, Gilles Leblanc? If we stay on this river, we will end up at Quebec. Then the Societé will have your precious Chosen Seed for sure.'

A tawny light glowed in the renegade's eyes. 'Even in that priest-ridden place we shall find powerful friends, Madame.'

Marie obediently laid herself down on the caribou hide, somewhat mollified at having so cleverly tricked the Acadian. *At least I know now where he is taking us. All roads and rivers in this land lead to Quebec, it seems. Well, that may not be so bad, after all. There will be roofs and doors, even hearths and shops to be had there. Who knows what may be possible? Perhaps we can even hide from the Black Robes among so many people. He hints that we shall find friends there. More mad men like himself, no doubt. But there will also be physicians or at least good French midwives. I shall give birth in a prop-*

er bed, not alone in the woods like an esqua. If only I can make it that far. Bien, I shall will it to be so!

Marie drowsed beside Mishikwit, dimly aware that Gilles Leblanc did not rejoin them. Indeed, her dream followed the *coureur de bois* till she lost him among the trees. He became a phantom so elusive that not even the forest-bred Maliseet sensed his fatal passing. Reassured despite herself by his lurking presence, she fell into a deep sleep.

The sun was sinking low when she awakened. Mishikwit was pounding pemmican. As usual, the Acadian was nowhere to be seen. It gave Marie pause to wonder what would happen to them if he chose never to return. *There are many Maliseet hunting us out there. Surely he knows what Teiskaret will do to him if we are caught. Don't even try to imagine what the Jesuit will do.*

Marie checked to make sure that the Acadian's canoe was still in its fir thicket. *He might leave us behind but never this. Yet where has he gone? What kind of man leaves two helpless women alone with all these savages roaming around? No wonder he lost his Claudine.*

Responding to a call of nature, the widow of Luigi Campagna left the camp and waded into a patch of giant ferns. She was about to take off her shift the better to wipe herself clean when she noticed something moving toward her through the gently waving fronds. 'Monsieur Leblanc, if you please! Be good enough to leave me to my toilet in peace!'

The frost-blackened fronds parted, unveiling a war-painted face. Stupefied, Marie froze as Old No Ears burst into view, tomahawk upraised. It did not reassure her to see his hostile frown transform to a friendly grin. She watched his eyes suspiciously probe the ferns for the jaws of a trap. Apparently satisfied, he began edging closer.

Marie screamed, then whirled and raced back the way she had come. As slow and clumsy as she was, the wary Maliseet did not overtake her till she stumbled and fell. Wrenching pain shot along her lame leg and brought an involuntary scream to her lips. She rolled sideways to stare upward into Old No Ears' amused eyes. He raised a palm to his mouth and made a warbling sound. Then that same huge hand seized her loosely gathered hair. She took perverse comfort in that familiar grip.

Something hard struck the warrior's shoulder: Mishikwit wielding Luigi Campagna's musket by its barrel. Unperturbed, Old No Ears looked round and grinned hideously as though inviting the M'ikmaq to strike him again. Marie twisted and kicked viciously beneath his breechclout with her good foot, converting the insane laughter into a startled yelp.

The Maliseet crumpled the M'ikmaq with one swipe. He belted his tomahawk and again seized Marie's hair. She looked upward into maddened eyes as the smock was ripped from her breasts and swollen belly. It was not animal lust she sensed coming at her. Pursuit of some wild justice drove her assailant on.

The Maliseet struck Marie to the ground. *Stop! You will kill my beloved! No! You are spinning round me, silly savage. Stop! Do you not know I am with child? Dear God, your breechclout is awry. Did the Jesuit not warn you I am a witch? Oh God, would you risk your manhood within the bearer of Satan's seed? What is this absurd new ear you have grown?*

Old No Ears whooped fiercely and fell upon her, knocking the wind from her lungs. Marie felt something hot and sticky trickling down her neck. The rolling eyes blazed into hers for an awful moment before the glaze of death sealed them.

'Stay down, Madame!'

The pregnant widow lacked the breath to chastise Gilles Leblanc for his pointless instruction. Casting about frantically to free herself from the dead man, she glimpsed two familiar Maliseet warriors emerge from the ferns. Each leapt high in turn, kicking like a rabbit with steel quarrels through their throats. Gurgling sounds in the underbrush betrayed their death throes.

The Acadian crouched down beside her, but he made no attempt to rescue her. Anger flooding over her like the hot dripping blood, Marie listened to the ratcheting of the crossbow. It was Mishikwit, lurching dazedly, who finally dragged Old No Ears off her. And still Gilles Leblanc did not take his eyes from the waving sea of fronds. 'Are you all right, Madame?'

'Small thanks to you, Monsieur!' Marie sat up gasping for air. What bothered her more than the blood soaking her shift was awareness of how much she did owe the Acadian. *Why think that? We would not be in this mess if not for him! Look, a new welt rising on Mishikwit's poor face! It's a miracle Old No Ears did not bash out her brains with his tomahawk!*

Marie heard the sickening sound the Acadian made wrenching his weapon from the skull of her assailant. He wiped brains and blood upon the white sphagnum moss before scalping the Maliseet with the bit of the tomahawk. 'You are even more of a savage than these Indians, Monsieur Templar!'

'Certes, Madame, do not think I take any great pleasure in doing this. Thomas Ironhand was a brave warrior who took many English scalps in his time.'

It shocked Marie to know that the dead Maliseet possessed a full Christian name. 'Monsieur, this brave warrior died in the act of violating two defenseless women!'

'Defenseless, did you say? Madame, you gave the poor man good cause to do what he did. I take only his scalp but you tried to take his manhood!'

'What? You stood by and watched us struggle with the brute? Mishikwit might have been killed while you dallied!'

Gilles Leblanc tied the oozing scalp lock to his belt. 'Please try to understand, Madame. If I had not marked Thomas' companions before making my move, it might well be us lying here.'

Shivering, Marie watched the renegade wade through the ferns to retrieve more scalps. *How many times has he done this before? Dear God, why did you send this terrible man to be our deliverer? Is there something you wish revealed in him?*

The muffled scream of a man in his death throes choked off. *Merciful God, how much longer must this nightmare go on? Must You keep soaking me in blood to make me see whatever it is you want me to see?*

The Acadian emerged from the ferns with two muskets slung from his back. A pair of powder horns dangled among the bloody scalps. Her face drained of all color by pain and anger, Marie tried to stand, but her twisted ankle buckled under her weight.

Gilles Leblanc and Mishikwit joined hands to form a kind of bosun's chair in which to carry Marie down to the water's edge. Without waiting for night to fall, the fugitives pushed off into the river. All night long, the paddles hurried them westward. All night long, the widow of Luigi Campagna tried to lose herself in the foaming phosphorescence, but her ankle throbbed too painfully for sleep.

Marie's only consolation was a gentle stirring deep within, as though her baby sought to calm her. She willed her womb muscles to subside and brought the Hohenstaufen ring to her lips. *Tarry yet awhile, my beloved. I know thou art anxious, but thou must give me time to reach a better place in which to bring thee into the light of day.*

Finally, a familiar shadow passed over Marie. *I began to think Your Majesty had deserted me!*

Centuries ago we promised our grandson never to do so, Marie of Hohenstaufen.

Your grandson? His name was Conradin, was it not?

Indeed, Conradin, son of Conrad. He was the last Hohenstaufen king of Germany. We spoke to him briefly on the eve of his execution in Naples.

His execution, Sire? Yes, I remember now. Why would they execute a boy not much older than Philippe?

For being our grandson, of course. What greater crime in the eyes of Holy Church than to be the Antichrist's seed? The Pope and the Angevin usurper of our throne together struck off his head on a public scaffold. He was not yet seventeen years old, but he died like a true Hohenstaufen. We promised him that those who bear his seed should never wander through this world alone.

Well, Sire, I appreciate the chivalrous gesture. Without your visitations I think I should have taken leave of my senses long ago. And upon that thought Marie passed into dreamless sleep, remaining oblivious even when Mishikwit covered her with the caribou robe.

It was already morning when she awoke. The Acadian was drawing the prow of the canoe from the hidden creek. She tried to rise, but pain punished her presumption so cruelly that she fainted again.

That day unfolded as one long blur of agony and fever. The widow of Luigi Campagna was only dimly aware of Mishikwit's freshly bruised face. The M'ikmaq packed bruised leaves about her injured ankle and made her drink hot tea and steaming broth. As usual, Gilles Leblanc was nowhere to be seen, but Marie did not miss him this time. *I would as well fall prey to the scheming Jesuit as endure more of the Templar's butchery. Ma pauvre sauvage, this wilderness is so large! Find us a place to hide forever from them both!*

The Acadian emerged from the forest at the fall of dusk. He gently helped Mishikwit lift Marie into the canoe. She no longer smelled blood and death upon him. She did not even notice the drying scalps hanging from his belt. Only the pleasant scent of woods and tobacco clung to his buckskins; yet she marked him with relentless loathing. *Your crossbow is well named, Templar, for you are the angel of death himself! You sweep across the land reaping lives like sheaves of corn.*

Silver light bathed the river as the moon thrust forth from its cloister of clouds. Marie glimpsed her own pale face in the clear water. A bruise darkened both her cheeks and eyes. *Mishikwit and I wear the same kind of mask. We are initiates into some pagan sisterhood, but the meaning of our enduring all this remains as much a mystery as ever.*

Next morning, Marie awoke to find herself alone in the tethered canoe. The sound of a babbling creek filled the hidden glen. Then she heard strange rhythmic noises emanating from a nearby copse of trees.

She pulled herself under an overhanging limb and dragged herself ashore. Using a musket as a crutch, she hobbled several feet till she espied the renegade's prone back. His buckskins cast aside, Gilles Leblanc wore only his homespun shirt. His naked buttocks heaved up and down.

The doe like eyes watching her over the Acadian's shoulder rendered the scene intelligible. *Behold what men do to women! For this is how babies are made. So much for the husband of Claudine resisting temptation! Yet you are no more to him, ma pauvre sauvage, than this white moss on which you are so fiercely pounded.*

Mishikwit, I brought you to this to keep Teiskaret from slaying you that hot spring night. In my pride, I thought I could guard you from harm. I even persuaded this renegade to do this to you when all you wanted to do was die. Why do your eyes not reproach me? You are a bottomless well accepting all that is or ever was.

Marie limped back to the ashes of a dead campfire. She poked the coals and revived a tiny flame. *I am made of the same stern stuff as you, Mishikwit. God shaped us women to bear all things.*

The river bore them westward through four glorious nights of Indian summer. The three voyageurs seldom spoke. A look or gesture sufficed, for they were grown single-minded now. Nothing mattered but to ascend the endless river. Marie's desires narrowed down to her need to reach civilization before the birth of her baby. 'Acadian, how much further to Quebec?'

'God knows, Madame, for I have never traveled this way before. Two nights should bring us to our grand portage. On the next day we cross to the Chaudière, God willing. Three days more down that river to Quebec.'

It struck Marie that the voyageur did not much care where they were.

Another day of hiding came and went. Marie watched the Acadian take his bearings upon the river. 'This is Abenaki territory, Madame. Now we can risk traveling in daylight.'

That evening, there began a persistent drizzle that chilled and soaked Marie to the bone. Morning would not come as she shivered to warm herself under the caribou hide. The nights had grown noticeably longer as autumn took hold of the wilderness. She felt herself sinking to a new depth of despair. *Marie Campagna, you will not make it to Quebec. You will die giving birth upon this endless river.*

The Acadian pressed on when morning came. White water often barred their way, but the canoe never turned aside from the narrowing stream. Marie passed between fits of light sleep and miserable wakefulness. She watched lines etch themselves ever deeper into the faces of her companions.

Not endowed with exceptional strength or stamina, the Acadian endured through the sheer power of his will. As for the M'ikmaq, the rhythm of her paddle only faltered when fending off a rock or poling past a sandbar. That evening she made camp and gathered roots and berries before snatching a few hours of sleep. *Ma belle sauvage, I think you grow stronger each passing day. What are you made of? Not even your loathsome master can wear you down.*

Next afternoon, they reached the portage to the Chaudière. A beaten track led up from the landing place into the birch-wooded hills. Marie felt her child grow restless. *If we can only make it from water to water, my beloved. Then it is down river all the way to the Saint Lawrence not far from the City of Quebec. Not far ahead waits a soft bed and friendly French faces, God willing. It is so near, my beloved, and yet so far.*

Crossbow ready at his hip, Gilles Leblanc stepped ashore and knelt to study the ground. 'The Jesuit passed here yesterday, Madame.'

Marie refused to believe such a dismal thing. 'How do you know that, Monsieur?'

'See, Madame: the cross of nails on either boot-heel? And beside it, see this moccasin print with two toes missing? That is why Teiskaret cannot abide French boots. I think he wishes us to know that he waits for us somewhere ahead on the portage.'

'Is there no other way than this to reach Quebec, Monsieur?'

'Not for you, Madame.'

'Monsieur, I have enough blood on my hands already! I do not need yours!'

'Teiskaret brings only two canoes this far, Madame. I make it five warriors and the priest who stand in our way. Worse odds than this I have survived before.'

'Monsieur, I tell you again: I wish this trail of death I leave behind me to end!'

'The end of the killing is near, Madame; that much I promise you.'

A sonorous voice floated up from the birch trees as Marie eased herself out of the canoe. 'Stand and give heed to God's word, O my children!'

Chapter XXVII

VENGEANCE

Rivière Chaudière, September 1756

Marie would have capsized the canoe if Mishikwit had not held it steady. Flailing about in knee-deep water, she caught a glimpse of the Acadian crouched behind a rock. He held his crossbow thrust forward in frozen menace like a snake coiled to strike.

'In the name of God, I come alone!' Advancing out of the trees with crucifix held high, Father Gabriel tipped back his hood and smiled serenely. 'Have no fear, my wayward children!'

Marie relived the massacre on Sanctuary Island during the few moments Gilles Leblanc took to scan each tree and rock. *Do not be fooled by him, Acadian! Somewhere near, Teiskaret and his warriors wait in ambush for the Jesuit's signal to attack us!*

In truth, the advancing priest frightened the Huguenot widow more than all the Maliseet she imagined lurking among the trees. The warding crucifix stabbed deep into her heart as the Jesuit intoned. 'I come to minister unto you in the name of Our Lord and Savior, Jesus Christ!'

With a sideways glance at Marie, Mishikwit scurried forward and flung herself down before the priest.

Father Gabriel laid a hand in benediction upon the M'ikmaq's glossy hair. 'Be at peace, Hagar. Do not fear for your lady. She shall have both my priestly benediction and my protéction for the birthing of her child. My brethren at Quebec shall welcome her as a lost sheep returned to the fold.'

'Hold, Black Robe!' The Acadian stood forth from his hiding place, but *L'Amanita* did not waver. 'Forfeit shall be the life of any man or priest who tries to take Madame Campagna from my keeping!'

'May God have mercy on you, Gilles Leblanc!' Father Gabriel shook his head sadly. 'I know only too well you make no idle boast. Have I not followed your grisly trail all the way here from La Pointe de Sainte Anne? Do I not pray both night and day for the souls of those you have scalped and left me to bury along the way?'

'You do well to be wary of me, priest. Who will pray for your soul when I spring it free of its mortal coil?'

'Gilles Leblanc, I charge you to stop taking Christian lives!' The Jesuit couched his crucifix like a shield before him. 'As priest of God, I call upon you to repent your many sins! You stand in peril of eternal damnation. Go down on your knees beside Hagar and plead for divine forgiveness!'

'Take not another step, Black Robe!' The renegade's stance gave warning of readiness to kill. 'You are no priest of the True God; those foul hands of yours have already caused more blood to flow than mine ever will.'

The Jesuit drew back more in pained surprise than fear. 'My son, remember what you are! Your Acadian people were ever true to Holy Church. From generation to generation, they follow faithfully those shepherds she sends to watch over them. The venerable Abbé Le Loutre himself welcomed you into this world. Did you not receive your wife and children in holy sacrament from these very hands?'

Gilles Leblanc tore the toque from his head; long straight hair tumbled about his shoulders. 'Look well upon me, Black Robe; my ancestors came here long before Jesuits abominated this land. Look at me and see the truth revealed, you false priest!'

Father Gabriel held up his crucifix to the renegade as though it were a glass that enabled him to see more clearly. 'Indeed, Gilles Leblanc, you are somewhat swarthy for a pure native son of France. Despite our counsel, there has been much mixing of Acadian blood with that of Hagar's people.'

'Yea, Black Robe, I believe some M'ikmaq blood does course in my veins. We also mingled with the Normans and Bretons who came here, but you must look much further back than the Acadians to discern my true lineage.'

'What talk is this of lineage?' The Jesuit furled his brow. 'It ill behooves a mongrel to brag of its pedigree.'

'Certes, Black Robe, it is true that I am sprung from the loins of a Kurdish slave sold into the harem of the great Sultan Saladin, himself born a Kurd as you will remember. He was the nemesis of priests of the cross like you. He drove you all from the Holy Land.'

'What? You claim to be a Saracen?' Father Gabriel hissed between his teeth. 'That is utterly absurd!'

'Listen to me well, priest! Five centuries ago, a daughter of that Kurdish slave was sent as gift to the Holy Roman Emperor at his court in Palermo. There she became a member of the royal harem. Eventually, her Templar son returned to Cairo and became a master of engineering.'

Father Gabriel chose to be amused by this revelation. 'Ah, so you would have me believe not only that you yourself are seed of the Antichrist, but that your Saracen ancestors came here with Templar renegades. Next you will be telling me it was they who built that den of Satan on the Accursed Isle of the Huguenot!'

'Think about it, Black Robe! Who else ever to set foot on that island could have done such a thing?'

Marie caught the flash of the Jesuit's eyes as he began to believe in spite of himself. He made a tiny gasping sound deep in his throat and dropped to his knees. 'Could it be that you speak the truth? Certainly none but the infidel minions of Lucifer could have performed so diabolical a deed. Even more diabolical to have hidden yourselves all these years like wolves among our Acadian sheep!'

'Yea, Black Robe, we learned to baa at the behest of false shepherds such as you. Like the Marranos and Moriscos of Spain, we have waited vainly, generation after generation, for deliverance from such as you. So long have we waited for the Chosen Seed that the hope of it became no more than a fable among us!' Gilles Leblanc lowered his crossbow as though tired of standing *en garde*. He held out an arm to the widow of Luigi Campagna. 'Behold, Black Robe, the Bearer of the Chosen Seed has come!'

Father Gabriel turned upon Marie a visage replete with despair. 'Alas, I find no remedy for this man! My priestly vision tells me that he is eternally damned! My daughter, you must not lend your unborn child to his fiendish purposes!'

'Black Robe, think you I prefer to end as did my mother?' Marie used both hands to support her swollen abdomen. 'Think you I wish my beloved to be buried deep in some Jesuit prison, just as I was buried?'

'Do not despair of Christ, my child! Holy Church grows gentler and more filled with Christian love with each passing age.'

Marie's laughter was not a thing of beauty. 'Forgive me, Father, but I have a great fear of burning alive!'

'My child, the Holy Office no longer ordains that heretics must be cleansed of their sins with fire. Once brought to sincere contrition, a heretic may hope to live in the bosom of Holy Church.'

'But I know only too well, Monsieur Jesuit, that your brethren would never trust me out of their sight. As for my beloved — what would you do with her?'

'Her? O my daughter, how you make me fear for your soul! Tell me, how was the sex of your unborn babe made known? Truly, it could have been no angel of God who made such revelation to you.'

Marie came forward to stare down at the kneeling priest. 'Do not try my patience further, Black Robe. Answer my question truthfully, if you can. What will happen to my child if she be given over to Monseigneur Gérard at Quebec?'

'I will not lie to you, Madame: the fate of the child you carry is of great concern to Holy Church. For centuries the enemies of the True Faith have used the myth of the Chosen Seed to work great injury among the Faithful. Imagine what would happen if such an Antichrist should rise again! The whole Christian world might come undone!'

'Monsieur Priest, I only care that you would take my beloved from me!'

'Your child needs sanctuary from such as him, Madame Campagna!' The Jesuit indicated the Acadian with an exorcising wave of his cross. 'You yourself have been stolen away by Templar heretics twice now; we must never let that happen to you again!'

Marie felt tiny kicks beneath her fingers. 'I thank you for at least speaking the truth, Father Gabriel. Perhaps even a Jesuit can understand why I cannot go with you now. Better for me to trust this murderous renegade than accept living death for this child I carry.'

The Jesuit's throat worked convulsively, but the Acadian stepped forward and thrust Mishikwit aside. 'Enough of your priestly raving, Black Robe! You have heard the lady's last word on this matter. Have you news to give me of Teiskaret ere I send you back to Satan in hell?'

'I took my leave of your rightful master and waited here for you in good faith, Gilles Leblanc.' Father Gabriel feverishly signed the cross as he rose to his feet. 'He and all his warriors portaged ahead. It pleases him to capture his runaway slave somewhere further along this trail of woe.'

'Say rather, it pleases him to choose his place to die.' The renegade aimed *l'Amanita* pointblank at the priest's chest. 'Just as it pleased you to chose your place to die!'

'Wait!' Marie struck down the Acadian's crossbow. 'What need is there to kill this priest? Too many have died along this river already. Save your bolts for a time of need, Monsieur Leblanc.'

Father Gabriel had spread his arms abroad as though inviting the bolt from the crossbow. It may have been his eagerness to die that stayed the Acadian's hand. 'Madame, perchance you have the right of it. I think Teiskaret will not wish to lose his fine priest. Very well, Black Robe, I will let you live for the nonce. Take up one end of this canoe and follow me.'

The Jesuit folded his arms with an air of disappointment. 'I took no vow to serve the Devil, Monsieur Leblanc. Go ahead and strike me down if you will.'

'My decision has been taken, Black Robe. Think not that I will oblige your desire to rejoin your master in hell.' The renegade drew his wide-bladed hunting knife. 'I will simply strip you of all you hold dear. With your crucifix and beads, your scribe's case and breviary, I will defile the river. Even your filthy cassock I will cut off you and spread upon its waters. Your vermin will drown or perish from the cold. And your Achilles' tendons I will sever lest you follow us.'

The Jesuit's eyes opened wide. 'You would do this to a priest of God, my son?'

'Yea, Monsieur Jesuit! It pleasures me to gall the servants of false gods!'

Without another word, Father Gabriel rose from the ground and shouldered the inverted canoe. Gilles Leblanc hung a reeking sack of sagamite about the priest's neck and turned to Mishikwit. 'Let the Black Robe follow behind you, Esqua. Let him see only his feet in front of him.'

Sparing of her tender ankle, Marie shouldered a few of the lighter bundles and followed the canoe up the beaten path. The renegade brought up the rear, strung crossbow mounted on his left hip. Two loaded muskets dangled from his right shoulder; a small pack hung crosswise from the other. All else he abandoned at the water's edge.

They marched all day, pausing only to rest for Marie's sake. She dreaded each convulsive stirring within her, knowing it would not be long till her baby forced its way into the world. She sucked salt from the rawhide headband of her pack and held on.

The Acadian often stumbled to his knees beneath his heavy burdens. As for the Jesuit, it was truly a cross he bore along that winding trail. His face took on the pallor of death itself, and fits of coughing racked his hollow chest. Sometimes he also stumbled and would have fallen if not for Mishikwit leading him onward.

The silent M'ikmaq was the only one of the four who never faltered on that grim portage. Though her load was heaviest of all, she gave no sign of fatigue. At each halting place, she quenched their thirst with water from the Acadian's canteen. With bear grease, she ministered to their blistered shoulders and feet.

A golden moon ghosting upon a silver lake marked the end of their trek. The Acadian chose a granite out-crop jutting out into the stream for a campsite. The sealskin canoe he weighted and sank deep lest it be stolen or wrecked during the night. He bid the two women be ready to use the primed muskets he posted among the rocks. Then he bound the Jesuit's wrists with rawhide before vanishing into the trees.

Mishikwit lit a tiny fire under an overhang. Marie helped her roast a pair of ptarmigan struck down with stones by Gilles Leblanc during their portage. They heated a flat rock and baked bannock. The caribou robe they stretched out as a makeshift shelter, for the M'ikmaq said it would rain that night.

Sweat-soaked tonsure capping his skull, Father Gabriel took refuge in prayer. Trembling with fatigue and fasting, he rocked to and fro on his knees. Marie heard only the clicking of crucifix and beads against the rocks. From time to time his fetid stench assailed her nostrils.

The sky had turned pitch-black when the Acadian congealed out of the shadows to partake of their simple fare. In the campfire glow, lines of fatigue furrowed his gaunt face. Raindrops from his nose and brows sputtered into steam among the coals and flames.

'Madame, I found something out there that I believe belongs to you.' The Acadian opened his pouch and pulled out the prize Teiskaret had given to one of the young Maliseet scouts. Marie did not need to look at his belt to know that yet another fresh scalp hung there. 'Be careful, for the pistol is primed and ready to fire.'

Marie lodged the weapon between her swollen breasts. Gilles Leblanc grunted with satisfaction at sight of the Hohenstaufen ring hanging there. A familiar passion flickered in his eyes. Marie was struck by his likeness to the lustful satyr: both damned forever to chase their elusive prey. She fought to keep from stealing glances at him as he leaned napping against the rock. When she finally yielded to temptation, she found that he had already vanished once more into the thickening gloom of the storm.

The child within Marie stirred more restively than ever before. The rebellious sphincter cramped and tightened ominously. *So, my beloved, thou wouldst depart from me in this awful place? Why am I so afraid? Will I never be ready to let go of thee? Would God permit us to come so far to no avail? Well then, come forth, if thou must.*

No, Marie of Hohenstaufen, do not let go. Your time is not yet!

Marie could have sworn that hard smooth fingers grasped her shoulders in the darkness. *Sire, some things even an emperor cannot gainsay. I pray you tell me something, if only to distract me from the pain I'm in.*

We are at your service, Princess Mine.

Be it true that the ancestress of Gilles Leblanc belonged to your Majesty?

Indeed, Princess Mine. The priceless white star you speak of came to us as a gift from the sultan of Egypt. Hence the name we bestowed upon her: Estelle Leblanc.

This Estelle Leblanc was a Dread Maiden?

Indeed, Princess Mine! Her mother had been trained by the Old Man of the Mountain in the Assassin fastness-es of Syria. At the time it seemed to us that the old Kurd had trained her rather too well. It gives even an emperor pause to know the woman who warms their bed could kill him with a single flick of her wrist.

It would seem such apprehension did not prevent Your Majesty from siring children upon her!

As for that, Princess Mine, propagating one's seed is a royal duty. One might almost call it an instinctive reflex for a Hohenstaufen to perform such duties, no matter how dire the circumstances. Our blood enemies and the clerics stop at nothing to kill us, so we are driven to multiply ourselves as best we can.

So eventually your Templars planted your wild seed here in the wilderness?

Wild seed? We take exception to your implication, Princess Mine! Say rather, a cadet branch of the family was planted here. In case of the main stem of the family

411

being cut off, we deemed it prudent to propagate bastard shoots in far away places.

Marie began to laugh through the waves of her pain. *So this Acadian renegade out there stalking Indians in the rain bears your royal blood in his veins? He is my distant cousin?*

Indeed, Your Highness! Gilles Leblanc is a throwback to our earliest age! We Hohenstaufen were once fierce hunters stalking our prey through Germany's black forests. Did you suppose that a wolf rises to lead the pack through fair words and deeds?

There is one more question I need you to answer for me, Sire.

I swear you grow more demanding each day, Princess Mine! Oh very well, we always did like that imperious quality in our women. Pose us your question if you must.

Tell me what purpose our lineage serves. Your Majesty's time is long gone. Memory of the Hohenstaufen perishes from the world! What matters it whether my beloved is truly your precious seed? Why do so many others sacrifice their lives so that we may live or die?

Our memory may perish but not our seed, Princess Mine! Our family stands for the oneness of all mankind. We sought to build a world to which all humanity belongs. We stood for Reason in an age of superstition. We sought to build a true Science that discovers and upholds the balance of man and nature. We were before our time, that's all!

This world is still not ready for such things, Sire!

Yes, but there comes a time when it will be ready for us to rise again, Princess Mine.

You delude yourself, Sire! I want nothing more of your lofty schemes! I only want to bear this child and rear it in peace!

The Bearer of the Chosen Seed is not born to peace, Marie of Hohenstaufen! There comes a time of the great-

412

est peril the world has ever known — far worse than nomad hordes and plagues and the burning of witches and heretics. Then according to the prophecy of Yolande, the Chosen One of the Hohenstaufen shall be needed to deliver mankind from self-destruction. It will be the time of the end for mankind if that Chosen One should fail to rise up! That is why you and your child must endure.

You are mad, Sire! And I am mad for listening to you!

The Emperor laughed, and she felt the cool tips of his fingers brush her temples as he took his leave. *Indeed, Princess Mine, we are both mad. Madness runs in the family.*

The Maliseet came for them just before dawn. They did not wear their French boots, but one of them scraped a musket on the slippery rock. Mishikwit's fingers drummed a tattoo on Marie's arm. Nearly blind in the darkness, she searched for the Acadian but found him not. She rose up with her companion and groped her way to the muskets. The loose sealskin wrapping the flintlock gave way to her numb fingertips, but the cold dampness of the metal made her despair. She drew back the hammer and set both forefingers upon the trigger.

The night filled with whispering rain. Marie's ears heard only the rhythmic rattle of the Jesuit's snore. Then her eyes began to distinguish shades of gray. Below the sighted gun barrel, ghostly shapes glided toward her. The hoot of some strange bird violated the stillness.

The eerie call still echoed when there came a punctuating cry. *The throes of a dying man! Yes! The Acadian is out there, still alive and killing! May God help these poor wretches!*

There came visions of her burning home and the scalping of Nicole and Luigi Campagna. Again she witnessed little Guillaume batted through the air. She felt the knife stab deep into the breast of Waksitanou's son.

What treason to pray for the souls of men who do such things! They live by the tomahawk: so now let them perish by it. Be glad that the angel of death stalks them through this night!

Yet she could not bring herself to hate those about to die. She smelled their fear drifting on the wind. She tasted their horror on her lips as though it were falling with the rain. Never before had she seen so clearly into the souls of men. *It is one thing to die locked in battle with a fierce enemy: there is some kind of brotherhood in such a death. It is quite another to have one's soul taken by a demon who knows no fear. Maliseet, be gone, or the Acadian will slay you all this night! Even you, Teiskaret, shall not stand before him.*

Then an invisible force struck out of nowhere. Falling, she wrenched the musket barrel upward and squeezed the trigger with all her might. The muzzle flash lit the painted face grinning down at her. A deep voice swore softly in French. Something heavy fell and struck her hand. 'Madame Campagna! Did you think Teiskaret could be killed by a woman?'

A snarling animal turning at bay, Marie snatched up the fallen tomahawk and scuttled against the rock wall. The Maliseet grabbed at her but she struck at him and pulled the satyr from between her breasts.

'Madame Campagna, 'tis but a trifling wound you have given me, but I must see to it. Tell my slave that Teiskaret will return to avenge his treason.'

Remembering how the war chief had often tricked Philippe, Marie crouched in the darkness and waited for the death strike. She held the satyr steady with both hands before her. So it was that Mishikwit nearly came to grief. 'Madame Marie, do you still live?'

A flash of lightning gave Marie a glimpse of two women groveling on their knees in the pitch darkness: Mishikwit, bare hands resting on her friend's shoulders, her huge dark eyes flashing; herself vastly pregnant and still trembling with fear and anger. She put down the big tomahawk and returned the smoking pistol to its secret place. 'Yes, I will live, ma pauvre savage — and you?'

The M'ikmaq chuckled deep in her throat. 'I will also live, Madame Marie, although that demon pistol of yours came close to slaying me!'

A cold chill swept over Marie. Her trembling lips shaped a mute thanksgiving that the woman she had once called friend had not been added to her long trail of death. 'I am sorry, Mishikwit. I thought you were Teiskaret!'

'The Maliseet is gone. I also thought to kill him for the sake of my father and brother, but I feared striking you in the darkness.' The two women rested their heads on each other's shoulder; they clasped each other in a feverish embrace.

Thus Gilles Leblanc found them in the dawning light. Blood flowed freely from a knife wound in his shoulder. The empty crossbow hung limply from that disabled right hand, but the long tomahawk stood ready in his left. 'Certes, Madame, this night of killing was closely run. I thank God you are still alive.'

'Quick, Monsieur, let Mishikwit bind your wound.'

'Madame, forgive me for letting Teiskaret escape.' Gilles Leblanc sank down and let the M'ikmaq cut away the homespun shirt from his shoulder. 'He is hard to kill, that Maliseet. He almost slew me in the darkness, but I am also hard to kill.'

'He swore vengeance, Monsieur. He will not rest till he has slain us both.'

'So let him come.' The Acadian winced grimly as Mishikwit probed the wound. 'He is alone now and twice wounded. I can still shoot *L'Amanita* if you will reload her for me.'

'So that you may collect yet another scalp, Monsieur?'

'Enough, Esqua!' The renegade drew away from Mishikwit's sucking mouth before turning again to face Marie. 'Would you rather so many die in vain, Madame?'

Marie thought of the father and mother she had never known. Of Guy de Bouillion and Luigi Campagna and Nicole. 'Bien, Gilles Leblanc, I will load your angel of death one last time for you, but you must promise me to spend your bolts with care.'

They found Father Gabriel praying deliriously. Blood from the blow of a tomahawk caked his face. His crucifix and rosary were gone. In the darkness, the Maliseet had nearly slain their priest.

The Acadian freed his wrists with a slash of his knife. 'You are a fortunate man, Jesuit. I cannot paddle a canoe, so I will let you live another day.'

'Vengeance is mine, saith the Lord, and I shall repay!' The Jesuit stared up unblinking at the graying sky.

The M'ikmaq came close and peered into the priest's face. A powder scorch from the satyr marred her cheek and brow. 'Ahh-eeeh!'

Marie caught at the woman's doeskin tunic as she turned to flee in terror. 'What is it, Mishikwit?'

'The Goddess has taken back the Black Robe's spirit, Madame Marie! His eyes can no longer see!'

Chapter XXVIII

NATIVITY

Rivière Chaudière, September 1756

Marie bound up Father Gabriel's wounds and chafed his wrists till blood flowed again to his fingers. She raised him, blind and stiff, from his knees and led him to a swamped canoe. Its sole occupant had died attempting to escape the renegade. The priest eased the body over the stern to lie awash in the shallow river. *'In nomine Patris et Filii et Spiritus Sancti.'*[1]

The faithful kayak was too small to carry all four of them down the Chaudière. Marie watched the impassive Acadian wreck its sealskin sheathing with a left-handed swing of his tomahawk. 'You astonish me, Monsieur Leblanc!'

'How is that, Madame?'

'You did not take the scalps of all these men you have slain!'

'The time for taking scalps is past, Madame.' Gilles Leblanc unhooked a dried clutch from his belt and let the wind stream through their coarse hair before scattering them upon the water. 'I took these because they

---

1. In the name of the Father, the Son and the Holy Ghost.

make my enemies fear me. A man is much easier prey when he's afraid of you.'

The widow of Luigi Campagna would not rest easy with that. 'You have more of the same hanging over your shoulder, Monsieur.'

'These are English scalps, Madame. The French at Quebec pay well for them.'

'Cast them in the water with the others, Gilles Leblanc.' Marie was somewhat taken aback at the calm authority she exuded. 'Put them behind you for the sake of your soul.'

'A man has to live, Madame.' Anger stirred in the Acadian's voice, but he tossed the scalps into the river.

Borne upon the rushing current, Marie fed her companions scraps from their meal of the night before. The Jesuit ate little, but he paddled with a will, grateful to occupy his hands as he chanted to himself. *'Introibo ad altare Dei.'*[2]

They made good time that day of Indian summer although the Acadian kept fretting about not being able to paddle. Mishikwit steered the canoe down rapids, through narrow passages and along shallow reaches till their small stream joined the broad Chaudière. Marie marveled to see the priest fend off boulders and half-submerged logs without once taking his eyes from the sky. 'See, Monsieur Leblanc? We do well enough without you to paddle our canoe.'

'Indeed, Madame! At this rate, Teiskaret's revenge may have to wait.' The Acadian smiled grimly and put down the crossbow Marie had cocked for him. His right arm hung like a cast-off thing from his bandaged shoulder. She watched him as some bird might watch a serpent coiling round her nest. *When next will you strike, renegade? Who will be the next victim of the terrible demon lurking inside you?*

---

2. I will go to the Altar of God.

The shadows were creeping across the river when Marie's birth pangs began. This time nothing could further stay her beloved from reaching for the light. Gasping for breath, she groped behind her and urgently gripped Mishikwit's knee. The M'ikmaq warbled a note in her throat and made a sign to the Acadian when he turned. 'Paddle for shore, Black Robe. We shall camp beyond that spit of rock on your right hand.'

The Jesuit closed his sightless eyes and spoke to the sun. *'Si libenter crucas portras portabit te!'*[3]

Already, Marie's contractions were quickening. She screamed aloud when her water broke. By the time Mishikwit helped her ashore, she felt herself drowning in the uncontrollable, irresistible frenzy of childbirth. 'Find me a bed, Mishikwit!'

'This is no time for lying down, Madame Marie. You are not in France now, so do as we M'ikmaq do.'

Marie appealed the matter to the Acadian. 'I am a civilized woman, Monsieur! I demand to birth this child in a bed. We are almost to Quebec, are we not? Is there no French settlement near?'

'We pass through an empty land, Madame, but it is an easy day's journey to Le Saut de la Chaudière. We will meet up with fur traders and their esquas tomorrow for sure.'

'Tomorrow?' It afforded Marie some relief to rail at the wretched man. 'Gilles Leblanc, attend me well! I need a proper bed and a good French midwife sooner than tomorrow!'

The renegade applied himself to tethering the blind Jesuit. 'Madame, the service of my esqua is the best I can offer you.'

Father Gabriel meekly offered up his scruffy neck to the noose. *'Ad majorem Dei gloriam!'*[4]

---

3. If you bear the Cross gladly, it will bear you.
4. For the greater glory of God (Motto of the Society of Jesus).

Marie despaired of obtaining any satisfaction from either man. 'Mishikwit, take Teiskaret's tomahawk and cut me a bed of spruce boughs. Hurry!'

The mild M'ikmaq left off making a fire. 'Madame Marie, I will not be of much use to you lying down.'

'And why not? Surely you don't expect me to birth my baby squatting in the woods like an esqua?'

'Madame Marie, you may take your ease if it pleases you while your man does the planting, but bringing the seed into the world is woman's work. No one can do it for you.' Mishikwit took up Teiskaret's heavy tomahawk in both hands and began lopping spruce boughs. The sullen set of her shoulders and jaw spoke more eloquently than words.

More than anything, what Marie wanted was one of her own people to stay with her. She looked again to the Acadian, but the man had obviously learned from past experience that women in labor were best avoided. As for the Jesuit, he was treading circles of oblivion at the end of his tether. As if to perfect his misery, he had begun flailing himself with a green sapling. *'Monstrum horrendum, informe, ingens, cui lumen ademptum.'*[5]

The pile of spruce boughs mounted higher, but the M'ikmaq went on trimming trees as though the work would never end. Overwhelmed by a renewed onslaught of birth pangs, Marie gingerly lowered herself upon the pungent needles and flipped open her ring. She gazed long upon the cameo portrait of her mother, but the Emperor did not come. Instead, her sphincter contracted with a vengeance, making it unbearable to remain in her prone position. She screamed and scrambled to her knees. 'God save me! Tell me what to do, Mishikwit!'

'You are doing it the right way now, Madame!' The M'ikmaq lodged the tomahawk in a tree trunk and

---

5. A monster horrendous, hideous and vast, deprived of sight.

came trotting back to Marie through the spruce boughs. 'That's it! Call out to God with all your might!'

'What good will that do? He never answers me!'

'Perhaps you call upon the wrong god, Madame Marie! What would the Christian God know of birthing babies? He and his brother Glooscap are merely Her sons. Listen to the wind and you will surely hear Her voice calling you.'

Only there was not the slightest breeze stirring. Perspiration trickled down Marie's thighs and arms. She held her breath and tried her best to humor the M'ikmaq. 'I do not know your Goddess, Mishikwit.'

'Madame Marie, it cannot be just M'ikmaq women who feel Her presence within themselves. All of us belong to Her — even Frenchwomen like you.'

'If you say so, Mishikwit, I will believe you! Pray tell me Her name that I may call out to Her!'

'Women call her by many names, Madame, but there is only one true Mother of us all.'

'Alas, the nuns never taught me such things!' A new spasm of pain engulfed Marie. 'Call out to Her for me, Mishikwit!'

'It is a thing each woman must do for herself.' The M'ikmaq drew close and put her hands on the French-woman's shoulders. 'Still, I think it pleases Her that we are as sisters, you and I. Come, Madame Marie! If we join our voices together, our Mother is sure to hear us.'

Mishikwit took the caribou robe and draped it over Marie's shoulders, forming a makeshift wigwam with herself kneeling inside. 'The Goddess, ma chere sauvage! What does She say I must do?'

'She says you are to squat like an esqua, Madame.' Mishikwit's voice came muffled from inside the thick hide.

'Bien! I will do as She says!' Marie surrendered to the firm hands grasping her straining thighs. Mishikwit began to chant in the M'ikmaq tongue.

The widow of Luigi Campagna gripped the two thick braids of the woman kneeling before her. 'Mishikwit?'

'Yes, Madame Marie?'

'If I should die this night, promise me you'll look after my beloved.'

The M'ikmaq's voice sank deep and rose again, calling upon the Goddess in her native tongue. Marie took a deep breath and followed after. *O Holy Mother, help me for I am indeed the most wretched of women! An orphan become a widow that let herself be robbed of her stepsons only to perish while giving birth to a bastard child. Please understand I am not used to praying to a heathen goddess! It does not behoove a good Christian to do so, but you and this M'ikmaq woman are all I have left! For the sake of my beloved, see me though this. Help me be brave at least once in my life!*

Merciless, the awful constricting pain coiled tighter around Marie. She tried to vomit, but only retching gasps passed her lips as her friend chanted on, lulling her down into unsounded depths. She wandered there till she lost all sense of time, conscious only of steamy breath upon her wet thighs. Then spasming pain thrust her to the surface once more. She screamed aloud and pulled at Mishikwit's pigtails. 'Hi-yah, Madame, time to push! Here, clench my headband between your teeth!'

Marie glared down at the invisible M'ikmaq. 'Push, you say? I cannot help but push, you silly esqua! Can your Goddess think of nothing better than to bid me squat and push?'

'Forget all else, Madame! Only you yourself can do this thing.'

The pangs lulled, letting remorse turn aside Marie's fear and anger. 'Dear Mishikwit, I am sorry for all the trouble I have caused you!'

'Are not kin-friends meant to bear each other's burdens, Madame?'

'Yes, my kin-friend, but will the Goddess forgive a poor stranger for not even knowing Her name?'

Mishikwit permitted herself a peal of laughter. 'Who better to forgive the ways of women than She who shaped us the way we are?'

'Bien! I am glad She knows that I have reached the end of my earthly tether, Mishikwit. I cannot endure much more of this woman's hell!'

'Ah Madame Marie, what can our Mother's daughters not endure? Hi-yah, Kin-friend, be ye joyful that your beloved is coming into the world this day!'

'I fear both of us have too far to go! Oh-h! What are you doing to me, Mishikwit? It feels like you are cutting me with a knife!'

The M'ikmaq chuckled to herself. 'A scalping knife has many uses, Madame. You and your next husband will both be glad that my mother taught me how to use it on a woman.'

'Mishikwit, do not even speak to me of taking another husband! If I had known a man could bring me to such agony as this, I would never have let one of them touch me at all!'

'Hi-yah, Madame Marie! Your pain would be less if your husband had been more of a man to you! You remain almost a maiden!'

The widow of Luigi Campagna was nothing if not loyal. 'Hush, Mishikwit, my husband was always a kind and gentle man.'

'I can well believe it, Madame Marie, but it is not a kind and gentle man that a maiden needs to be made a woman.'

Waves of dizziness and nausea swept over Marie. 'My dear Mishikwit, I would fall down without you to hold me up. Don't you think I should ask Father Gabriel to pray for my beloved and me?'

'Better that you use your breath to push, Madame Marie! Better that you push!'

'Alas, my friend, I can push no more. Nothing is left of me but a great bleeding wound. Please, Mishikwit, beg the priest to commend my soul and that of my beloved to the Christian God!'

The M'ikmaq poked her head through the caribou robe to stare Marie in the face. 'Push, you cowardly esqua! Push, or I swear by the God of Christians that I shall rip the babe from your belly with this scalping knife!'

And Marie pushed as she had never pushed before. A searing molten mass tore down through her. She felt her tissues rend, felt her bones and sinews split in twain. *So close and yet so far, my beloved. All for naught our long journey together! At least this way God will spare you from suffering as I do.*

'Push, Madame! Push!' Marie's leg muscles arched; her molars ground deep into the stiff headband. Again and again, she met Mishikwit head to head, for the M'ikmaq would give her no quarter till the deed was done.

And still the baby lodged deep inside her like a dead thing. 'Sauvage, you are right! It is time to make an end. I am all used up! Cut my beloved free with your knife before she dies inside me!'

'What silly talk is this, Madame Marie? I am touching the head of your beloved!'

'Do not lie to me, Mishikwit! True kin-friends do not lie to one another!'

'Push one more time, Kin-friend Mine! Push as you have never pushed before!'

Marie willed it be done, but she felt nothing ensue, not even pain. '*Ma chere sauvage*, I am sorry to disappoint the Goddess, but you must use your knife. Take my beloved from me before it be too late!'

She felt Mishikwit's hands groping her, felt the cold steel of the knife. Then came to her loins the most profound voiding sensation. 'Madame, you have done it! Your beloved just slipped like a fish into my hands!'

'I know, Mishikwit, I know!' Marie slumped forward, quite overwhelmed by relief and joy.

'Hold, Madame, do not fall down!' The M'ikmaq broke free of the caribou robe. 'Take your little girl in your arms like a mother should!'

'Ah-h, ma chere sauvage! Thank you for all these lovely spruce boughs! May I lie down now?' The M'ikmaq gently lowered the new mother and child to the bed of needles. She drifted upon them in darkness till she heard her baby cry. The helpless wail sent fresh blood surging through her veins. She freed her left breast from the smock.

Marie felt Mishikwit sever the umbilical cord, felt something slither from within, felt her babe's thirsty suck. Her hand came upon her cameo ring dangling open. As she closed it and tucked it between her swelling breasts, a vivid sensation swept over her of having come this way many times before. She sank down into merciful dreams that echoed with the M'ikmaq's haunting song.

Your deed is well done, Marie of Hohenstaufen! Arms akimbo and dressed in full regalia, the Emperor towered over Marie.

She raked together what little fire remained in her. *Your Majesty deserted me! You promised to be here in my time of need!*

Do be reasonable, Princess Mine! What does an emperor know of birthing babies? Discretion is the better part of masculine valor when it comes to crossing such dire feminine straits. We thought this native woman handled your travail magnificently!

Marie would not forgive him. *Yea, Sire! No thanks to you, my race is run!*

Run? Yes, perhaps it is run, but 'tis not yet won, Princess Mine.'

I have done all I can, Sire! I can do no more even if the life of my beloved depends upon it!

Oh come now! To quote a crude-speaking man of Albion: methinks the lady doth protest too much!

And you jest too much, Sire! I can hardly move my legs! I am numb from the waist down!

God's truth! A woman complaining is like a staghound with a wet nose. It is time enough to worry when the nose dries up. Have we not followed you across half a millennium? Never once in all these centuries have you given birth without making a fuss about it! It is part of your indomitable nature! A most worthy consort you have proved to be, Yolande of Brienne!

A thousand flashes of light pierced Marie's veil of darkness. *What did you just call me, Sire?*

A slip of the tongue, Princess Mine. Now is not the time to confuse you! The Emperor furrowed his high-templed brow. *More worrisome than your health is this bastard offshoot of ours. We cannot deny that Hohenstaufen blood flows in his veins, but he has not lived many lives before like us. Newcomers to this universe yearn for what they may not have. There's no telling where desperation shall lead this Gilles Leblanc.*

For once, Marie felt smugly certain she could resolve the Emperor's quandary. Even so, she couldn't quite credit the words that came to her mouth. *It's a simple matter really, Sire. Gilles Leblanc loves me!*

Oh do be careful what our bastard scion loves, Princess Mine! His is neither a simple love for your person nor even an honest lust for your body. It is the Bearer of the Chosen Seed that he covets.

He comes by his devious motives honestly enough, Sire! Was ever a woman more to you than a receptacle from which to take pleasure or in which to deposit your seed?

Must you still think us a villain because of a few youthful peccadilloes? Marie felt a sea-change sweep over the phantom of her dreams. *Princess Mine, you accused me thus when we first laid eyes on one another. It was on our wedding night, remember? The guests were all assembled around the nuptial bed, waiting for me to consummate the marriage. After all we've been through together since, you ought at least by now to call me by my Christian name.*

Marie stared up at the figure in stunned silence. His regalia had been cast off, revealing an intimate garment frighteningly familiar to her. *Bien, Sire, I shall think of you as Frederick, if that pleases you.*

Marie awakened to find the Acadian standing over her instead of the Emperor. Writ large upon that face of darkness was an intense passion. It wreathed his thin lips; it distended his feverish eyes. 'Certes, Madame, you have done well this day!'

His words set up an unsettling echo in her mind. 'Yes, Monsieur, my womanly deed is done.'

Gilles Leblanc shifted his stance to use his crossbow as a crutch. He carried his right arm slung from his left shoulder, and his cheeks were flushed with fever. *So, renegade, your wound worsens. What a sorry pair we are, you and I. Do you still think to stop Teiskaret when he comes for us?*

A sound she had never heard before made Marie look where Mishikwit knelt near the glowing campfire. The M'ikmaq was drying the squalling newborn with a towel. *Surely, my beloved, she did not immerse thee already in icy water! And what has she done to thy poor navel? At least she has not circumcised thee! Our Savior may have been born in a stable, but even so, his birth was better accommodated than thine has been. There are no shepherds or wise men here.*

'The child is female.' Gilles Leblanc watched carefully as the M'ikmaq began tucking the infant into the swaddling furs. 'The Grand Master will be pleased, Madame!'

The Acadian himself did not seem that pleased. *Why do you look at me like this, renegade? Who is this Grand Master you speak of?*

'A healthy babe, Master.' Mishikwit held up the bundled infant for the Acadian to see. 'She shall live long and well, I think.'

'If God so wills it.' The Acadian turned quickly aside and began untangling Father Gabriel from his tether. 'Time we were on our way. Esqua, help the Black Robe lift Madame Campagna into the canoe.'

'Master, we must let Madame Marie rest here today!' The M'ikmaq was careful to keep her body language submissive. 'As you can see, she is too weak to travel.'

The Acadian turned his back on the M'ikmaq and looked down at Marie where she lay among the spruce bows. 'Certes, Madame, I would indulge your need for rest if I dared.'

Marie felt a black void enfold them both. She struggled to see what was hidden in the darkness between them. 'Mishikwit is right, Gilles Leblanc: I cannot move off these spruce bows this day! I bid you leave us behind if you fear Teiskaret catching up with us.'

'Quickly, Esqua, prepare Madame Campagna for our journey! We must reach Le Saut de la Chaudière before nightfall.'

'It cannot be, Master!' The M'ikmaq handed the infant back to its mother. 'To birth this child, Madame Marie crossed the Great Water. She is a delicate Frenchwoman. She has lost much blood. And still she bleeds a little.'

'Esqua, I hear you, but we dare not loiter here. Teiskaret may come after us with his good friends, the Abenaki. Help the priest place Madame Marie in the canoe. She is not heavy.'

'Nay, Master, we must stay here this day! You yourself require rest and tending.'

The renegade dropped his crossbow and backhanded Mishikwit to the ground. 'Esqua, you will do as I command! Put the woman and the baby in the canoe.'

The M'ikmaq rose to her knees. The fine bones of her cheek and temple gleamed ivory-white through the scorch marks and powder burns. 'Master, Madame Marie has no milk to give. Without rest, she cannot feed her babe.'

'What matter's that, Esqua?' The Acadian kicked the cringing woman with a stiff moccasin; his left arm arced up like a snake to strike her again. 'Have you not suckled grown men these many nights? You yourself shall wet-nurse the babe.'

Marie feebly raised her head from the spruce boughs. 'Gilles Leblanc, you are a killer of men and abuser of women! I will not go with you to Quebec!'

The Acadian laughed, turning upon Marie his feverish eyes. 'I've no longer any thought of taking you to Quebec, Madame. Your girl-child lives! The Grand Master may have his Chosen Seed to do with as he will, but I claim you as mine to have and to hold.'

Marie sank back from the terrible presence of the man. 'One day of rest, Monsieur. That's all I ask. Grant me only this, and we will go with you wherever you choose to take us.'

'How I did love thee, O Bearer of the Chosen Seed, when thou didst wade among the lilies.' Gilles Leblanc put his hand to his sheathed scalping knife as he came for her.

Marie fumbled her bodice open and exposed a dry breast to her baby. 'I remember no lilies, Acadian. Do you forget Claudine and her children?'

The renegade started back as if in wonder from the reclining woman. 'I am a born Templar, Madame. In my veins flows the same pure blood as quickens this child. I have waited long in this wilderness for your coming. That wait shall not be in vain.'

Marie felt his passion transfix her like a butterfly upon a pin. 'Did you bring me here to plant seed in my accursed womb?'

The Acadian turned to stand over the M'ikmaq once again. 'Esqua, you will take this babe to the Grand Master in Quebec. It will not be hard to find him. Guard her with your life.'

Mishikwit sidled close to Marie. She took the infant from her arms and whispered in her ear. 'Madame Marie, just now I caught the scent of Maliseet drifting heavy over the river!'

'Monsieur Leblanc, do not part me from my beloved!' Marie tried to rise up, but she was unable even to turn upon her side. The baby's piteous wail made the M'ikmaq halt and look to her master.

'Madame, we shall do as you say. You and I, we shall wait for Teiskaret here!' Perspiration beaded the brow of the Acadian. 'Something tells me he will not keep us waiting long. And when he is dead, we shall go where no one shall ever find us.'

The blind Jesuit wandered past. Holding up his skirts like a dowager, he waded out to the bobbing canoe and declaimed to a flight of geese honking across the sky. *'Quem fugis, a! demems? Habitarunt di quoque silvas.'*[6]

Mishikwit lingered at the riverbank. 'Madame Marie, I do not want to leave you here!'

The widow of Luigi Campagna laid down her head. 'Esqua, do as your master bids you!'

The M'ikmaq waded out to the canoe and handed the baby to the priest. Then she splashed back for her basket. Marie fumbled for her father's ring, watching as the Jesuit frowned down at the strange object in his lap. *If only he knew what is entrusted him! Dear God, preserve him from dropping my beloved in the river!* 'Before you go, Black Robe, I pray you christen my beloved!'

A luminous smile wreathed the Jesuit's lips at the thought of familiar things to be done. His fingertips found

---

6. Ah, madman, whom are you running from? Gods too have lived in the woods.

and caressed the newborn's brow. 'I seem to remember that this child is the offspring of the dead Huguenot. What name would you give his daughter, Madame?'

Marie hinged open the ring and looked into the dark haunting eyes of her mother. 'Lizé! Let her be called Lizé.'

'Lizé Campagna!' The Jesuit pulled back the swaddling clothes from the baby. 'Given such a name, people are bound to call her Lizette. Be that as it may, the name sounds Catholic enough.'

Reverent, he took up the baby by her ankles and dipped her naked in the flowing river. *'Ave verum corpus, Natum ex Maria Virgine!'*[7]

'Foul priest, leave the Chosen Seed alone!' Leaving *L'Amanita* lying forgotten on the ground, Gilles Leblanc drew his tomahawk and headed for the canoe. Father Gabriel smiled at him expectantly.

And then a bloodcurdling war-whoop burst upon the little encampment. Marie remembered how a similar sound had greeted her dead husband when he went to their door. Frozen, she watched the Acadian crouch down and then charge past her into the trees. She heard the sound of men fighting and then the sound of men dying. She clutched Mishikwit's hand and waited for the victor to emerge.

He came carrying a naked saber in his right hand. Mishikwit set up a wail at sight of the dripping scalp. It occurred to Marie that this was Chosen blood. 'So, great Teiskaret of the Maliseet, you have slain Gilles Leblanc at last.'

'Yea, Madame. The renegade will not break faith with me ever again!' Teiskaret flourished Deborah's sword. 'Yet let the campfire songs sing that he died well for one who was not Maliseet.'

---

7. Hail the True Body, born of the Virgin Mary.

Marie looked where Father Gabriel still held her baby in his arms. 'I ask of you what I asked of him, Teiskaret. Give us a day to rest before you take us to Quebec and claim your reward.'

The Maliseet threw back his head and laughed. 'The renegade has slain all my best warriors, Madame. Even the two Abenaki who came here with me this day he has slain. Your blood is needed to settle the debt to my people. I dare not return to Deborah without the scalp of the woman who birthed our children.'

He flourished the saber again as he drew near; Marie composed herself for the final stroke. Instead she heard the satyr bark close beside her. Felt the invisible fist slam the war chief down. Watched the bloody heels of his moccasins beat the sand.

For a long time it seemed that nothing moved in the little glen. Then the Maliseet sat up and gazed down in amazement at the crimson rose blossoming on his massive chest. 'Esqua, you have slain me!'

'Maliseet, I have avenged my father and my brother this day.' The M'ikmaq held the smoking pistol steady in both hands as if it could be fired again like the Acadian's crossbow. 'My ancestors may now rest in peace; that is enough. I will not give them your scalp, Great Teiskaret.'

The war chief's fierce eyes rolled to Marie and transfixed her with their waning light. 'When you see Deborah, Madame, tell her that I slew the Acadian in accordance with her command.'

The Sagamo of the Maliseet slumped forward and let go the saber. The Jesuit rocked the wailing infant till it fell asleep. *Requiem aeternam dona eis, Domine: et lux perpetua lucent eis.*[8]

---

8. Grant them eternal rest, O Lord; and let perpetual light shine upon them.

*

Marie of Hohenstaufen, your prophecy will be fulfilled. Rest easy, for now your race is indeed won.

And what about you, Frederick of Hohenstaufen? Have you learned nothing from witnessing all this?

Only that I must summon the courage to wander in this world again as you do, Empress Mine. God knows I've little stomach to relive such things.

Nonsense, Sire, I see the same old fire in your eyes! You intend to try saving the world again!

Nay, Queen of Jerusalem, for it little profits a man to save the world if he loses himself along the way. I would rather find my old friend Piero. He also wanders here somewhere, waiting for me to return and ask his forgiveness. The world shall have to save itself. It is not a thing a single man can do anymore.

A long silence ensued between the star-crossed pair. *Frederick of Hohenstaufen, I forgive you for disappointing me. There was a time I expected you to make the world perfect, you know.*

You wanted it made over in your image, my dear. The emperor laughed. *Perhaps I shall return next time as a woman. I think you women have all the advantages in this dawning new world.*

You would make an incomparable woman, Sire! Marie managed a smile. *If you become a woman, that would mean that we are finally free of one another, would it not?*

Indeed, Empress Mine, we are already free of one another. But we can still be friends, can we not?

As I remember, Frederick, we were lovers but never friends!

Then let me begin again, Marie of Hohenstaufen. Fading, she felt him kiss her cheek.

*

It was early morning of a new day before Marie became aware of Mishikwit helping her to drink steaming broth. There were new marks of mourning painted on the M'ikmaq's face. 'Sauvage, did I dream it? Are Gilles Leblanc and Teiskaret both dead?'

'Yea, Madame Marie.' Mishikwit broke off feeding her and went to pick up the fussing baby. 'The Black Robe is feeling better today. He said a mass for the Maliseet's soul.'

'Did he not also say Mass for the Acadian?'

'Nay, Madame Marie, for he says my master would rather burn in hell. I buried them both deep in trackless sand so no man may steal their scalps.'

The M'ikmaq picked up Lizette and bared her ample breast. Marie smiled ruefully at seeing this. 'Lizette has two mothers now, Sauvage.'

'There is only one Mother, my kin-friend, and we are all but shadows of her. Finish drinking your broth and rest so that your own milk may flow.'

'I fear I shall never make a proper wet-nurse, Mishikwit. You saved both our lives today.'

'Let me stay always at your side, Madame Marie.' The M'ikmaq poked her nipple in the infant's mouth. 'Let me stay with you lest harm come to you or this Chosen One.'

'It cannot be, Daughter of Waksitanou, for you must return to your people and bear more children.'

'Nay, Madame Marie, for I have shed a man's blood this day.'

'Mishikwit, my dear friend, do not let me steal life from you as I have from so many others!'

'Hi-yah, Madame Marie, my father, my husband, my brother and my son are all slain. Even my Acadian master is gone from me. The Goddess commands me to stay with you.'

'Ah, Mishikwit, I am too tired to argue with you just now. Let us be gone from here before more priests and warriors come.'

'All who were coming have already come and gone, Madame Marie.' The M'ikmaq set the sated child at the widow's meager breast. 'I do not smell any more of them upon the river.'

'Still, let us be gone from here.' Marie felt for her Hohenstaufen ring, but it was gone. Yet it did not make her afraid to be without it. 'I can feel something stalking us out there.'

Darkness still shaded the forest when the Jesuit and the M'ikmaq carried Marie down to the canoe. She took her baby in her arms and looked back at the unmarked graves. 'Be at peace, ye men of the wild. Next time you pass this way, try not to kill one another.'

Father Gabriel signed the cross and took up his paddle. *'O matre pulchra filia pulchrior!*[9]

Then Mishikwit pushed off the canoe, and they passed into the mists drifting over the river.

---

9. What a beautiful mother, and yet more beautiful daughter!

Chapter XXIX

FULL CIRCLE

Quebec City, September 1756

From high upon the citadel's stone ramparts, the Marquis de Saint-Véran squinted down at the autumnal forest stretching to the horizon. Only the blue ribbon of the Saint Laurent gave some relief from the cloud-shadowed brilliance of it all. Fresh from his maps and charts, his mind's eye easily followed the great river to the five inland seas lying at the heart of the continent.

From time immemorial, the native peoples of the land had plied this route to trade with their friends and war with their enemies. As they reckoned the passing of the seasons, it was only yesterday that a handful of French adventurers had sailed up the river to trans-form their world forever. Those intrepid priests, wan-dering *coureur de bois* and professional soldiers had quickly carved this virgin wilderness into one of the largest empires in history.

Much too quickly, I fear!

It was no more than a house of cards that the French King had sent Louis-Joseph de Montcalm-Gozon to defend. Already, millions of English colonists were encroaching upon New France like a plague of locusts. Vaudreuil, that imbecile of a governor, might talk of driving those land-hungry heretics into the sea, but the general knew full well that a thousand Indian raids would not suffice to stem the Yankee tide.

As one of France's most decorated soldiers, he would do his considerable best to fend off the Anglo-Saxons, but it could only be a matter of time till this empty river filled with Union Jacks and redcoats. Then would come the final battle to determine the fate of a realm larger than all of Europe.

This particular morning, the Commander-in-Chief of His Most Christian Majesty's Armies had something much more immediate on his mind than geopolitics. Once more, he mentally ran through his special emissary's verbal report. *So she is come back to me at last. And the girl-child is born to her exactly as the Dread Maiden promised.* 'Did you speak with the lady, Sayadana?'

'Master, she was still too weak from giving birth to even know I was there.' The voice came forth from a figure set like a carved wooden effigy in a niche among the walls. 'We arrived too late to be of any service. All we could do was help the daughter of my brother bury the Acadian Templar and those who slew him. Then I hurried back to bring you word of their coming.'

'You left those two women and the child alone in the wilderness with a Jesuit?'

'The Black Robe is no longer himself, Master. I much doubt he could harm anyone. Even so, I left my three most trusted Montagnais to watch over them from afar. Did I do wrong?'

'No, my friend, it was I who did wrong. I kept Gilles Leblanc waiting alone in the wilderness far too long. If I had not been so late arriving here from France, many of your people and mine might still be alive. But what good are "ifs" to men such as us? At least your brother's daughter still lives. How goes it with her?'

'As I told you, Master, the English rangers slaughtered her husband and child. As if that were not enough woe, the Maliseet chief slew my brother Waksitanou and his eldest son. Mishikwit lives now only for the sake of the Chosen Seed.'

'Ah yes, the Chosen Seed! That is the cause for which so many of us have lived and died these several centuries, is it not?' The general heaved a heavy sigh. 'But the burden was given my people to bear, not yours. I am sorry for the loss of your kinsmen, my friend.'

'Master, it is not your place to feel sorry for us. No one forced us to do what we have done.' The effigy detached itself from the wall and came forth to lay a hand on both the general's shoulders. 'On behalf of my people, I ask only that our sacrifice shall not have been made in vain.'

'Ah, Sayadana, so many dead voices sing that same refrain!' The general closed his eyes and put his hands to his ears as if he indeed could hear voices whispering to him. 'The children of my faithful servant, what news bring you of them?'

'The sons of Luigi Campagna are kept safe at La Pointe de Sainte Anne. An Ottawa she-bear guards all three with her life.'

'They will not be safe there for long, my friend. The English will be driving in our Maliseet pickets soon. We must bring those boys to Quebec as soon as possible.' The general's animated features turned to stone at the rattle of an approaching saber. The M'ikmaq stepped back into the shadowed niche.

The gaunt young captain clicked to a halt on the parapet and saluted smartly. Scion of a family that traced its lineage back to an indiscretion of Hugh Capet, the Chevalier de Grisay risked his life as recklessly in battle as he spent his nights in drunken revels at the taverns. 'Mon général, His Eminence has arrived.'

'Capitaine de Grisay, must you persist in according Monseigneur Gérard the honor due a cardinal?' The

Marquis de Saint-Véran could not bring himself to return the aide de camp's salute. 'He is an envoy sent to us by the Societé's général, nothing more.'

'Monsieur le Marquis, a young man has to make his way in the world as best he can. The Societé's Black Pope is perhaps the most feared man on earth. It cannot hurt to gain the favor of his right hand.'

'Chevalier, it might impress the Monseigneur more if you were to curb your visits to La Belle Bergere.'

'Two of my uncles are Jesuits, Monsieur le Marquis.' De Grisay flashed his perfect teeth in an insouciant smile. 'The brethren are holy priests of God, but they understand men of the world like us very well. It must come of hearing our confessions.'

'Like us?' A faint grimace was the only sign that the general gave of remembering what it was like to be young and free of heavy cares. 'Enough of this banter, Capitaine de Grisay. Please conduct Monseigneur Gérard to my staff quarters.'

'He already awaits you there, mon général.' The aide de camp snapped to attention and bowed from the waist. 'I took the liberty of having your steward light a fire for him. You understand, these cold September winds!'

A shiver running along his spine, the general did not begrudge the fire he found blazing in the great stone fireplace. The cleric stood with both arms extended to the burning faggots as though embracing them. *Bien! It would seem this good priest has not yet sufficiently mortified his flesh with this cold barbaric land. It may therefore be hoped he will take his leave of us before winter sets in.* 'Monseigneur Gérard, how good to see you!'

The Jesuit turned to warm his nether side. 'My dear Marquis, it is good of you to receive me at such short notice!'

'Your Reverence knows I am ever at the service of Holy Church!' The general bowed with all the precision that years spent at Versailles had schooled into him. He remarked in doing so that the cleric's calotte and mantle were of black satin, that his crucifix was carved from African ebony. A large blood-ruby adorned his left hand. A gold signet ring weighted his right index finger.

'Then, my dear Marquis, I trust that the Society of Jesus may count upon your services as well!' Despite his soft-spoken words, the priest's aquiline features hardened as he cast a glance at the fleeting shadow that followed the general into the room.

'Indeed, Monseigneur!' The general smiled pleasantly at his distinguished guest. 'I often ask myself, where would the Church be without its formidable Jesuits?'

'Where indeed?' The cleric returned a facsimile of the general's smile and added the faintest hint of a bow. 'My brethren in Jesus are famous for coming to the point, Monsieur le Général. I understand that you redeemed yon M'ikmaq from prison before he could be tried. Did you not know he stands accused of spreading heresy? What does it profit us poor priests to tend God's garden if you insist on replanting the Devil's weeds?'

'I have assumed personal responsibility for Sayadana's salvation, Monseigneur Gérard. Rest assured that I fully appreciate the importance of the task entrusted to your order by His Holiness.'

'Then Your Excellency will understand the urgency that brings me to you this morning.' The Jesuit drew forth a seal-broken envelope. 'This report comes from one Father Gabriel, a scholastic of our order based at La Pointe de Sainte Anne.'

'Yes, I read his name in dispatches only this morning.' *For once, dear Jesuit, my own military intelligence has managed to hold a candle to yours!*

'Then, Monsieur le Marquis, you already know that Father Gabriel has just returned from a mission behind enemy lines, bringing with him a pregnant Huguenot captive.'

The general could not resist so rare an opportunity to correct a Jesuit's understanding of things. 'According to our own reports, Monseigneur Gérard, there are actually two women and an infant in the priest's party.'

'The native woman is of no concern, my dear marquis.' The priest shot an uneasy glance at the M'ikmaq. 'However, the Frenchwoman and her child are quite another matter. The Societé requests that both be turned over to us at once for due canonical process.'

The general lifted a finely arched eyebrow. 'Before that can happen, Monseigneur, I believe there is some question of legal custody to consider. As reported to me, your scholastic was gravely wounded by hostile savages and only kept alive by the efforts of his female companions. Therefore, Madame Campagna and her child can hardly be considered his prisoners. Indeed, your Father Gabriel made it clear to my courier that the situation is, if anything, quite the reverse.'

The Jesuit gave another curious glance at the M'ikmaq. 'My dear marquis, please accept my assurance that the woman and her children were taken prisoner during a raid by our Maliseet allies behind British lines. Unfortunately, both the native commander of the raiding party and our coadjutor seem to have been lost in the line of duty. As for the blinded scholastic, I know not what to make of his behavior; I do know that the woman has already been judged a dangerous heretic by a properly convened ecclesiastical court.'

'You allege that this Frenchwoman is a Huguenot, Monseigneur?' The general drew forth his lace handkerchief from his sleeve and coughed gently into it.

'Actually, Your Excellency, she was abducted by Huguenots, who suborned her reason, which is of course no valid excuse in the eyes of Holy Church for making heretical professions. It appears a Huguenot heretic by name of Luigi Campagna forced her to marry him.'

'Monseigneur, may I presume this Luigi Campagna was a casualty of your recent mission in L'Acadie?'

'Such are the fortunes of war, Monsieur le Général. Not that it need concern us. This Campagna had been proscribed an outlaw in France.'

'Monseigneur, need I remind you that L'Acadie was ceded to the English under the terms of the Treaty of Utrecht more than forty years ago? This Huguenot Campagna must have been a subject of His Britannic Majesty.'

'A moot consideration given that France is now at war with Britain, Monsieur le Marquis.' The Jesuit stepped to one side, having found the fire too hot for comfort. 'We have every confidence that French arms will prevail in this oncoming conflict, that you will restore L'Acadie to Louis Quinze, its rightful owner.'

'Your confidence is much appreciated, Monseigneur, but who knows better than the Societé what great odds are stacked against us?'

'We have God on our side, Monsieur le Marquis, so who shall be against us? That is why our own General has sent me to New France. To give the signal for what you soldiers call *la petite guerre*. Our Indian allies are to be unleashed as never before. You may believe me when I tell you that my brethren shall give you every assistance in accomplishing your great and holy task of driving the English into the sea.'

'Oh, I believe you well enough, Monseigneur Gérard.' A dark flush suffused the marble countenance of the general. 'Along the thousand leagues of our fron-tier with the English, your *petite guerre* has already begun. Innocent men, women and children like these Campagnas die cruel deaths as we speak.'

'Innocents, Monsieur le Général? I beg you be more precise in your choice of words. Those about to die are all heretics of the most pernicious stripe! Damned Calvinists or worse, every last one of them! Would you have these heretics come sweeping over the walls of your citadel?'

'Monseigneur, the Societé is France's staunchest ally in our war against the English heretics. But that need not prevent us from regretting the barbaric measures needed to defend La France and true religion. This Huguenot widow is much to be pitied, would you not agree?'

'Monsieur le Général, the Societé will give her and the child all due consideration, I assure you.'

'My dear Monseigneur, I do not doubt your word for a moment!' The general feigned a moment's hesitation, although he suspected a simple soldier's artifice of being wholly transparent to so accomplished a student of human behavior as this Jesuit.

'My dear Marquis, do oblige us in this matter and thereby be assured of the enduring esteem of the Societé. I take ship for Le Havre in a week's time. I shall personally deliver Madame Campagna and her child to our proper authorities at Paris.'

'Monseigneur, I fear what you ask is impossible. Madame Campagna and her child are French prisoners of war. They must be interned here at Quebec in accordance with military regulations.'

'Monsieur le Général, perhaps I did not make myself clear: this woman is a dangerous heretic.'

'Monseigneur, my prisons here are full of heretics. As for the newborn child, I raise no objection to the Societé providing religious instruction when she reaches the age of understanding.'

'That is less than what I seek, Monsieur le Marquis!' The Jesuit visibly struggled to keep his voice and manner pleasant. 'Perhaps you still misunderstand me: the Societé demands custody of this woman and child in the name of Holy Church.'

'Monseigneur, even my dull wit can see this must be no ordinary woman to so provoke the interest and concern of the Societé. Perhaps you would be so good as to enlighten my understanding so that I may better give judgment in the matter.'

The general watched the shades come down over the eyes of the cleric. 'All souls are important in the eyes of God, Monsieur le Marquis. Perhaps Governor Vaudreuil would be more understanding of my humble petition.'

'Unfortunately, Monseigneur, His Excellency travels up the river to Montreal.'

'Surely Your Excellency will not oblige me to wait for his return!'

'I am sure Governor Vaudreuil would bend over backwards to accommodate you, Monseigneur. However, both his high regard for the Societé and his absence from Quebec are irrelevant to the case before us. As you will recollect, the company of fusiliers at Le Saut de la Chaudière are French regulars, not Canadien militia. Therefore, they fall directly under my command, not his.'

The Jesuit's manner lost all semblance of civility. 'Monsieur le Général, may I take it that this is your last word on the matter?'

'It is, indeed, Monseigneur.' The marquis clapped his hand to the hilt of his sword with an air of military finality. 'You may rely on me to keep the widow and her child safe from all harm while you appeal their case to higher authority in France.'

'Monsieur le Général, be assured I will do so, but I feel it is my Christian duty to advise you that you make formidable enemies this day.'

The marquis smiled his most innocuous smile. 'Monseigneur Gérard, permit me to offer you a friendly word of advice in return.'

'Certainly, my dear marquis! Offer away for what good it will do you!'

'Be careful when you return to France, Your Reverence. We are entered upon what the philosophes call "an age of enlightenment".'

'You call it enlightenment, Monsieur le Marquis? You might better call it an age of darkness when godless men like Voltaire peddle their writings freely.'

'Your Reverence, I fear that winds of change begin to blow against our respective estates. The noblesse and the clergy can ill afford to quarrel at such a time. Forget not Philippe the Fair and the fate that befell the Knights Templar. They were once as influential in affairs of church and state as Jesuits presently are.'

'The Templars were heretics and demon-worshippers all, Monsieur le Général! I reject your analogy. His Holiness joined King Philippe in condemning them!'

'Is it ever otherwise when the mighty fall? I say again: beware of what is to come! But who am I to lecture you? It ill behooves a simple soldier to instruct an eminent churchman in such matters! Forgive me my impudence. I wish you bon voyage, Monseigneur Gérard. I shall pray for your safe return past the English blockades to La Belle France. Give her my heartfelt love, for something tells me I shall never see her again.'

When the Chevalier de Grisay had conducted Monseigneur Gérard away, the general re-opened the dispatch pouch from Le Saut de la Chaudière. The M'ikmaq's expressionless eyes watched as he retrieved his gold signet ring. Stifling his cough, he hinged the lid open and gazed upon the hidden cameo. His left hand trembled as he held up the tiny portrait to the streaming light. He could see ghosts shimmering all around him. 'Lizé!'

The M'ikmaq gestured at the blank wall as though welcoming someone into the room. The general looked up but saw only the play of shadows. *Is it you, Frederick of Hohenstaufen?*

Yea, Grand Master of Templars, I am come one last time to make known that the ancient promise is kept. Behold, the Chosen Seed is born anew. Guard her well.

Sire, the Societé is hot on her trail. At great cost, I have won her the barest reprieve just now.

It will suffice for the moment, and that is all that matters. The Societé's time of great power grows short. You prophesied truly to the Monseigneur, Grand Master: the hubris of the Templars overtakes them. They will be swept away in a time of troubles such as our old world has never seen.[1] It will be many years before the Societé rises to great power again. They will forget that the Chosen Seed and her Bearer are safe in our hands.

Sire, they will forget because what we do no longer matters. You Hohenstaufen dreamt of a world in which all men are united, but that dream is dead and gone. I regret that we have sacrificed so many lives in vain.

Do not despair, Prince Mine. Sparks rose up from the fire and illumined the face of the M'ikmaq and the Frenchman. *Forgive me the familiarity, Monsieur le Marquis, but you remind me so of my grandson, Conradin. We are both relics of a fading world, you and I. It is five centuries since I had to give way and watch my world dissolve. Prepare yourself, for your time of passing is soon upon you as well. Even so, I say to you once again: do not despair of what comes after. Something new arises in the consciousness of men.*

The Grand Master of Templars smiled ruefully. *Do you set the Chosen Seed free, Sire?*

Indeed, my son, let us scatter the Chosen Seed to sprout and prosper in this fertile new land. Those in

---

1. France, in concert with most other Roman Catholic countries, suppressed the Society of Jesus in 1764. On July 21, 1773, Pope Clement XIV issued a brief, Dominus ac Redemptor ("Lord and Redeemer"), suppressing the Society for the good of the church.

whom the blood runs true will take our place soon enough. The future awaits such Chosen ones, for the world cannot unfold itself without them.

Chapter XXX

SURFACING

Sanctuary Island, June 2001

Hey, what's that little patch of pale stars doing way up there? It's the middle of the day, isn't it? How can there be stars? Let's see, it was still morning when I stumbled into this pit. I closed my eyes to shut out the blinding sun and took that big step straight down. Feels like I took a blow to the back of my head. That's what I get for listening to voices.

Yet what I've lived down here in this Place of Dreaming is far more vivid than anything I ever lived through before! Like I'm the Pythia entranced in the spring-caves under the temple at Delphi listening to voices and seeing visions. But I can't have been out of it all that long. One can't stay immersed in water this cool more than a few hours without succumbing to hypothermia. Remember good old Leo trying to convince Mom and me that breasts are built-in life preservers and that women develop an extra layer of fat to keep them warm!

When I crane my neck way back like this, the stars fade out, and I just barely catch the halo of the sun. Which would make it somewhere past high noon. Question is, how much of all this am I hallucinating? It is a dream, isn't it? So maybe I'll just wake up and won't have to live this out to the bitter end. Except I don't want it to be just a dream.

Not to worry, Girl! You're too full of pain and sensation for all this to be just a dream. Face it, Girl, you're really down here alone in this fucking well! Wonder how many people have ended their lives like this.

Nicole didn't even say good-bye. Like one moment you're retracing the lines of her nose and cheeks. Velvet over steel, you could feel her cool palms soothing your temples. But next moment she's gone from you. As if just coming together and reliving your story after all these years has finally set her free of you. And set you free of her! Aye, there's the rub, for it means that this time she's not here to get you out of this mess you're in. Neither is dear Mishikwit. Even Frederick II Hohenstaufen is gone. So who in hell do you think you are, anyway: the eternal damsel in distress?

Definitely time to get yourself out of here, Twenty-First Century Girl! Better do it while your limbs and muscles still work. You can thank your lucky stars nothing seems broken! Just a few new scrapes and bruises. Time to make something more of this toehold than just using it to keep from treading water. There must be other chinks in this stonewall those Lüneburgers built for Luigi. As he used to tell the good doctor, about all they're good for is busting up sod with a plow! So just make sure you don't bring their whole damned well down on yourself, okay?

That's it! Brace yourself against the wall and take a step up. Trouble is, everything's so slippery-slimy down here. Don't even think about what these jagged stones are doing to your poor back.

There's the hole in the rock you've been searching for! Now, imagine you're walking on eggs and pull yourself up to it ever so careful-like. What's that white thing floating in the water? The bandage finally soaked off your forearm, that's all. All these scraps of rotten

wood are the sticks you broke through when you fell
into the well. You're as naked as the day you were born,
Girl — except for Frederick's ring.

Easy does it! Just step across, stick your toes in the
crevice and straddle the well! Now you're only knee-
deep in water. And there's the next handhold up you'll
be needing. Real careful now! That stone beside it is
loose — don't dislodge it or you might bring the whole
well caving in on you!

Now look up — can't be more than another four
meters to the surface, right? Christ, that sun is bright!
Better find yourself another chink before you fall back
down!

There, that's got it! Now step up to your handholds
and do it all again! It's great to be finally out of the
water except that now you're shivering cold. And
you're a whole lot heavier. Got to keep your muscles
under control or you'll fall back down for sure. Only
there doesn't seem to be any more handholds up here.
It's all smooth above you! So where the hell's Leo? He
ought to have found you by now. If only you hadn't left
your clothes on the beach. 'Leo! Leo!'

'Marie! Where the hell are you!'

'I'm down in Luigi Campagna's well, that's where!
Just be careful you don't fall in like I did!"

His head and shoulders block out the sun. 'For the
love of Christ, Marie! Are you all right?'

'A little the worse for wear, but nothing serious. I'm
very cold, but I think I'll live if I can just get out of here.
You didn't bring a rope with you, I suppose.'

'No, but I've got my cane. Here it is! If you stretch
up, you should be just able to reach it! Grab hold of the
handle and I'll pull you up.'

'Leo, you don't really expect me to trust my life to a
man with a cane!'

'Why not? You don't really think I'd ever let go of
you, do you?'

'I'm naked, for God's sake! You're my father!'

'Well, I'm glad you finally conceded that point!' Your eyes meet his as you catch the gnarled blackthorn handle. It pulls you loose from your toeholds; you hang dangling from those powerful wrists and hands of his. 'Did you find what it was you've been looking for this time, Sorcière?'

'I think so! Much more than I knew I was looking for. You knew it was here waiting for me all these years, didn't you, Leo?'

'Oh, I knew it was here all right, but I could never dig it out for myself. It takes a sorcière to do that.'

'It's the breasts and extra layer of fat, I suppose.'

'Yeah, maybe! Whatever it takes, I knew you had it.'

'Well, are you going to keep me dangling here all day?'

'Oh, right! Sorry! It's just that it's not often I get to talk to you like this. Okay, get ready! I'm going to pull you straight up. Try helping me by clambering up the rocks with your feet, if you can.'

'Leo, there's something I'd like to say to you before we do that.'

'Oh? What is it?'

'I knew that someday you'd come back for me, Dad!'

AUTHOR'S NOTE

Some readers may wish to know something of the historical basis on which this fictional novel has been erected. First of all, it needs to be pointed out that actual events spread over several years have been compressed into the period of human gestation.

Luigi and Marie Campagna are based on my ancestors, Louis Payzant and his second (and much younger) wife Marie. I am descended from their child Lisette born either during the last stage of the canoe voyage to Quebec (according to family legend) or soon thereafter (according to French documentation).

The Payzants were Huguenots who fled religious persecution in France. They lived for several years with their <u>four</u> children on the island of Jersey before obtaining a land grant in Nova Scotia. A knighted uncle, a shadowy figure long in the service of the British crown, seems to have been instrumental in obtaining this land grant. The characters Philippe, Jean and Louis are drawn from their three sons of the same names. For literary reasons I chose not to develop a character based on their daughter Mary. Nor is there any reason to believe Marie was not the birth mother of all four children. There were other children by the first wife who did not come with them to the New World.

In 1752, Louis Payzant sailed his own vessel across the Atlantic to take up possession of his island in

453

Mahone Bay. This merchant sea captain and his wife set up a trading post on the island and proceeded to establish amicable relations with the new "German colony" at Lunenburg. My research indicates that Payzant's nautical and entrepreneurial skills may have helped an essentially peasant people adapt to their strange new environment and become famous seafarers.

Maliseet raiders attacked the island settlement on May 8, 1756, just as the Seven Years War was getting officially underway. Nicole and Guillaume are based on a one-line reference to the maid and child slain in the attack. Indeed, all those living on the island were killed except for Marie and her children. This "massacre" by French-led natives from what is now New Brunswick prompted the proscription placed on the M'ikmaq less than a week later by the British governor at Halifax. The evidence indicates that scalp-taking bounty hunters killed many aboriginal people during the proscription.

Father Gabriel and the other Jesuits figuring in this novel are fictional characters. Their presence is inferred from the role that priests commonly played in instigating Indian attacks against the British and also in fomenting passive Acadian resistance to British rule. *La petite guerre* was a concerted French policy often orchestrated by Catholic missionaries for driving the English colonists into the sea. The role which the Church played over many centuries in persecuting Huguenots suggested the fictional plot line.

The Holy Roman Emperor Frederick II Hohenstaufen is a favorite historical character of mine. I think of him as the prototype of modern human consciousness. He was excommunicated three times, was probably assassinated by Catholic agents, and his descendants were systemically eliminated by the Church. His Empress Yolande is recorded as having died in childbirth. Her grandson Conradin suffered the fate depicted in the